SAVED BY THEIR ONE-NIGHT BABY

LOUISA GEORGE

MILLS & BOON

SAVED BY THEIR ONE-NIGHT BABY

LOUISA GEORGE

REDEEMING HER BROODING SURGEON

SUE MacKAY

MILLS & BOON

First Published in Great Britain 2019
by Mills & Boon, an imprint of HarperCollins*Publishers*
1 London Bridge Street, London, SE1 9GF

Saved by Their One-Night Baby © 2019 by Louisa George

Redeeming Her Brooding Surgeon © 2019 by Sue MacKay

ISBN: 978-0-263-26981-9

MIX
Paper from
responsible sources
FSC® C007454

This book is produced from independently certified FSC™ paper
to ensure responsible forest management.
For more information visit www.harpercollins.co.uk/green.

Printed and bound in Spain
by CPI, Barcelona

PROLOGUE

Black. So much black.

Black and cold and something heavy pressing on his chest.

So cold.

Pain in his head.

A sickening creak of steel cut through the thick silence, making his gut tighten and panic creep through every cell in his body.

Black.

So cold.

So cold.

So cold.

'Johnny? Nick? Eddie? Ethan? Anyone?'

Me. That's my name. Ethan Reid.

Uncontrollable shaking spread from his gut through his bones and over his skin. His heart thumped and his head ached. Someone was shouting his name, someone out there in the blackness.

'Cold. Head.' He'd said it out loud, he was sure he had, but he couldn't hear his own voice. He tried to take a deep breath, but something was on his chest and he couldn't move. Something pressing down on his chest, his legs, his arm. He blinked. Again. Tried to make out something, any-thing. His heart rate doubled, trebled. He tried to move but

he was pinned to the cold, wet ground. There was space above him, enough to lift his head up, but when he did he made contact with something big and immovable.

Where was he? What was happening? He couldn't move? Where…?

Think. Think. Think.

Blackness everywhere. Time slowed and the blackness started to eat at him piece by piece. Blackness that was so tight and choking he thought he was going to drown in it.

Falling. Falling. Blackness.

'Cold.' He tried again. Cold and wet and black and… he was shaking. Every part of him. 'Cold.'

'Ethan? Thank God. Stay with me. Ethan!'

A warm hand on his. He couldn't see… Wait, over there…a pinhole of a light.

'Ethan? Ethan, can you hear me?'

He tried to nod but he couldn't move his head. Everything hurt so much, the light and his head and his legs.

'Squeeze my hand if you can hear me.' Chase. Chase Barrington. It was Chase's voice, right? And he wanted him to squeeze his hand. Why? Why the hell would he squeeze Chase's hand?

They'd had a fight. Hadn't they? They always fought. The last thing he'd do was squeeze his hand.

But, sensing this was important, Ethan did as he was told.

'Hey, Ethan? I said squeeze my hand if you can hear me.'

He just had. Hadn't he?

The warmth disappeared, as did the voice. Then, from somewhere far away, he heard Chase again. He strained to hear what he was saying. 'It's Ethan. Yup. Look, some of the others are…' Chase paused. His voice had fractured, pain filling every word. 'Accounted for. And Ethan was in the drying room the last time I saw him, before… No, I

can't get him out, he's under about three storeys' worth of bricks, plaster and a massive beam that's snapped in half. And he's unresponsive.'

No! I'm here. I'm here. Help me.

Somebody else said something. Muffled.

Then Chase again, 'Nick? You've found him? He's… where? Where? But that's completely totalled. Oh. No.'

More muffled voices. Raised.

'No, I'm not going to stand out here and wait. Who knows how long it'll take them to get here? Nick or Ethan or just stand here and do nothing? What kind of a choice is that? No, just shut the hell up. Ethan's right there and I know I can get to him, okay? He's going to freeze to death or worse.'

Death? Wet. Black. Cold.

Foggy images flickered into Ethan's head as he tried to stay focused. Snow? Yes, he was always in snow.

Try harder.

In a ski lodge. Somewhere? France. The world champs. Yes. Drying room. Chase. Clenched fists. An arm pulled back to swing.

He blinked and saw a tiny blue light getting bigger and in the bluish glow he saw wires hanging down. Broken beams. Part of a wall.

Shit. There's half a wall on my leg. 'Help! Get me out. Help! Someone!'

'Ethan? Did you say something? Hey, don't move, seriously, you'll bring everything down on top of us. Stay still, okay?'

Chase Barrington again. Why him? Why him of all people?

Stay still. Stop shaking. 'Cold.'

'I've got a space blanket. It's just hard to reach around…'

Warm air feathered across Ethan's face and something that

made a scrunching sound was shoved up against his right side. 'Can't get it across you, Ethan. But they won't be long.'

'Who?' It was Chase talking, right?

Remember. Remember.

'Search and Rescue. They're coming, but there's a blizzard…' Chase's voice was weird. Kind of softer than normal, which was definitely weird for a seventeen-year-old kid who was usually full of himself. 'You have to stay awake, okay?'

'Heavy. Chest. Stuck.' Pain shot through his head and he wished he could rub the damned place it hurt but he couldn't lift his hand. 'What happened?'

'Avalanche. Took out the lodge.' Grunting, Chase curled into an impossibly large ball in the tiny space, pressed his feet against the rubble and bricks and broken beam and pushed. Nothing moved. 'You're kind of trapped.'

Ah, yes. Now it was coming back. Junior team ski trials. The lodge. A huge roar and a breeze and then he'd been falling. Then black. 'I'm cold.'

'I know. It's the fricking Alps and it's almost midnight.' Chase laughed but it didn't sound right. Forced. Cold. Damn, it was so cold here.

Chase grabbed at something on the ground and pushed it out of the way, shone his head torch at the ceiling and shook his head. 'I know it hurts, but try not to think about it.'

He paused as the haunting creaking of steel broke into the night. Then a crash and a plume of dust caught in the blue light. People screaming somewhere.

Ethan's heart pounded and he tried to move his legs to scuttle back away from the noise. But he was pinned to the floor. *Get me out of here.*

'What's happening?'

'Just a bit of movement. It's fine, it's the other side of

the building. Don't panic.' There was an edge to Chase's voice now.

'I'm not panicking. I'm so cold. And wet.'

'Always moaning,' Chase tutted, but he didn't sound angry or hostile—which was new. 'Here, take my hand.'

Ethan heard the scrape of a ski jacket against wood and then felt Chase's hand close over his. The warmth made Ethan's hand stop shaking just for a minute or so.

More loud creaks and Chase's hand stiffened. A couple of breaths until the creaking stopped. 'It's okay, Ethan. Breathe.'

That was the problem…he couldn't get enough air into his lungs. 'How long have I been in here?'

'Seven hours? Maybe eight?'

'So long?' No wonder he was cold. Maybe this was just a nightmare where he was dreaming he was trapped with the guy he hated most of all in the world in a space so cramped he couldn't breathe. Maybe he'd wake up soon. 'Where's everyone else?'

There was a silence long enough to make Ethan's chest hollow out.

'Out.'

'Out? Thank God.' He breathed away the dread of hearing anyone in the squad was injured or worse. 'Everyone?'

'All except you and… Nick. But he's…he's going to be fine.' Chase's voice did that weird soft thing again, but it also broke a little, telling Ethan that Nick wasn't fine at all.

'Why are you here, then, and not with him? You guys are such good mates you're like an old married couple.' In fact, it had been Nick they'd been arguing about outside the drying room. Same old stuff. Who was chicken, who was going to win, who was going to wipe out on the slalom. Just banter to fuel the competitive teenage aggression. That, and the fact Nick was always so damned sure of himself.

He was a shoe-in for the British junior team, and Chase

and Ethan and everyone else were fighting for a place alongside him. A couple of beats passed before Chase answered. 'Sucks, right? But until help gets here you're going to have to put up with me. Lucky for you I'm just the right size to belly-crawl through the one tiny hole between you and the outside.'

'Lucky? I have a wall on my legs.' But the others were safe. That was one good thing. Not choked up in here like him. Wait…if he was lucky then did that mean Nick hadn't been? Had Chase chosen to help him and not Nick? What the hell? His head hurt too much to make any sense of it.

'You're talking, that's something.'

A sharp pain funnelled through Ethan's lungs as he tried to inhale. It felt as if the blackness was filling him up from the inside too, stopping his breath. 'I can't breathe.'

'If you can talk you can breathe.' Chase tapped his hand. 'When we get out of here, Reid, I'm going to whip your arse down La Sache.'

'Yes, you will.'

'Whoa. You always beat me down that run. Every single time. Where's the fighting talk you like to give me? Bring it on, Reid.'

'I can't feel my feet.'

Silence.

Chase swore. Everyone knew a skier couldn't ski if they couldn't feel their damned legs. 'Probably just the cold.'

The panic he'd thought he'd got a hold of bubbled up through Ethan's belly to his chest. He couldn't feel his feet or his back. He couldn't stop shaking. There was so much ice and wetness and blackness he was suffocating with it. He wanted to breathe fresh air. He wanted to be outside. Would he ever be warm again? He gripped Chase's hand as water seeped through his clothes. 'I don't want to die. Not here and not like this.'

Seventeen was way too young to die, he had a whole lot of living to do. Right?

The next moment was filled with another ominous creak and the drip, drip, drip of snow melt. Chase inhaled loudly then huffed out as their world, which had shrunk to this twisted leaning lodge, stopped moving. 'You're not going to die, man.'

'Face it, I'm freezing. I'm hurting. I'm stuck in a collapsed building.' The parts of his skin that he could feel stung with such intensity it felt as if he was on fire. 'Is it hot in here? I'm starting to burn up. Can you take the blanket away?'

'There is no way you can be hot, it's probably hypothermia. Listen to me, you have to hang on. Someone's coming to get you out.' Chase rubbed rough hands over Ethan's palm. He stretched and wound his arm through the tiny gap between body and wall, and rubbed Ethan's torso, encouraging blood flow. Then over his leg. Chest. Cheeks. And then he started again at Ethan's hand. He worked for a few minutes then murmured, 'Don't you ever tell anyone I did this, okay?'

'Your secret's safe with me.' Time to be honest. Because if you're going to die, then why not? 'I'm scared.'

Ethan's heart thumped and he fought to control himself, wishing he hadn't said something so weak. He had to pretend he was okay, right? That he wasn't scared. That everything was going to be fine, just as Chase had told him it would be.

Chase beat him to it. 'So, we're ripping it up down La Sache. It's one of those perfect days, you know, where the sky is so cloudless and blue it's almost as dazzling as the powder. And you've got your best form, right? Everything's going perfectly—'

A deafening crash broke him off. The earth shuddered

under Ethan as more of the lodge—close enough for them to feel the whip of air and backdraught—collapsed.

'Get out, Chase. Go. Before the whole place comes down.'

But instead of retreating, Chase edged closer, holding Ethan's hand tightly. 'You've got your best form on, right? La Sache. You make three perfect turns. Whoosh. Whoosh. Whoo—'

Another crash. Chase's breathing got faster. 'Okay. Looks like we've got to do something. Fast.' Chase directed his head torch onto the beam. 'Right. Let's try this again.'

Turning tightly in the cramped space, he lifted his knees, pressed his feet against the broken beam and heaved. Heaved some more. 'Anything? Any movement at all?'

'No.' Ethan pushed and tried to wriggle his body free, but every time Chase moved, clumps of dust and ceiling fell around them like confetti.

'On my count…' Chase glanced up at the ceiling, such as it was, illuminating it again, and they both saw the whole thing ripple like a wave as he moved. Any minute now the place would come down on top of them, suffocating them. 'One. Two. Three.'

The beam shifted enough for Ethan to drag one leg free. 'Yep. Almost.' Another creak. 'Go. It's too dangerous. Leave me here. Get the hell out, I don't need you on my conscience.'

But Chase shook his head and tightened his hold on the beam. 'The rents are going to be so relieved when we get you out of here. Can't wait to see their faces.'

'My parents are here?' Ethan knew Chase was trying to distract him from the task in hand, keeping him talking, keeping him alive.

'Mr Wheeler said he was going to call everyone's parents. They're flying them all out here.'

'Okay. Tell them…' What to say? He doubted they'd even turn up, but just in case they did Ethan chose his last words to his parents very carefully. 'Tell them I forgive them.'

'I'm not passing on any message, you can tell them yourself. And there will be media too. There always are at things like this. You're going to be famous. The boy who lived, right?'

'And who are you? Freaking Hermione?'

'In your dreams, Reid.'

Little falls of dust trickled over them. Outside someone was shouting at everyone to keep still.

'Ne bouge pas. Attendez! Attendez!'

More French.

He hated French. He hated snow. He hated being trapped. He didn't want to die.

Panicked voices. A siren. More sirens.

But Chase caught Ethan's eye. Determination shone there as he nodded. 'Right, let's go again. I never thought I'd say this to you but, Ethan, I need you to work with me. Everything you've got, okay? Or you and I will die here and that, my man, is not the way I want to go. One. Two. *Three.*'

Next thing he knew Ethan was being dragged over brickwork and snow and something he didn't even want to imagine but which felt soft and yet bony. And then he was hauling fresh air into suffocating lungs and watching the place where he'd been two seconds earlier disintegrate into rubble and dust and nothing.

And he breathed, sucking in huge gulps of air.

He breathed.

He was alive. Chase Barrington had saved him.

And that was something he'd never have believed possible.

Later, as the paramedics worked on him, he watched Chase talk to one of the newly arrived search and rescue guys.

Saw the slump of his shoulders. The hand whisked across his eyes. Then his view was obliterated by a sudden convoy of vans. Tearful parents pouring out, screaming and sobbing. He craned his neck for his mother or father.

No.

As he'd imagined. He wondered what he'd have to damned well do to get their attention at all.

Then, as he was being shunted into the ambulance, Ethan saw Chase walk away from a woman, leaving her sobbing into the dark night. Ethan called out, 'Chase! Chase.'

Chase turned and looked, then he turned away and walked into the darkness.

'Chase!'

But then he was there. Looming up in front of him as he had in the tight, dark prison a few minutes earlier, but the bravado from before had gone. He had red rings around swollen eyes. A gruff expression. Hell, he was just a seventeen-year-old kid living a nightmare. *Like me.* 'Look, Reid, I gotta go.'

Ethan held up his hand to stop the paramedic from closing the ambulance door. 'And Nick?'

Chase shook his head and his words came out on a sob that he coughed away. 'He didn't…make it. That's his mum. She's broken. He was her only child.'

The paramedic fiddled with the drip and then said softly, 'My count was four. I'm so sorry, buddy.'

Four dead? Four of the team? His brothers in sport, if nothing else. Ethan's heart twisted as his gaze settled back on Chase. 'But you told me they were safe.'

'I told you they were out.' Chase shrugged. Empty. His best friend had been in danger and he'd chosen to save someone else's life. How would that make you feel? You had a chance and you didn't take it. You bet on someone else. On the someone you didn't even like.

'But you made me think they were alive. I thought they were safe.'

'You needed something to hang onto.'

And he'd hung on tight. 'I'm so sorry about Nick. I heard the conversation. I heard you make a choice. No one should ever have to do that.'

'You were closest.' Chase's face clouded, the way it did when they fought. The way it did in their stand-offs. The way it had just a few hours ago when he'd been trying to make Ethan apologise in their stupid argument. Chase's hands fisted as he wrestled some emotion or other away. His best friend had died and maybe he could have done something to prevent that. God knew how that felt. 'You'd better be worth it, Reid. Make it worth it.'

Judging by the way Ethan's parents had treated him to date, and knowing what a great guy Nick had been, Ethan doubted he could ever be worth it. But this was a second chance and he was going to make the best of it. 'I damned well will. Chase, I owe you my life. Thank you. If you ever need me, anything at all, just find me and I'll be there for you.'

But the way Chase looked at him told Ethan that he'd never call. And, worse, that he believed he'd made the wrong choice after all.

CHAPTER ONE

FRANCE.

Not a place he'd ever thought he'd return to, and he'd done everything in his power to avoid it. But sometimes honour and duty overrode everything else, even good sense.

Dr Ethan Reid dropped his khaki holdall onto the hotel bedroom floor and chanced his luck for a minibar. After opening all the cupboards and drawers, he grunted. Seemed his luck was all out. But if he was forced to be in France he was going to drink, at least tonight, and then he'd have some chance of sleeping.

After a quick shower and change out of flight-weary clothes he took the stairs down two at a time from the eleventh floor, courting the usual looks of astonishment from anyone he passed peeking out from the generic hotel corridors at a tall, lumbering, sandy-haired and probably sandy-coated—given he'd been in Africa for the last four years—guy gunning down the stairs instead of sedately hitching a ride on the elevator. Seemed no one walked these days.

Never mind. Or, as they said around here, *tant pis.*

After spending years living under canvas his first instinct was to sit outside on the terrace in the fresh air as he was used to, but the thunderstorm that had threatened

as his plane was landing had become a reality, so he was forced to stay in the bar. Even so, the place was quiet with just a few suited singletons dotted at the tables staring at smartphones and laptops, probably in Marseille on business given the outfits.

The end of April was too early in the season for the sun crowd, though he suspected the port city would be busy all year round. He ordered his whiskey and soda, and slumped down at the bar, trying not to engage in extended conversation with the bar staff, which left him plenty of scope to chill and get his head round being back here, in the place that still gave him nightmares.

His instructions were on his phone. He tugged it from his pocket and ran through them again with the same trepidation he'd felt the first time he'd read them. How had he agreed to this?

6.30 a.m. Orientation with Medicine For All Search and Rescue Co-ordinator Chase Barrington on the bridge of the *SOS Poseidon*.
7.00 a.m. Pre-launch safety briefing
7.30 a.m. Under way

So that was it. A six-week deployment to pluck refugees from the Mediterranean Sea, assess and treat those with medical needs and transport them to a receiving port.

And somehow survive.

'Aperol spritz, *s'il vous plaît*.'

A woman's voice behind him cut through his thoughts. After his initial knee-jerk disquiet at hearing the French language again he was impressed to realise he still understood it a little.

'*Merci*. It's a beautiful night. I love thunderstorms. I know...crazy.' As she seamlessly switched from French to English she laughed, a soft sound that breathed life

through the dull, stale atmosphere in the bar, and continued her conversation with…whoever. 'Here's to freedom, excitement. Adventure.'

A strange toast that conjured up all manner of stories in his active imagination. Curiosity getting the better of him, Ethan turned to see who the laugh belonged to and who needed all of those things. A little further along the bar was a petite woman dressed casually in contrast to the suits in a dark blue flared skirt and a navy-and-white-striped T-shirt, a dark silk scarf looped loosely round her neck and a small black leather backpack slung over one shoulder. Very chic. She had large, dark eyes and loose honey-coloured waves framing her face. Pretty too.

As if she felt him looking, her gaze sought him out. Whoa. So much more than pretty. She had the kind of face that pulled you to her, a heady charisma, eyes buzzing with energy, a generous smile, olive skin that had him thinking of cloudless skies and skinny-dipping. And now he was just getting carried away.

Glancing around the room, he noticed all the single suits watching her too.

Ethan looked away. No point getting in any deeper than one look. Tomorrow he was facing a demon or two and he had to keep his head straight. He tried to shrug off the trepidation of meeting up with Chase after all these years, and spending the next six weeks rescuing refugees. The doctoring part he could do in his sleep, but living on a ship would only add more spice to his nightmares. He looked down at the menu but the gnawing sensation in his gut had nothing to do with hunger.

She laughed.

Oh, what the hell? He chanced another look, because he couldn't not. Something about her compelled him to take a second viewing. And there wasn't anything else to look at in this place other than a baby grand piano that no one

was playing, dark velvet drapes and that bar menu, which he'd scanned and disregarded a dozen times already.

She was talking to, but standing a little away from, a guy who had about fifteen years on her. Thin, wiry. Like a stoat. No, a weasel, in a shiny, cheap suit that was clearly tailored to bulk him up. They seemed oddly matched. Too old to be a boyfriend, too young to be a parent.

The weasel leaned in, leering. Unsteady. He had the kind of smile that was all mouth and no eyes. Greedy. He said something to her.

Her body snapped taut as she stepped back. 'No. I'm not interested, thank you.'

Something about her reaction and the fleeting shock in her eyes had Ethan on high alert. He edged closer to listen.

Weasel guy's empty smile kept on giving as he ran a bony finger over her hand. 'I'm sure you are. A drink. Some fun. Maybe I just need to persuade you?'

Persuade? Nausea roiled in Ethan's gut, he'd seen way too much fallout from men *persuading* women in his line of work. But this wasn't his business. He sat back.

Sure, it wasn't his business, but he kept a watchful eye open.

Another step back, a flick of her hair as she shook her head. 'I said I'm not interested. Please, leave me alone.'

'Oh, *chérie*. Come on, let's have some fun.'

Knowing he beat the guy hands down on height and strength and definitely smarts, Ethan walked over and tapped him on the shoulder. When the weasel wheeled round and looked up at Ethan he gulped. Swallowed. Paled.

Ethan stepped into his face. 'She said leave her alone. So do it. When a woman says no, she means no. And even when a woman says yes to a guy like you, she means no. Okay?'

'I wasn't trying anything.' The man raised palms slick with a sweaty sheen. 'Just being friendly.'

Ethan shook his head. 'No. It's not friendly, it's creepy. And you're not trying a thing, mate, because you're leaving.'

'Okay. Okay. I get it.' The wiry man shook his head back, imitating Ethan. Then he nodded sharply to the woman. 'I'll leave you to it.'

'Merci.' The woman breathed out as the weasel disappeared out the door. 'But I was handling it.'

'I know you were, but I also know men like him. It's just easier if we outnumber them.'

'We?' Her eyebrows lifted. 'For a minute there I thought you were going to play the part of my boyfriend. You know how it goes… *Hi, honey, sorry I'm late.* Big *bisous*. That would have given him a definite hint to leave too.'

'Big kisses.' There was a thought. A highly inappropriate thought given the circumstances. He caught her eye again and this time she looked away, two red spots blooming on her cheeks. He reached for an excuse to make her smile again because he liked it when she did that. 'Just checking my French. For a minute I thought you said *bison*. And I wondered if it was normal in France for a boyfriend to bring buffalo along to a date.'

'Buffalo are great on dates, don't you do that in England? You're all so weird over there. Yes, *bisous* means kisses.' As she laughed, her gaze settled on his mouth and that stoked something deep in his gut. Then she was back to eye contact again. 'Your French is good.'

'I'm very rusty, it's been a long time since I was in France.' Not long enough. 'Your English is far better.'

'My mother is English. French father.' She drained the luminous orange drink and put the glass on the bar. 'Okay, Monsieur Knight-in-Shining-Armour, that's me done. Time for bed, I'm heading up to my room. Thanks again for rescuing me when I didn't need it.'

'Hey, any time you don't need rescuing, I'm your guy.

I'll walk with you to the lift to make sure he's gone.' He
kept a healthy distance but caught the fresh scent of co-
conut and hibiscus. She smelt good. She looked good. She
made him laugh. In another life he might have made a
move. But not tonight. She looked too sweet to want what
he could give her; which was a one-night stand and noth-
ing more.

As they reached the lift she nodded goodbye politely
to him, stopped and pressed the button and he headed
towards the stairwell door. Which didn't move when he
pushed it. He pushed again. No. No movement. He heaved
his right shoulder against it, but no. 'Strange. It can't be
locked. It's a fire door.'

'Maybe there's something leaning against it on the other
side? Or perhaps it's jammed?' The woman called to him.
'The lift's on its way down. Hop in.'

'No, thank you.' He tried the shoulder heave again.
No dice.

A ping. 'Quick. Going up. Come on.' She ran over,
tugged his hand. Tugged again and laughed. That soft
sound had his gut contracting. He gave one last long look
at the closed fire exit door and shrugged. It was just an el-
evator. It would be a matter of seconds, a minute at most,
and he'd be on his way to bed.

It was just an ancient elevator with one of those con-
certina doors that he'd seen in black and white movies. As
he tugged the heavy lattice across she asked him, 'Floor?'

He controlled his raging heartbeat. It was just a damned
elevator. 'Eleven. Please.'

'Oh. Same.' Her gaze snagged his and she smiled as
if there was some meaning there. 'Funny coincidence.'

He didn't believe in coincidences. 'At least there isn't
any muzak playing, like the Beatles on strings or some
such crime against our eardrums.'

Filling his lungs with as much oxygen as he could, he fixed his eye on the green LED display.

'Lifts aren't your thing?' There was laughter in her voice. 'Or is it the music you don't like?'

'I prefer stairs, that's all.' He couldn't be in here and do small talk and breathe all at the same time.

Floor One.

She tapped her foot. She was wearing flat black shoes with a little bow on the front. Like something a ballerina would have. It was amazing to see something so dainty. Most of the women he'd spent time with over the last few years had worn hiking boots or had bare feet. It was weird being here with no dust, and with regular things like reliable electricity and running water, clean clothes. Elegant shoes. A beautiful woman who smelt of fruit and flowers instead of dry dust and sweat. A body that looked fit from exercise but not too much. Just enough curves that in that fictional other life where he'd consider making a move, he'd relish exploring. Her hair shone and was shot through with wisps of gold and light.

And, *man*, he really needed to get to floor eleven before he got carried away on pointless poetics which were so unlike him he forced himself to do a quick reality check.

France. Lift. Tomorrow. Which was enough to send any wayward thoughts scuttling back to where they'd come from.

Floor Two

'So why is a knight in Marseille? Business? Holiday?' she asked, her smile refreshingly open and unguarded.

'Business.' If he said out loud what he was here for it might actually make it real, and he wanted to live in the

blissful pretence that he wasn't going to set foot on a ship tomorrow and meet up with a ghost from years ago. 'You?'

Floor Three

'An adventure, actually.' Her eyes lit up, her dark brown irises dilating a little. Whatever she was going to do in Marseille, she was certainly looking forward to it.

Floor Four

'Ah, yes. How did it go? Freedom, adventure, excitement?'
'Oh! You heard me?' She pressed her lips together and chuckled again.

Floor Five

He nodded. 'It sounds intriguing. Have you just been released from prison or something?'
Her hand hovered over her mouth. 'I can see how it could have sounded like that. Yes, I'm a mysterious, elusive thief who's just escaped from gaol.'
'If you were elusive you wouldn't be in gaol, or telling me about it.' She was good value, that was for sure. A woman who didn't take herself too seriously. A delicious distraction.
'Good point— Oh!' The elevator jerked sharply and she grabbed his arm to steady herself. There was a weird thumping sound. The gate rattled. A bump. Another jerk. Then…nothing. No sound. No movement. Nothing.

Floor Six

Kind of. Maybe? Who knew? *Just an elevator. Breathe.*
Her hand was still on his arm and he realised he didn't

want her to let go, not just yet. She turned her face up to
him, eyes still lit by excitement. 'A power outage? Must
be the storm. It happens. In France.'

'It happens everywhere.' So much for reliable electric-
ity. And why she was excited by this he couldn't fathom.

'At least the light is still on, that's something.' But her
smile faded as the bulb flickered and fizzed and died.
'Wait, wait…damn.'

Was it him or was it hard to breathe right now?

'Hang on.' He slid his phone out of his pocket and
flicked on the torch. An eerie glow lit the tiny space and
he fought back the memories that still walked through
his dreams.

Broken walls, bare wires, the weight and the pain.

Her grip on his arm was a little tighter now. Maybe she
had a thing about lifts. He needed to show her that it would
be fine. He covered her hand with his and looked into her
eyes, trying to ignore the little fizz of electricity that shot
over his skin at that slight touch. Geez, what would his
body's reaction be to something more intense, like kiss-
ing her? Getting naked?

And that was such an inappropriate thought that he let
go of her hand. 'It's going to be okay, we just need to get
it going again.'

All would be fine. He hammered a fist on the number
eleven button. Then on the gate. Then back to the eleven.
Eight. One.

'Hey, are you all right?' She touched his back, mak-
ing him pause.

Not wanting to look too deep inside himself, he busied
himself with pressing the red security button. 'I'm fine.'

'Sure. Me too. I love getting stuck in lifts.'

'We're not stuck.'

'Okay. I love getting not stuck with a man who wants
to not rescue me. Too many nots.' She put her hand to the

back of her neck and moved her head from side to side, as if soothing the knots there too.

'No one's answering, I don't think the help button is working. There's usually a phone somewhere.' He stabbed at a metal plate on the wall. It swung open, revealing a loose wire hanging over a shelf where a phone had once been. Little beads of sweat pricked the back of his neck.

'No phone. *Tant pis.* I'll use mine. Call the manager. Bring your light over here so I can see.' She tapped her phone. Twice. Two little lines appeared on her forehead. 'No signal. Looks like we'll just have to wait. I'm sure it won't be long.' She slid to the floor and pulled him to sit next to her, but not before he'd put his phone in the metal box where the real phone should have been. A shaft of pale light hit the far corner and the rest of the elevator was shadows. 'By the way, my name is Claire.'

'Ethan.'

'Pleased to meet you, Ethan. I'm a...' She grinned and bit her bottom lip. 'What am I, if I'm not a thief? What could I be? I always wanted to be a singer in a rock band, but I can't sing a note. Or a ribbon acrobat, but I'm not keen on heights. Who should I be today?' She thought for a moment. 'I know, I'm a princess of a small principality. I have wealth beyond measure but I work endlessly to help people less fortunate than me. You?'

'I'm not a princess, no.'

That sparkling laugh again. Heat suffused his skin. He'd never found a woman's laughter particularly sexy before but hers had a direct line to his groin. 'Play the game, Ethan. Come on. You don't know me at all so you can pretend, make something up, be anything you want to be. How would I ever know the truth? Let your imagination wander. Hmm... I know, you're a dashing knight who likes to drive racing cars. Very fast. Very rich. From...somewhere exotic. You have that look about you. From...?'

'England, actually.'

'No. Play the game. How about Monte Carlo? Somewhere fabulously rich where they won't let you live unless you have at least thirty million in the bank.'

'I'm not big on games, Claire.' Unable to just sit there, he powered back up the wall and hammered on the gate, managing to stop himself from shouting because that wouldn't get them anywhere.

'Why not?' At his silence she said, 'I'm just trying to distract you from the fact we really are stuck in a lift and no one seems to be rushing to our aid.'

'I don't need you to distract me. I'm not a child. It's just a damned elevator.' If he said it enough he'd believe it.

'Don't waste your energy banging and cursing. If the electric's out, we'll be here until it's fixed.' Her hand snaked into his and she tugged him back down next to her. 'Tell me, why does a man insist on taking the stairs, and get frustrated when he can't? Why does he hesitate to get into a lift with a woman he's having fun with?'

'Maybe I just wanted some exercise.' Ethan shuddered. How could she see through him? It was unnerving. 'Maybe I didn't want to make you feel uncomfortable after that creep was coming on to you.'

'And maybe there's a lot more to your story, but you clearly don't want to talk about it.'

'No, I don't.'

She shrugged. 'So now you do want to play the game. A mystery man who doesn't like broken lifts.'

Hot damn, why did he feel a need to explain? 'It's a normal, natural reaction to being trapped. I'd prefer it if we weren't at the mercy of mechanical things.'

'You've had a bad experience in one before?'

'Something like that. A long time ago. I was stuck under a collapsed building.' He breathed out. He'd never said anything about this to anyone in over fifteen years and yet

here he was saying this to a stranger. Maybe it was easier to say these kinds of things to someone you knew you were never going to see again, who wouldn't call you out on the fact that sometimes you got a little jittery in a tin box. That just happened to be broken. 'It took a few hours to get me out. Other people died. I was lucky.'

Lucky. Yeah, he should be grateful for the nightmares—at least he got to wake up. But grateful wasn't the emotion he generally experienced, not when guilt fitted him like a second skin.

She put her hand on his arm. 'I'm sorry. I shouldn't have pushed you. I don't even know what to say to that. It must have been so frightening.'

Understatement of the year. He blew out a slow breath. 'Yes, well, as I said, it was a long time ago. I'd prefer it if we changed the subject.'

'You want to forget it. I understand.' A beat. Two. Then her sing-song voice again. 'Hey, do you want a drink? I have a secret stash.' She dug into her bag and pulled out a silver hip flask, unscrewed the top and took a drink. Coughed. Wiped the top with her palm and handed the flask to him. 'It could be a long night so we might as well make it a good one. Luckily my *papa* knows his cognac.'

'Yup.' Ethan enjoyed the burning sensation sliding down his throat and he felt some of the tension ease. 'You're the kind of person I'd like to be stuck with on a desert island.'

'You're the kind of person I'm enjoying being stuck with in the lift. And, for the record, you don't make me feel uncomfortable at all.' She looked at him through wisps of hair that he ached to touch. Then she smiled and it was so uninhibited and free that something in his chest expanded.

She made him feel hot and a damned sight less stressed. Awareness flared through him as he tried to find words that weren't filled with innuendo. That wasn't who he was or what she needed so he tried to get the conversation on

to safer territory. 'Good to hear. And, yes, I'm from England but I've been working in Africa for years.'

'Ah. That explains the tan. You like it there? I've never been but I'm pretty sure I'll get there one day. Some of those places sound amazing.'

'It's perfect for me.' Not wanting to tarnish the romantic image she clearly had of the place, he didn't mention the work he did there. 'So what's this adventure you're embarking on?'

'Oh, nothing too major.' But her grin told him otherwise. 'I'm running away to sea.'

CHAPTER TWO

'WHAT THE HELL…?' Ethan almost choked on his second mouthful of brandy. He'd expected her to say a holiday or a new job, not something so…out there. Plus, the prospect of going to sea seemed to excite her whereas the thought of stepping on that ship tomorrow filled him with dread. Given what he knew of her so far, she could probably make watching paint dry sound like an adventure, but then she was most likely sailing the Med on one of those super-yachts, or a cruise round the Greek islands. She was ethereal, unreal, a dream. A fun-loving, beautiful, laughter-filled dream. 'Why would you choose to do that?'

'I've just had a lucky escape from a crappy relationship with a man who made a million promises and then let me down on every single one of them. We had everything worked out—the wedding, our future, how many kids we were going to have and at what intervals. And it's gone. All gone. *Pouf!*' She brought her fingertips to her lips and blew out, splaying her fingers. 'When I looked at what had happened to us I realised we'd been so caught up in the mundane we'd kind of lost all the fun. So I'm grabbing my freedom with both hands, doing things I've only ever dreamed of doing. Kind of like a bucket list, but not because I'm dying, because I'm living. Starting again. My girlfriends made me write it as therapy to get

over him. I was, like, how do I want my life to look? Who do I want to be?'

'What's on the list?'

'Run away to sea. Get a tattoo. Drink *kava* in Fiji. Swim with sharks. Blah-blah…the usual things.'

Oh, yes, he'd heard it all before. Many of the volunteers he worked with had come to the refugee camps because of their own bucket lists. Whereas he'd started doing the voluntary work precisely because he liked *not* having lists, not being tied to anything or anyone or any place. 'So I'm guessing being stuck in a lift with a stranger isn't on there?'

'Dance with a stranger is there, but getting stuck with one never crossed my mind. Maybe it should have.'

'Maybe it should.' Possibilities ran through his head— kisses, his hands in her hair. Her up against the wall. Something hot bloomed in his gut.

'And there's bigger things too, like grasping opportunities, taking risks. I was always too scared to step outside my comfort zone, but here I am.' Her eyes brightened, shimmering with life and excitement, and he couldn't look away. God, she was breath-taking in every way; beautiful, sexy as hell, seriously funny.

'Here you are. I hope they get the lift working soon so you don't miss your boat.' He hoped they got the lift working soon, period.

'It's not leaving until tomorrow.' She shrugged, but her gaze caught his and the awareness tightened and tugged. 'We have all night, Mr Knight.'

'Looks like we do.'

'Can I tell you a secret?' She leaned closer and he wasn't sure who held whose hand first, fitting fingers together, skin sliding over skin. Him? Her? Both at the same time? Awareness turned into an urgent need, as if all his nerve endings were heightened and sensitive to her touch. This

dream was getting real and for the first time in his life he wasn't praying it would end.

He stroked her palm. What were they doing? *Don't ask questions.* They were consenting adults. 'Sure, tell me your secrets, Claire.'

She smiled coyly. 'I'm a fake really. I might sound as if I've got it all sorted, but I'm wobbling. I feel as if I'm walking—running even—on a tightrope and there's no safety net. The girls said it'd be fun to have an adventure and I'm trying to work out whether I'm wildly excited or whether the bubbles in my gut are made from pure terror.'

'Sometimes it's the same thing. Two sides of the same coin. Here…' He pulled her to standing and positioned her in one corner of the lift. The space was so damned cramped. He fought the rising sensation in his gut. *It's just an elevator.* They'd be out of here soon. He wasn't pinned down. He wasn't trapped. He wasn't staring death in the face. He was looking at the prettiest women he'd seen in a long time and thinking about kissing her. He wasn't going to let his stupid panic take over. He would take a leaf out of her book and just fake it.

So he took her hands in his and started to walk backwards across the floor. 'Walk with me. I've got you. Right now. Just don't look down. You can do this.'

She took his lead and put one foot in front of the other gingerly, as if she really was walking on a thin rope. 'I'm scared.'

'You can do this.' His grip tightened and she squeezed back.

'I can do this.' She laughed, looking about as far from scared as anyone could be. She pretended to look down and to wobble. 'Uh-uh.'

He pulled her to him, anchoring her against his chest, nuzzling into those luscious curls. Her delicious scent stoked the unfurling need in his gut. He wanted to kiss

her. To strip away those layers and find the real Claire underneath this act.

For a few seconds they stayed crushed together, holding on as if neither wanted to let go. Then she ran her hands over his shoulders and down his back and fitted herself into his arms. She leaned her head against his chest and then swayed slowly.

'You want to share the tune?' He laughed into hair that smelt of lemons. 'Because I can't hear a thing.'

'Something slow.' For a few moments she swayed and smiled, her head tilted against his jaw as her hands stroked across his back and over his arms. Then she pulled away slightly and looked up at him, hands locked on his biceps. As she gazed up her eyes misted with need. The atmosphere in the lift crackled and pulsed. She put her cool palm to his cheek, then ran soft feathery fingertips across his lips. His gut contracted with need.

'Dance with a stranger; I can tick that off now. Tell me, Ethan, are you married? In a relationship?' she whispered, even though there was no one else to hear her. 'Are you the kind of guy who would cheat?'

'No, no, and definitely, no.'

'Good.' Closing her eyes, she pressed his lips against her fingertips, the pressure on his mouth tantalising, excruciatingly sexy. He could feel her breath coming fast and soft. The scent of hibiscus filled the air. 'Then, yes, yes, and definitely, yes.'

Torn by his warring conscience and the sharp tang of desire, he groaned and fisted his hand in her hair.

So close. So close.

Swallowing hard, he tugged her hand from his mouth. Geez. Any guy would think he was an idiot for stopping kissing a beautiful woman who wanted him. 'Claire, what are you doing?'

Her eyes flickered open and she smiled. 'I'm kissing

you. I'm taking a risk and I like the way it makes me feel. I like you. You want to take a risk too?'

Hell, yes. He didn't need to ask her to clarify, the intent was there in the way she pressed against him and in the thick need in her voice. Words seemed to have got lost between his brain and his mouth, but he dredged them up, because he had to make sure she understood. 'You need to know that tomorrow I'm gone. I'm not…reliable.' He broke things apart rather than built them up. But he wasn't a saint either. 'I'm not going to make a million promises and break them. I can't promise you anything at all.'

'Good. I don't want promises.' If she'd been paying attention, Claire would have noticed the way admiration had tucked itself into a corner of her heart. He wasn't going to break her because she wasn't going to let him or give him the chance to. He wasn't going to break her, but he was going to kiss her. And hopefully more if she could convince him. Because from what she knew of him already, he was a good honest man, unused to being seduced in a lift.

As if she did this kind of thing every day! The cognac had taken the edge off her nerves and she could barely believe the words coming out of her mouth. But if she was going to be the person she wanted to be—which was independent, self-actualising and free—then she had to start making changes. This was as good a first step as any.

Besides, the guy clearly hated confined spaces, so she was just doing her civic duty by distracting him, right?

She looked up into beautiful eyes that were denim blue and hazy with lust. Lit by the white light of his phone, he looked like something she'd dreamed up—tall and toned, gorgeous strawberry-blond unruly hair and two days' growth on his jaw that she wanted to scrape her skin against.

He wasn't cocky or arrogant, but the very act of pushing her unwanted admirer away and then walking away

himself—no come-on, no smart moves—had made her heart trip and her imagination run riot. Who was he? Why had they held hands not once, twice, but three times? Why had his first touch made heat pool low in her gut? How could a man make her feel so sexy when she barely knew him?

'You can be my first adventure. I don't want to know anything more than your name: Ethan, the racing driver.' She took his phone and killed the torch app, throwing them into a sensual muted darkness.

'Claire.' He powered her back against the wall. He may have been chivalrous, but he definitely knew what he wanted. 'You want to show me some of your acrobatic moves now?'

'Kiss me first.'

Claire Durand! Asking so blatantly. Her friends would be proud. The first touch of his mouth was scorching. There was no hesitation, no gentle learning. He was exactly what she needed. This kiss was what she craved, the hot, sweet stroke of his tongue turning her limbs almost to liquid, the press of his hand on her face, then her throat, then her breast.

She ran her hands round his neck, breathing in the scent of fresh air and something exotic.

He slid his hand under her bra and stroked her nipple. 'You like that?'

'Yes.' She was so turned on she could barely manage to speak. Any minute now the lift could start. Any minute now they'd have to stop. She didn't want him to stop.

He breathed against her neck. 'Any other items on your list?'

'This.' Running her hand over his jeans, she felt the outline of his erection. 'Sex with a stranger. I didn't write that, Marianne did.'

'I like Marianne. She sounds like a good sort.' He drew

back, ran his hand up her thigh, making her laugh and squirm. His fingers played with the lace edging on her panties, making her writhe against him. 'But I like you a whole lot more.'

'I like you too.' With a flick of her fingers she had his zip down and then she had his length in her hand. He was so hard. For her. To know she'd made him like that made her feel powerful, strong and almost unbearably turned on.

Kissing him hard, she barely noticed as he tugged her panties down. As she stroked his erection he groaned curse words at her throat, intensifying her need.

'Do you have a condom, my knight?'

'Here.' Discarding his jeans, he reached into a pocket, unwrapped the condom and sheathed himself in a matter of seconds, though it felt long enough to drive her crazy with longing. Then he lifted her to sit on a rail she hadn't even noticed was there, cupping her bottom with strong hands. 'You sure about this?'

'Yes, but space is limited.' She felt his back ripple with what she imagined must be anticipation, but she wasn't so sure. 'Now's the time for the show and tell acrobatics.' She curled her leg round his waist and tugged him closer. His erection was tantalisingly close, nudging against her opening. 'I want you to know I don't usually do this.'

His forehead was against hers. 'Neither do I. Never.'

'It's just… I want you. I don't even understand why. I just do.' She couldn't explain it, didn't want to understand why she'd been attracted to him the second she'd seen him. Lust at first sight. And more…there was a lot about him that intrigued her. She just knew she wanted him. Now. She took his hand and encouraged him to lift her other leg around his hips. 'Please.'

He nudged into her, pausing briefly for her to open for him. His words were like a balm on her throat. 'To freedom.'

'Yes. More.' Her mind misted with him. His smell, his touch. This stranger. This man. She wanted his hands and his kisses all over her skin. She wanted him deep inside her.

He palmed her breast, stoking hot need. 'Excitement.'

'Amen to that,' she sighed. 'More. More.'

He thrust again and again. 'Adventure.'

'God, yes.' And, heck, what an adventure this was. She had never felt so alive, so carefree, so beautiful.

His rhythm kicked up and as he pushed inside her over and over he kissed her thoroughly until she was moaning for more, feeling him pulse higher and faster, then lose control, taking her with him.

A distant rumbling had her coming to her senses. Breathless and satiated, she lowered herself to the floor.

A bump and a shudder. She grasped his arm, her limbs limp. 'What was that?'

What the hell had she just done?

He wrapped her close and held her steady, pressing soft kisses over her mouth, her nose, her throat. 'Electricity.'

'And then some.' She breathed out, tried to slow her raging heartbeat.

A thump. Another bump. The whirr of electricity. A jolt and they were on the move again. He pressed his forehead against hers and laughed. 'Did the earth move or was that just the lift starting up?'

'Both?' She laughed with him. The fun was in the risk, not just in the man. At least she hoped it was, because there was something about him that called to her. Something that connected with her on a deeper level than random elevator sex.

Floor Seven

Her heart thumped hard as she retrieved her panties and stuffed them in her bag. *Ask him to stay the night.*

But then she might want him to stay for longer. He'd said no promises.

He had skin that had been kissed long and thoroughly by sunshine. He smelt of exotic lands and he would return there, she knew. A man like him couldn't be caged by a relationship. She'd lose him to the heat and the sun and the swirl of sand.

He quickly dressed as she straightened down her skirt, ran her hand over her hair…but he was there too, running a palm over her cheek, distracting her, mesmerising her. Caring for her. She ignored the clutch in her throat. 'Perfect timing all round, I think.'

Floor Eight

Ask me to stay the night.

'Perfect.' He tilted her chin and slid his mouth over hers again. He tasted so sweet and hot, of brandy and kisses and a fantasy, and a small part of her wished…

No wishes. Freedom. Excitement. Adventure.

Floor Nine

The doors pinged open and she jumped away from Ethan. The hotel manager dragged the gate open then made a show of bowing and clasping his hands. *'Je suis désolé.* So sorry for the inconvenience. Electric. Thunder. *Kaput.'*

'Merci beaucoup. Ce n'est rien.' It's nothing. She chanced a glance at Ethan, who was trying hard not to laugh. 'No inconvenience at all.'

What had they just done?

How had they gone from a simple conversation to the

most sensual sex in her life? It was as if there had been some sort of weird inexplicable force pushing them together. Or it might just have been the Aperol.

She sneaked a look at him and her heart slipped into tachycardia. He really was the most gorgeous man she'd ever seen, all mysterious and a little pent up. How interesting it would be if she could spend more time peeling those emotional layers away, but it had been fun to help him unwind; he certainly looked a lot more relaxed now. Smiling, she tried to get rid of the hotel manager as quickly as possible.

A million apologies and handshakes later she was alone once more with Ethan.

Floor Ten

Say something.

Floor Eleven

The gates rattled closed behind them and he slipped an arm around her shoulder. 'You want a nightcap?'

Yes. And whatever that led to. Every part of her craved more of his touch and it would be so easy to take him up on his offer, but she couldn't let herself do this. No more. It was over before it had begun. It had to be. She was starting a new life of independence and the last thing she needed or wanted was to fall for a man who could take that away from her and then leave her with nothing but a smashed heart. She'd been there before and there was no way she was going back.

Claire was going forward.

She took a deep breath and gave the only possible answer. 'No, thank you. I've got a big day tomorrow.'

'We could just sleep.'

'Somehow I doubt that.' Images of waking up to that mouth and that body had more heat swirling round her veins. She tugged out from under his arm but tiptoed back to kiss his cheek. 'I want this to be my perfect memory. Just this. I don't want morning breath or regret. I don't want things to be awkward over breakfast or to sneak out in the early hours as if what we'd done was somehow shameful. I don't want to ruin this with mundanities or disappointment.'

'That would never happen. Not after one night. I don't think you and disappointment could be in the same sentence, Claire.'

You don't know my ex. 'I'm not taking that chance. But thank you, that was amazing. I have a very nice memory to take away with me to sea.' Her smile spread through her body. God, this take-charge thing was a really positive boost to her confidence. Tonight she was amazing Claire. Tomorrow she was going to try to emulate that in her new job, in her new life, where she knew there'd be no chance of losing her heart. 'Goodnight, good knight.'

'I never thought I'd enjoy being stuck in a lift but I certainly did.' Ethan grinned, although the smile looked as if he wanted more too. More sex, more of her. *More of her.* She liked the way that made her feel, that there were men out there who wanted her. Sexy men. Strangers. Ethan... Who was he really? Who was the man who could melt her with one look? Her heart contracted and she wondered... another time, another life? *No. Don't spoil it with wishes.* One last smile from his sexy mouth. 'Goodnight, Claire. Have a good adventure.'

'I intend to.' *I just did.*

Mentally fist pumping, Claire smiled to herself as she

slid her key card into the slot and crept into her dark hotel room.

Day one of her new life. Freedom, excitement. *Adventure*. Mission accomplished.

CHAPTER THREE

HAVING CLEARED PORT SECURITY, Ethan swung his bag onto his shoulder, stepped onto the dock and breathed in fresh sea air. The *SOS Poseidon* loomed in front of him and he put a hand on the cold steel gangway.

Six weeks and counting.

Even though he knew this assignment had an end date he felt his heart pound hard against his ribcage, and for the briefest moment he contemplated running back to the hotel and finding Claire.

And then what? She was adventure bound and he couldn't take that away from her. He didn't know her surname, he knew nothing about her except how she felt in his arms and how she tasted. The sound of her laugh.

He smiled to himself. Hell, last night was one memory he'd tuck away to help him through the endless nights on board ship.

Right. Do it.

He put a foot on the gangway but hearing voices behind him he turned, and faced a ghost from sixteen years ago. Chase Barrington.

His blood pounded in his veins as memories whipped him back to a place he never wanted to revisit. Cold. Snow. Death.

'I'd have known you anywhere.' Chase stepped forward,

bridging the gap. Same old smile—fleeting, then gone. The intervening years had been good to him. He'd grown into himself: tall and strident, standing on the dock as if he owned the damned ship. Typical Chase. But, then, as SARCO for this medical rescue mission, he certainly held a lot of responsibility.

'Same.' Ethan wasn't sure what to do next. Shake his hand? Thank him for giving him his life? God knew, he owed him everything, but at the same time he knew how much Chase had regretted that choice in the end.

Standing with his arms loose by his sides Chase wasn't giving out any clues on what next either, so Ethan did what he'd do to any old friend and gave him one of those tight guy handshake-hug things. Then sprang back. Unsure. After all, they weren't exactly old friends.

Chase glanced at the woman he'd been strolling along with and gave her the backpack he'd been carrying. His eyes were misted and that hit Ethan hard in the chest. Was that a reaction to seeing him or to the woman?

But maybe he was reading too much into all of this, because when Chase turned his focus back to him he was all business. 'Come on up to the galley. With a bit of luck there'll be coffee. And I should thank you for saving our bacon—we were let down at the last minute and were desperate to find a replacement. Paediatricians with refugee experience are thin on the ground this season.'

'No problem, I go where I'm needed.' *Desperate.* Of course Chase would only have asked him as a very last resort. And Ethan had only responded because he owed Chase his life. Owed him two.

How to be good enough for a life lost? Could you ever be? How many lives did you have to save to make up for the one you stole? He'd spent the last decade and a half working on it and it still didn't feel adequate.

He wondered whether he should say something about

their shared past, but decided against it. He was here to do a job, pay a debt, and then he was going. There was a reason they hadn't been in touch for sixteen years.

Ethan took in his surroundings. As ships went, it wasn't exactly luxurious, but it had been a safe haven for so many he imagined beauty was in the eye of the refugee.

'You've just been in Sudan, right?' Up in the galley Chase poured coffee from a battered metal pot and handed it to him, indicating a sugar bowl and a plastic bottle of milk on a tray atop a pile of papers.

Ethan added milk and wrapped his palms around the cup. It might have been April but the early mornings were still cool. That, and the fact he hadn't acclimatised from the desert heat yet. 'Sudan, Darfur, Ethiopia. Anywhere the earth is baked I'll go.'

He didn't add that he avoided all things cold and wet and snowy... He didn't need to. Chase was the only person who would understand why. He'd also, no doubt, think him weak for letting what had happened all those years ago still affect him now. Chase was the kind of guy who moved on.

Like the woman last night.

The memories bombarding him now were of warm eyes, a hot body and a feeling of regret that things had ended so abruptly. Which was all kinds of weird given that connections weren't usually things he coveted. So why he felt he'd missed a chance last night he couldn't say. It had been a long time—probably never—since he'd felt such an immediate attraction to a woman.

He blinked and brought himself back to today. He had enough to deal with, working alongside Chase, without adding into the mix pining for a woman he was never going to see again.

'You haven't worked out of a ship before?' Chase asked, but his voice sounded over-polite.

Okay, Ethan could do that too. Maybe it was better if

they never cracked open the wound that bound them. But
on the other hand maybe it was better if they got it all over
and done with now. He tested a little and smiled. 'These
days I prefer being on firm ground.'

There was a flicker of understanding in Chase's sharp
nod but he appeared not to want to go back there either.
'Right, well, you'll soon get used to it. The first couple of
days are the worst but we have plenty of anti-nausea meds
to get you through the seasickness. It's easy to pick up the
routine, you'll learn it as we go. First, I'll show you to your
quarters…shared, unfortunately. You're in with Akil, one
of the crew. I'll introduce you later.'

'I'm used to living in a tent or a lean-to, so commu-
nal's not a worry.'

'Good, because it's all we've got.' Chase gave him a
brief tour of the ship and the sparse medical space he'd
be working in. Ethan ducked his head as he descended
steep metal steps and opened the door to what looked like
a cupboard but which was, in fact, his cabin. There was
just about enough space to turn around between the bunks
and the door. No porthole. Ethan tugged at his throat and
hoped Chase wouldn't notice.

Seemingly oblivious to Ethan's unease Chase pointed
to a small cubbyhole that looked as if it had once had a
door on it. 'There's a couple of T-shirts with our logo on
hanging there in the closet—you've to wear them all times
when you're on duty. Wet-weather gear on the right-hand
side. The shared bathroom and toilet are down the corridor.
We'll go through all the safety stuff at the briefing, but use
the rope to get around the deck when there's a heavy swell.
Sorry it's not the *QE2*, but we save as much space as we
can for the refugees. We need safe, private spaces for preg-
nant women, nursing mums and anyone that needs isola-
tion. All the men we rescue and anyone else well enough

has to live and sleep on deck—depending on how many we have on here at a time.'

'It's all good.' Six weeks. That was all. The ship lurched. Ethan grabbed the wall as his stomach roiled.

'Looks like we're under way. If you need anything just ask. And…' Chase frowned. He looked as if he was about to say something but changed his mind with a quick shake of his head. 'See you on deck in ten minutes for the safety meeting. You can meet the gang then.'

Ethan threw his bag onto the bunk that looked the least slept in and inhaled. This was fast turning into a trip from hell. An old adversary, moving on from the past, the smallest cabin in the history of tiny cabins. Water. Cold. Could it get any worse?

Oh, yes. It was a dry ship too. He laughed to himself. That was a tautology if ever he'd heard one, but there was no alcohol allowed, for anyone. Not that he was desperate for a drink, but sometimes it helped to chase the demons away.

Like last night; the hip flask. A flash of sparkling eyes. And the rest…

He blew out a breath. Scrubbed his hand over his hair and went to meet the team. With a bit of luck he'd be too busy to care about anything other than saving lives.

When he arrived on deck he found a group of around ten people, all wearing the same logoed white T-shirts, chatting and laughing. They seemed completely at ease and there was a sense of camaraderie he knew well and had seen often in groups of volunteers. No one vied for power, everyone made the mission their priority and aimed to carry their weight as a team member. Seemed that was just the same on a ship as it was on dry land.

Chase introduced him to the captain, an American surgeon, some of the ship's crew, a Danish midwife called Freja and Akil, Ethan's Egyptian cabinmate.

'Hope you don't snore, man. Good to have you here.' Akil shook Ethan's hand firmly and a smile formed between an impressive dark moustache and beard.

Ethan doubted he'd be in the cabin much anyway. At least, he hoped not. 'No promises, mate, I'm sorry.'

'This is Kristina, a GP on her first mission.' There was a softening in Chase's voice as he introduced the woman Ethan recognised from the dock.

Interesting.

Or maybe it had been his imagination, because Chase walked away then and didn't give her a second look.

But two red spots flamed on Kristina's cheeks as she smiled and Ethan knew they were nothing to do with him. 'Hello, Ethan. I hope you're remembering all our names, we're going to test you in a minute.'

'And I'm probably going to fail, but don't hold it against me—' He was cut off in mid-sentence as a door swung open and a breathless woman ran onto the deck wearing a regulation white T-shirt and dark blue shorts, honey-coloured hair whipping round her face and large brown eyes glittering with smiles. 'Hello, everyone, sorry I'm late. I was just helping one of the crew with a nasty abrasion on his hand.'

The scents of coconut and hibiscus filled the salty air and Ethan did a double take as his heart damn near thumped out of his chest. He remembered the way she'd moaned, the way she'd kissed, and his whole body strained for her. What the hell…? 'Claire?'

'Ethan?' She took a step back, mouth open. Her eyes widened and the only emotion Ethan could read on that pretty face was horror.

This was her adventure? This was freedom and excitement? A refugee boat with no luxuries, no personal space and little comfort? He'd pegged her to be choosing something else entirely. And not with him.

Chase's eyebrows rose as he watched their interaction. 'You know each other?'

We had sex in a lift then walked away.

Ethan eventually found words. 'We've met.'

Judging by the way his body was reacting with heat and muscle memory at last night's escapade, and her stiff body language telling him to back right off, it seemed that things could definitely get a whole lot worse.

It had been a one-night stand, they'd both agreed. Strangers, never to meet again. A game played well. Until now. Claire sucked in air as she walked towards the group, trying to look as nonchalant as anyone could with a high heart rate and embarrassment whipping through her at sixty knots.

Ethan. Was this for real?

In the fresh morning light he looked even more gorgeous than he had in the dim bar lighting and elevator shadows. She didn't know his full name or what he did for a living, but she knew how he looked in the throes of an orgasm. She knew what kept him awake at night...or at least she could guess after what little information he'd given her under duress. She knew how he kissed, how he held on tight and how easily he could let go. And she knew that was just the warning she needed to heed.

His eyes narrowed ever so slightly as he admitted to the group that they knew each other, and that small frown was enough for her to know he wanted to forget last night as much as she did. But now that they were face to face and doomed to spend the next few weeks together, she wasn't sure forgetting him was going to be possible.

'It's a small world,' she mumbled to her new boss Chase, and prayed the heat rising from her chest wouldn't materialise as a full-body blush. Unfortunately it did.

Luckily, one of the women handed her a bottle of water

and a smile and made space to stand next to her in the semi-circle to hear the safety briefing.

'Thanks for the water. I'm Claire,' she whispered as they walked over to see how the lifeboats were released.

'Kristina.' The woman smiled and stuck out her hand. 'Hello.'

Claire shook. 'First-timer too?'

'Yes.' Kristina looked so confident it was hard to imagine this was all new to her. 'But at least you know someone here.' She nodded towards Ethan. 'That's got to make things easier.'

'Oh. I don't really know him. We've only just met. I mean…last night. We were at the same hotel. We bumped into each other in the bar.' Claire winced. Now she was just gibbering and making everything seem worse.

But Kristina smiled. 'He seems nice anyway.'

'Nice. Yes.' 'Nice' wasn't necessarily the word she'd use. Sexy. Orgasmic… She bit the smile from her mouth. 'I don't know him that well.'

'I think we'll all know each other far too well by the end of this mission.'

'Oh? What kind of a mission is this exactly? What do you know that I don't?' Claire laughed, wondering what she'd signed up for.

'I'm ex-military,' Kristina explained. 'Living in close quarters like this for weeks on end can get claustrophobic. We'll probably all have cabin fever by week four.'

Great. Stuck on a ship with a guy who made her hot and want to know the answers to too many questions with no reprieve. Claire chanced a look over at Ethan, who was chatting and laughing with one of the team, and she wondered how the hell he'd come to be here when his favoured place was Africa and he appeared to be more comfortable outdoors than in the cramped conditions they had on board. No wonder, given what he'd told her about his past

last night. How did a person even come back from a life-threatening situation like that?

She watched as he bristled and his back snapped straight when Chase called for everyone's attention. More questions formed in her head. Why the sharp reaction to the SARCO? Did Ethan not like playing second fiddle to another man? Did he want to call the shots?

And why was she interested? He was not her business. She'd come here to find out who she was and to take the lead in her life for the first time in years. Doing her thing, for herself, by herself. Like she had last night when she'd had sex with a man because she'd wanted to, and she'd liked the way putting her own needs first had made her feel. She'd liked the way Ethan had made her feel too. Which wasn't helping her right now.

Not wanting to spend any more time thinking about him she refocused on Chase, who was reading from a clipboard giving everyone their duties for the morning. 'We have a specific area we're allowed to patrol between here and as far south as Libyan territorial waters and we're heading out there today. We patrol and we wait. We listen to reports from other ships, the coastguard or aircraft sightings. We respond. Sometimes it takes days to hear of something or someone needing help, sometimes it's only a matter of hours before we get alerted to a raft or a boat in trouble.

'In the meantime, we keep busy. I've left an inventory in each of the medical rooms and everything should be in order, but we do daily checks so we can radio for more supplies if we need them. Kristina, can you go with Freja and check the meds? Claire and Ethan, I need you to check the surgical room, make sure the oxygen cylinders and ECG machine are working, the resus trolleys are stocked and acquaint yourselves with the layout. When there's a squall things can move about and we all need to know

exactly where the emergency equipment is so we can put
our hands on it when we need to.'

Brilliant. If Ethan had been allocated to work in the
clinic area then he must be a medic of some sort. Now she
was going to spend awkward one-to-one time with him,
and probably work closely in a team. But if he registered
that inconvenient fact he didn't give anything away; he
didn't meet her eye when he heard their names mentioned
together, no partners-in-mischief wink.

Her mouth suddenly dry, she followed his taut back and
long hurried strides across the deck, through the medical
suite and into the surgical area, apparently also known
as the operating theatre, resus, birthing suite, morgue or
whatever it needed to be as required.

He held the door open, let her go in first then closed
it behind them. Then he turned to look at her, those blue
eyes wide with shock. He sighed heavily as if he'd been
holding his breath since the moment she'd rushed onto the
deck. 'Claire? This is surreal.'

It wasn't accusatory, he just sounded confused, amazed,
maybe a little freaked, as she was. It was one thing to have
a one-night stand but something altogether different when
that one-night stand turned into a six-week co-habitation
on a mission bound to be fraught with emotion for the
people whose lives they were saving. There wasn't space
for anything personal. She looked at him and hoped being
with him twenty-four hours a day for too many weeks
would stop the flutter in her belly she got just by looking
at him. 'Doctor? Paramedic? Nurse? Why are you here,
Ethan?'

'Paediatrician. You?'

'Nurse.' So things were going to get cosy here, at least
in geography if nothing else. 'How long are you here for?'

'Six weeks.' His eyebrows rose in question. *You?*

'Nine.' At least she'd have some time without him when

she'd be able to breathe. 'So, when I said I was running away to sea, you didn't think about casually mentioning you were too?'

'Believe me, there was no running on my part.' He ran a hand through that lovely sand-coloured hair that she imagined she could still feel under her fingertips, as if he'd been somehow branded onto her memory—touch, scent, taste. 'If I remember rightly, Claire, you didn't want to discuss real life. Besides, Marseille is one of the biggest ports in France, you could have been going anywhere...chasing racing drivers.'

'That was a joke. I'm not chasing anyone. The opposite, in fact.'

'I know, you made that very clear. But I imagined you on some fancy super-yacht sailing around the Med on holiday. Or...' He shrugged and there was a hint of a smile. 'Okay, to be honest, I didn't imagine you anywhere other than in that lift. I much prefer reality to games and dreams.'

His eyes settled on her mouth and she saw the flare of interest and felt it resonate deep in her belly. The attraction was still hot and intense and very inconvenient given this was her fresh start. 'Not that I need to explain, but I was badly hurt by my cheating ex, my self-esteem fell below zero and I needed to feel strong again. Last night I did. I took control and did what *I* wanted and I'm not ashamed of that.'

He shook his head, interest morphing into concern. 'I don't want you to feel ashamed, not at all. We were consenting adults and last night was amazing. Trust me, I'd much rather be there doing that than be here doing this. I'm just surprised to see you.'

'I can tell. You didn't exactly look thrilled when I walked onto the deck.'

'I have a feeling things are going to get busy and complicated and probably messy on this ship. And once the

six weeks is up I'm heading straight back to Africa.' He turned and busied himself with checking the valves on the oxygen cylinders and writing things down on the clipboard Chase had given him. 'I don't think we should take things any further.'

'I wasn't going to suggest we did.' She spoke to his back, glad that he couldn't see the two hot spots spreading over her cheeks. 'I know how one-night stands work, Ethan. We were both very upfront about what we wanted yesterday, I'm not about to hold you to anything. Relax, you don't have to warn me off.'

He turned to look at her, his expression troubled. 'I'm explaining, not warning.'

'You're doing both.' There was a crushing feeling in her chest that told her she felt a little hurt that he was flipping her off like this, which was weird because she had thought about saying the same thing. She should have been relieved. The last thing she needed was emotion involved in all of this and she had a feeling there'd be emotion aplenty if she got to know Ethan more.

His shut-down in the lift halfway through a story about being crushed under a building demanded questions and they required answers, as did his love affair with Africa, but then there would be more connection and she'd be falling for him and before she knew it she'd be back at square one, having her heart broken by someone who couldn't love her back. 'Don't worry, I'm cool with drawing a line under last night and I have no desire to step over it.'

Liar. Her head had it all sorted, she just had to get the memo to the rest of her body.

He nodded. 'Good, because I don't want there to be anything awkward while we're here.'

'Not from me.' She raised her palms.

His shoulders relaxed a little and he smiled. 'Or me. Friends, then?'

'Yes. I think we could both do with a friend in a place like this.' She didn't want to admit that her body strained for more than that.

His smile grew. 'And I'm glad I added a little of the excitement you're looking for.'

'Oh, believe me, you did.' Heat rushed over her skin at the memory of his hands and his mouth and how he had felt inside her. Keeping on the right side of the line was going to be a damned sight harder with those memories flitting back every time she set eyes on him.

The door swung open, interrupting her thoughts. Ethan snapped upright and his smile fell as he looked towards the door. Chase breezed in and as he caught Ethan's eye his jaw tensed.

What was it with these two? They were like two stags locking horns.

'We need everyone on deck,' Chase said. '*Moonbird* has radioed a sighting of an overloaded vessel in distress eight nautical miles south-south-west. First visuals estimate around fifteen people on board, no obvious life jackets, thick smoke coming from one side of the boat.'

Her heart kicked up a gear. This was why she was here—to save lives, not to moon over out-of-reach men or analyse relationships that were none of her business. 'Sure, Chase. We'll finish this up later.'

'Wind's getting gnarly, it could be a bumpy ride. Make sure you grab your life jackets.' Chase nodded and just before he left he added, 'We have crew who are experienced in retrieval. We do an assessment of each person as they come on board. There's a translator who documents everything with you. You'll soon get to grips with it all.'

As they followed him out Ethan turned to Claire and frowned. '*Moonbird?*'

'One of the humanitarian planes that patrols the area. Whoa.' The boat lurched forward and she grabbed onto

the rope that made walking around the deck much easier
and safer.

'How do you know that?' Ethan was at her shoulder,
one hand at her hip making sure she didn't fall.

Friends do that, she reminded herself. 'I did my re-
search. When I applied I treated it like an exam—studied,
got to know the subject inside out, learnt all the nautical
terminology. Didn't you prepare?'

'I only agreed to come at the last minute. They were
desperate.' The way he said the last word made it sound as
if he had a bad taste in his mouth. Or maybe it was because
the boat pitched again, forcing him to grab the rope too.
'I do have a file they emailed me but I haven't read it all
yet. Okay, stay there. This is getting hairy.' He ran to the
life jacket stores and brought two bright orange ones back.
He handed one to her and tugged one over his head. If she
wasn't mistaken he was looking about as green as she felt.

She fastened the jacket round her waist. 'Is it bad form
to throw up when you're in the middle of a rescue attempt?'

'I would say so.' He laughed, pulled something from
his pocket and held it out to her. 'Mints from the flight.
Might help.'

'Thanks.' But he wasn't looking at her any more. His
gaze had landed on Chase, standing on the bridge with
binoculars at his eyes, and he was back to looking trou-
bled again. 'Ethan, have you and Chase worked together
before?'

'No.' He frowned. 'Why?'

'You both seem a little, er...tense around each other. Is
that the alpha male thing playing out?'

'I barely know the guy.' He shrugged as he held the
rope more tightly, his knuckles white. 'I'm sure he's ex-
cellent at his job.'

'That doesn't explain anything.'

Spray washed over starboard side, making the wooden

deck slippery, and she tried to get purchase with her train-
ers. Her stomach felt as if it was being turned inside out.
'How long does it take to travel eight nautical miles?'

'Don't ask me. You want to go sit down somewhere?'

'Yes, but I'm not going to.' Nausea rippled through her,
from her stomach to her head. She did not want to throw
up in front of him, or anyone else, for that matter. 'I think
we must be sailing into last night's storm. *Eugh.*'

As if he could read her mind, he briefly tipped her chin
up and smiled. 'Apparently they have meds. Do you want
me to get some?'

She shook herself away from his hands and checked to
see if anyone had been watching this interaction. The last
thing they needed was for people to think there was some-
thing going on between them, or be made to feel awkward
around them. But they were hidden by the life rafts. Alone.
Her heart tripped. Last night being alone with him had felt
like heaven, now it felt dangerous and illicit. 'No. I'll be
fine. But thanks anyway.'

'You don't have to fight it. What use will you be if you
feel ill?' He smiled softly. 'Can I tell you a secret?'

'Oh? Okay.' She was thrown back to the lift when she'd
leaned against him, all alcohol-fuelled bravado, and told
him she was scared. The first touch of his skin against
hers had sent tingles through her body. The scent of him
as he'd wrapped her close had driven her crazy with lust.
More tingles zipped through her now. It would be too easy
to reach for him but she couldn't. Just couldn't.

He gripped the rope with both hands as the ship tipped
hard to port. 'I'm pretty sure I'm going to throw up any
minute too if I don't have a tablet. Wait here.'

'That's your secret?' Laughing, she watched him slide
across the deck as the ship crashed over a huge wave, and

wished he wouldn't be quite so nice to her. Being a friend was all well and good, but not when your body wanted to hurl itself right over that line.

CHAPTER FOUR

WAS THIS THE karma he'd been waiting sixteen years for? Slip-sliding on a creaky ship in close proximity to the man who'd chosen to save him instead of someone more worthy. And Claire. And the damn attraction to her that he couldn't act on either here or when they were back on solid ground.

If he were a religious man he'd have thought it was some kind of a test. One he was most likely to fail if Claire stayed on his radar. He tried to hurry back to her but spray showered him and cold seeped through his bones as he fought to keep upright and moving forward. As he peered across the bow he saw Chase watching him inch his way back towards Claire. Ethan raised a hand. *All good.*

Chase nodded then turned away.

If the tension between them was obvious to Claire then it was going to be obvious to everyone else. It wasn't his intention to make any of the team feel uncomfortable, so he'd have to find time to speak to Chase and blow through the uneasy connection that had brought them to this point.

But not today. He barely had time to hand a strip of pills to Claire when the ship's engines quieted and someone shouted for the rescue raft. Someone else stumbled past, dragging a box of life jackets. Two people lowered

the boat landing for the rib to attach to when it came back
with rescued passengers.

'Okay?' he asked Claire.

'I will be.' She nodded, took the tablets with a gulp of
the bottled water she'd been gripping since he'd first seen
her that morning. At one point he'd had a feeling she might
hit him with it.

Ignoring the almost overwhelming nausea, he dredged
up a smile. 'Come on, then, let's really get this adventure
started.'

From where he was standing he could see crew mem-
bers, balancing precariously on turbulent rafts, setting up
a human chain. He scanned forward to the sinking dinghy,
which was lurching up and down in the thrashing waves
and to two small and shocked-looking children at the front.
They needed to be off that flimsy boat now.

What was the hold-up? As always in the early stages
of any mission he felt stymied by inaction. But there were
protocols they all had to follow to keep everyone safe and
he knew the crew was doing its best to work as quickly
as possible. But his hands were itching to do something.

He pushed forward to the boat landing but was held
back by Akil. 'No, Ethan, this is your first time. Just watch
and wait for us to pass you the children. We need you on
the ship, not in the water.'

One of the kids was strapped into a life jacket then
picked up and hauled over sloshing angry water into the
hands of an aid worker, then another and another until
Ethan was handed the shivering, soaking boy who looked
about six years old. His rich ochre skin was ice cold and
his huge brown eyes screamed of panic but he didn't utter
a sound.

In contrast, the next bundle passed along was a wrig-
gling, screaming little girl who was handed over to Claire.

'Hey, buddy, you're safe now.' Ethan wrapped the boy

in a space blanket and tried to soothe him, his words translated through a Libyan translator called Fatima. 'It's okay, you're safe. Where's Mum? Dad?'

Having done this for years he knew how children were often either insatiably clingy to whatever surviving parent they had, or were so inured to loss and separation it made his heart twist. No child should ever have to go through this, but if they did he wanted to make things better for them. Always.

The boy pointed a trembling hand to a woman who was being helped onto the ship and Ethan breathed out. 'Mama?'

The boy nodded. One less trauma for him if he had a parent alive and walking. 'Great. Let's get you all through to the clinic room.'

The girl's screams punched the air, rough and raw despite the translator's and Claire's best efforts to reassure her. The mother was wrapped in a thick blanket and brought with them. No possessions came up from the sinking boat, not a toy or a single bag with documents or spare clothes. Nothing that was theirs. They had nothing except each other.

Better make damned sure they're going to be okay, then.

He sat the boy on an examination couch and made a quick assessment. Hypothermia. No doubt a degree of starvation and dehydration; his ribs were visible and his wrists were impossibly thin. His heart was pumping a little too slowly for Ethan's liking; one of the sure signs of a too-cold body. A quick history from the mum—over her daughter's incessant screams—told of no immunisations so they were at risk of common childhood diseases too. The boy was called Hassan, the girl Aya.

'Can you explain we need to get the wet clothes off, then go grab them all some fresh things from the clothing cupboard next door? Mum can get changed there too,

it's more private,' Ethan said to the translator. 'I'll give Hassan a hand. Then I'll take a temperature reading and we'll need to get some fluids into them all pretty quickly.'

Fatima explained everything to the little mite, who just stared up at Ethan blankly with those enormous dark eyes. Ethan tried a smile and helped the boy tug the life jacket off, followed by a soaking thin cotton top from his shivering body. Hassan was compliant and almost sleepy, so Ethan rubbed his little arms and legs to get his blood flowing. He was immediately thrown back to an icy dark space where Chase had done the same for him.

He battled the memories away. Time enough for that in his dreams, he didn't need them interfering with his work too. He winked at the kid. 'Come on, mate, we need to get you warm.'

'L'était une petite poule grise...' Claire sang softly as she rocked little Aya, swaddling her first in a space blanket then a thick wool cover.

A loose lock of hair swung forward to frame Claire's face as she softly sang the words of what appeared to be a lullaby that his schoolboy French wasn't up to translating. He remembered the way her hair had slid through his fingers, the lemony scent of the strands, and he felt a hot jolt of lust skim across his skin, arrowing to his groin.

Eventually she came to the end of the song and stopped rocking and her gaze caught his across the room. For the briefest moment something passed between them—a look that slowly heated from friends to over-the-line hot. A flash of need.

He wondered if she was thinking the same thing he was and whether her mind had gone back to the lift and the sensual kisses, the press of bodies in the shadows and the soft moans in the air. Or whether she was thinking about that line she'd talked about and if it would give under a little strain.

Looking at her now, he was sorely tempted to rub the damned line out completely, find somewhere private—if such a place existed here—and kiss her again.

Hassan tugged on Ethan's hand, making him remember just what he was supposed to be doing. Tearing his gaze from Claire, he helped the boy into the dry clothes Fatima had brought in, then took his temperature. Too low. 'We need to warm this lad up from the inside too. Hey, buddy, do you want a drink of hot chocolate? That'll warm your tummy.'

The mum came back wearing fresh clothes and stood close, speaking in a language that occasionally sounded familiar, although he didn't understand most of what she was saying. It was the language of refugees: *Thank you... My babies...help my babies. Food, please. I want to live.*

Geez, he knew how that desperate panic bloomed raw and hot in the centre of your chest and how easily it spread through every cell. How easy it was to give in to it instead of using it to fuel your actions. How you clung to anything, any hope, anyone.

You'd better be worth it, Reid.

He damned well hoped he was.

Then he wondered if being on a ship with Chase and Claire was sending him quietly mad, because nothing else could explain how easily his mind slipped from the present to the past and then further back into ancient history where the roots of his nightmares had been sown.

Fatima pressed a cup of warm chocolate to the boy's lips. Ethan watched the shock and surprise, and their first smile of the day was won. Chocolate; the friendliest language on the planet.

'Some for Aya too?' Claire asked in a measured soft voice, holding her spare hand out for the cup Fatima was passing her. Claire was the calm they needed, but he liked

to hope his efficiency and attention to detail saved lives as much as hope. In essence it was teamwork.

As the little girl gulped down the warm drink, he prioritised. 'We need to know how long they were out there and what they managed to eat or drink. Past medical issues and brief history—anything we need to be aware of until we can get them to safety. And she needs to get out of those wet clothes.'

Claire nodded. 'I'm just holding her a minute longer so she knows she's safe.'

'She needs warm, dry clothes.'

'I know that.' Claire shot him a confused look. 'She's starting to settle and she's slowly warming up. When she's calmed down enough I'll get her into dry clothes and then we might be able to do a thorough assessment. We won't be able to do anything with her screaming her head off.'

They were working from two sides of the same plan and that was okay. Claire's body heat would warm the little girl and she could do some quick core assessments just by observing her. Ethan was more act first then explain, knowing from experience how the cold and wet bit into your bones and how quickly you wanted it to stop.

'Okay. Once they're fed and calm we'll have a longer chat with them about their medical needs. When the families come to the camps we usually leave them a day or so to settle in then we do the best we can to get them immunised at the very least, fed as well as possible. Sometimes they've been for weeks with little food, particularly the parents.'

Claire's face fell. 'How bad must things be to need to risk your life and that of your children like this?'

Having seen it over and over in various camps across Africa, he knew exactly how bad life could be. 'Many are fleeing torture or war, some are escaping human trafficking. Sometimes the risk of leaving is worth much more

than staying. It's not our place to judge, we just have to help them rebuild something better than what they left behind.'

'I wouldn't dream of judging. I'm here to help them.'

Claire was holding a snotty-nosed child dressed in rags, her hair had been whipped in all directions, her cheeks red from windburn. She had jeans with holes in the knees and a regulation baggy T-shirt and he couldn't help smiling at her, because if he was ever asked to describe what beautiful was he would remember this moment. 'Not quite the luxury cruise I had you pegged for.'

'I think, Ethan, you had me pegged all wrong. Funny how we make assumptions.' She smiled back and there was a tease that reminded him of last night. 'I like to be proved wrong, though.'

'What do you mean?'

Her eyes sparkled. 'I'm glad you're not a racing driver.'

And for the first time since he'd left Africa he was ridiculously pleased to be on this ship, with her.

But then Akil appeared at the door with two grubby children on one side and two on the other. 'Four more for you, Doc. And another couple just coming off the raft now.'

'Okay. Good. Right. Yes.' Claire's eyes grew wide and she took a deep breath. As an old hand at this kind of thing Ethan knew how that kick of anticipation felt, how the adrenaline surged and got you through. Although it was a whole lot different on a boat. And with that, the adventure was turning serious and all thought of anything but saving lives fled Ethan's brain.

It was impossible to sleep in the dark cabin. Shadows flared on dull white bulkheads that crowded in closer and closer. The rhythmic crash of waves against the hull and the constant hum of the ship's engines should have lulled him, but they made his gut churn instead. And Akil's snoring was bordering on cataclysmic.

No matter how much Ethan tried to still his mind, it kept tumbling over the day's events. He couldn't get rid of the image of hope shining in Claire's eyes as she'd soothed the little girl and the way his harping at her to get Aya into dry clothes had made her second-guess herself. It wasn't his job to make her question her efforts; as a team member he was supposed to boost her.

The walls pressed closer and he tried to focus on counting his breaths but Claire's face floated to the forefront of his mind. Again.

No point in thinking about her. Or what her words had meant; that she was glad he was there and how much that had made him smile for the rest of the day.

The elevator sex had been amazing.

He'd had enough one-night stands to be able to handle the aftermath well. But he was on full alert whenever she was around, and wondering where she was when she wasn't in his direct line of vision. Not just because he wanted to see her but because he needed to know she was safe and well and…hell, this wasn't working, on so many levels.

He sighed, tugged the pillow out from under him and wrapped it over his ears. But the restlessness wasn't outside. It was deep inside him, making his mind whirr and his legs twitch. Sleep wasn't going to come. Again.

He threw the covers back and stole quietly out of the cabin, hoping a walk round the boat in the fresh air might make him tired enough to sleep.

As if. But, hell, it was worth a try.

Once on deck he held onto the rail and filled his lungs with huge gulps of salty air as he looked across the water. There was nothing out there but a thick blackness that was almost tangible. A million stars slicked across the sky. Murmured stirs and a harmony of snores floated to him from the area where the rescued men were sleeping.

Otherwise there was no sound apart from the swoosh of the water against the hull.

It was almost peaceful but for the lurch in his gut. A couple more days and he'd have that under control, which was probably more than he could say about his interest in Claire.

Five weeks and six days. He closed his eyes and imagined lying perfectly still under canvas, arms behind his head, the dry heat of the day warming his skin…

'Hey.' It was Claire, rocking back and forth with a sleeping Aya on her shoulder. 'You awake too?'

He was surprised at how much his heart kicked up at the sight of the woman he'd only met again yesterday. She looked tranquil and relaxed as she lulled the little girl and something fisted tight in his heart. He breathed it away. Tried to. The problem with Claire was that she had him imagining all sorts of out-of-reach things, like what it would be like to wake up with her and way…*way* down the line, what it would be like to wake up with her *every day.*

He breathed out and focused on here and now instead of fairy-tale land. 'I never sleep well the first night in a new place. I guess it must be all the new sounds and smells and the lumpy beds, but I always crash from exhaustion the second night, so I'm just holding out until then. How's the seasickness?'

She grimaced as she gently patted the little girl's back. 'Just about bearable. You?'

'I'm told it's better if you can see the horizon and I was hoping some fresh air and a walk would help too.'

'Lovely.' She smiled her entrancing smile. 'Where shall we go? Up the Champs-Élysées? Hollywood Boulevard? What about Oxford Circus?'

'We're in the middle of the Mediterranean Sea. But I was actually in Darfur.' He'd been around her for less than twenty-four hours and her quirks were clearly start-

ing to rub off on him. If you didn't like your current circumstances then you pretended you were someone else and somewhere else, and hoped life would become more bearable.

Her eyes grew wider. 'Darfur? Tell me about it. What's it like?'

Hell on earth some days, but he'd been trying not to think about that. 'It's dry and dusty and flat, and in the early morning it's so peaceful and still you can almost imagine that there is nothing bad in the world. A new day, a fresh start and just as the sun begins to rise you can see the red earth stretching out before you. Then the sounds start: babies crying, a call to prayer, mothers begging for food, the expected tensions of overcrowded communal living spilling into fights and, in the middle of it all like some kind of miracle, there are children playing.' He thought about Hassan and the mute shock that had enveloped the boy. 'The kids are the most amazing. No matter what they've been through or seen, their smiles are enough to put your whole day straight.'

'Wow. You clearly love it.'

'Don't get me wrong, there's unimaginable poverty and grief there but you have to believe each day is going to give you something positive or else you can't survive it.'

'So you think of a place like that to help you get over being here?' Claire shook her head. 'You must hate boats as much as lifts.'

'About the same. It's not the vessel as such, it's the cramped space. The wet and cold.' He wasn't going there. 'Do you often make things up? Last night you were all about being an escaped prisoner.'

'When reality's looking crappy then, yes, why not? I used to do it with my little brothers and sisters when they had nightmares or were upset.'

'You have a close family?'

'You bet.' She smiled. 'Too close at times. Two sisters and two brothers. Always noisy, always chaos, no privacy. They're all still living in the same village we grew up in… some still at school, one left to go to university and then came back. When I ran away to sea I wasn't just escaping my ex, I was escaping my crazy family too. My youngest sibling is four years old and I'm the oldest, so when Mum wasn't available for something they always turned to me.'

'Wow, how old are you if your sister is that young?'

'Twenty-six. Élisabeth was one of those little change-of-life mistakes and a complete shock for my parents. We all love her completely, though. Then there's Eric, who is ten, Camille, sixteen, Marcus twenty-two. And me; sister, second mum, babysitter and entertainment all rolled into one. It's lovely on a good day, but pretty claustrophobic, to be honest.' She was still rocking gently, her feet anchored wide to keep herself steady on the moving ship. He imagined she'd done that soothing motion a thousand times before; it sat well on her, easy and calm. And briefly he had an image of her and him and… He shook his head. Goddamn, now he was starting to fantasise about happy families, which was ironic given he hadn't any experience of one.

He wondered how it would feel to live in a messy life like hers instead of in the sterile one he'd grown up in—no noise, no chaos, just his parents locked away in their study discovering important things for their important university jobs… And in the process ignoring their, oh, so unimportant son and leaving him to get on with things on his own. 'So that's why you can make things up so easily, it's a defence mechanism. Escape of the mind if not the body.'

'Probably. When the younger ones were being stroppy I needed to be able to create some peace and quiet in the middle of anarchy. So why not do it now too, even though we're adults? This ship is churning like a roller-coaster

and I'm not getting used to it fast enough. I don't like the way it's making me feel, so why not pretend I'm somewhere else?'

'Like in a lift?' The words shot out before he could stop them.

'Ethan. We agreed.' She fired a warning look at him, but not before he saw the memory cloud her eyes. If he wasn't mistaken she still wanted him as much as she had last night and the feeling was very definitely mutual.

Heat flared through him and he wanted nothing more than to wrap her in his arms and slide his mouth over hers again. 'I was trying to distract you. It worked on me well enough last night. It happened, Claire, we can't pretend it didn't.'

'But we don't have to keep talking about it.' She was right, there wasn't anywhere they could take it, especially on a ship with little privacy. But he'd had enough trouble trying to get to sleep tonight knowing she was only a few doors away. Knowing what she tasted like and aching to taste her again and again.

'If we were somewhere else…' He swallowed hard and tried to erase the memory.

And then what? He'd had plenty of flings, but had never had the compulsion to get to know any of the women better. But, then, they'd all been on the same page as him: sex was for fun, a release, a game. Something you walked away from with a smile on your face. It wasn't about getting to know someone better or falling hard.

Claire grimaced. 'We're not somewhere else, though, are we? And in this particular instance I'm not prepared to pretend otherwise. We're here and we have to leave the past in the past.'

'If only it was that easy.' Ethan sighed. He'd been trying to put the past behind him for too long already. It wasn't working.

'We have very different futures planned, Ethan. If we're going to survive the next few weeks living in such close quarters we're going to have to agree that we forget about last night. Please, let's not mention it again.'

'Okay. You're right.' But, regardless, everything about not touching her again felt wrong.

'It's not that I don't want to, it just makes sense not to. I'm here to work, not mess around with an unsuitable man.'

He couldn't help laughing. 'Well, you definitely have the measure of me.'

'I know. Okay… I think it's safe to put little Aya down now. I wanted to give her mum a break. They were all exhausted and I imagine they have a long road to walk until they find some peace.' Shrugging, Claire walked over to the women's sleeping area and laid the little girl next to her mother, and just like that last night was put in its place and the line heavily drawn over in thick vivid pen so neither of them could forget where it was. Right there between them.

He saw how carefully she placed the child down into the crook of her mother's arms and almost couldn't bear the hope in her eyes. 'It's hard not to get attached, but they'll be gone in a matter of hours.'

'I heard there's a problem finding a port we can go to, so it might be a few days.'

'We're here to help them rebuild their lives, Claire. This is their first step; we make them safe and then we let them go, to whichever receiving country we can find, and that's where it ends for us. It has to, we can't keep track of them all. I know how easy it is to want to know what happens to them—we all want to believe in a happy ever after, right?' Even though they both knew that might never happen for some of the people they rescued. 'I had to keep reminding myself not to get involved when I first started this gig.'

'It's hard not to.' She glanced back at little Aya before they started to make their way on a walk around the deck.

The sea was a little calmer now and walking was substantially easier. 'It's hard knowing they're at the mercy of strangers.'

'I know, but we're strangers too and we care. That's the most important thing. And at least we hand them over to agencies who can help.' As it was her first mission she'd need to know she was valued and that she'd done a good job. No doubt what she'd seen and done today would live with her for a while. And there was, inevitably, more to come. 'You did well today, Claire. It takes a lot of guts to leave everything you know and come here to do this kind of work. It can be harrowing and difficult, but also very rewarding. Was your trouble sleeping because your mind was going over today's events?'

'Totally. I feel as if I'm never going to sleep again because there's so much going round in my head. It's certainly been a day of surprises.' She rubbed her hand over her neck and moved her head from side to side as if easing out knots in her neck. Ethan had to clench his fists to stop himself running his hands under her hair and massaging the tension away. But it didn't escape his notice that he wanted to, regardless of what they'd agreed.

'It has indeed.' He paused as they came across Chase sitting on his own in a dark corner of the deck, staring out to sea. He had that troubled expression again, as if he was trying to solve the problems of the universe. 'You okay, Chase?'

'Fine.' His old adversary raised a hand and waved them on, but Ethan didn't want to leave him alone like that. He stopped and looked at the SARCO, caught his eye and raised a question. *You really okay?*

Chase huffed out a breath and turned away.

Ethan didn't want to walk away but Claire shook her head and pulled his arm and he had no choice but to follow her.

Once out of Chase's earshot Claire whispered, 'He's been there for about an hour. Akil said he sits there every night, just staring into the distance. They just let him be. I guess we all have different ways of coping.'

Or not.

Did Chase ever think back to that night? Did he ever wonder why he'd been left on this earth when those four boys had died, when the building had collapsed on them and not him? Did his head threaten to explode the way Ethan's did when the words spun round and round like some sort of torment? *Why me? Why me? Why me?* Did Chase believe there had been a higher reason for choosing him over Nick?

And what kind of measure was he using to see if Ethan had been worth it after all? Was it the same measure Ethan himself used? Numbers tallying into the hundreds? Lives saved. But never enough.

'Hey, are you okay?' Claire's hand was still on his, tugging him back to the present. So much for leaving the past in the past. Her smile was soft and concerned and like a punch to his heart. 'Don't tell me…back in Africa? Somewhere warm and dry and sunny?'

'No.' Ethan shook away the rank memory. 'Sorry, not Darfur this time, but I *was* miles away.'

'It's okay. It's all okay.' Soothing and soft and sensual. 'Want to talk about it?'

It wasn't okay at all but he shook his head, because talking certainly wouldn't fix anything. 'No. But thanks.'

'You have to let it go.'

'What?'

'Whatever it is that's eating you up from the inside.'

He scrubbed his hand over his hair, amazed she was so perceptive and so vocal. 'This is what they mean about living so closely with people—they get to know you too

well.' And it hadn't ever bothered him until a particular someone had started probing into his thoughts.

'You want some privacy? Yes. Sorry, I should have thought. It is claustrophobic, not just in lack of space but with the number of people here.' She took a step back. 'I was just trying to help.'

'You are helping. Like you wouldn't believe.' The way she was looking at him, with a mixture of empathy and compassion, just about undid him. The temptation to talk to her about that night and about Chase and about being here was growing stronger with every minute he spent with her.

But what would that achieve? Absolutely nothing, apart from opening a can of worms he'd screwed closed sixteen years ago. Some things were best not discussed with anyone other than those who had been involved. Maybe Chase? Maybe one day. Certainly not today and not with Claire within listening distance. She didn't need to hear that.

It was weird how he felt so drawn to her. He wanted to tuck back a stray lock of hair that had been whipped up in the wind, but thought better of touching her; their connection was only getting more intense. It was made even more so by the thick cloak of darkness that seemed to cocoon them, and their lowered voices that spoke of an intimacy he was attracted to and yet overwhelmed by. So he took a step back too.

'You should try to get some sleep. It's going to be another big day tomorrow.'

She smiled. 'Yes, I'll give it another try. You should too.'

'*Try* being the operative word. Good luck and goodnight.' He walked behind her down the steel steps, keeping his eyes pinned to the space above her head and not paying any attention to the sway of her hips or the swing of her ponytail. Not breathing in that coconut scent. Not

wishing he had a time machine that could dial back twenty-four hours and press pause.

Then he crawled onto the tiny bunk and lay back with his hands behind his head, listening to Akil's wheezy snoring.

The refugee work was second nature, but it was everything else that made Ethan feel all kinds of confused. The only thing he knew for sure was that the longer he was on the ship the harder everything would get.

CHAPTER FIVE

By the next afternoon they'd reached Malta and Claire had waved goodbye to Hassan, Aya and their mother, and the other refugees, with a happier heart. Happy that they'd got to that point in their journey safely at least.

Then they sailed right back into international waters and fished more refugees out of the unforgiving sea. Rinse and repeat. And again. And, like the raging storm, the continual stream of people felt like it was never going to stop.

Sixteen days passed and they'd rescued four hundred and thirty-two men, women and children and found places of safety for them in various ports around the northern Mediterranean. And every single minute had been a mix of wonder and hell. Wonder at the resilience of these souls who'd had absolutely nothing but a desperate sense of survival as they'd fled atrocities so bad they often couldn't speak of them.

And the hell of spending sixteen long days where she saw Ethan for about fifteen hours a day, and the torment at being around him was driving her crazy.

Sure, it made sense for them to keep their distance but they were constantly tiptoeing around each other, like right now when they were heading to another rescue. It was a situation that could literally throw them together at any given moment and it made their conversation stilted. The temp-

tation to touch him was almost unbearable but ever since
that first night on the ship, when they'd agreed not to talk
about what they had done in the lift, he'd kept his distance.

And she'd kept hers. So she was down to just skirting
around him as they worked, but the more time she spent
with him and the more she saw his care and efficient com-
passion, the more she fell just a little harder for him.

'Claire? Claire, come, quick.' Ethan was taking the
weight of a heavily pregnant woman as he tried to help
her over to the medical room. 'She's in labour.'

'Oh. Okay.' This was going to be a challenge. 'Hello,
there. Let's get you somewhere more comfortable. What's
your name?'

But the woman kept moaning, one hand on her belly, the
other trembling and pointing towards the refugees' boat.

Claire took the woman's arm, and spoke to the translator.
'Fatima? Can you translate? Is she with anyone else? Hus-
band? Partner? Other children? Anyone to support her?'

Fatima, who was also Claire's cabinmate, spoke to the
woman. Paused. Tried a different-sounding language.
Eventually they ascertained she was from Eritrea and her
husband was one of the bodies they were now loading
onto the ship. Claire bit down the terror and distress rip-
pling through her, because it was nothing compared to
what Mariam—they'd discovered her name—was going
through. 'Is there anyone else with her?'

Fatima shook her head.

'Right, then. She has me.' With Ethan guiding, Claire
helped Mariam up onto the examination couch. Then she
snapped on gloves and with gentle coaxing Mariam re-
laxed enough for an internal examination. 'Does she know
her due date?'

Fatima asked and then translated. 'End of June, she
thinks.'

Claire did the maths and didn't like what she worked

out. 'So, eight weeks early, with ruptured membrane, seven centimetres dilated and very regular contractions. This baby is coming.' She looked at Ethan. 'Is there anything we can do to delay things?'

He shook his head, no doubt knowing as well as she did that once a baby decided to come there wasn't a lot to stop it, especially when they weren't medically equipped enough to have a full-blown obstetric service. 'Doubtful, but let's offer the betamethasone injection to help baby's lungs.'

'If only we had Freja.' Their midwife had been amazing just the other day with a mum who had been in a similar situation, but she'd had to leave the ship at the last port for a family emergency and their replacement midwife hadn't materialised yet. Typically poor timing. And, worse, Mariam was malnourished and exhausted. Claire couldn't imagine what horrors she'd endured up until now.

They set up a drip and gave her the injection, but Claire couldn't help noticing that her hands shook a little. This was another life at stake, one not even born yet, and the weight of responsibility hung heavily on their shoulders.

'Stress brings the babies early but we can do this. We can,' Ethan said so reassuringly and with such conviction that she couldn't help but believe him. Or wanted to, at least. 'I'll ask Chase to radio the base and airlift her out.'

'In this weather? They'll struggle to get a chopper out here and I'm not sure we have enough time. But baby's going to need an NICU for sure.' *If he or she survives.* Claire wouldn't give that thought more space in her head. This child was going to survive.

Fatima nodded. 'I'll go and ask him.'

'Wait.' Ethan looked up, anguish etched into his features despite his positive words. 'Tell him it's a preemie baby and that I said we need a chopper. Tell him we need to save this baby, there isn't a choice here. Say those words.'

Claire's heart did a little jolt as she watched him working. She liked it that he genuinely cared, that this seemed to be more than a job to him. He strapped a monitoring belt onto Mariam's belly and tried to get her to relax. 'Okay, Mariam. It's okay, baby's coming soon.'

'No. No.' Mariam held her belly and cried.

'We're going to need you to stay strong, honey, because this baby's coming whether we want it to or not.' Claire stroked Mariam's hand but Mariam clutched Claire's fingers. 'No.'

It was clearly the only English word she knew but she also understood smiles and soft voices. 'We'll help you, Mariam,' Claire crooned. 'Stay strong for the little one.'

Mariam's breathing changed and she became more focused as the contractions came fast and furious. She wriggled off the bed and stood up, pressing down on the examination couch as she moaned long and hard, then started to pant.

At the start of the next contraction Ethan held up his hand and counted with his fingers, waiting for the right moment. 'One. Two. Three. Push.'

Mariam bore down with a grunt.

No baby.

Claire squeezed her hand. 'It's okay, you're doing fine, Mariam. We'll just wait for the next contraction and you can push again.' Claire did the actions of panting and pushing, hoping Mariam would understand and follow her lead. 'That's right. Pant. Pant. Pant. Push. Push. Push for me. *Push.*'

No baby.

The heart rate that had sounded so clear and strong a few minutes before was starting to slow, which meant the baby was getting into distress. Claire took a deep breath, trying not to worry. Labours could be long and tough, especially

with first babies. 'Can you push again, Mariam? Yes, I know it hurts, but it'll be over soon.'

When the next contraction started Ethan positioned himself and counted. 'One. Two. Three. Push. Again. Push.'

Still no baby. No head crowning. Mariam started to cry again. 'No. No.'

'Okay, we can wait a little longer.' Ethan smiled, but Claire knew that giving birth on a rocking ship with strangers was not a formula for a relaxed birth. She fished out her phone and found some soothing music. It won her a smile, and then another. She stroked Mariam's hair back from her face, massaged her lower back and tried to make her feel as relaxed as she possibly could.

As the next contraction gripped their patient they waited for the count. Waited for the push. Waited for the head.

Still no baby.

The foetal heart rate was decelerating. And at the same time Claire's was increasing.

'She's exhausted, look at her.' She held Mariam's hand as she slumped back onto the bed, face screwed up tightly in pain and fear. Her breathing was accelerated and she was limp and clammy. 'We just need some time.'

Mariam pushed again and again and again. But each time she became more and more despondent. Claire was starting to panic inside, but tried to keep as calm as she could. 'One more time, honey.'

They were running out of time and Mariam's energy was draining fast. She lay back on the bed and closed her eyes. 'No. No.'

Claire took a deep breath and blew out slowly. 'If we were in a hospital we'd have everyone on standby now, we'd have all the equipment. If we don't do something they're...' *They're both going to die.* She didn't need to

say it but the words hung in the silence. 'We need this baby out.'

Ethan closed his eyes briefly, said something quietly then nodded. 'Okay.'

Claire was intrigued. 'Was that a prayer or something?'

'No. I was just going through all the possible reasons why labour doesn't progress. Common things occur commonly, my guess it's a nuchal cord compression. Right. Mariam, one more time.' His voice was gentle and if there was any worry at all in his mind he wasn't showing it to their patient. Luckily Fatima came back in at that moment and was able to help with the translation.

Claire took Mariam's hands in hers. 'Just wait for Ethan's instructions. For your baby's sake. Please. He's going to help.'

'A big push now. Please.' And Mariam pushed and Ethan calmed her and encouraged her.

And then baby was there.

And silent.

No. Claire's breath stalled in her lungs.

Breathe.

With a calmness Claire certainly didn't have, Ethan clamped and cut the cord, and placed the floppy baby into the little incubator. He rubbed its tiny chest, suctioned mucus. Listened to its heartbeat. Said a few choice words that were barely audible. Administered oxygen. Rubbed the tiny chest again. And Claire held Mariam's hands— because the new mum just wouldn't let go. She was holding onto Claire the way Claire wished the baby would grab onto life; tight and hard.

Come on.

Thirty-two weeks or thereabouts, a starving, grieving mum and a terrible sea voyage. Stress. Fear. They had rudimentary suctioning and resuscitation equipment and excellent medical expertise, but what they needed was a miracle.

Breathe, little one.

Breathe.

Then the faintest of squawks. And again.

Claire breathed out as Ethan caught her gaze and nod-ded. He may have been giving the impression of calm but the relief in his eyes was obvious as he said, 'Here you go. A girl. A lovely baby girl.'

Mariam took the baby in her arms and stared down at her, dry-eyed and shocked. So much had happened to her in the last few hours it must have been hard to reconcile it all. A death. A life. Survival against the odds. 'She's so small.'

'She's beautiful.' Claire couldn't disguise the emotion in her voice as it wobbled and broke. She fisted away tears, because if Mariam wasn't crying then her nurse couldn't. The baby was indeed beautiful but so small and at risk of respiratory problems, infection and so much more. Claire busied herself with helping skin-to-skin contact for mum and babe and attaching a pulse oximeter to the baby's foot. 'This is just to check her oxygen level.'

'I wish your father was here,' Mariam whispered. Fatima's voice cracked as she translated and they all stood and stared at this scrap of life that had come from such a terrible situation. 'But I'll love you enough for both of us. I'll do any-thing to keep you safe.'

Even travel hundreds of miles across raging seas to start a new life.

Chase appeared at the doorway. 'Chopper coming. ETA one hour. Taking her to Marseille. All okay?'

'Too small but, yes, so far so good.' Ethan nodded. 'And thank you.'

Chase managed the smallest of smiles. 'I'm not the lunatic taking on a storm in a helicopter. Don't thank me.'

But she noticed a slight softening in the way the two men looked at each other across the tiny baby and doting

mum and for a moment allowed herself to believe everything was going to be all right for them all.

As they waited for the helicopter, Claire helped Mariam into new clothes and listened as Fatima translated the mum's story. 'My husband suffered beatings and torture to earn enough money to pay for this journey. We needed to escape.' She closed her eyes and refused to say why. 'There were too many of us and we realised the boat wasn't going to make it to land. People panicked and tried to get the captain to send out an alarm for someone to come and help us, but he refused because he didn't want to get caught. A fight broke out and my husband pushed me to the front of the boat for safety. But then he was hit and fell overboard. He couldn't swim. There were no life jackets.'

He had paid the ultimate price for his love for his wife and unborn child. 'How will you cope in a strange place with a new baby?'

Determination shone from Mariam's eyes as she spoke through the interpreter. 'My husband died to save us so we will survive. I'll fight every day for my child. She will be my hope. I will call her Awate, which means victory.'

'Go safely, Mariam and little Awate.'

Claire silently prayed she would never be faced with such a situation but, if she was, hoped she'd have half the courage of Mariam. As she listened with wonder, Claire caught Ethan watching her. His words came back to her: *Don't get involved.* But it was too hard, she loved too easily. And, besides, how could you not get involved with such stories and such courage?

But as she waved them off she felt the pressure of the day creep under her skin and suddenly all her energy drained from her. She hugged her coat around her and ached to climb into a soft bed, pull the covers over her head and sleep.

Ethan stepped closer and the exhaustion morphed into

an ache to lean her head against his chest and feel his arms around her. Sharing this with him had only brought them closer. He smiled generously. 'You okay?'

'I don't know.' There was too much emotion here. Lives too tragic, a blessed new birth. And too much Ethan. 'I just wasn't expecting to feel like this.'

'Come with me.' Ethan walked Claire to the galley and sat her on one of the metal stools by the serving hatch. In contrast to the dimmed light in the medical room, the chrome fittings glared. Blinking into the brightness, she looked shocked and shivering and if he could have pulled her into his arms he would have. Instead, he made her a drink and pushed the warm mug into her hands. 'Drink this. I'm sorry it's not cognac.'

He knew he shouldn't have made a reference to their night, but what the hell…

Her hair had shaken loose from her work-smart ponytail and she looked exhausted with eyes smudged with shadows, but she managed a sexy slow smile that connected with his gut.

It's not that I don't want to do it.

More than two weeks had gone by and Claire's words had been going around his head. If only they'd known back then how they'd be thrown together and have to somehow ignore the need inside them, maybe they'd have stopped before they'd got so carried away. Or maybe they'd have thrown caution to the wind and spent the night together too.

She took a sip and sighed. 'Cognac dulls the senses, but hot chocolate cures all ills.'

No, kissing you would.

He'd kept his distance and watched her initiation into this kind of life from afar. He'd seen how it took pieces out of her, how she gave her all for these people. He saw

how deeply she cared and there was something about it that struck a chord deep inside him. More than amazing sex. More than sultry kisses. She was kind and compassionate and made him believe there was still a lot of good in the world.

It helped too, that she was utterly unaware of how beautiful she was or what just looking at her did to his gut, his head and his groin. But he was still sticking to his side of the line even if it killed him.

He sat on one of the stools next to her, close enough to chat but with enough distance that indicated *friends and nothing more*. 'You want to talk about it? Or do you want to go somewhere? How about Fiji? Tahiti? An exotic island where you get cocktails with umbrellas and calm, clear seas?'

'So very tempting, especially the calm seas, but sometimes you have to stay exactly where you are and just let things settle. I need to process what's just happened.' She shook her head and hugged the mug against her chest. 'I didn't think she was going to make it. That tiny thing. I swear I was breathing for her.'

'You and me both.' All he wanted to do was wrap Claire in his arms and comfort her. But right now she looked like she just needed someone to hold her. She'd shown endless courage and had supported Mariam in ways she didn't even realise. She'd given her hope and faith in good people and that would steer Mariam forward. 'You did well today.'

'Doesn't it break your heart?'

'I don't let it.' He shrugged, pushing the image of the floppy baby to the dark part of his brain where all the other shitty thoughts went. It was probably getting quite crowded in there. 'I'm probably immune to it now.'

'No, you're not. I saw the way you looked at Hassan and at Mariam. You were desperate for her baby to survive and for her too. You're not immune, you care very

deeply but you just won't admit it. How many people have you saved, Ethan?'

'Eight hundred and eighty-two direct interventions. Many more where I've helped.'

'You actually counted?'

'Yes.' He didn't offer any more explanation.

'And you will have given every single one of them the same care and attention, but you don't let yourself talk about it. You swallow it up and bury it deep.'

'Trust me, I'd go mad if I allowed it to get to me.' Nevertheless, Ethan felt the weight of responsibility square on his shoulders, always. More lives saved to add to his tally but it would never be enough to fill that yawning hole in his gut.

What would Nick be doing now if he'd lived? Would he be doing something like this, the way Ethan and Chase had steered their lives to rescue work? Or would he have a cushy suit job in the City? Or be the gold-medal-winning sportsman he'd been destined to be? Ethan scrubbed his hand across his jaw and decided not to think about any of that. 'Unless I'm already mad, of course.'

'I think we all are, just being here doing this instead of a safe job on dry land. Maybe it's a weird seasickness… of the head.' Claire laughed, and as if sensing his unease steered the subject away on another tangent. She seemed to have a second sense about what they should talk about; enough but not too much. Whisking him away to exotic locations instead of facing the reality of being on a jumped-up trawler.

'Okay, Mr Knight, why did you decide to do this kind of work instead of following the money? A lot of doctors just do private work.'

Mr Knight. His gut contracted at the memory that seemed from so long ago and yet was imprinted on the back of his eyelids every time he closed his eyes. The lift.

Her. The feel of her skin. 'I wanted to give something back and help people who aren't as fortunate as me. I had an inheritance a few years ago that means I don't have to be too concerned about living pay cheque to pay cheque.'

Most people said how lucky he was not to have to worry about money but Claire frowned. 'An inheritance means someone died, though?'

'Yes. Parents. Six years ago.'

'I'm so sorry, Ethan. Did they die at the same time? Oh, were they in the collapsed building too?' She put her hand over his and squeezed. Her skin was hot from the cup and her skin so soft.

But the thought of the collapsed building had ice running down his spine and he should have moved his hand from under hers but he let it stay just a little longer. For the warmth. 'No, they weren't in the building. It was a car crash, years later, on their way back from a dig up north.'

'A dig? What is a dig? It's something you do. To dig?'

'They were archaeologists'

'I see. I'm so sorry they died. In some ways it must have been better for them to go together. But it must have been so hard losing them both at once.' She laced her fingers into his and her thumb stroked the back of his hand. 'You've had a rough time over the years.'

At her concerned expression he shrugged. 'It's okay, we weren't close.'

'They're your parents, of course you were close.'

'You had a very different upbringing to me, Claire. Let's just say my folks had a hands-off approach to parenting. They were passionate about their work—they were academics, both professors and absorbed in a whole world that didn't involve me: ancient history. Present-day stuff didn't register. They preferred me to be away at boarding school rather than in their lives. They paid people to care for me while they were away. A stream of nameless baby-

sitters who had no interest in anything but the money. And strangely my parents were very money savvy. They invested a lot of their earnings in stocks and shares that have paid out well, and they had really great life insurance.'

She shuddered. 'I couldn't imagine being completely on my own in life.'

'It means you can be very flexible about where you go and what you do. No strings, nothing to bring you back.'

Her eyes brightened. 'I want that too. No one to think about apart from me. Bliss. Don't get me wrong, I do really love my family, but I just need to get away from them and from the village and do my own thing.'

'If you're so hell-bent on adventure, what happened to all those family plans you had with your fiancé?'

'Oh. Him.' As if she'd only just realised they were holding hands, she slid her fingers out from Ethan's. The broken connection with her ex clearly had her deciding there'd be no connection with anyone else either, at least not for the foreseeable future. She went back to cradling the cup. Probably a much safer option, given that the cup wasn't likely to kiss her any time soon.

'I'd known him since primary school. We'd grown up together in the same village. It was all we knew. Then I went away to do my nurse training in the city and we started to grow apart a little. But we still had those promises we'd made to each other, still had plans to settle down. I was going to get a community job in the local medical centre, he was going to run his parents' car mechanic business. We'd planned it for so long I couldn't see beyond that.

'But I'd spent my life looking after my siblings, being a homebody, and part of me craved something more. When I met people who'd travelled it sounded wonderful and I thought maybe we could do it for a while and then go back to the village. The thought of splitting up was the furthest

thing from my mind, I just wanted to see some of the world before we grew into being our parents.

'But David didn't want any of that. His parents are getting old and he's taking more responsibility in the business and he didn't want to leave them. So I agreed to stay for him—for us—but the arguments became more frequent and he became more distant and then one day I found him with one of our mutual friends. He said that with my big ideas he didn't trust me to stay around, so he'd moved on. It broke my world apart.' She finally smiled. 'But in the end it gave me the gift of freedom.'

'How's that working out for you?' The fiancé must have been the world's biggest idiot to have let her walk away. But, then, if he'd kept his promises she wouldn't be here with *him*.

'I love it. I love being free and having no ties, no responsibility for anyone but myself. I love making decisions for myself and myself alone.'

Her smile was as free as the status she was chasing. 'Independence suits you.'

'Yes, well it's hard work too.' She tugged her cardigan across her belly and visual signs of the strains of the day reappeared back under her eyes and in her expression. 'The past few days have been an eye-opener.'

'You chose a hard route. Like you said, there are easier jobs.' She was a giver and for once he wanted to give something back to her. So he came a little closer and tentatively put a hand on her shoulder.

'Ethan...we said we weren't going to do this.' The cup hit the counter as she turned to look at him. 'I shouldn't have touched your hand. I'm sorry. I was just sad for you.'

'It's just a shoulder massage, okay? You have knots on knots here.'

'Shoulders only?'

'Yes. Unfortunately. Shoulders only.'

She relaxed back against his hand and moaned softly. 'That is so good. So...damned...good.'

He could smell the hibiscus scent and he closed his eyes, trying to maintain some semblance of calm when his heart was raging and every part of him strained to touch her. He even managed to sound quite civil as he asked, 'Better now?'

'Yes. Oh, God. Yes. Now, that is so damned good.'

Her moans rattled his resolve. There was a perfect moment where his hand touched her skin and her breathing became ragged and the atmosphere in the room heated. If he pressed his mouth along that collarbone...if he turned her round he could kiss all the way up her throat to her mouth.

He turned her a little and his gaze snagged on hers and in that moment the memory of all the kissing, all the making love in the lift, all the moans and the fun rolled through him.

He wanted her.

And judging by the way she was looking at him, she wanted him too.

It could have been as simple as that, just as it had been in the lift, but it wasn't simple at all. She had dreams and he wasn't going to smash them. And he had promises that took him far away from here and didn't include anyone tagging along. She snapped upright, again apparently mind reading. 'Ethan. God, what are we doing? What if—?'

'What if what? What if someone comes in and sees you drinking hot chocolate and debriefing about a tricky medical emergency with a team member? Shock! Horror! It's okay to debrief after something like Mariam and Awate. In fact, all the research says it's imperative to talk after something like that.'

She gave him a wry smile. 'With a team member who has his hands on me.'

'Hand, singular. One hand.' Reluctantly he took his hand away. 'And now it's gone. More than once you've wanted to make me feel better and you've helped. I was reciprocating. But...' How to put it into words when they weren't allowed to talk about it? 'You know...'

'I do.' She looked up at him from under lashes that were impossibly long, framing dark eyes that were serious and laughter-filled at the same time. She was so achingly beautiful it made his heart hurt. 'It seems that we can't be trusted to be on our own.'

He laughed, but she was right. One more moment and things could have got seriously complicated. *More* complicated. 'It seems that way. Probably a good idea if we travel in packs from now on, so we're not in a position to get carried away. If you're feeling better I'm going to head back to the medical room and see if they need me.'

With a bit of luck he'd be kept busy for the next twenty-six days.

'I'm feeling a lot better. Wait—' She grabbed his closed fist and brought it close to her lips. Kissed each knuckle. Her gaze latched onto his with so much wanting it almost had him stripping her naked right there. Not touching her was one of the hardest things he'd ever done. She swallowed. Breathed out slowly. 'Thank you for the hot chocolate. And... you know, everything.'

'My pleasure.' And it was. But he walked away before he did something reckless, like kiss her again. She had too much to lose by getting involved with him. He had nothing to give her except a life of sand and dust and restlessness.

CHAPTER SIX

A FEW DAYS later the sea was starting to calm and they'd picked up no more refugees since Mariam's boatload. The sun was peeking through thin clouds and Claire was enjoying sitting on deck reading a book, taking advantage of the quiet morning.

Well, she was making a good pretence of reading while watching Akil teach Ethan the intricacies of tying sailing knots with a huge coil of rope they used when they moored at port. From this vantage point she could see the concentration on Ethan's face as he tied and untied the knots, the look of relief and pleasure when he got it right. Determination when he got things wrong. When he concentrated, a lock of hair fell over his face and he pressed his lips together in a tight smile. His hands held the rope as if he'd been born a sailor, wide shoulders capable of carrying far more than his fair share of the workload—and he did. He was compassionate and yet sexy. Funny and serious...

It wasn't just his physical appeal, there was a connection that felt like that thick coil of rope tugging her to him, and resisting it was exhausting.

Well, she'd just have to be exhausted, because she wasn't prepared to put everything on the line for him. She'd almost given up her freedom for one man and she wasn't going to jeopardise it again now that she actually had it.

Still, there was no problem with window-shopping. The man was gorgeous to watch.

And kiss.

See? Exhausting.

Akil said something and both men laughed. As Ethan tipped his head back he turned and caught her watching him.

Oops. She snapped her book up in front of her face, but that didn't stop the hairs on her arms prickling. He was coming over and she felt as giddy as a schoolgirl with her first crush.

'Hey. Claire.' The sun was directly behind him and as he was shadowed she couldn't see his face. But she didn't have to look at him to know the finer details of his skin; she had them burnt into her memory along with the sharpness of his cheekbones, the dazzling eyes, that reluctant smile.

She put her book down as her heart gave its regulation Ethan leap. 'Oh. Hi. I didn't see you there. Beautiful day.'

'Nice to have a few days' respite and enjoy the ride for a change.' He tilted his head to one side. 'Where do you fancy going today?'

'I'm not sure I need to go anywhere right now, thank you.' She laughed and pointed to the expanse of calm blue sea stretching behind them, further than the horizon. In their brief evening talks when the ship had pitched and rolled until they'd both turned green, they'd 'virtually' visited the deserts in Rajasthan and the cool interior of the Taj Mahal, snorkelled on the Great Barrier reef and had a quick sojourn to the Amazon River.

But Ethan hadn't actually been there in real life so they'd just made details up, which had made it even more fun because they'd started off serious and had dissolved into silliness and fantasy and play that had made them completely forget about the sea and the sickness. 'It's actually starting to be pleasant on here.'

'So you don't fancy a quick trip to Naples?'

'Oh, Neapolitan pizza, yes, please. Anything's better than the food on here. Can we pretend it's a sunny day in July too? The wind's just a little too cold for me right now.'

'How about a sunny day in early May?' He grinned. 'Seriously, I heard we're going to have a quick stopover in Naples.'

'For real? You're not pretending?' The seasickness that had dogged her at the beginning of the trip had gradually eased, but lately it had come back, not as fiercely as before but enough to make her feel queasy. Time on shore would be brilliant.

He shook his head. 'We're stocking up on supplies and Freja's meeting us there to come back on board. Rumour has it we get a few hours on shore. So real pizza.'

'Oh, amazing! And red wine.' But even as she said it Claire's stomach tumbled at the thought. Strange...she usually loved red wine. Perhaps a *digestif* would settle things. 'Maybe Aperol.'

'And gelato.' His eyes widened greedily. 'The ice cream in Khartoum is pretty average.'

Fatima wandered out from the bridge, securing her hijab round her neck. 'Did I hear the words *pizza* and *gelato*? Count me in, I know the best places for authentic Italian food. Akil will come too, if he can get the time off. He loves ice cream, and let's bring Kristina, I'm sure she'd like a break.'

'Pizza and ice cream. Excellent. A party!' Claire jumped up and turned towards the bow of the ship, inhaling in surprise. There in the distance were the umber and cream stone port buildings, overlooked by an imposing castle on a hill. The mighty volcano Vesuvius loomed large to the right, and between there and *SOS Poseidon* were lots of little white yachts. 'Oh, my goodness, I never thought I'd be this excited to see dry land.'

* * *

Although getting used to walking on tarmac was an altogether different prospect as she stepped off the gangway and waited for her brain to catch up with her body. Her legs were shaky and she had to concentrate to put one foot in front of the other. That hint of nausea still laced her gut. 'Is there such a thing as ship lag? Like jet lag but from ships? I feel like I'm drunk!'

'Hopefully we will be soon.' Kristina laughed. 'It is so good to be off the ship, right?'

'It will be when I can walk properly.' Claire giggled. 'Such a shame the others have to stay on board while we get to play.'

Kristina looked back at the vessel and at Chase, who was standing on deck, waving them off, and her smile grew wistful. Claire could tell there was something interesting going on between them; they circled each other from a distance but Claire noticed there was a certain amount of care taken between them when talking. Kristina's smile was a little sad as she waved. 'Yes. A break for all of us would be nice.'

Claire noticed Ethan looking at Chase too, but his expression was less interested, more pensive and she wondered what the heck the tie was that bound them. Which was a foolish thing to wonder because after the other day when she'd almost kissed Ethan again she'd vowed to keep her distance and that had to mean in thought as well as proximity. Fatima looped her arm into Claire's and Kristina took the other side as they wobbled up towards Fatima's favourite food street.

But they weren't the only visitors to have had the same plan to visit Naples's best pizza restaurant, and the narrow cobbled street was packed with tourists all jostling for a table. Fatima sighed and stood at the end of the long queue. 'I know a good trick. The wait is usually around

thirty minutes this time of day, so a group of us can stay in the line here while some go to the kiosk next door and buy some beers.'

'I'll go.' Both Claire and Ethan spoke at the same time.

'Excellent.' Fatima clapped. 'We'll wait. Large, cold beers for everyone, please.'

The queue for the beer wasn't much shorter, but luckily they were on the sunny side of the street and Claire basked in the rays while she looked at the multicoloured tall buildings that lined the winding street. On a balcony further down a man was singing opera into a microphone to the enjoyment of everyone below. When he finished he winched down a large bucket for the spectators to pay him tips—of which there were many.

'Opera and pizza, could it be any more Italian?' She laughed, glad to keep the conversation strictly non-personal, and Ethan seemed happy to do the same, which was a relief. All she wanted was to start feeling normal again, and to have some fun.

Eventually the beers arrived and they wandered back to the group. Or to where the group had been standing, but now they were gone. Ethan frowned. 'Where did they go?'

'Are they inside? Wait here.' Claire pushed forward and tried to speak in her best Italian to the swamped restaurant host but he shook his head and said he didn't understand. She nudged her way back, trying not to spill the beer in her hands, and found Ethan. 'They won't let me in to look. Hold these beers while I check my messages.' She checked her phone. 'No. Nothing from any of them. I'll call them.'

She called Fatima, and then Kristina and Akil. No reply. 'The reception's not very good. What shall we do?'

'We can put our names down on the list and hit the back of the queue again.' Ethan sighed and didn't look happy about that idea. 'Or we can go somewhere else.'

'I'm hungry.' In actual fact her belly had been alter-

nating between starving and nausea for the last few days. 'But I'm not bothered about drinking these.'

'Okay. Neither am I.' Ethan handed all their beers to a group of thirsty-looking Americans further down the line. 'Let's get out of this maelstrom and find somewhere quieter, otherwise we won't get any pizza or ice cream before we have to be back on board. Let's play tourist and wander the back streets, that's usually where the best food is.'

Which sounded lovely in principle, but went completely against their plan. Claire's heart thumped at the prospect of a few stolen hours on her own with Ethan. It was like a delicious treat, and an exciting temptation. 'Are we allowed to be out in public on our own?'

He grinned. 'Claire, look around. There are a few thousand people here who can act as chaperones. I think we'll be safe.'

She just hoped he was right.

Or not…

The back streets of Naples were quieter, although motor scooters zipped back and forth, navigating around people and the odd stray dog. Little cafés and pizzerias spilled onto the cobblestones; above them were windowsills bedecked with pots of scarlet geraniums interspersed with the Italian flag. It was a feast for the senses: cooking smells and bright flowers and the hum of regular everyday life that they'd missed on the ship.

Keeping Claire's comfort at the forefront of his mind, Ethan picked a restaurant that wasn't overtly advertising to honeymooners. Although, considering he'd known her so intimately, he felt like a teenager on his first date. His heart was happy to be with her regardless of the restrictions they put on their relationship, and it was good to see her relaxing and not exhausted from work. They ordered all the things they'd been talking about—pizza and wine—and

planned gelato for dessert. A band was playing in the bar next door, its lively tunes spilling into the early evening.

'I love it here.' Claire took a sip of the local red wine then put it down. 'Not sure about the wine, though. I think I'll stick to water.'

'You okay? Don't you like it? Do you want something different? White? Bubbles?' He knew she liked Aperol and cognac but not what wine she drank or what food she liked. There was so much he didn't know about her. They'd skipped that *getting to know you* part and succumbed to desire, clinging to each other for comfort and release and sex.

Although it had been more than sex and they both knew it.

'Water is fine. I'm just getting over my ship lag and still feel a little wobbly, so adding wine into the mix might be a recipe for disaster. I am, however, ready for this.' She bit into the freshly made pizza that had a perfectly crispy crust, fresh mozzarella, slices of ripe tomato and shredded basil leaves. She pretended to swoon, her eyes rolling back a little in the same way they had when she'd been in the lift and reaching orgasm. No matter how much he tried, he couldn't erase that memory.

She was also rocking the outfit she'd been wearing in the lift too. Too many memories from that skirt, and so much temptation. She groaned in delight. 'Oh, wow, Ethan. I did not know pizza could ever taste this good.'

'Eat your fill, we can always get more.'

'I wonder what the others are getting up to.' She giggled, wide-eyed. 'Do you think they'll suspect something?'

'Suspect what exactly? They were the ones who left us stranded. We're just having dinner in broad daylight.'

'In a side street so no one can find us.' Her eyes met his and they didn't need to frame what they were doing.

Excitement. Adventure.

She licked her lips. And that simple action had him

curling his hands into fists to stop him from pulling her into his arms.

'Claire, you have no idea how much just looking at you turns me on. I mean…we can say that, right? We know there's an attraction here, there's no point in pretending there isn't. We just have to work on stopping it. There is no way we can carry on like this on the ship. I'm going to explode with frustration.'

'Okay, so how do we stop the attraction?' She put down her pizza and smiled as if enjoying the effect she had on him. He liked it that she was growing in confidence and finding out what she liked, especially when what she liked was him. For now.

'I'll tell you my trigger points and you tell me yours and then we can make sure we don't do them. For me it's your mouth. And your eyes, and your…' His eyes roamed her body and he tried not to think about how she'd felt in his arms. How good it had been to be inside her. He wasn't sure this tactic was going to work, but he'd been honest when he'd said he was going to explode soon. Being around her was hell. And heaven. 'Let's just stick with your mouth. Please don't lick your top lip.'

'Like this?' She ran her tongue slowly over her lips and laughed.

His laugh was strangled by a hot surge of lust. 'Exactly like that. Fair warning, Claire. It's a trigger for me.'

Her eyes glittered. 'So no licking lips.'

'No. Thank you.'

She smiled and took a sip of water. Her tongue darted out and ran along her bottom lip.

He inhaled deeply. 'Claire, what part of don't lick your lips do you not understand? You want me to explode right here?'

'Sorry. Force of habit.' She laughed. 'Okay, my turn.

Please don't do that thing where you smile just a little bit, with one side of your mouth.'

'You don't want me to smile?'

'Not the way you did when you were…' She swallowed and fanned herself with the menu. 'When we were…in the lift.'

'Okay, no smiling.'

'*Half* smiling. Or smelling so good.'

He sniffed his underarm. All seemed fine. 'You want me to smell bad?'

'No, just don't come too close because I love the way…' Her cheeks turned almost the same colour as the potted geraniums. 'Never mind. Right. Change the subject.'

He was so turned on he was almost lost for words so he took a bite of food and focused on chewing.

She picked up another piece of pizza and eyed it greedily before asking, 'So what's going on between you and Chase? Honestly, what's the story there? I've been trying to fit the jigsaw pieces together, but I'm not sure I can. You guys had some sort of argument before you came on board or something?'

'We go a long way back.' This certainly wasn't what he wanted to talk about. Rewind? Licking lips was a lot more fun.

She frowned, pizza still in the air midway between her plate and her mouth. 'I thought you said you didn't know the guy.'

'I barely do. I mean… I used to.' He could talk about this. He could. It was just conversation, it didn't need to probe any deeper. 'I haven't seen him for sixteen years but we were in the same ski squad together.'

'Skiing? Mr Sunshine and Sand who thinks of Africa as home? You ski?'

'Not any more.'

'Why not?' She put the half-eaten slice back on her

plate and her eyes grew dark. 'What? What is it? Why are you looking so...troubled? Why am I scared about what you're going to say?'

Would this make a difference to how she saw him? How she interacted with him and Chase? Hell, she could just as easily ask Chase for the details, although he got the feeling his old adversary wasn't in the headspace for talking about their joint past any more than he was. He took a breath. 'Remember I told you about the building that collapsed? It was a ski lodge and Chase and I were in it.'

'How? Why did it collapse? I've been wanting to ask, but didn't know how to or whether you'd want to talk about it.'

'I don't.'

'Okay. That's fine. But you need to talk to someone, probably Chase, because you both look so... Now I think about it, you both look sad. Haunted. And that's not good for anyone.' Her smile was soft and concerned. How easily she shaped her moods to him, as if she felt what he felt, or at the very least understood him on a deep level. 'So if you don't want to talk to me, that's okay, but please talk to someone.'

He'd been carrying this with him for so long it fitted him like a second skin and he'd thought no one had noticed, but if she had then others must have too. The last thing he wanted was a *keep out* sign on his forehead, especially in his line of work.

'It was an avalanche that destroyed the building. It was a long time ago.' He tried to sound casual, as if every day since then hadn't been some sort of penance for him.

'Oh. Yes.' She snapped her fingers, looking as if she was trying to remember something. 'I heard about that. Boys on a trip...in a team. Some people died.'

'Four.' Why was he even telling her all this? He never talked about it.

'And Chase? What happened to him?'

So much black. And cold. 'He pulled me out. He saved my life.'

'Oh. Wow. That's…that's huge.'

'Yes.' He didn't know what else to say. Couldn't say much actually because of the thick weight in his throat that was spreading to his chest, making breathing difficult and his thoughts blurry. And all of a sudden he was there again in the suffocating dark and cold, with the crushing sensation in his thighs and his chest. And he wanted to flail out his arms and push off the feeling, but it was inside him. He sucked in air.

Italy. Pizza. Claire.

Sea air. Rock music. Claire.

Italy. Pizza. Claire.

Claire.

She frowned. 'I'm trying to remember the details. They had problems getting the rescue team there, a long delay, and there was a lot of media noise about it. Parents complained and some sued. There were court hearings and investigations. It was in all the French newspapers. Was that you?'

'Suing and complaining? No. I didn't want to think about it. No point blaming someone for an act of nature.'

Somewhere during the conversation her hand had found his and she gripped it. 'How long were you stuck in there?'

'Hours. It felt like for ever. It was dark and cold and I was hypothermic with a beam on my chest and legs.' He hung onto her hand. 'It was tough, but Chase…well, he kept me sane and I owe him my life.'

'So what's happened since then? Did you have an argument or something? Because I would have thought an event so big would bring you together, but you act weirdly around each other, like you're annoyed or mistrustful or something. How come you're now working together?'

'That night I told him I owed him a favour and to ask if he ever needed me. He said they needed a paediatrician urgently. He asked. I came. Simple.'

'Why now, I wonder?'

'I don't know. That's been bothering me too. He hasn't said a word about it, in fact we've both avoided the subject like the plague. So maybe it was a subconscious thing.'

She cupped his hand with both of hers. 'There's so much you need to say to each other. I haven't seen you talking. There's no camaraderie there, not really.'

'I guess neither of us wants to go there again.'

'Maybe you have to. Maybe you have to push through it.'

'I don't know what headspace he's in. If it's anything like mine, I pity the guy.'

'You'll only find out by trying.' She made it sound as if breaking that silence might actually be a good thing, that it could be as simple as starting off a conversation. Maybe it was.

'Until I arrived here I hadn't seen him since that night. I know it's weird, but we didn't get along before the avalanche, and there was no need to have some kind of faux friendship afterwards. His best friend died there and he wasn't looking for another one to fill the spot, well, not me anyway. He had to make a choice about who to save and he picked me,' he explained.

'Wow. That's intense, Ethan.'

'You could say that.' *You'd better be worth it.* Those words had framed everything Ethan had done since then. 'To be honest, I couldn't walk for a while afterwards and was in hospital for months. I damaged my spine a little; it's fine now but I spent a long time in rehab and lost touch with everyone from the team.' Rather, he'd purposefully pulled away from all that, not wanting to face the other survivors. 'It was all a mess. Everyone was grieving the

dead and in such shock. It was just easier to fade away and concentrate on getting better.'

'You went home to your parents? Surely they made an effort for you then?'

'I was in the spinal unit and then at home for a while, but it was frustrating for us all, to say the least. They weren't suited to being nurses and I was the worst kind of patient.'

'They must have been heartbroken when you were so badly injured.'

'Some of the team's parents flew to be with us in the French hospital, but mine were *unable to get away* and just wanted updates.'

Claire swore in French and shook her head. 'How could they be like that?'

'We never discussed it, of course, but I'm pretty sure I was a mistake, an unplanned baby and very much in the way. I left for medical school as soon as I could, never put on skis again; in fact, I haven't been near snow again either.' Just the thought of it made his body feel like ice. He shivered and tried to cover it up.

But she noticed. He got the feeling Claire noticed a lot. She nodded and smiled kindly. 'Now I understand.'

'I wish I did. You think you're over it and then you get palpitations and sweating, like in the lift, a few minutes of blackness or being hemmed in and it all comes rolling back.'

She watched him for a moment. 'So you know more about wanting to be free than anyone. No wonder you do the work you do.'

He knew more about being locked into guilt and fear than about freedom.

Her fingers stroked his jaw. 'I'm sorry, Ethan. You look shaken up.'

He forced the memories away. Stupid to ruin such a

great night with that. 'It's just weird, going back there. Being with Chase has pushed it front and centre again.'

'I get that. Do you want to go somewhere else?'

He wanted to haul her against him and find comfort in her, with her. To wipe away the stale tainted memories and fill his head with new ones of her. He didn't care what the geography was. 'You want to leave without getting your gelato?'

'No. We can do both. I mean, we can pretend we're somewhere else and eat gelato here.'

He thought for a moment, listened to the early evening laughter, the upbeat band, the hum of the scooters, Claire's laughter. *Italy. Pizza. Claire.* He breathed off the heavy weight and breathed in the light and the laughter and Claire. 'I'm happy to be right here.'

'Me too.' She smiled and it was honest and pure, and instead of always wanting to be on the move he actually wanted to stop. Right here.

His heart hummed for her, his body too, and he wondered how it would feel to give up everything he knew and find a way to be with her. Then he stopped himself from getting carried away because she had to do her thing, on her own, and he had to repay his debt for as long as that took.

He couldn't ask her to come to Africa and relentlessly try to save people for ever and ever and ever, making a tally, wondering what infinitesimal number would ever be able to fill the gap Nick's death had left. Or whether it could ever be enough in Chase's eyes. No, he couldn't push his burdens onto someone else and make them bear that weight with him. And he couldn't take on someone else's.

But it didn't stop him wondering how it would be if he stopped.

Impossible. He ordered the gelato, hoping the cold would freeze some sense into him, but when it came,

Claire's eyes were so full of life that all he wanted to do was rock into her and keep that shine in her irises bright. This was no good. The more time he spent with her the more time he wanted to spend with her. As she scraped the last drop of ice cream from her bowl he checked his watch. 'It's getting late, we need to go.'

'Back to reality.' She sighed. 'Okay, time to activate the trigger point plan.'

'It's been activated for the last few days as far as I'm concerned.' He laughed and started to tick the list off on his fingers. 'So don't forget, no smiling. Smelling. Licking lips.'

'*Half* smiling, that's the killer. Yes, that's exactly what I mean. Stop it, Ethan.'

'I can't help it.' He gave her his full-beam grin. 'You make me smile.'

She sighed again, but her smile grew and as she stood she swayed a little towards him. 'If you don't stop saying things like that we're going to have to add talking to the list too.'

After they'd paid the bill they walked through the maze of dark streets, trying to find their way back to the port, but all that seemed to happen was they'd come across another narrow alley instead of the main road down to the ship. It was getting dark and the streets took on a different hue. Ethan steered her down an alleyway that looked vaguely familiar. 'Pretty sure it's the next left. Then right and straight down to the dock.'

She came to a halt at the end of the street. 'No left turn here. I think we're lost. Let me get my phone out, I can find a map or something.'

'It's fine, Claire. Don't worry, we're not lost.'

'I'm not worrying.' She leaned against a terracotta-coloured wall under a streetlight and gazed at her phone,

tapping and tapping. 'There's something exciting about trying to find your way, don't you think, along a new path?'

She was so goddamned beautiful in this light his heart almost couldn't take it. As she concentrated on looking at the screen, the tip of her tongue ran along her bottom lip.

'Claire…' It was half warning, half a hymn to her. Then he was cupping her face and sliding his mouth over hers.

There was a moment when she hesitated, inhaled the shock. Then she softened against him, moaning his name, and opened her mouth to him. She tasted of lemon gelato, her lips still cold. She tasted of freedom and excitement and everything good.

She wound her arms round his neck and pressed herself hard against him and he hung on, deepening the kiss, grinding her against the wall. His hands skimmed her breasts and she panted at his touch, a light mewl escaping from her throat that was like oxygen to burning embers. Desire sparked through his veins, setting every nerve cell alight. He wanted her naked. He wanted to rock into her, to watch her come, to hold her until the morning.

Someone on a scooter tooted as they sped by, dragging him back to reality.

This was insanity.

He tugged his mouth from hers, tried to control his breathing. Failed. '*God*, Claire, I've been wanting to do that for so long.'

'Me too.' Her lips were plump from the kiss and a jolt of pride shot through him: he'd done that; he'd made her lose control. He'd tasted and teased. She put her palm to his jaw and her smile was all sex and wanting, and if he had been a weaker man he'd have found somewhere close by where he could have taken her and…taken her. 'At this moment I can't think of anything more exciting than kissing you, Ethan.'

He ran the back of his fingers down her cheek. 'We said we shouldn't—'

'We said not on the ship. We didn't say anything about not down an alleyway in Naples.'

'You did that tongue thing.' He rested his forehead against hers, his heart rattling at the rightness and wrongness of kissing her.

'You smiled. You smiled when you kissed me and I was lost. It's just a little excitement on dry land. That's all.' They both knew it was a whole lot more than that. She laughed softly then glanced at her phone and cursed. 'We need to hurry, the ship's leaving soon.'

'So now it stops.'

'Yes. Now it stops.' She tugged her clothes back into place and sighed, as if stopping the physical could stop the emotional. *As if.* 'Still, Ethan, that's something to think about tonight when I'm in my bunk.'

He groaned at the image in his head of her naked, wearing only him. 'Don't. I don't want to think about you in a bunk. Or naked. It'll drive me crazy.'

'It'll be harder working with you every day and not being able to do it again.'

And saying goodbye at the end. It was better to put a stop to it all now, rather than trying to break off something even more intense a few weeks down the track. He started to walk down the alleyway, resisting the urge to hold her hand. 'I think it's this way. Trigger points activated?'

'I'm being serious, Ethan.' She tugged him to stop. 'What's going to happen?'

'Nothing.' He shrugged and saw the fun die in her eyes. 'Nothing can happen, Claire, we both know that.'

CHAPTER SEVEN

LIFE BACK ON the ship was so busy Claire almost didn't have time to think about Ethan and the kiss they'd shared. And...everything. At least, she tried not to think about it because she was even more confused now. But with sixty-four new refugees on board, her medical skills were being well used and her free *thinking* time was mercifully limited.

It had been four days since those wonderful few hours of freedom but now the medical room had become her new home. Today she was working on a patient who, like many of the others, was suffering from the effects of poor nutrition, dehydration and exposure to who knew what bugs on a tiny boat with people from almost as many different countries as the number of passengers.

Claire gave the details to Kristina, who'd just finished a stint with a woman suffering from horrendous chemical burns. They really did have to be ready to deal with whatever was thrown at them, or at least get the patient basically stabilised until they could dock somewhere.

'This is Fuaad, aged forty-two, from Somalia. His temperature's thirty-nine point seven. He's got rigors, low blood pressure and a thready pulse. There's obviously some sort of infection going on but nothing obvious.' Claire looked at the emaciated man, who was shivering despite

the warm spring day, and touched his hand to give him some comfort. 'He just says he aches all over, but reports no pain in any specific area.'

'Could be anything. Make sure we maintain strict infection control protocol.' Kristina did a quick examination of Fuaad with the help of a translator. 'He's badly dehydrated but his chest is clear. Grab some normal saline, will you? We'll set up a drip, give some antipyretics and see if that brings the temp down. We'll have to start him on some broad-spectrum antibiotics too, until we can get a positive result from a swab or urine sample. If only we had a blood culture machine.'

'Dream on, Doctor.' Claire smiled at Kristina as she slid an IV canula into a vein in the man's arm.

It was so different from working in a hospital where you had everything to hand. Here, often the only option was to reach some sort of working differential diagnosis and hope.

They worked on him for a while, checking and double-checking his temperature and response to the fever-lowering drugs. Claire noted his observations. 'He's a little more comfortable now, although we still need to know where that infection is.'

'It's like a game of pin the tail on the donkey, but we don't even know where the donkey is. We'll just have to keep an eye on him until we get to port.' Shaking her head, Kristina washed her hands and dried them. 'I need to go and see the baby that's not keeping anything down, so can you apply a dressing to Geesi's foot laceration? He's waiting outside. Then there's the blood-sugar check on Ahmed, he's all over the place at the moment. This last group have all been quite sick.'

'Sure. It's definitely gone crazy.' Claire glanced at the wall clock. They'd been working non-stop for hours and every part of her ached with exhaustion, her stomach growled with a mix of nausea and hunger... She couldn't

remember the last time she'd eaten anything. But even though regular breaks didn't happen, it helped to have her head full of work instead of other things. 'I would have thought Ethan would be here by now. Do you know where he is?'

Clearly *other things* still squeezed into her brain.

Kristina threw a paper towel into the bin and frowned. 'Oh, didn't you hear? He's swapped shifts. He's working nights from now on.'

'Really?' Claire's heart thumped a little too hard. Why? Had he changed shifts because he didn't want to be around her?

No, she wasn't that important in his life that he'd move things around. They'd just been messing about, two consenting adults having some shore fun. At least, that was what she'd been trying to tell herself. She tried to sound nonchalant. 'Since when?'

'I think he talked to Chase about it yesterday. It may have been the day before.'

After they'd got back from Naples. Was he actually activating the trigger plan and just avoiding her completely? She felt unaccountably upset all of a sudden. 'Lucky we're the dream team, then.'

But Kristina just smiled and went to see the sick baby, leaving Claire discombobulated. She hadn't realised how much she'd enjoyed seeing Ethan every day and how easily they'd learnt to work alongside each other, how his care and compassion towards their patients brightened her day. How he made her laugh. The places he took her to in their down time.

Now their paths were only going to cross at handover. It was what she'd wanted, right?

'Claire?' It was Fatima. 'Fuaad is saying he has a bad headache.'

A simple cold? Flu? Dengue fever? Malaria? Zika?

Meningitis? Claire's gut clenched. That could be dangerous with so many people on board. She ran to Fuaad and
ascertained he had no rash or sensitivity to bright lights.
His temperature had dropped enough to be out of the danger zone but he was complaining that his vision was like
shattered glass.

'Now it sounds more like a migraine, but he had rigors
so it can't be,' she explained to Kristina when she came
back after settling the baby. 'But we need to keep an eye
on him in case it isn't something as simple, especially with
so many people on board. The last thing we need is for an
infection like that to spread.'

Claire set up a makeshift isolation unit as best she could
with the scarcity of cabins available, and made sure she
was the only person going in and out. Strict infection control was a pipedream in a place like this but she did what
she could.

The next two hours dragged by slowly and gave her way
too much time for her mind to wander. She tried hard not
to think about Ethan and the reasons why he might have
asked to change his roster.

She tried not to think about him, but she couldn't help
it. How could one person have become like oxygen to her
in such a short time? And why did her stomach feel so
unsettled at the thought of him? Was he having a physical
effect on her too?

'How's Fuaad doing?' Kristina asked when Claire came
out of the isolation room just before her shift ended.

'Much better. Brighter. No neck pain, just a dull headache, which he says is much less painful. No rash. Maybe
we were being over-cautious?'

'You can't be too cautious. Imagine what would happen
if meningitis or some other virulent infection got hold of
everyone on here. Thanks for going the extra mile with

him.' Kristina grinned. 'I am so glad today is almost over. Got any plans for the Marseille stopover?'

They were all leaving the ship tomorrow and having a break. Claire sighed at the thought of no more seasickness. 'Three whole days to do nothing but sleep in a proper bed, eat *pain au chocolat* for breakfast and drink decent coffee. Maybe the *pain* and the coffee actually in bed. Oh, and a hot shower that I don't have to keep to a four-minute time limit. Bliss. I never thought I'd be wanting all those things I've taken for granted my whole life. You?'

Kristina shrugged. 'Oh, I'll just see how it goes. Sight-seeing would be good. And yes to decent coffee.'

'Are we all staying at the same hotel? The St Martin?'

'I think so. Pretty sure they make a block booking.'

Which meant Ethan might well be on the same floor as her again so things wouldn't be as relaxed as she'd hoped. Either they'd get together again or they wouldn't... either option would give her a lot to think about, mull over. Dream about.

But three days off was probably the best thing she could wish for right now. Since being back on the boat she'd felt weird. It wasn't just the longing looks at Ethan and the ones right back at her from him, she felt physically exhausted and queasy and just...strange. She figured what she needed was space. From him. From this. From her thoughts, really.

The end of the shift eventually dragged within her grasp and after writing up all her notes she climbed the metal steps and stepped out onto the deck. The gentle breeze billowed her jacket and she tugged it close, wishing it was Ethan's arms around her and then berating herself. Because what part of freedom and adventure was falling for a guy who was walking off this ship and heading straight to his comfort place without her?

Her stomach roiled and she clutched the railing, hauling greedy gulps of fresh air deep into her lungs.

Did sexual frustration give you nausea?

'Hey.' It was Kristina, carrying two mugs of steaming coffee. She offered one to Claire. 'I hope you don't mind me bringing this over. I saw you from the galley and wondered if you might need a debrief. Or a hot drink. Or both.'

'Thanks.' Claire took a sip of coffee and felt her stomach turn over. Holding her cup against her chest, she grimaced. 'Maybe water might be better.'

'Everything okay? Only you're holding onto the rail as if it's a life raft.'

She just couldn't shift this gnawing ache in her belly. 'I don't know. Do you think it's normal for seasickness to keep coming back?'

'You're not feeling well?'

'A little queasy and my head feels mushy, like I have to work hard to concentrate. Must be seasickness, right?'

'Claire, this is the calmest sea we've sailed on.' Kristina used her cup to indicate the flat turquoise water, with barely any waves, just the gentle swell from the ship's wake. Her friend's eyes narrowed a little as she smiled kindly. 'Maybe there's another reason why you feel sick?'

Claire shrugged. 'Food poisoning? A bug? It must be a bug I just can't shake. There's been enough people on and off this boat, I could have caught it from anyone.'

'Sure. But no one else has a stomach bug.' There was something else in Kristina's eyes. She was looking at Claire the knowing way a woman looked at another woman. 'But maybe you're right. Maybe it's…something else entirely?'

What did she mean?

Then the penny dropped. Claire's stomach tightened and her heart rate thudded. When was her period due?

If she was honest, being on the ship she hadn't paid any attention to her regular routine but surely it was due any time around now. Everything had been turned upside down, including her heart. She checked the calendar on

her phone. She was late. *Three. Days. Late.* She stared at the little boxes of dates on her screen and breathed out, hoping this was a mistake or a nightmare, that this wasn't happening. When she looked up Kristina was still there, smiling softly.

'No,' Claire said, a little more vehemently than she'd intended. She couldn't be pregnant. Couldn't. 'It's not that. Honestly. I've got a few cramps now, actually. A bit of PMT too.'

Which may explain the weird mood swings, nausea, sore boobs. Yes. Sore boobs now she thought about it. Definitely PMT.

'Uh-huh. Okay.' Kristina put her hand on Claire's back. 'It's none of my business, but if you want to talk or anything I'm here.'

'Thanks. Just the change of routine, right? That happens.' They'd used protection.

Kristina nodded. 'It certainly does.'

Pregnant?

No. No. No. No. No. Claire briefly squeezed her eyes closed and forced the threat of tears away. 'No. It's fine. I'm not...you know.' She couldn't say the word out loud. 'I'm sure of it. I can't be.'

Luckily Kristina was a mind-reader. 'Okay, as long as you're sure.'

It had been one time. *Once.* 'Please don't say anything to Chase or anyone else.'

'Of course not. It's none of my business.' Kristina's eyes flicked to the place where Chase sat every evening and she looked torn by loyalties. 'But I have to say this as a friend and a medic, so bear with me. If you ever were pregnant you'd have to tell him as soon as you knew for sure, because there's too much of a risk to you and the baby here. You know how it is—it can be dangerous if we hit stormy seas and you get thrown about, plus infection, diseases...'

Kristina was right. If she really was pregnant then her job would be over. This adventure. Excitement. Freedom.

God. Freedom with a baby in tow. It just wouldn't be possible. 'I'm fairly sure women have been pregnant on a ship before.'

'They have, and we'd look after you, but I don't know about being on a rescue ship, Claire.' Kristina smiled, her voice soft in the same way she spoke to traumatised patients. 'Do you want to do a test just to make sure?'

'No. It's fine. It's probably too early anyway.' Claire pressed her palm to her belly—as flat as a pancake. If she concentrated hard she could feel soft cramps, right? Her period would start in the next day or so; she was just late. 'I won't be. Seriously, I can't be. I want this job too much. I have a whole new life ahead of me.'

Not in me. Please.

'Okay. Remember that I'm here to talk to.' Kristina nodded, gathered both cups into her hands then started to walk away. 'Any time.'

'Thanks, I know.' At least there wasn't any judgement there. Not like she'd get if she went home with her tail between her legs and a baby in her belly after all her talk of escape. How would she face her ex then? And her parents?

It couldn't happen. She stared out at the beautiful calm sea that stretched for miles and miles, and the excitement she usually felt at the view didn't even register. Now all she saw was distance between her and everything she wanted to do.

Impossible. Claire shuddered and turned away from the water, her head reeling with shock. She needed to get her thoughts around this on her own. Luckily Fatima was still working so Claire would have the cabin to herself to think, rest, hope. She marched across the deck, but a sandy head appeared at the top of the metal steps she was about to descend.

No. Her heart twisted. She couldn't deal with Ethan now. Not with this. What would he think? What would he say? A pregnancy would scatter everything they both wanted to the four winds. They hadn't planned for that. But he was heading up the steps towards her and she couldn't turn and walk away without looking rude or inviting further questions.

She raised her eyebrows in salutation, trying to be polite and calm when inside she was a panicking mess. If she had his baby then she'd always have a connection to him wherever he was—and it likely wouldn't be with her, probably not even in the same hemisphere, but he would always be in her heart and in her head. She'd never be able to forget him or put him down as a fun fling, not with this kind of consequence.

Even so, his smile warmed her as he stopped near the top of the steps. 'Claire. Hi. How's your day going?'

To total crap. Worrying about whether I have your child inside me. 'Oh, you know. Busy.'

'You okay?' He frowned and little lines formed round his eyes. He had sleep creases on his cheek as if he'd not long woken up. And the thought of him being in bed made her upset stomach feel a little more giddy.

She grabbed the stair rail just for something to hold onto that wasn't him. 'I'm fine, thanks. Why?'

'You seem tense.'

Perceptive. Her blood pressure was probably reaching crisis point. What should she say? Anything? Nothing until she knew for sure? A pregnancy test might not be accurate right now and she didn't want a false positive to put them both into a tailspin. It wasn't fair to push them into a situation neither of them wanted until she had definite information.

So she stuck with work stuff. 'We had a guy with a nasty fever earlier. We managed to bring it down but I

don't know for how long. Hope it turns out to be nothing. I know you mainly deal with the kids, but if you get a chance could you look in on him? He's called Fuaad.'

'Sure. There's a very hazy line here. I do what's needed regardless of the patient's age.' A little frown line appeared on Ethan's forehead. 'You seem upset. Is something wrong? Did something bad happen?'

Bad? The thought of being pregnant was insane. She shook her head. 'I thought you were rostered on the early shift with me, so I was confused when Kristina turned up. She said you'd swapped to night duty now.'

'Ah.' He shoved his fingers through his hair. 'I should have said something to you before. Chase said he was short of night staff and I thought, Why not?'

'So it's nothing to do with…' She hesitated. 'Us?' Trying not to think that *us* may well be more than just the two of them.

He slowly blew out a breath. 'I thought we could do with some space. You know, the trigger thing. Just a precaution.'

'Sure. Of course. Good idea.' So it *was* because of her. Her heart fisted tight in her chest. His eyes roamed her face, first her eyes then her mouth, and heat spread through her, making her already uneven heartbeat jitter and thump. How could she feel upset and turned on at the same time?

His frown deepened. 'I'm thinking you don't agree.'

'I do. We talked about it. It's fine.' It wasn't fine. Truth was, she felt immeasurably shaken and she needed to get away for some headspace. But he was putting so much space between them it would never be breached and she was trying to work out how to tell him she might need that space breached—for the rest of their lives.

He was doing that half-smile thing and his words were at odds with his eyes and with the kiss. And all she wanted was to kiss him. But she didn't and he kept on talking. 'Be-

cause if wc don't rein things in we'll both be out of a job and bang goes that freedom and adventure you're having.'

'I see. Right.' Her throat felt raw. The job could well be on the line anyway because of giving in to her foolish desires. She stepped aside to let him come up to the top step, then started to go down. 'Got to go. Have a good shift.'

But his hand went to her back and he turned her to face him. 'Hey. I thought it was what you wanted. Why are you dashing off?'

'Heading for a shower then some rest.' Tears were threatening so she hurried down the stairs. *Just giving you the space you want.*

CHAPTER EIGHT

ETHAN DROPPED HIS bag at the hotel reception desk and waited to check in, watching Fatima, Kristina and Claire in the line ahead of him, laughing. But Claire turned and when she saw him she smiled, giving an eye roll that seemed to say, *This place, eh?*

Did she think it was dangerous to be here, the way he did? The next few days were going to be torture if he couldn't touch her—and he couldn't. He'd stepped back and he was going to stay on the right side of that line for both of their sakes.

Claire said something to Fatima and Kristina and they nodded and wandered towards the lift, then she came over to him.

There had been a group lunch down at the marina to kill time before check-in and he'd managed to sit at a different end of the table to her, but now she was impossible to avoid. She smiled warily and he knew it was his fault she felt she had to tiptoe around him after their conversation yesterday. But swapping shifts had seemed the best course of action if they were going to get out of this assignment unscathed. 'Hey, Ethan. I...er... I'm sorry I ducked off so quickly yesterday, I was knackered.'

'Understandable. It's been chaotic these last few days.' After the way they'd once melted into each other's arms

he hated the stiff politeness between them now but it had to be done, especially here where the spectre of that lift and the sex hung over them. 'Fuaad said to say thank you for looking after him.'

She brightened and some of the stiffness melted. 'He's okay now?"

'His temperature's still very labile but he's being transferred to Marseille hospital and hopefully they'll find out what's wrong with him.'

'Just a weird bug then?'

'Probably some kind of systemic tropical infection. You see it a lot in Africa.'

Something slid across her eyes. Fear? 'Do you think it's contagious?'

'Depends what it is. I assume we all used the right infection control protocols?'

'Of course.' She ran her hand across her belly and frowned. 'I was just wondering if we could find out the specific diagnosis.'

'We'll probably never find out. Once they leave our care we generally don't get to see them again, unless they come back to work with us, like Akil and Fatima did. I'll do some digging, though, if you're worried.'

'It would be good to know what we were dealing with.' She bit her bottom lip. 'For future reference, you know. So we can spot the symptoms more quickly next time.'

There was more to it, he thought, but didn't know what. Maybe this was her first contact with such an illness. 'Are you feeling better? You seemed on edge yesterday.'

'I'll be fine once I get my legs to work properly. Ship lag again.' She gave a mock stumble and her smile was as wobbly as her legs. 'You?'

'As good as I can be.' He rolled his eyes, the way she had. *This place, eh?*

'Oh. Because you're in France? Of course.' Then she

looked across the foyer and smiled that sexy smile that had every part of him straining for her. 'And the lift?'

'All of the above.' There were many things here to make him uneasy, not least the memories of pleasure and pain.

He took his key card from the manager and wandered towards the door to the stairwell, preparing his weary legs for the climb to the eleventh floor and hoping the prospect of exercise might make her step away. Then he wouldn't be so tempted to put a *Do Not Disturb* sign on the lift, crawl in there with her and have a repeat run.

He'd never ever believed he'd be craving to crawl into a tight space like that again.

But Claire was still by his side. 'Just wanted to mention that the girls and I are going out shopping, but then we're heading to a restaurant in the marina for dinner. Do you want to come? I think Chase will be there, and Akil and some of the crew, so you wouldn't be outnumbered by women.'

Chase, who had sat silently throughout the lunch and who had disappeared before anyone could invite him out later. Wise man. 'I've had no sleep. I'm just going to hit the sack and see what time I wake up.'

'Should I text you the name of the restaurant?' Brighter eyes. Hopeful smile.

'Sure.'

Her smile wavered. 'You won't come, though, will you?'

'I don't know.'

Trouble was, he wanted to. Everything about spending three glorious days with Claire appealed, but after their kiss he knew he was getting in too deep and he could see she was too. If him swapping shifts had upset her then she'd be even more affected when they said goodbye at the end. This was her fun adventure and he didn't want to turn it sour, so it was better to haul up that barrier to protect them both from hurt further down the line.

He said his goodbyes and ran up the stairs. The shades were down. The sheets were cool. And he tried to sleep.

But sleep wasn't coming any time soon and he tossed and turned and tried to get rid of the images flicking through his head like an old movie reel; the lift, her smile, snow, blackness, her smile...

Or maybe he did sleep because he found himself waking with a start in the darkened room. *Nine forty-two.* He'd slept the afternoon away and half of the evening, and had missed dinner. And she was probably thinking he'd done that to avoid her.

Had he? He'd been intent on keeping Claire at arm's length, but in distancing himself from Claire he'd inadvertently removed himself from his team—which was never a good thing to do. Camaraderie was important on missions like this and group outings usually enhanced team spirit.

He imagined them all out at dinner and wondered whether he should just lighten up and join them; Claire laughing, little glances in Ethan's direction. The excruciating pain of desire, and not being able to touch her. Fatima making everyone's conversation easier with her knowledge of so many languages and slick interpretation skills. Akil the joker. Kristina with her solid calm. And possibly Chase.

Chase sitting a little distant from them all, watching and not saying much, as was his style. He hadn't always been like that. Once he'd been fiery and forthright. He'd been assertive bordering on aggressive in his competitiveness. He'd been a fierce friend to Nick and a hard adversary to be around.

By isolating himself in his room, had *he* been avoiding the possibility of getting closer to Chase too? Of finally breaking down the barriers that were so huge between them?

Claire had said he should. Was it even possible?

It never seemed so on the ship, but maybe it was possible now they were back in France, where it had all begun. And ended. And perhaps, if they managed to speak about any of it, they could both move forward.

Ethan looked up at the ceiling, but instead of seeing the hotel light fitting he saw rubble and wires and darkness. *Black. Cold. Ice.* The beat to his life these past years. *Stop.* He sat up and flicked the lights on. *It has to stop.*

Was this what filled Chase's thoughts as he sat alone on the deck? Was this what walked through his dreams, his life? Was this what he wore as armour every single day, fuelling every thought and action and tainting everything? Because if the future was going to be all this on repeat, Ethan didn't want any part of it.

Feeling suddenly wide awake and fired up, he showered and dressed. No time like the present. If Chase was anything like him, Ethan knew exactly where to find him.

Ignoring the lift that seared images into his brain, igniting lust throughout his body every time he passed it, he tugged open the fire exit door and took the stairs two at a time, and soon enough found himself in the bar, with the velvet curtains and single suits staring at screens. And Chase sitting exactly where Ethan had three weeks ago, contemplating the mission and the past and trying to find answers in the bottom of a tumbler.

'Thought I might find you in here.' Ethan slid onto the bar stool next to Chase and ordered. 'Whiskey and soda for me, and same again for him.'

Chase nodded his thanks with a lift of his eyebrows. 'Just enjoying the peace and quiet.'

He did enough of that on the ship. Ethan shrugged. 'You want me to leave?'

'You have a drink ordered.' He didn't say stay, but he didn't tell him to leave either. 'How're you finding it?'

Which bit? The ship? The work? The woman? 'Oh, you

know. Colder and wetter than I like, but I'll cope. Halfway through already, it'll be over soon enough.'

Chase nodded. 'We couldn't have set off without you. I know you dropped everything to come here.'

Which Ethan guessed was a thank you in Chase-speak.

'Truth was, I was in between jobs.' He'd been wasting time in bars similar to this one in Khartoum, pondering how his life was panning out when he'd got the call from *Medicine For All*'s head office. 'I owe you. I told you that. That night.'

Something flickered across Chase's eyes. *Don't go there*. His head gave a minuscule shake and emotion leached from his face. But they had to go there no matter how much they didn't want to. Either that or self-destruct.

Ethan pushed. 'I never thought our paths would cross again.'

Chase stared into his glass. 'I'm thinking you made sure they didn't. You didn't come to the funerals or the memorial service.'

Imagining the hopelessness surrounding all of that, Ethan shuddered. Four lost lives, so much gone, too young. The grief-stricken parents. The minute's silence that felt like it had stretched across Ethan's whole life. He hadn't needed a service to help him remember the dead; they walked with him everywhere. 'I was in hospital, getting fixed.'

Chase nodded, emotion sparse, voice hoarse. 'I heard you had a couple of fractured vertebrae.'

'Took a while to mend. Plus a duff leg for a while too. I had a lot to get my head around.' But this wasn't just about him, it was about what Chase had had to do too. How the hell did a seventeen-year-old live with making a decision about who to save and who to leave? Chase had just been a junior skier, not a SARCO back then. 'Not sure if you can get over that kind of thing, you know? Not properly.'

Chase blinked and went on studying his glass. Not once since Ethan had sat down had they made eye contact.

Chase might not be ready to talk about this but Ethan had a few things he needed to get out while he had the chance. Blackness and cold whipped round him but he breathed it away. If he didn't say something soon, his whole life would be black and cold. He took a deep breath and blew it out slowly. 'I need to say thank you for saving me, Chase. I need to say I'm sorry about Nick. I don't know if I said that before. I don't remember much, to be honest, apart from the dark and the cold and the pain and your voice. But I know you had to choose between saving me or saving your best mate and you chose me. I can't get my head round that.'

Chase's shoulders sagged. 'No. Ethan—'

'You have to know I'm trying to make it worth it. There isn't one day that I don't think about how things could have been different. How Nick might have survived. And how bad I feel about that.' Guilt ate at everything he did.

You'd better be worth it.

Chase shook his head then lifted his eyes and met Ethan's. Survivor's guilt bound them together. The whole thing was messed up. So damned sad Ethan's heart almost snapped in two.

'He wasn't ever going to survive, Ethan. He was crushed under three huge beams. There wasn't anything I could do except maybe say goodbye and make sure he wasn't on his own when he died. But I couldn't do that when I could actually save you. Right?'

Pain arrowed into Ethan's heart. 'But I thought you'd had to choose who to save?'

'There wasn't a choice. Nick was almost certainly dead and you were gripping onto something. You were a pain in the arse, Reid, but you had spirit and a will to survive. You were the only one who had a chance.' Chase's eyes

misted and he blinked again. 'I didn't know how to cope with it all back then. I was angry and broken and I'd lost my friend.'

'But I thought…' He'd imagined Chase looking from one dying kid to the other, torn in two over who to help. That much was probably true, because he would certainly have died if Chase hadn't pulled him out. But he'd thought Nick had died *because* Chase had saved *him*. Not that Nick had already been too far gone.

Eyes back to the amber liquid, Chase cleared his throat. 'I shouldn't have let you believe there was any kind of choice or that I blamed you for Nick's death. Because I don't.'

Ethan let that settle for a few moments. He'd spent sixteen years believing he'd been the reason another guy had died. Knowing he wasn't should have freed up some space in his chest but it still felt as if the beam was crushing him. Although maybe it was a little lighter now. Maybe.

He had a finger of bourbon left to drink. 'You heard anything about the others? I saw something about Eddie getting a silver medal in Whistler. And Cam's a bigshot human rights lawyer.'

Chase sat up straighter, his mouth set in a line. 'Mr Wheeler's doing charity work or something in a garden centre. Fat lot of good he was in an emergency, but at least he's doing something good now.'

'No one knows how they're going to react in a moment like that. He must have been in shock.'

'Something like that.' Chase's eyebrows rose. 'Seems most who survived have gone on to do work that helps others.'

'The world needs more people like that, right?'

Chase shook his head. 'Not if it means they have to live through what we did.'

'You think about it a lot?'

'All the time. It eats away at me. How come I came away with barely a scratch?' He took another drink of his bourbon. 'Why me? Why not Nick?'

'Yeah.' Ethan's heart twisted as he felt the pain he saw in Chase's face. 'And why can I walk and talk and breathe and live and have a future when they can't? Why?'

Another shake of the head. 'There isn't an answer to that.'

Better be worth it.

He was trying, for God's sake. He was goddamned trying. Because even if Chase hadn't meant the words, Ethan walked the sentiment, lived it. He'd survived when others hadn't. 'We've got to live for them too, right?'

'That's a lot to live up to.' Chase swirled the last of his whiskey in the glass and looked deep into it as if it had all the answers.

And Ethan knew then exactly what Chase thought about every night as he stared out to sea.

Ignoring the razor blade pain in his throat, Ethan raised his glass. If they couldn't yet raise a glass to each other, the least they could do was toast those who had gone too soon. He managed to squeeze the words out. 'To Nick, Liam, Mac and Johnny.'

'Rest in peace, lads.' Chase blinked.

Another flicker of eye contact. A sharp nod of the head as the glass hit Chase's lips. Then the drink was gone and, a few seconds later, so was Chase.

Feeling far too shaky and awake to go back to bed, Ethan ordered another drink to steady his nerves.

It was still as raw as hell, but it had been a conversation.

It was a start.

CHAPTER NINE

ETHAN HADN'T TURNED up to the dinner, but Claire wasn't surprised. Just like everything else he did, when Ethan pulled back he did it properly.

Standing in the hotel foyer, waiting for the lift with Kristina and Fatima, she took a huge breath and tried not to think about what had happened in that little metal box, and that it wouldn't happen again.

Her period still hadn't arrived and at some point she was going to have to take a pregnancy test. Bad enough that she'd had to find excuse after excuse as to why she wasn't drinking the copious amounts of wine they'd bought between them, but she hadn't had five minutes alone to slip out and buy a pregnancy test, so she was in limbo. She'd have to make an excuse and head off on her own tomorrow and get one.

How far back would he step if it was positive?

'Hey, Claire.' Kristina was tugging the lift gate open. 'Are you okay? You seem miles away.'

No. For a change, Claire's head was exactly where her body was. Right here. 'I'm tired, actually. I'll be glad to get some sleep.' Claire stepped into the lift and refused to allow her thoughts to go back to that night.

This time there was no problem reaching floor eleven and she stepped out, taking a long deep breath. Sharing a

room with Kristina meant they would no doubt chat late into the night and hopefully she'd be too exhausted to be kept awake by her thoughts.

But suddenly, a little further along the corridor, the fire door blasted open and Ethan powered through it a little unsteadily, his face dark and haunted. Clearly something had happened to him and her first instinct was to reach out to him and hold him close, to soothe away whatever pain he was feeling.

'Ethan…' She breathed his name like a sigh and then felt the colour start to rise into her cheeks. Damn her stupid hopeful body.

He looked surprised to see them all and did a double take. 'Oh. Hi. Sorry I didn't make it to dinner.'

Claire opened her mouth to answer him but couldn't find any words. *I think I'm pregnant* was hardly suitable. Neither was *Kiss me*. And they were the only words in her head.

Finally, with her cheeks burning red hot, she croaked a brief, 'You missed a good night. Sleep well.'

'Goodnight.' Without really looking at any of them, he brushed past and headed towards his room.

She felt Kristina's eyes boring into her back as she watched this stiff exchange so she turned away from him. 'So, Kristina, are we going to draw straws to see who uses the shower first?'

Her friend laughed. 'I'll race you.'

He was sliding his key card into the lock.

Say something.

Not in front of the others.

He was opening the door. She held her breath.

He closed it behind him.

''Night, all!' Making Claire jump, Fatima slipped into her room to a chorus of *Sleep well* and Kristina slid her card into the door lock.

He was in his room, two down from her. He had no idea what was running through her head, what might be growing in her belly. Okay, she had to admit, probably *was* growing given the lack of her period. He had no idea how his life could irrevocably be changing. If he stepped back from her, would he step up for his child?

But there was no point giving him a sleepless night too, not until she was sure. Claire breathed out and was about to step into the room when Kristina whispered, 'He looks like hell.'

'To be honest, we probably all look as tired as he does.'

'It's not like him to stalk off without a smile, though. Maybe one of us should just check he's okay.'

Claire shivered. No way was she knocking on that door and making a fool of herself. 'I'd go talk to him, but it's... complicated.'

'Should I go check on him, then?' The look she gave Claire was an ultimatum that Claire didn't want to respond to.

He had looked like hell, Claire relented. It wasn't hard. 'All right, I'll go. Just to check he's okay.'

Before she lost her nerve, she tapped on his door. He answered dressed only in a pair of boxer shorts, his broad chest bare. In the lift she'd hung onto those shoulders, she'd run her hands over that sun-kissed chest, but she hadn't seen it in the dim light and shadows. On the ship he wore the regulation T-shirt and shorts. She'd spent hours watching the way his skilled hands worked on patients, dealt with medical equipment, tied those ship's knots, admired the way his calves moved like a symphony when he walked or ran his laps round the deck. But she'd never seen his body like this.

Half-naked, Ethan Reid was tanned and lean and all the things she'd dreamed he'd be. Her gaze wandered over his body, committing every muscle, every dip to memory.

She swallowed roughly as desire flickered to life deep in her belly, and she couldn't help checking out those dark boxer shorts.

Omigod. She was gone, just looking at him.

Then she remembered the triggers and their promises and she pressed her lips tight together. When she followed the smattering of hair upwards via his abdomen, his chest and then to his face, his eyes snagged hers. He'd stepped back to let her in. 'Claire? Did you want something?'

Yes, please. All of it. All. Of. It.

If she walked into the room she would be inviting further complications into her life. But something had happened to him and she just wanted to make sure he was okay.

Saying nothing, she walked past him and into the room. The light was dimmed, the curtains still open wide. From here she could make out the lights of the port and the hulking shadow of their ship. She'd come up in *their* lift with the prospect of *their* baby in her belly. Somehow their lives had become irrevocably intertwined and she was half hurting because he was now holding her at bay, and half driven mad by desire.

She dragged some semblance of sense into the forefront of her mind. 'Um. Yes. Are you okay? You look…' Beautiful. Exhausted. Haunted. 'I was worried. *We* were… worried when you didn't come to dinner. I told the team you were probably asleep, but we just wanted to make sure you were okay.'

His eyes were dark and that haunted look seemed to cling to his whole body. 'I spoke to Chase.'

'You did?' Her hands felt restless. She didn't know what to do with them, where to sit, how to act. Because all she wanted to do was hold him and she couldn't do that. 'Did you talk about the avalanche?'

A sharp nod. 'We talked about that night.'

'And how was he?'

'Guarded. Raw.' Just the way Ethan was looking now. He poured two glasses of cognac from a bottle she'd seen for sale in the hotel shop. 'He's racked with guilt and beats himself up about it every day. Sixteen years and it's still right there front and centre of everything he does.'

'That makes two of you.' Taking the glass but not drinking from it, just in case, she sat by the window on the only armchair in the room and he perched on the end of the bed, cradling his liquor.

'I don't know if we'll ever be able to put it behind us.'

'But it was a good first step. You can't expect everything to be fixed after one conversation.'

He took a sip from the glass, grimaced, then put it on the nightstand. 'I've probably had enough. Too much maybe. I'm wired, to be honest.'

The subdued light threw shadows on the walls. She could see his large frame and hers. In the shadow they were so close they looked as if they were two halves of a whole, embracing. 'Tell me what he said.'

'It was weird. Like he didn't want to go back there, but it was the only possible thing to do. We might never get the chance again, we're always too busy or never alone on the ship, and we needed to just talk.'

Ethan closed his eyes and he looked so exhausted and wrung out she knew she couldn't add to that by telling him something she sort of, might, kind of think she maybe... and then having her period arrive in the middle of the night and having made a big fuss over her stupid misfiring hormones.

Tomorrow she'd buy a test and do it just to be sure. If she was pregnant she had the rest of their lives to tell him, one night wasn't going to make a difference. But being here for him for right now might make a difference to him.

He shrugged. 'I'm just trying to make sense of it all.

He said something that surprised me, that he hadn't had to choose between the two of us and that Nick was already dead when Chase came to rescue me.' Ethan blew out a deep breath. 'Or as good as dead anyway. There'd never been any chance of him surviving.'

'So you weren't the reason Nick died? That's good, then, isn't it? It frees you?'

His eyes grew darker. 'I've spent so long trying to make up for Nick's death, thinking I was somehow to blame, and suddenly I'm not. I've committed my life to proving my-self, so knowing the facts should be freeing, but I don't know, Claire. I don't know how to feel. Because there's still that need in me. Deep down. I need to keep on proving—'

'Hey, you are enough.' She put her glass down on the windowsill and took his hands in hers, because she knew this wasn't just about Nick and that night, it was about the lack of love from his parents too. He'd been waiting for someone to tell him he was enough, then when that hadn't happened, he'd tried to prove it to himself and to the world. 'Look at the work you do, tirelessly.'

He dropped her hands and skimmed the top of his head with his palm. 'It's been a hell of a few weeks.'

'It sounds as if it's been a hell of a life, Ethan.'

'The thing is, I remember lying in the dark, thinking I was going to die. And hearing Chase say something about having to make a choice between me and Nick. But...' He sighed. 'I had so much going through my head, maybe I heard it wrong. The building was creaking and any minute the whole place was going to completely collapse on top of me. I was panicking. I was in so much pain and it was so dark and when I heard his voice I just wanted to shout, *Choose me. Choose me. Don't choose Nick. I'm here. I'm here.*' He closed his eyes. 'Yeah. Gutless.'

'Not gutless. You wanted to survive.' Her heart twisted as she imagined him as a young man, trying to come to

terms with losing those team members. Riddled with guilt and panic, turning to his parents for support and receiving nothing. Then finding his own way, making amends the only way he knew how—by fixing broken people. It wasn't fair that he'd had to deal with all of that on his own. And yet somehow he'd come out so strong and capable and compassionate. He'd survived and gone on to do great things, which was a miracle in itself. 'No one would ever think badly of you for wanting to survive.'

'Except me.' He reached for his glass and gulped some cognac. Shook his head. Then his eyes sought hers and she wanted so much to stop the ache in his heart.

She found him a smile and had an inkling as to how she could help. 'Hey, you want to be somewhere else? Back in Africa now? Or how about just lazing on a beach in Tahiti with bottomless cocktails again?'

'No, Claire.'

'Then where?'

Time strung out. He stroked his thumb over her lip, sending shivers of need through her that arrowed deep in her belly. His eyes sought hers and for a few moments he said nothing. He just stroked her lips and edged closer as the room filled with unmet need and longing.

He was so close now, so close she could feel the hitch in his breath, the heat thrumming from his skin. The palpable desire.

'Where, then, Ethan?' Her voice cracked the spell but didn't break it. She wanted to kiss his pain away, to be the thing that put that half-smile back on his face. The one he turned to when he needed someone. But there was so much at stake now.

He shifted closer, his mouth at her ear. 'I want to be in a lift in Marseille.'

Her heart rattling with conflicted emotions, she moved away from his hand. 'Don't do this, Ethan.'

But he closed the distance and stroked her cheek with his fingers. 'I know my swapped shifts upset you, but it was the only thing I could do that made any sense. I had to put you out of reach because from the moment I first saw you in the bar I wanted you. Over and over and over. I can't work side by side with you and not want to touch you, kiss you, hold you. I put you out of reach, but this makes more sense right now, Claire. You. Me. Here. Close.'

She had no doubt he meant it, but things would change once he knew about her late period. The heat would steam out of his eyes, he'd get that trapped look he'd had when he'd first stepped into the lift, when he'd first seen her on the ship, always when he was inside looking out, as if every muscle strained to break free, and now she understood why. He'd been pinned to the floor and looked death in the face and since then he'd fought to be unrestrained.

There'd be no more cheek stroking or stolen kisses, but no matter how much she didn't want to she had to stop this and tell him. She put her hand to his cheek. 'Listen, Ethan, I have to tell you something—'

'No.' He put his finger to her mouth briefly. Smiled.

'Ethan—'

'Enough talking. I have plans for that mouth.' He slid his lips over hers and her words were caught between her throat and her head, then lost altogether as everything in her brain blurred.

He whispered her name into her mouth then she felt the stroke of his tongue and she was lost in his taste and his scent and the strength of his hands on her face. There was the real world beyond that door and there was here, no space for words, just feeling and touching. No time except for this. No promises or truths. Just his mouth and his hands in her hair, on her breast, removing her clothes.

Her hands on his skin, running over muscles. His kisses. His kisses that made her heart race and her limbs melt and

the fire in her belly spark bright and fierce. His kisses that deepened as his tongue danced with hers, that drew a slick trail to her throat. Then to her breast, as he sucked in a nipple, making her buck against him.

She tugged at his boxer shorts, stroked his hardness through the fabric and went to touch him, but his hand stilled hers. 'The last time was too fast. I want to explore you. We have all night.'

All weekend if they wanted, before they got back on the ship. She wanted more, she realised with a shock. One night wasn't going to be enough. She wanted everything but, knowing that was impossible, she would take every precious damned second she could get tonight.

He laid her on the bed and slid down next to her, his erection jutting against her thigh.

He stroked between her breasts, his gaze almost reverent. 'Claire, you are amazing. You blow my mind. Completely. I can't think straight when you're around. I just want to do this. All. The. Time.' He gave her that sweet, sexy smile as he stroked her skin. 'Makes being around you in polite company pretty damned difficult.'

She squirmed under his touch, desperate for his hand to clamp her nipple. Hand. Mouth. She didn't care which. *Both. Please.* But he just smiled some more, knowing he was driving her crazy with need.

Magnifique. 'Bel homme.' Beautiful man. She sat up and cupped his face, pressed her mouth to his again as tears threatened. *You'll break my heart.*

She knew that already, because his type always did. But there was no going back. She needed his touch, needed his drugging kisses. Needed him inside her. She'd come here to comfort him, but all she craved now was the comfort of his touch.

He smiled and tugged her hair tie, letting her hair fall around her shoulders. He shook his head, eyes light and

glittering. 'Claire, *you* are beautiful. So damned beautiful it makes my heart hurt. I can't make sense of it, I can't stop thinking about you. About the way you feel and the way you make me feel.'

He leaned and slowly sucked her nipple into his mouth. She slid her fingers into his messy hair and moaned as he sucked first one bud then the other. He laughed as she tugged him back to her and kissed him hard.

Laughed again as he made her lie back and kissed down her throat to her belly. She felt the roughness of his jaw against the soft skin on her thigh and then delicious heat on her slick core as he explored her with his tongue.

She had never felt more aroused in her life as he slid his fingers inside her, sweet torture that was both too much and not enough. She writhed against him, wanting him on her, in her. But the pressure and the pleasure built and built as his fingers probed and stroked, until she couldn't hold on any longer and she shuddered against him, her scream loud and raw.

Overwhelmed by the white-hot intensity, she kept her eyes closed but felt him move, and then he was there, cradling her high against his chest. And she held onto him, afraid of the feeling in her heart, afraid he'd see it in her eyes.

But one orgasm wasn't enough and she could feel his erection hard and tight against her thigh. She was emboldened by his kisses and wanted to feel that release again. Wanted him to have it too. She sat up and slid his boxers off, straddled his thighs and stroked his length.

He groaned as she kissed the tip, called her name as she took him deep into her mouth again and again. But then his hand covered hers. 'Stop. I want to be inside you.'

'Please?' She laughed.

'Now,' he growled, but she refused to move.

'Please, Mr Knight. Don't forget your manners.'

'Claire.' Another growl and she wondered if it would ever be possible to tame him. To anchor him to a place, or a time, or a promise. But he laughed as he flipped her onto her back in one swift move. Then a few moments drifted as he sheathed himself with a condom.

As she waited, her hand went to her belly and for a second everything came back to her and she wanted to tell him, to just say the words. To tell him a condom wasn't needed. But all sense was gone when he turned and looked at her with such intense desire. And she nodded.

He kept his eyes locked on hers as he pushed into her.

'Yes,' she whispered, as he filled her deep and tight.

'Yes.' Holding her hand against his heart, he rocked into her, a slow sensual rhythm that held her in a state of torment and bliss. His eyes blazed freedom and excitement and adventure. And something more. Something that connected with her on a deeper level, in her heart and in her soul.

Then his rhythm changed and he tilted her hips and his thrust went deeper and faster, and she gripped his arms then his buttocks, pulling him closer and ever deeper. And then there was no more holding on as pleasure overrode everything. He held her steady as she let go, calling his name into the darkness. He anchored her in his arms and against his heart as she shattered around him. Then he was pulsing deep inside her as he succumbed to his own release.

But his eyes never left hers and raw honesty was there. This was perfect and irresistible and crazy and wild and there were no answers and no questions. Just this.

And then he kissed her again, long and slow and with such need it was as if she were *his* anchor and everything slotted into place in her head and in her heart. Being here with him made complete sense. It made all the sense in the world.

CHAPTER TEN

SLICK WITH THEIR SWEAT, he lay back on the pillow and breathed deeply. 'Wow, Claire. That was…wow. I didn't know two people could make each other feel like that. You are really something.'

This is. What we have here. She couldn't find any words as she slid into his embrace, laying her head on his chest. It had been the most intense, the most meaningful sex of her life and she wasn't sure her heart was going to recover.

He nuzzled the top of her head. 'Kristina won't mind if I borrow you for the next few days, will she? I'm not quite finished with you.'

'Sounds interesting.' She sighed, imagining the next two days of nothing but him and room service. Such a wonderful dream, but that was all it was, a dream, because the minute reality hit them everything would come to a grinding halt. Reality was basically everything: her missed period; the ship; geography; plans.

'I'll certainly make it interesting,' he growled into her ear.

'I know you would.' The stroking was intoxicating. 'But we'd planned to do some exploring. I promised to take her to this amazing *chocolatier* I know, and the best place for *bouillabaisse* in Place Jean Jaurès. You can come with us if you like.'

'I have no desire to see any more of Marseille than this room. Preferably with you in it.'

Of course. He hated France. He wouldn't want to be tied to the place or get to know it better, he just wanted to lock himself in this room until it was time to leave. And why not? He'd suffered badly in this country and being here brought back horrific nightmares. Her heart knotted as she wondered how things might work out and she couldn't see a positive way through. She dredged up a laugh, which sounded hollow and sad in the darkness. 'You need to get out more.'

'I need to be inside you more.' His fingers drew small circles down her belly, sliding to her thigh.

'Already?'

'You drive me crazy. Yes. Already.' His fathomless eyes drew her in and she wanted to stay there for ever. And she wanted more, oh, she really did, but it wasn't fair being here without being honest.

She put her hand on his. 'Ethan, listen. Stop.'

'You okay?'

'I think I'm pregnant.' It was probably cruel to blurt it out like that, but she'd screwed up her courage and there was no going back.

'What? After five minutes? So soon? Are you psychic or something?' Laughing, he snaked his arms underneath her and drew her near, spooning his body around her, snuggling against her neck. When she didn't say anything more his body stilled. Froze, in fact.

'It's not a joke.' She didn't want to see his reaction and watch that trapped panic slide into his eyes so she spoke to the blackness, the weight of it almost crushing her, because too many lives depended on these next few words and his reaction. 'My period's late, Ethan. After the first time, in the lift. I haven't done a test yet because I think it's too soon...' and the truth was she was too damned

scared to '…but I'm never late. I'm always regular, on the dot. Twenty-eight days. Always.'

Still nothing. Barely a breath. 'Say something, Ethan.'

'We used a condom.' Which wasn't exactly what she'd wanted to hear.

'I know.' She didn't need to explain that no contraception was one hundred per cent safe; he was a medic, he knew that.

More silence, almost painful to breathe and to feel.

First his leg moved away, then the rest of his body inch by inch, and he lay back on the pillow with his head on his hands. She was left with nothing but an aching heart and cold space where he'd been spooning her. 'And it's mine? Are you sure?'

'Yes. It's yours, Ethan. Of course it's yours.' She squeezed her eyes shut to stop the tears from spilling down her face. This was not the adventure she'd been craving. Or the excitement. Definitely not the freedom. 'You're the only person I've made love with in almost a year.'

'And…what are you going to do?' His voice was cold and she imagined him working out how the hell to extricate himself from it all. 'If…'

'If I am pregnant I will keep it, of course.' There were options and she'd considered them all, but she'd made that decision at least. In her family babies were welcomed, even if inconveniently timed.

'Right.' He blew out slowly and she felt a wave of relief shudder through him. 'Of course.'

'*If. If*, Ethan. Nothing's definite.' Why had she opened her mouth and blurted it out? Why hadn't she waited?

'I know you well enough that you wouldn't have told me if you didn't think there was a high chance of it being true. You're not going to play games about something like this.'

'I told you because I'm confused and I couldn't stay here and act as if everything was fine when I had this going

round in my head. I thought you should know.' And she
was hormonal and had post-sex brain. 'But now I wish I
hadn't said anything until I was certain one way or the
other.'

'I'm glad you told me.'

'I don't think you are.' He wasn't a very good liar.
Words were all very good but his body belied them, tense
and taut and what felt like miles away from her now. She
sat up next to him, glancing at his dark expression and
confirming her suspicions. 'But that's fine. I can manage
without your support.'

She made a decision. She was not going to rush out and
do anything yet. They had two more days here and she was
going to try to relax because stress wasn't good for any-
one, and not for the baby, if it was in there somewhere, try-
ing to survive. She was going to go out with Kristina like
they'd planned, she was going to breathe and take some *me*
time. Although she wasn't sure how long she could keep
pretending it wasn't real; she had to face up to the truth.

'I was going to go out and buy a test tomorrow but I
won't do one until I'm back on the ship, Ethan. You and
I both know about false positives, there's no point in get-
ting into a spin over nothing.'

He nodded. He hadn't touched her since she'd told him,
he hadn't smiled, he'd just developed a deep frown and the
haunted darkness he'd worn when she'd knocked on his
door earlier had taken up residence again. 'That's your
choice and I can't do a thing about it, Claire. But if you are
pregnant I don't want you setting foot back on that boat.'

'And then what? Leave my job and ruin my life just be-
cause I may or may not have a baby in nine months' time?
You and I both know there is a chance of miscarriage and
all sorts of things that could go wrong. It's very early days,
if any days at all, so let's just give ourselves some time to

get used to the idea and see what happens. All that sea-sickness might have just messed up my cycle.'

He clicked his fingers as if trying to remember something. 'Fuaad. That's why you were concerned about Fuaad's fever. Because it might harm the baby?'

'Yes, among other things. But I had all the vaccinations before I came and we have good protocols in place. And I'm fine. Look at me. I'm fine. Please don't say anything to anyone. Please.'

'How can I? It's your body, and your life, I have to respect that. But as soon as we know for sure you have to talk to Chase about it and decide whether you can stay or not.' His eyes glittered. 'But if I think for a second that you're in any danger I'll be rowing you to shore myself if I have to.'

She registered the way he was already trying to protect her and the baby, and that gave her a little hope that she wouldn't be on her own through this journey. But, if necessary, she was just as determined as Mariam to protect her child at all costs. 'I know how to look after myself and anyone else who comes along. We'll be fine.'

We? We? But no matter how much she tried to convince herself otherwise, she was sure there was a tiny little life inside her and it was going to need every ounce of its mother's strength.

Even though he was trying to protect them his expression was hard set. 'I'll make sure you're both well provided for.'

'Sure, you'll wire money from your camp in Darfur or something? You'll provide for your child from there? This isn't the nineteenth century, you know, I don't expect anything from you. I can manage just fine.' She'd hoped for something more. What, she didn't know, because she knew any kind of declaration was beyond Ethan right now. He

was reeling from the shock while she'd had days to come to terms with it.

He hadn't had the kind of life where babies were loved and expected and part of every day. He'd been isolated and neglected and a burden. And even though he'd try his best to take care of his child, he would always see it as a burden too. He didn't know any different. Her heart hurt for them all as she pushed the sheets back and climbed out of bed.

He sat up straighter, his hand outstretched. 'Where are you going?'

'Back to my room.' Tugging on her clothes, she fisted tears away.

'Claire, stay here.' It was the first time he'd ever raised his voice around her.

But she needed some space. 'I can't.'

A *baby*?

What the actual hell? Ethan couldn't get his head around that thought. And yet his eyes had kept darting to Claire's belly as if staring at it for long enough might give him some answers. For the record; it didn't.

But if Claire was pregnant then life would never be the same again.

He bunched up the sheets that smelt of her and tried to make sense of it all. He'd always prevented this happening in the past, so why it had happened now, with Claire, was beyond him. They'd been careful. *He'd* been careful that night and ever since. The moment he'd realised he'd been getting in too deep with her he'd ramped up the barriers. She'd broken them down with a smile. He'd re-fortified them, she'd shattered them with a kiss. And then last night she'd come to him, sensing he'd needed to talk, and making love with her had blown his heart wide open.

But this? A child? This was another level of complication. He wasn't father material, he certainly wasn't husband

material. A nomadic life in an African desert wasn't the right place for a family. But neither was France. Not for him. She'd want to go home, for sure, to be surrounded by the people who loved her.

And what the hell did he know about childrearing? Paediatrics, yes, he'd written papers on the damned subject. But being a father? Nothing at all.

He threw the pillow that was imprinted with Claire's citrus shampoo across the room. There was no way he was going to get any sleep now. If ever.

Because, despite the panic, deep down in a corner of his heart a light had flared when she'd said the word *pregnant*. A light that had given him the first sense of hope he'd had in a long time. But the hope had wilted as he'd worked through the ramifications.

He tried a warm shower. A run. A cold shower. But nothing stilled his mind. He was too jittery for meditation, too wired for more alcohol. Too strung out for a conversation with anyone else but Claire.

He didn't see her at all the next day or night, even though he'd knocked on her door and half expected to hear from her. His text suggesting they talk went unanswered, so he presumed she'd done the sightseeing thing with her friends and was keeping her distance. He didn't see Chase again either, so early on the last evening on shore he took to pounding the streets once more, trying to see if exercise might help get his mind straight about any of it.

It didn't. Fifteen kilometres, three babies in pushchairs, a toddler gleefully splashing in a fountain and one set of identical eighteen-month-old twin boys tottering along La Corniche later, he arrived back at the hotel. Suddenly the world was full of babies everywhere he looked.

And each step had stamped out a regular beat: Claire and a baby. Claire and a baby.

It wasn't helping. A father? Like his own? Distant and difficult?

But that was the only way. Surely? It was all he knew.

As he ran up the fire exit stairs he examined the adrenaline flowing through him and was surprised to feel excitement there as well as panic. Had his own father ever thought about Ethan like that? With some excitement?

Don't get ahead of yourself.

After a quick shower and change he was examining his dinner options when his phone beeped. It was a message from Kristina.

There's a visitor for you in reception.

From Kristina and not from Claire, he noted. She was hurting and it was his fault. He should have reacted better, but he'd been too shocked to temper his response. Not that that was a justifiable excuse for freezing her out like he had, and for being cold and short-worded instead of supportive. After all, not that he would but if he chose to he could walk away from this, but Claire had to live with it for ever. And what then of her bucket list of plans and dreams?

He headed down to Reception and found himself face to face with '*Mariam?* Hello! And little Awate. Good to see you both.' It really was. He didn't often get the chance to catch up with his old patients.

And there was Claire. His heart panicked at the sight of her, so beautiful, hesitant, wary. So unlike the free, uninhibited Claire he'd made love to twice. And, judging by the way his body prickled and his heart squeezed, wanted to make love to again.

But her eyes darkened when she looked at him and, in

contrast, shone brightly as she turned and gazed at the bundle in Mariam's hands. With his careless, unrestrained reaction to her news he'd done a lot of damage to her heart.

Fatima was there too. She smiled and stepped forward to translate. 'Mariam heard the ship was in dock and went down to see if you were there. The crew told her to come here.'

'Is she okay?' He did a visual assessment. Mum and baby looked fine. Claire didn't.

Always Claire. His first thought in the morning, the last image in his head before he slept, not that he'd been doing much of that recently.

Fatima smiled. 'Mariam is doing well. She just wants to say thank you to you both for saving her child.'

Claire threw him a hooded look that said, *See, we do get to find out what happens.* And, probably, also a whole lot of curse words. 'And Awate? How is she?'

'Here.' Mariam grinned. 'Hold her.'

'I'd love to.' Claire took the baby from Mariam's out-stretched arms and her eyes misted. 'She's adorable. She's put on a good amount of weight. I can't believe how much she's grown.'

He watched as she cooed at the baby, the whispered voice, the softened features, and he imagined a future. His heart twisted. Not a future that could include him.

He snapped back to reality. They hadn't had a positive result. No result at all, in fact. They were living in limbo. 'So, Mariam, how are things for you?'

He waited as she spoke and Fatima translated. 'They were discharged from hospital two days ago. Awate is doing fine. She's still tiny, as you can see, but she's going in the right direction. Mariam has to take her to the clinic to be measured and weighed three times a week and her milk is coming through well. Baby is hungry.'

Claire nodded. 'Excellent. Where are they staying?'

'In the refugee centre. She says it's okay. She'll be fine. She's hoping to look for a place to live and get a job if her asylum request is granted. She has strength for her child.'

'I know she has.' Claire gave the new mother a wobbly smile and Ethan wondered exactly what was running through her mind right now. 'Tell her I'm so pleased to see her and that I'll call in to see her next time I'm in Marseille. I'll give her my number in case she needs anything, or just a friend. We can all do with those, right?' After she handed little Awate back to her mother, Claire wrote down her number on a piece of paper.

He wanted to tell her again about not getting involved, but it wasn't his business. Yet he felt a responsibility to her. And who was he to advise against involvement when he'd gone and done it himself with her? And whose life he'd mess up if he allowed things to get any more serious between them. He could possibly navigate being a father, but being her long-time lover? *Husband?*

But his heart fisted at the thought of walking away from her.

'Mariam says she's tired now. I'll walk her back to the centre.' Fatima smiled. 'It's not that far. Then there's the group dinner at Rafael's. See you there?'

Claire glanced at Ethan and then back at Fatima. 'Not sure.'

Fatima looked from one to the other and he wondered whether Claire had confided in her or not. 'Okay. See you bright and early back on the ship, if not before.'

Then it was just the two of them standing in the reception area. He didn't know what to say next so he waited. But Claire just looked at him, her eyes smudged and sad, and he felt a thick weight crushing his chest. He grasped at something. 'What did you do yesterday?'

'I showed Kristina the sights, had an early night. Shopping today. You?' Her tone was clipped.

'Thinking. Running. Sleeping. But not sleeping.' He paused, not knowing where to begin. Then decided to just talk about it. 'It's not what you wanted.'

'No, having a baby at this point in my life isn't on my bucket list, Ethan. But we don't always get what we want, right?' She shrugged resignedly and he ached to hold her tight, but got the feeling she didn't want that from him. 'But the good thing about being a human is that we can be flexible and respond to circumstances when they are thrown at us. If it turns out there is a child in here, I'll adapt.'

She patted her belly and something fierce bloomed inside Ethan's chest. He stepped towards her. 'I want to—'

She put her hand up. 'Please don't talk about it any more, not until we know for sure. It's all I can think about and I'm so tired. This is supposed to be a nice break before we get back on the ship to work non-stop for another three weeks, and I'm not relaxing at all. I need a distraction.'

There were so many ways he could relax her, but he doubted she'd agree to any of them. 'Maybe we can find some common ground to just relax without being stressed? You want to take a little time out from it all?'

She looked completely lost, her eyes lined with shadows. 'If only that was possible.'

'You said something about the best *chocolatier* in town?'

'With you?' There was a glimmer of lightness in her eyes for the first time since he'd held her tight against his chest the other night. 'You want to actually leave the hotel?'

It hadn't occurred to him that he'd be out there doing things in France, his only impulse had been to make her smile. He was a lost cause. 'Yes, of course.'

'Of course? You don't sound so sure.' She looked at him with narrowed eyes. 'And you honestly like chocolate?'

'It's my one vice.' He smiled, because smiling was easy when he was with Claire, even when everything else was difficult. 'And gelato, of course.'

She smiled back at him. Finally. 'And cognac.'

And you.

Trouble was, she was his vice and his virtue. And he was stuck between the two, not knowing where to go next.

CHAPTER ELEVEN

IT WAS STILL light as they strode through the La Plaine district of the city and the last dying rays of the sun had a little warmth left in them. Claire was surprised she'd even agreed to come with him after the way he'd reacted to her pregnancy suspicions, but here was the thing—something about Ethan made her heart sing and she needed a little of that right now.

Being with her new friends had been lovely, and they'd laughed a lot, but everything had been marred by her lack of a period. Somehow she felt she could bear the grumpiness and lack of focus on anything else with him, because it was as much his fault as it was hers. They were united in one big fat mistake that was going to change the course of their lives. Or hers, at least.

And she was supposed to be distracting herself from all that.

'There's a lovely morning market here with food from all corners of the world. You name it, we probably have it.' She pointed out the closed stalls in the square and the fruit and vegetable shops spilling out onto the pavement. Then another shop front with huge bowls of ruby- and jade-coloured olives glistening in oil and another with brown hessian sacks holding as many different spices as there were days of the year. Basically, she was using her

hands to point to as many things as possible to stop herself from grabbing his.

His eyebrows rose a little and he smiled. 'It's not like the France I remember. This is warm and dry and buzzy.'

Good. She wanted to help him have better memories of her home country. 'France isn't just mountains and snow.'

'Of course I know that. I just…' He shrugged. 'Funny how one thing can colour your life in so many ways.'

Don't I know it? She rubbed her tender breast, believing now that these weren't her normal PMS symptoms.

'Can you smell the cinnamon?' Her stomach growled loudly. 'Not only is this the place with the best hot chocolate in the world, there are amazing Moroccan cafés here too. They made me want to visit Morocco and North Africa just by their cooking smells and flavours.'

He laughed. 'I'm getting a hint here, aren't I? Do you want to eat something? Is that why you're talking so lovingly about food?'

'Yes, I'm starving, and then I feel sick and then I'm starving again. Sometimes only chocolate will do.' She grabbed the last vacant table on the terrace and signalled to a waiter to bring over a menu. 'I don't know why I'm asking for a menu. I know it off by heart. *Un morceau feuilletée du chocolat lait, s'il vous plaît. Deux chocolats chauds.* Sorry, Ethan, I'm a philistine. Only milk chocolate will do and I've ordered you a drink. Don't argue about that. You'll never want anything else for the rest of your life.'

'I doubt that.' His eyes were all tease and she imagined what was going round in his head. It hurt that the sexual attraction was intense, along with a tenderness borne from their intimacy, but it also hurt that she couldn't see how they could get over this massive hurdle.

'Ethan Reid, honestly. When I said I wanted a distraction I didn't mean that.'

'I want to make you smile.'

'You do. Mostly. Which is why all this is so hard.'

'Okay, stick to food.' His eyes glittered as he smiled and she knew how they'd got to this point from that first smile in the bar. His smile was everything; a joy, a picture, a pleasure. 'I'm not a chocolate purist. To be honest, I'm grateful to get decent chocolate at all.' He sipped his drink and sighed as if he'd fallen in love. He probably had, the owner really did have the best ingredients here. 'Do you know Marseille well? Did you train here?'

'Yes, it's like a second home. I was here for four years on and off, then I went back home.'

'Which is where? I can't believe I don't even know that about you.'

She laughed. 'We missed the getting-to-know-you stage, didn't we? I'm from a *commune* on the edge of the Gorges du Verdon. It's called Moustiers. Moustiers Sainte Marie, to be precise.'

'Verdon? Near the mountains?' He visibly shuddered.

'*Oui*. It's beautiful—if you like nature and churches. But a little dull after you've lived there your whole life. I'm not a country girl, I don't think. I don't know. This is all I've ever known. The road from here to home and back again.'

'You didn't travel on holidays with your family?'

She laughed, incredulous. 'There are five kids, Ethan. We couldn't afford to travel. Our holidays were spent running around the fields and mountains and messing about in the river.'

'Sounds idyllic.'

'So does sailing in the Greek islands, seeing kangaroos in the wild and riding horses in California.'

'You can still do it.' He paused for a minute and they both knew what he was thinking about. Suddenly the conversation became serious again. 'You can do anything you want.'

Claire's stomach churned and she wasn't sure if it was the prospect of what she was facing or genuine morning sickness but in the evening. Or maybe just too much chocolate. 'When you spoke to Chase, did he mention anything about Kristina?'

Ethan frowned. 'So we're not talking about you?'

She ignored his question, hoping he'd take her lead. 'Only whenever they're in the same room they seem to take it in turns to look at each other, then quickly look away. I thought maybe he might have mentioned something. Kristina's never said a word.'

'He didn't mention anything. But, then, talking about his private life isn't exactly the kind of territory we're in. Early days and baby steps, I think.' Ethan drained his cup. 'It is perfectly possible to travel with a child, Claire.'

'I know that. It just isn't on my radar.' Freedom had been.

Across the square a man started to play a guitar, slow, sultry music befitting the clammy evening. They stopped talking for a moment to listen. An old couple walked into the middle of the square and started to waltz, laughing, whispering, so sweet. As she watched them Claire wondered how many obstacles they'd overcome. What they'd had to give up to get to this point of dancing close, grey-haired and still together.

She'd never been *together* with Ethan. This hadn't been a courtship, it had been lust a million times over, but he was right, they hadn't learnt about each other. And now they were going back onto the ship and any intimacy would have to cease. Again.

He was sitting so close to her, his hands inches away from hers. Yesterday he'd been inside her and today she felt like a teenager with her first crush, not knowing where she stood or what to do with her hands.

He glanced at her. 'You want to dance?'

'Yes. No. I don't know. It's all so complicated.'

'It's just a dance.'

'It isn't. Be honest, Ethan, you know it isn't just a dance. It's connection and kissing and getting closer and closer and then there's this huge problem we can't ignore. And I didn't want to talk about it, but everything circles back to that in the end. What if the test is positive?' She looked deep into his eyes, trying to find answers she knew he wasn't capable of giving. 'What then?'

One man had already let her down badly. She couldn't stand it if another one swore to be with her and then just couldn't let go of his nomadic life. And what would that mean for a baby? A father who randomly dipped in and out of their lives? She didn't want that.

He shoved his hands into his pockets. 'We'll work it out.'

And it was so tempting to believe him.

But *we'll work it out* wasn't any kind of answer, because he was addicted to the volunteer life and she could see why he'd be like that. Dealing with such intense and desperate situations meant you didn't have to examine your own thoughts and feelings. He'd been all but abandoned by his parents, had almost died in an avalanche. He'd been broken and the only way he knew how to fix himself was to fix other people and hope that some of it would rub off on him.

What he wasn't addicted to was any kind of family life, or doing what he loved doing with a wife and child in tow. Not that she wanted to be a wife. That hadn't been on her radar since she'd left her ex in Moustiers.

'I think you've got an admirer,' Ethan murmured, and it was so unexpected and strange that she frowned.

'What?'

He tilted his head towards the old man, who was still dancing with his wife but also beckoning Claire over. 'I

think he wants to swap partners.' Ethan grimaced. 'I'm guessing you'll dance with him?'

'Jealous? Really?' She loved the thought of dancing with Ethan to the romantic music in the pretty evening light, but that would create more problems. But she wasn't going to refuse the old guy's offer either. And a bit of jealousy wouldn't go amiss. Grinning, she walked to the middle of the square and took his hand as Ethan offered his to the woman.

As Monsieur Cabot chivalrously twirled her round they chatted. He was here on holiday with his wife of sixty-two years. They had three children and eight grandchildren. They'd owned a *boulangerie* until he'd retired, only ten years ago. He was surprised to hear Claire wasn't *with* Ethan as she told him they were just friends.

'He's a fool, then,' M. Cabot said as he gamely twirled her around again, doing a little shimmy as he kept hold of her hand. Claire laughed. The man was clearly trying to impress her. 'I snapped my wife up as soon as I could. It was love at first sight.'

She didn't want to tell him she didn't believe in it. Love took time to grow. You didn't fall in love with someone when your eyes met across a room. Or a bar. Or a lift. That wasn't how it worked. You didn't fall in love like that. Her mouth was suddenly dry. 'That's very romantic.'

M. Cabot grinned and looked softly over at his wife, who was dancing a lot more sedately with Ethan. 'The minute I met her I knew she was mine and I made sure she knew it too. I stole her from another man. Just a boyfriend, but you know how it is. If you find it, you hold onto it.'

She didn't want to ask him how you even knew you'd found it. Her heart thrummed and she glanced over at Ethan, looking so strong, so beautiful, so...out of reach.

Heart hurting just a little, she turned back to M. Cabot. 'You stole her? How so?'

His breathing was a little ragged and his face red from exertion as he laughed. 'He wasn't serious about her… wasn't treating her right. I could see he wasn't making her happy. So I walked right over to them and said, "We're going to…"'

'M. Cabot?'

He stopped dancing and closed his eyes. 'Uh…head. *Head.*'

Suddenly Claire felt the whole weight of him against her as his legs sagged. 'Oh! M. Cabot. Ethan! Quick!'

'Hold on.' Ethan was with her in an instant, taking M. Cabot's weight and lowering him to the ground. 'Okay. Let's get you safe. Can you talk to me? Er…?'

'Henri. Henri Cabot. He was fine, chatting happily, and then he collapsed against me. Said something about his head.' Claire's heart was pounding, but not just from the medical emergency. You didn't fall in love like that. It had been a whole lot of lust, that was all. Right?

Ethan patted the man's face gently, trying to get him to focus. 'Henri? *Peux-tu m'entendre?*'

'Do you want me to translate?' Claire asked.

'Was it that bad?'

'It was excellent.' She didn't think that Ethan could do anything badly—not where medicine was concerned at least. She wasn't sure about his sticking power in other things, though. 'There may be things he says that you don't understand. His speech is slurred.'

'Tell him I'm a doctor. That he needs to try to stay calm and that I'm going to call an ambulance.' Ethan's eyebrows furrowed. 'I don't like the way his face is drooping at the corner.'

'A stroke, do you think?' She was aware that neither of them was looking after Madame Cabot, who was hovering at the side with her hand to her mouth.

Ethan was completely focused on Henri. 'We can't be

sure, but it looks like it. Can you hold the fort while I get someone to call an ambulance?'

'I'll go. It'll be easier if I tell them in French.' Claire ran to the café, told a waiter to phone for an ambulance, brought a blanket to cover Henri and keep him warm until help came, and dragged over a rattan chair for Madame Cabot to sit on.

'Does he have any medical problems?' Claire asked Mme. Cabot—Adele.

'Blood pressure. He's on tablets.' The older lady's hands shook and she was pale and shocked. 'That's all, and he's not very good at taking them because…' She rolled her eyes, but they were so full of love and panic that it almost stole Claire's breath away. 'Because he's a man and I can't tell him to do anything without a fight. He won't go to a doctor unless I push him.'

Not visiting a doctor didn't mean you didn't have problems. Claire relayed the information to Ethan, who was loosening Henri's shirt collar and tie while asking questions about everything and nothing, just to keep the man talking. She was impressed to see him trying to use his rudimentary French, even if he was woefully wrong at times. He asked Henri to raise his *brasse*. The old man shook his head and looked as if he was trying to swim with his right arm.

'Ethan, you mean *bras*. Arms? Right? Not breaststroke? Look, his right arm is moving, but not his left.'

In another situation the language confusion might have been funny but Henri clutched at his head and Claire could see the pain on his face. It was mirrored in his wife's expression.

'Help him, please.' Mme. Cabot begged, her voice weak with worry. 'What's wrong with him?'

Claire held the lady's trembling hand. 'I don't want to

make a diagnosis without proper tests, but I think he might be having a stroke.'

'No. He's not.' Mrs Cabot shook her hands free, knelt down and smothered her husband's face in kisses. 'Come on, Henri. Get up. Come and dance with me.'

Henri closed his eyes. From this angle one side of his face was definitely affected and drooping.

'No, Henri. Don't ignore me. Get up and dance.' Mrs Cabot stroked his cheek and a tear landed on his skin. Oh, to have such a fierce love for someone that you thought you could will them better with the sheer strength of it. 'Now, do you hear me? Get up. Please. *Please*, Henri.'

More tears fell onto Henri's shirt. Claire's throat was raw and she gently rubbed Mme. Cabot's shoulders. There was nothing medically they could do without medication and equipment so they just needed to be there and be ready in case Henri's condition deteriorated. 'I think he needs a little rest. The paramedics should have some drugs to help him. He said you have children. Are any close by?'

'No. Paris, Quebec, Rennes. Not here. He loves dancing. We met at a dance.' She took his hand in hers. 'He just walked up to me and whisked me into his arms and I've been there ever since. Henri, hold my hand. Henri! Why can't he hold my hand?'

Claire squeezed the threatening tears away. 'He might be able to use his other one.'

'Don't let him die.' The woman's face crumpled. 'He's the only man I've ever loved. How will I cope without him?'

Claire's heart nearly broke in two. 'It won't get to that. The ambulance is on its way and they'll take care of him. Let me call someone to be with you.'

'No. No. I don't want to worry anyone.'

'They need to know and they'll want to support you and Henri. That's what families are for.'

In a rush of affection Claire realised she'd want her family around her too, if what she suspected became a reality. She'd need their support. She didn't want to go home, but she'd have to because there was no one else. She'd left her nursing friends here in Marscille, but none of them were the settling-down type.

Ethan wouldn't care where she was, most likely, as it wouldn't affect him. But her family would help her, after they'd recovered from the shock, the way she'd helped her *maman*. Yes, she'd go home to the mountains.

She was shaken out of her reverie by the sound of the ambulance siren. 'Okay, we'll need to give them some space while the paramedics work on him.'

It took them a few minutes to assess Henri, and Claire translated for Ethan. Their patient's blood pressure was very high and it was, as they'd guessed, a stroke that was affecting his speech and causing the facial droop. There was a long road ahead for both Mr and Mrs Cabot.

Claire embraced the older lady before helping her into the ambulance. 'Best of luck. Take care, Adele, and give him a hug from me.'

'I will. *Merci pour tout.*' Mrs Cabot cupped Claire's cheek and smiled weakly. Then she glanced towards Ethan. 'Hold him close tonight.'

I'd love to. She watched as Ethan gently embraced Adele and told her to look after herself and managed to coax a smile from her at the way he expertly dealt with a scared Henri and gave him courage. She saw the way he handed over information to the paramedics as calmly as any professional she'd ever seen.

He was everything she'd ever desired in a man. She wanted to breathe him in, kiss him hard and make love again. But things were far too serious for that and since her conversation with Henri she'd felt discombobulated.

She felt Ethan slide his arm around her shoulders as they

waved the ambulance off and the temptation to hug him close was almost overwhelming, but she pulled away and gave him a smile that she hoped said, *Stop*. And he did, letting his hand drop to his side with confusion in his eyes.

They walked along in silence for a while and she tried to get the image out of her head of Mrs Cabot covering her husband's face with kisses. That woman had not been willing to let her husband give up.

Claire imagined how it would feel to have a love so strong and unbreakable that you couldn't bear living without it.

Love doesn't happen with a look. It happens with time and connection and shared experiences.

It didn't happen in three short weeks. And not, if she had any sense at all, with the most unattainable man she'd ever met. Trouble was, she had a bad feeling she was already halfway down that road, so no matter how funny and smart and compassionate Ethan was, she wasn't going to allow herself to fall for him any more than she already had.

She didn't love him. She didn't. Her heart was hurting for the Cabots and not for herself.

Suddenly the night didn't seem quite as temperate as before. A cool breeze floated in from the sea and she pulled her jacket around her shoulders as she started to walk quickly back to the hotel.

But Ethan was by her side. 'Wait. Claire?'

She upped her pace. 'There's too much going round in my head. I can't wait, Ethan.'

He touched her elbow. 'I want to make sure you're okay. That was pretty intense.'

'It's all intense. And it's not okay.'

'I know it isn't.' His eyes were bruised with hurt at her rejection. 'But I have just one thing to ask you.'

'What?'

'Do a test, Claire. Find out what the reality is and then we can start to make a plan. Okay?'

'As soon as we're back on the ship I'll do a test, I promise.' If she was back on the *SOS Poseidon* then there'd be less chance of Chase shipping her back to shore too soon, then at least she'd grasp a few more days, even weeks of freedom before she went back home to face her friends and family.

But the problem was, when she looked deep inside her heart, where Ethan was concerned she wasn't sure anything would ever be okay again.

CHAPTER TWELVE

THE NEXT DAY was torture. Three hours after they'd set sail they'd picked up a small deflating RHIB overcrowded with Sudanese refugees. At least, Ethan thought, he could speak with them in their own language, but the sun had been relentless and these guys—fourteen men with high hopes for a chance at a safe future—had been floating for days at the mercy of what little wind had reached them.

Severe dehydration was the most pressing problem, along with chemical burns from the cargo their boat had also been carrying. Some were barely able to speak because their lips were so cracked and their throats so raw.

Which, on a positive note, meant Ethan hadn't had time to think about Claire and the way his heart had thumped as she'd walked back to the hotel in silence last night. The look in her eyes as she'd refused a drink and slunk off to bed had stayed with him into the early hours.

One of the men was writhing in pain on the trolley and Ethan was trying to get an IV line into pretty collapsed veins. Ethan rolled out his best Arabic, and when that failed to get a response tried his pidgin Beja. 'Hey, Mustafa, this will work a whole lot better if you lie still.'

Confused and in pain, the man grabbed the cannula and tugged it out. Blood poured down his arm and onto the floor. Ethan stemmed the flow with pressure and strapped

on a wad of gauze. Finding another vein that he could use was pretty difficult. 'Lie still, mate. Come on.' *Give me a break, please.*

'Don't bite me! You're biting! Keep away!' The man was clearly delirious as he thrashed out, missing Ethan's jaw by a whisker.

He tried to calm the man down. 'Hey, buddy. That's a neat right hook you've got there, but please keep it for the boxing ring. I want to help you.'

'Oh. I didn't expect you to be in here,' a suddenly red-faced Claire said as she breezed into the medical room, and his heart thudded hard just seeing her—everything was tangled up in lust and need and something deeper, something that scared him. Their relationship had gone from sexual to serious and his body and brain didn't know how to compute it all. She came over to the trolley and smiled at their patient, unaware of the precariousness of Mustafa's mental state. 'Need a hand?'

'I need to keep him still.' His eyes flicked to her belly and he shook his head. 'Could you ask for Akil or someone to come and help?'

'I'm here.' Her eyes narrowed. 'What do you need?'

'Mustafa's hallucinating and I want to get some fluids into him. But he's scared and keeps hitting out. I don't want you to get hurt. Basically.'

'I'll be fine.' She gently took hold of Mustafa's hand and coaxed him to lie down and keep still. But as Ethan started to make headway with the cannula the man started to shout and pull his hand away.

'Keep still, honey,' she said over and over, her tone getting a little more assertive with each rendition, but always sweet and gentle. But just when they thought he was relaxing, he'd straighten again and start to cower and shake and cry.

'It's okay. We've got you. You're safe now,' she cooed,

stroking his hand and getting him to lie down again. 'I know you're scared but you're safe here.'

'No!' Mustafa kicked out, his foot narrowly missing her belly and stormed out. Heart racing, Ethan grabbed at her to move her out of harm's way but she shook herself from his grip and then rushed towards the door. 'Mustafa!'

'Do not go after him. Claire. Stop.'

'He's confused.' She briefly glanced back at Ethan and then opened the door. 'God knows what he'll do.'

'You are not to go after him, do you hear me?' And, yeah, he knew his protectiveness was annoying but he didn't care right now. Ethan visually tracked Mustafa across the corridor and into another room. 'He's just gone into the men's toilet and Chase has followed him in. If they don't come out in a couple of minutes I'll go in. Okay? There's not enough room in there for more than two or three people. Chase'll get a handle on it. If he doesn't, he'll call.'

Claire bristled. 'I could have handled him.'

'I know, but you shouldn't have to.'

'It's my job, Ethan.' She swiped the back of her hand over her forehead and breathed out sharply. 'And I'm confused why you're here instead of in bed, getting ready for the night shift.'

'My sleep pattern's all over the place so I thought I might as well come work here instead of lying on my bunk.' *Thinking about you and the what-ifs going round my head.* Grasping the opportunity of them being alone, he closed the door to block out the rest of the world and lowered his voice. 'Did you…?'

'Do a test?' Her eyes sparked a heated defence. 'Yes.'

'And?' He held his breath, praying, but for what he didn't know. Just praying he'd find peace with whatever she said. Having a baby might not have been on her bucket list until she was older, but it hadn't been on his at all.

Her chin lifted defiantly, but her eyes glittered with tears. 'It's positive. I am pregnant.'

'Okay.' Trying to get a grip on his rapidly spiralling life, he swallowed hard, his body fizzing with something akin to expectation and even excitement, but his head was reeling at the possibilities and problems this brought. And the hope.

A baby. His baby. *Their* baby.

Emotions charged at him and he couldn't name them all, panic mostly about a life he'd made. But warmth and strength and trepidation and pride hit him like a whirlwind. It was some kind of miracle. After all the crap he'd had in his life there was this. Maybe there'd been a reason he'd survived. Not anything to do with the lives he'd saved, his successes in the end, but to create something better. Something pure and perfect.

Claire looked up at him through eyes swimming with tears. 'I'm sorry.'

'Don't be sorry.' He just wanted to hold her and wipe the tears away, but the invisible armour she was wearing made him rethink that.

'You were supposed to be a fling, Ethan.' Her hands fisted by her sides and he got the feeling she was trying to summon all her strength to deal with the emotional fallout. 'I guess you can still be that. I won't hold you to anything.'

'You won't be short of anything, I'll make sure of it.'

Her shoulders sagged. 'Except a presence. That right?'

He didn't want to make promises he couldn't keep but he knew he couldn't walk away and never have any contact again. This child was a part of him. 'I want to be involved with my baby, Claire. That much I do know.'

'Just not with me, right?'

What would happen? After getting to know him better she'd eventually discover he wasn't worth it…in exactly the same way Chase had thought so, and his parents too.

He didn't want to put that sort of pressure on her. Surely it was better just to be a provider rather than a lover? 'It's early days. We don't know where you're going to be, where either of us will be.'

'I know where I'll be. I just can't be confident of where you'll be.'

See? She'd already got the true measure of him. 'What do you want from me, Claire?'

'I don't know. Something that says you'll be there when I need you to be, for our child. That you'll turn up if you say you're going to. That you won't let him or her down.'

'I won't.' But she kept looking at him as if not trusting his words. 'What do you want, Claire? A marriage proposal?'

Her eyes flared brightly as she looked at him, her gaze burning deep into his soul. 'Ethan, we both know that doing something as rash as that won't help.'

But something fierce bloomed in his heart and he wondered...could it be possible? Could he do it? Could he stop moving and settle? Could he do all the things normal people did? Could he be someone his child was proud of knowing? Could he stick with Claire, wherever she was? Even in France?

He just didn't know.

The door flew open and Kristina ran in. 'Hey, can one of you come and give me a hand with Mustafa? He's fitting in the men's toilet. Chase was there but he's had to go to another emergency, a fight or something.'

'Sure thing.' Claire looked relieved that they were no longer alone.

As Kristina held the door open she called over, 'Claire, can you bring the oxygen too in case we need it when he's post-ictal?'

Ethan shook his head vehemently and unlocked the chain around the large cylinder on wheels. 'No. I'll do it.'

But Claire glared at him. 'I can manage just fine.'

'I said I'll do it.' And then he'd make damned sure she was safe and well and back on shore as soon as possible. He wasn't going to let anything jeopardise that fledgling life in her belly.

His child.

His baby.

Bloody hell.

An hour later Claire was throwing up over the side of the ship when Kristina came over and rubbed her back. 'Better out than in, eh?'

'I'd prefer it to stay where I put it.' Claire moaned.

'Remember when we first came on board? It settled after a couple of days.'

This won't settle for months. Claire rinsed her mouth out with her water bottle. No point in keeping it a secret from Kristina. 'I don't think it'll just be a few days, Kristina. I'm pregnant.'

'Oh, honey.' Her friend wrapped her arms around her and it felt great to have a non-judgemental no-agenda hug.

If only she could have done this with Ethan instead of being both angry and besotted. Confused didn't even begin to describe how she was feeling. She still couldn't get Adele Cabot out of her head, and also Mariam with her single-minded determination to do everything as a solo mum.

Claire wiped a surreptitious tear away. 'It's okay. It's fine.' It would be. It would have to be.

'And Ethan?' Kristina squeezed Claire's shoulder. 'He's the father, right?'

'Yes.'

'And how's he taking it?'

'He says he wants to be involved, but I can't see it happening. I couldn't make him stay with me in France

because he hates the place and I couldn't imagine bringing up a baby in refugee central. Not until I know what I'm doing anyway. And besides all of that…we're not together.'

I love him.

Her heart felt as if it was snapping in two but it was her baby she was sad for. She knew not all marriages were happy ones and that millions of women had brought up children on their own—she just hadn't planned it to be that way for her. She didn't want their child to suffer in any way, and having a father who might or might not be around would be awful. 'Worse, he wants me to talk to Chase.'

Her friend nodded. 'I imagine he does.'

'I can stay here, right? On the ship? Until my stint is finished?'

Kristina sat back and wiped a tear from Claire's cheek. 'Tell me, honestly, do you feel this is a safe environment for a pregnant woman?'

'I can protect myself. There must be guidelines about this kind of thing.'

'There's what's called an offshore agreement.' Kristina nodded. 'It says you have to inform the vessel master as soon as the pregnancy is confirmed.'

'And…?' There was clearly more to come. Claire's stomach tightened, because she didn't think it was going to be positive.

'If circumstances are hazardous, we'd need to drop you off at the first port of call.'

Claire knew she was clutching at straws as she pointed out the calm waters. 'This isn't hazardous, we're hardly moving.'

'But there have been times where we've strapped ourselves down in a storm, remember?' Kristina smiled kindly. 'Only you can make that kind of decision but you have to be honest with yourself—how would you feel if

you put yourself, the baby and possibly others at risk in a storm or with unrest or a confused patient like Mustafa earlier? Ethan mentioned you were almost kicked in the stomach.'

'I know I have to start being sensible, I just don't want it to end.'

'What? The assignment, or whatever it is you have going on with Ethan?' Canny Kristina. Nothing much passed her by.

At least being here meant Claire saw him every day, every hour if she wanted. She couldn't imagine how she'd feel if she were miles away from him. Would he think about her the way she thought about him? Would his heart hurt the way hers did? She didn't want to admit it, but she'd fallen hard for him. Too deep, too hard. One look across that bar and she'd fallen.

Love at first sight. Maybe it did exist after all. For the dreamers and the believers.

But real *love*? The lasting, permanent, forever kind? Loving a man who was utterly unattainable and completely noncommittal? One-sided love wasn't enough where they were concerned. She squeezed her eyes closed. How could she have been so stupid?

Because he was kind and compassionate and funny and sexy as hell. With something to prove.

'Okay, to be honest, I don't want either to end,' she acknowledged to Kristina. 'I want both to keep on going and I know it's all going to come to a grinding halt the minute I leave this ship. My dreams, my hopes, my plans. *My heart.* All gone in a puff of smoke.'

Kristina tilted Claire's chin up. 'But you'll have something amazing to look forward to, right? That baby is going to be one heck of a cutie.'

Claire ran her hand across her belly and for the first time since she'd done the test she smiled. Because this

was a baby. *Oh, mon Dieu.* This was amazing. A new life, and part of her and Ethan. 'If he's anything like his father then…yes, he sure will be.'

Unfortunately, Chase wasn't quite so effusive and positive. 'Of course, you have every right to stay on board, but I have to caution you about the dangers.'

'I know.' Claire had waited until the next morning to both pluck up courage to face her boss with the news and do some research. Everyone knew the first trimester was the riskiest and her nausea was only getting worse. Today she'd had to run three times to the toilet and had lost her breakfast, morning snack and a cup of coffee. So she was exhausted now as well as frequently leaving her duties and dashing off. Why couldn't she be one of those women who didn't get morning sickness? And then, what if she was having an ectopic pregnancy and needed emergency treatment and they were too far from shore? What if Mustafa had actually kicked her in the belly? What if Fuaad's infection had spread?

And then…what if everything turned out just fine? Frustration rushed through her. 'Pretty sure plenty of women have been pregnant on a ship, though.'

'Indeed they have. But there are risks, especially on a ship like this. We're heading out close to Menorca this afternoon, then we're turning southeast where we're more likely to pick people up. There's a storm blowing through tomorrow, pretty fierce by all accounts, so we're going to take a battering. We could drop you off at Menorca. Why don't you have a think and get back to me? In, what, an hour? Then we can change course, get you off the ship and onto a plane to somewhere you want to be.'

'I want to be here.' She'd been on the boat in bad weather before, she could cope with this. But now she

knew she sounded like a petulant child. What she needed
and what she wanted were two separate things.

'Claire doesn't need to think any more about this.'
Ethan? *What the hell?* How dared he? He strode into the
room with possession in his eyes. 'If that storm is as bad
as the forecast then we'll all be vulnerable out here.' He
turned to her. 'It's a medicane, bringing severe weather. I
just heard about it on the radio and came to find you. We
need to get you off as soon as we can.'

She didn't know whether to kiss him hard for being so
passionate about her welfare or whether to tell him where
to get off.

Chase frowned. 'I think this is Claire's decision to
make.'

'It's my baby too.' Ethan stood tall and bold, pride shim-
mering from every pore, not backing down.

God, he was magnificent when he stood firm, protect-
ing his child. But for how long? Magnificent didn't change
nappies in the middle of the night, or rub feet after a hard
day, not when magnificent was on another continent.

'What? Your...?' Chase's eyes widened and he looked
at each of them in turn. Then raised his hand. 'This is your
private business. But it's my mission and I have others to
think about too. Let me know in an hour.'

'She's going. If you don't drop her somewhere safe then
I'll damned well release a RHIB and take her ashore my-
self.' Ethan clearly was not up for discussing this.

'Excuse me, I am here.' Claire knew they were both
trying to work out what was for the best. 'This is for me
to decide, not either of you.'

But her heart knew what her head was trying to com-
pute. A severe storm wasn't going to help her and, if any-
thing, she could be the one needing care. That was not
what she'd signed up for, she didn't want to become the
patient here. She had to admit defeat, or reframe it in a

positive choice of taking her first steps as a mother and protecting her child. That was a good thing. 'It's okay. I don't need an hour. Take me to Menorca, I'll make my own way home from there.'

Ethan nodded, catching her eye. She saw pain there and determination and she didn't know which caught her sharply in the ribs the most because she knew if she left there was a good chance she wouldn't see him again.

She turned and left the room as quickly as she could before she broke down in front of them. The dream was well and truly over, not just for her life as she'd planned it, but with Ethan too.

She didn't have long to fester in her cabin with her bad mood before he came and found her packing. 'Claire, I'm so sorry. I know you wanted more time, but that storm sounds like a howler. It's for the best.'

'For the baby, yes.' Her gut was in knots and her heart was twisting slowly and painfully as she folded up her '*Medicine For All*' T-shirt and put it in her rucksack. That one thing was her symbol of freedom. Packed away again for another time, another life.

He strode right into the room. 'I couldn't live with myself if anything happened to either of you.'

Her throat was so thick with frustration she couldn't speak, so she just went on biting her lip and stuffing things into her bag.

After watching her for a few seconds he took the folded-up sweater out of her hand and put it on top of the T-shirt. Bad enough that he wanted her to go, but he was helping her pack too. His voice was soft, though, and filled with care. 'Claire, I didn't expect it to get to this point.'

'You and me both.'

'I don't mean about the baby. I mean about you and me. Us. This.' Shaking his head, he took her toiletry bag out of her hands and slotted it next to her sweater. Then took

her hands in his. 'Claire, you're amazing. You're open and warm and caring and so damned sexy it makes me hard just thinking of you.'

That made her smile a little. 'The sex and the kissing weren't the problem. Just the end result, right?'

'I want you to know that I...'

Hope flickered in her chest. 'You?'

'I do care for you. Very much. I hope that's obvious. But—'

'It's okay. Please don't say it.' But. But. But. This was the kiss-off. She wanted to put her hands over his mouth and stop the words, better yet, put her mouth over his and swallow all his pain. 'Don't say the words, Ethan. I know what you think and it's okay.' If she wasn't enough to make him want to be with her, then she wasn't going to try to make him love her. 'I've written my contact details down. Please give me yours. For the baby.'

She had to concentrate on that now. Not on this or him or her breaking heart. She shook her fingers away from his, but not before she ran her skin over his fingertips. Then she handed him the piece of paper she'd put next to her bag.

He glanced at it and inhaled sharply. 'You're going home? To the mountains?'

It was no doubt the final nail in the coffin of their... relationship? Whatever it was, it had been short but so intense and deep and she wasn't sure she'd ever really get over him. 'I have people who love me there. This little one will have family to grow up with. It's a good place.'

'But claustrophobic.' His one fear.

'Only if you let it be. Not for a child.'

His smile was small but soft. 'I bet you'll be telling him or her stories about all the places you want to go. Pretending you're there with them.'

'I think, perhaps, playing games is over for me, Ethan.

It's time to get real.' She put her hand to her stomach and he followed with his eyes. Then he reached out. 'Can I?'

No. No. 'There's nothing to feel.'

But she closed her eyes as he pressed his palm over her abdomen. Clenched her eyelids tight to stop the threatening tears. One was on the verge of escaping so she palmed it away, hoping he wouldn't see how much he meant to her.

But then, tired of fighting it, she finally leaned against him, her head on his shoulder, breathing in his scent.

'Claire.' He said her name like a prayer as he wound his arms around her waist, drawing her close and nuzzling against her neck. And she clung on, forcing back the sobs in her throat, forcing back the words on her lips.

Je t'aime.

She loved him hard and deep and for ever.

And look what that had got her: a baby and a broken heart.

'Right.' She breathed deeply and pulled away from him. 'I have to finish packing. You were going to give me your contact details?'

'Yes.' He swallowed hard, his features haunted. 'Of course.'

She waited until he'd finished tapping into his phone. Nodded as her mobile beeped with his details. 'Right, I should go up on deck now. We'll be docking in ten minutes.'

'Claire…' His eyes misted and he tugged her close again and she prayed he'd say the words she had on repeat in her head and with every beat in her heart.

Je t'aime. Je t'aime. Je t'aime.

Someone whistling outside the door made her jump and she stepped away from him, out of reach. 'Someone might see.'

He shook his head. 'I don't care if anyone sees us. Chase

and Kristina know and others will probably guess, It's out there now.'

'I care, Ethan. I care because we haven't decided anything except that I'm being shipped home and you're going to be here and then who knows where.' The longer they were apart the more her heart would break and the more likely it was he'd forget the way they felt when they were together.

She couldn't tell him to stop roaming the desert looking for peace, she couldn't make him fall in love with her, but she had to say something for their baby's sake. 'You have the chance now to be a father. That's worth something, Ethan. Worth all those lives you saved, surely? More than that, it's the most precious job in the world. And…if you can't love me that's okay—'

'I…' He opened and closed his mouth, clearly not knowing the right words to say. She knew what they were. *Je t'aime.* But he didn't say them. He didn't say anything at all.

'Just please love this baby,' she begged, not wanting to hear anything that would hurt her heart, and she wanted to be able to tell their child that she'd fought for it. 'It will need you, Ethan. I know you didn't get the best upbringing, but things don't have to be that way. You can be a part of his or her life, a big part.'

'I will be.'

For the child, but not for me. 'So where will you go when you're done here?'

She wanted him to say Moustiers, Marseille, even just France, anywhere that meant he was within reach. He gave a little shrug. 'That depends on the agency.'

'You can't choose? You can't tell them where you want to go?' *You can't give it up for us?*

'I go where I'm needed.'

I need you. A lump formed in her throat and she could

barely force the words out. 'Eight hundred and how many lives?'

'Nine hundred and seven now.'

'Isn't that enough? When will you stop, Ethan?' But she knew the answer. It would never be enough for him. She sighed as her heart was crushed. 'Just don't disappear into the middle of nowhere and pretend we don't exist.'

He ran his thumb over her lip and gave her that half-smile she loved so much. 'I won't. This is my child and I'll be there.'

He didn't promise, though, she noted. He didn't swear on his grave or profess absolute certainty. And, oh, she could have let herself get carried away by the passion in his eyes. He believed it. Right now he truly did. But she couldn't believe him. Running away was all he'd known.

Ethan watched Claire's hesitant steps down the gangway. Every part of him wanted to call out to her that he wanted her. But she knew that. She knew he wanted her, he just couldn't give her what she needed.

When she stepped onto the dock she wobbled a little and he started to run along the deck to get to her, to pick her up and bring her back to him. But she rallied and walked confidently towards port security. His heart willed her to look back, just once, so he could see her beautiful face. Although it had been committed to memory over and over when he'd gazed at her during their lovemaking. When he'd watched her laughing, seen the enchantment in her eyes as he'd described all the places he'd been to.

As if she knew he was watching, she turned, shielding her eyes from the sun. She scanned the ship, stopped as her gaze caught his. He raised his hand in a wave but she turned away and disappeared into the port buildings.

She was gone. Gone because he'd made her leave and she probably hated him for that too. His heart was wrung

out and his chest felt as if something was crushing it. The way it had felt all those years ago when a building had collapsed on his ribs, only this time the pressure was from inside and he couldn't push it away. It stole his breath, clamped his gut and made his throat raw with bile.

He'd see her again; he'd make sure of it, because there was no way he'd walk away from his child. But holding her, kissing her?

That was a dream that had evaporated the moment he'd realised just how much he cared for her and that she was falling just as hard for him. Whatever else happened, he needed to make sure he protected her and that meant keeping her at arm's length, for her own sake. He couldn't let her fall further for someone who was chasing promises made long ago, making up for lives lost, making his life count for something. Making up for Nick, Liam, Mac and Johnny. Making up to Chase. He couldn't let her love someone who couldn't let go of the past no matter how much it cost him.

But judging by the single tear she hadn't prevented trickling down her cheek as she'd clung to him one last time, she'd already started to care for him. That had to stop right now, and making her leave was the best first step.

CHAPTER THIRTEEN

MEDICANE FRANCIS WAS worse than expected. Gusts of over ninety-five miles an hour and freezing, torrential rain meant the ship rocked and rolled and pitched, and for three days they could barely tell which way was up and which was down.

But Ethan didn't care. For him it was a perfect storm. Cold. Wet. Loss. All over again. And there was nothing he could do about it, stuck here on a moving target, battered and bruised and trying to administer medical care to people pummelled by flying debris, soaked through and seasick.

Rain lashed sideways across the deck and he clipped himself onto the rope, trying to keep upright as he did a check on his huddled passengers. The last boatload they'd picked up were in reasonable health. Trying to keep them dry was futile, but he didn't want hypothermia to hit.

'This is one hell of a downpour,' Akil shouted, even though he was standing right next to Ethan, head dipped against the lashing gale. 'Your girl got off just in time.'

My girl. Right. 'She's not my girl.'

'Hmm. Could have sworn there was something there. My mistake.' Akil's eternal optimism and cheekiness was wearing thin today. 'Hey, don't look so glum, mate. Plenty more fish in the sea.'

He didn't want anyone else. And he couldn't bear the thought of anyone else touching her. Hadn't been able to stomach that idea since chasing off that leech in the bar on the first night. He said something to Akil that he'd probably regret later and went to find some quiet, if not any peace.

It was his turn to be alone on the deck, and embrace the blackness as it shrouded them. Where was she now? Had she reached her home? How had her parents reacted? Had she bumped into her ex? How was the baby?

He tried to imagine a life without them in it and he was lost. But, then, he'd been lost a long time.

He missed her. He missed her so much he could barely breathe.

He picked up a coil of rope and started to practise his knots to keep his hands busy and to calm his brain with a repetitive action. He wasn't sure how long he'd been there when something moved in his peripheral vision and Chase was sliding down the rail to sit next to him. 'Is it okay...?'

'Sure. Take a pew. It's your ship.' Truly, the last thing he needed was a chat with Chase, but luckily they hadn't strayed into anything personal since that night at the bar. Hopefully they could sit and brood in companionable silence.

That lasted for about two minutes then Chase inhaled deeply and said, 'You seem a bit lost these days, Reid. I know we haven't exactly got along but if there's anything I can do...' His voice trailed off, but Ethan understood the sentiment. And clearly straying into personal territory was going to happen, whether he liked it or not.

'It's fine. Thanks.'

Chase nodded, didn't look at him. 'Do you love her?'

This wasn't the kind of thing they talked about, this was next level stuff nudging them from old adversaries to colleagues and now to...confidants? That was a huge step. But he was grateful for the chance to say out loud

some of the stuff that was going round in his head, driving him half-mad. 'Hell, Chase, I don't know. I can't stop thinking about her. I can't stop imagining a future with her and it half scares me and excites me at the same time. But love? That's a big ask.'

'I know. But maybe you do?'

Love? He'd never known what it felt like. But if it felt like you had pieces of you missing when you weren't with the person, or that your whole world was better just seeing them smile, then maybe.

He just missed her, right? He just needed to get used to thinking purely about himself again. He just needed to find someone for random sex, like before…before he'd ever met Claire.

But the thought of anything intimate with someone other than Claire made him feel colder than the cruel wind buffeting them in the Mediterranean.

He didn't want anyone else. He wanted Claire.

It hit him hard. Yes, he loved her and probably had from the moment he'd lifted his head over that menu and watched her in the bar. She made him want to stop chasing halfway round the world, as his world had become her and the child she was carrying. A family?

Hell. That was something he'd never have thought possible and now it was all he could think about. 'Yes. I do love her.'

'Does she love you?'

She liked him, he knew that. She kissed him like she was drowning in him. Little things—attention, glances, caring, her eyes that had looked so haunted and bereft as she'd left. But maybe that had been for the end of her dream? 'I don't know.'

'Go to her. Find out.'

'I can't. You need me here.'

'Is that what you want me to say? You want me to stop you?' Chase shook his head. 'You said you can't stop thinking about her. I don't want anyone on this ship who isn't one hundred per cent focused.'

If he went to her he couldn't do this and he *had* to do this. He'd made a solemn promise. 'I'll focus.'

Chase nodded. 'If you're so keen to come back then you can, when your head's in the right space. There's always a place for you here.'

'Because I owe you more, right?'

'No, you don't owe me anything. Except maybe to take a chance on something good when it comes your way, and start living. Maybe this is what your second chance is all about.'

Ethan ran the rope through his fingers, feeling the rough edges of splayed cord. If he ran the rope fast enough his palm would grow red and hot. He wanted to feel that burn as a physical ache rather than the one inside his heart. 'But what about Nick?'

'It's not about Nick, it's about you. You have to live a life worth *something*. That's all.' Now Chase turned his eyes on him, full glare. 'Having a family is a pretty good example of that, don't you think?'

Yes. But could he do that? Could he stop? Could he be enough as a father and a husband? Maybe he already was.

Reality hit him. He was just like all those refugees he saved; fleeing from something dark, trying to find something better, to be safe. But the truth was the darkness was inside him and the only light he'd ever felt had been when he'd been with Claire. Maybe it was time to stop running and tether himself to something good, something bright and light.

And just like all those poor souls, he had to take a risk. He dropped the rope and turned to Chase. 'How soon can you get me off here?'

Five days later...

'Élisabeth, run in and get a book, I'll read you a story.'

Claire sat on the veranda, looking out over the ancient village, which was bathed in a dusky pink glow. It had been a hot spring day and there was still warmth in the dying rays. She leaned back in the chair and relished being dry and not endlessly rocking.

And then her heart clenched as she wondered how they'd all managed through the reported storm of the century. How Ethan had managed, mostly. Because he was, always, the first and only person she thought of. For all the good it did it her. She hadn't heard a thing other than news reports but, then, she hadn't expected to hear from him. He was true to type, she gave him that. She only wished things could be different.

Her mother came out to check on her for the millionth time that day. 'Are you sure you're okay to read to her while I sort out dinner?'

'*Oui, Maman.*'

Her mother put her palm to Claire's cheek and smiled. 'I love you and I know you're not happy to be here, but we're happy to see you. And we're happy about your news.' Her parents' excitement about their first grandchild had almost overwhelmed her. It was good to know she was loved unconditionally regardless of anything she did, and Claire knew she'd feel the same about her little one.

He'll miss so much. But that was Ethan's choice. She'd get to see everything first-hand: first breath, first steps, first smile. And all the while wishing he was here and aching for him because she wanted him to know what it felt like to be loved and how wonderful it could be to give your heart and love to someone else.

And, selfishly, she wanted to be loved by him.

She took a breath and blew the hurt away. 'I am happy about the baby, Maman. Honestly.'

'*Becassine!*' Élisabeth came running out of the house and threw the book onto Claire's lap. How appropriate. A comic strip about a naive girl who had countless adventures. *And who didn't get pregnant in any of them.* Claire smiled wryly. 'Come sit still.'

She started to turn the pages, but her little sister was restless and kept looking down the huge limestone steps that wove through the village. 'Élisabeth, I can't read if you're going to wiggle. It's like being back on the ship.' Where her heart was, with him. She'd left a piece of herself there in his hands.

Her sister sat up straight and pointed down the hill. 'Who's that man? Why is he staring at you?'

'Which ma…?' Claire's voice faltered as she saw a tall sandy-haired figure striding up the steps towards her. Her heart skipped and jittered. 'Ethan?'

'You didn't tell me there were so many steps,' he called from about twenty feet away.

'Wait until you get to the chapel at the top. We're only halfway up.'

Ethan was here? In the mountains?

Her heart beat so fast she wasn't sure she would be alive by the time he reached her. Was he here for her? No, he was here for the baby. Surely. She wiggled her sister from her lap. 'Élisabeth, pop inside for a few minutes.' She was far too young to witness this, whichever way it went.

'Why?' Élisabeth wound a finger into her hair. 'You said you'd read a story.'

'I will. Later. Every book on the shelf. Just, please, please go inside.' Claire couldn't drag her eyes from him as he climbed towards her, but she managed to control herself and didn't run down into his arms. He wasn't holding them out. 'Ethan?'

She hoped it sounded unaffected, even though she knew it was filled with the pain and longing and love she felt for him.

He stopped a few feet from her, but there still wasn't a smile; instead he looked concerned and solemn. Terrified, actually, and she was immediately thrown back to how he'd looked when he'd first stepped into the lift. *Always the lift.* It had been both her downfall and the best thing in her life. 'How are you, Claire?'

'*We* are fine.' She made an effort to make sure she included the baby in this because if he'd come back for her he'd be kissing her right now, wouldn't he?

'Good. Great.' His shoulders relaxed but only a little.

Maybe he wasn't here for either of them? Maybe he had bad news? Her heart was thundering now. 'What's the matter? Why are you so serious?'

'Because love is a serious business, Claire. It needs to be done right.'

'Love?' She was concerned she might need a cardiologist soon, the way her heart was rattling along.

'I haven't done it right, Claire. I tried hard not to see it and to pretend I wasn't growing feelings for you, but I can't run away from them, not when they're inside me.'

'You love me.' It felt as if the sun was coming out inside her chest.

'I love you both.' His voice cracked a little and she could see his hands clenched and she knew he wanted to hold her, but was weighing up her reaction because she'd never told him her feelings either. 'I love you because of the way you grasp life and look for the good in everyone. The way you open your heart and give more than is needed. Not like me. I count the number of people I've saved, Claire. Not how well they live. Or how well I live. I closed myself off from feeling anything because I didn't want to have to face more pain, but what I didn't realise was that when you

block out pain you block out every other emotion too. You made me feel something for the first time and I couldn't fight it. Fear. Panic. Excitement. Desire. Love. I love you and I want to be with you.'

Wow. Her throat felt thick and raw. She cut through the distance between them and put her hands to his face. 'I love you too, Ethan.'

'You do? I wasn't sure...' He slid his arms around her waist and tugged her close.

He wasn't sure because he had never had it, he didn't know how love felt. She blinked the tears away. 'I love you and I'll prove that to you every day.' She pressed her mouth to his and showed him just how much she loved him in her kiss.

When she pulled away she asked him their question. The one that had bonded them from the beginning, because she had to know how things might work out for them. Love was one thing, but geography was very important too with a baby in tow. 'Ethan, I know you hate France and I'm so glad you're here for me, but where do you want to be?'

She held her breath, wondering whether he could truly give up his life for a family.

But he didn't hesitate as he took hold of her hand and held it to his heart. 'Right here. By your side. Wherever you are, I'll be with you and our child. I may not know anything about being a good parent, but I'm willing to try and to learn.'

'You'll be a wonderful father, Ethan.'

'And a good husband too, I hope.'

'A husband?' It was early days for them both, even though she knew he was her forever guy.

As if he'd read her mind, he whispered onto her throat, 'I know it's probably too soon and we'll have a lot to work out but I've been thinking...a lot.'

'What about?'

'It's weird, I've been chasing around Africa, trying to make everything right by Nick and my seventeen-year-old self, but there's something about this place that makes me feel like I'm me.' He shrugged. 'I lost who I was in France and now I'm finding things I want here too. I was thinking about applying for work at the refugee centre, maybe we could make a home in Marseille?'

'It is very claustrophobic here.' She pointed to the wide-open spaces between the mountains, the huge blue Alpine sky.

He didn't follow her eyeline, he just gazed at her. 'I only need to look at you anyway. You and the baby.'

'You might have to go out at some point.'

'If I can see the sea and the horizon and feel the space then I'll be free, Claire. Free with you. And then, maybe, some time when we're ready we can go visit all those places you want to go to. If you'll have me?'

'Of course I will, Ethan.' She pressed her lips against his, relishing his strength and his taste and the feel of him in her arms and the love in his touch. 'I love you so much.'

Always and for ever.

EPILOGUE

Eight weeks later...

IN THE END Ethan had insisted on a wedding 'as soon as bloody possible', because he wanted to do love right, and it had almost stopped her breath just knowing how hard a man could love when he allowed himself to.

But he'd been asked to help Chase out on the ship for a few weeks so she'd moved down to Marseille to be there whenever he docked for a few hours or a glorious weekend in their hotel, and then, when he docked for the last time, what a reunion that had been.

He loved the little town house she'd found for them to live in and had settled into a job at the refugee centre and their lives had been blessed with laughter and love and baby scans, which made everything seem so much more real and exciting.

But now things were getting serious. 'Your parents don't mind missing this?' Kristina pulled Claire's long braid forward over one shoulder and then fastened a small flower into her hair. 'Perfect. Beautiful.'

'Oh, don't worry, they have plans for a huge party when we go back home. But they know we wanted a private ceremony and living in a village like they do, it'd be filled to the rafters with people Ethan doesn't even know. No, I

much prefer it this way. Just us.' She took her bridesmaid's hand and tugged. 'Come on.'

Kristina chortled and followed Claire down the corridor towards the city hall reception area. 'You are one woman in a hurry.'

'I'm getting married to the love of my life, I don't want to waste a single minute—oh! There he is.' He was talking to the *adjoint au maire*, making a joke of some kind, and they were all smiling. But when he turned to her his smile changed into something that made her heart melt. Fun and games for everyone else, but a smile so pure and honest for her.

Just looking at him in a dark navy suit and tie stole her breath away. He mouthed, 'I love you. You are beautiful.' And she knew, in his eyes, she was.

Then the *adjoint au maire* called for silence and Kristina took hold of Claire's flowers and Chase handed over the rings and she became Mrs Reid-Durand after they'd made their vows.

'Congratulations, you two.' Kristina hugged them both.

'Congratulations, Reid.' Chase shook Ethan's hand and she could see a growing connection between them too. She was so glad and proud of Ethan and her heart filled more than she imagined possible, but then everything became a blur because in the next breath he was kissing her and cradling her tiny but definitely-there bump.

'This is nice and everything and I love you so much,' he whispered.

'I love you too.' However, she sensed a but...

'But I do have somewhere else I'd like to be right now.'

'Oh? Where?' She grinned, knowing his answer.

'Celebrating in the lift on the way up to the honeymoon suite.'

'We have to play nice first and then we get to play naughty later.'

'I like the sound of that.' He placed his hand over her bump and kissed her again. 'I didn't know life could be like this.'

'And I didn't know I could be so happy.'

But she knew, with Ethan, there would be a whole lot more to come. Adventure and excitement guaranteed.

* * * * *

REDEEMING
HER BROODING
SURGEON

SUE MacKAY

MILLS & BOON

This book is dedicated to all those amazing people
who give their time and skills
to helping those less fortunate.
You rock.

PROLOGUE

SCREECH. THUNK. METAL hitting concrete.

Men shouting.

'Accident!'

'Quelqu'un est blessé!'

'Aidez-moi!'

Bang!

A swinging metal chain swiped the crane it was attached to, swinging outward.

More shouts and yells.

'Cherchez le médecin!'

Kristina Morton spun around and began running towards the noise, her heavy pack bouncing on her back, aggravating damaged muscles.

'I'm a doctor,' she shouted to the security guard standing at the steel gate accessing the wharf where a freight ship was being loaded. Tapping her chest, she said, 'Doctor. Me.'

The man shook his head. *'Non.'* He pointed to another ship. *'Docteur.'*

'Oui.' Pointing in the same direction, Kristina uttered one of about five French words she knew. 'Yes, I'm a doctor joining that ship. *Doctor.*'

Rolling her shoulders back, she slid out of the straps of her pack and dug into a side pocket, handed over her

wharf pass. Written in French, it did say she was a doctor. Didn't it? She hadn't taken a lot of notice when she'd received it along with other documents at the hotel reception desk where she'd stayed in central Marseilles last night.

The lock clanged open and the gate swung wide, allowing a man in fluorescent overalls to run frantically towards the *SOS Poseidon*, the *Medicine For All* charity ship Kristina had been bound for.

The guard called after him with urgency and Kristina took the opportunity to slip into the sealed-off area, her pack knocking against her good leg. It wasn't hard to see what'd happened. Seventy metres along the wharf pieces of a metal cage were spread across a wide area, and from under what looked like a side of the crate protruded a pair of legs, while the man's helmet-encased head was under the edge bar. Men were clustering around, waving their hands and yelling at each other.

'Oh, hell.' She ran faster, reached the men and dropped to her knees with a hard thump. Ignoring the pain that set off in her injured thigh, she shouted, 'I'm a doctor.' 'Doctor' sounded similar to the French version; surely they'd get the message? Too bad if they didn't, she was already observing the man crushed under the steel strops meant to hold the side of the cage together, except they'd sprung apart on impact. 'What's his name?' she asked without thinking, and got a surprise when someone replied.

'Antoine. Is he unconscious?'

'I'm not sure.' Reaching under the metal for his wrist proved impossible, it was too far in, so she pressed a finger on his carotid. 'Antoine, can you hear me?' Damn. He wouldn't understand her. 'Can you talk to him, see if he's responsive?' she asked the man who spoke English, before focusing on the pulse rate. Normal. So far so good, but still a long way to go.

She couldn't understand what he said to Antoine but

she recognised the flickering eyelids. The helmet had done its job. A quick appraisal showed blood seeping through Antoine's trousers from his groin where a metal shaft had lodged. Her heart stuttered as the memory of a similar injury swamped her. Automatically her hand went to her thigh and rubbed down the ridge of scar tissue.

'I told him you're a doctor. I'll get some men to lift this.' The man now squatting next to her knocked the cage.

'Get them ready, but don't move it yet. Antoine's bleeding. Removing the pressure could cause a haemorrhage.' Bleeding out wasn't an option on her watch. Not again. The guilt at not being able to prevent Corporal Higgs dying had not dissipated so much that this didn't unnerve her. Not that she'd been in any position to help the soldier, being disabled herself, but doctors were meant to save people, no matter what. 'I need something to make a wad to press over the bleeding.'

Moments later Kristina was handed a small bundle of shirt pieces folded into squares, while another man was tearing his shirt into strips to tie the wads in place. She wouldn't think about the hygiene aspect, containing the bleeding was the priority.

'Thank you. *Merci.*' The odd angle of Antoine's left leg indicated a fracture above the knee. 'Be careful, don't hit this when you take the grill away.' She pointed to the rod.

'It's attached. It'll pull out.'

She hadn't noticed that. Now she'd prefer the man unconscious. He needed morphine, fast. 'Can you send someone to the *Poseidon* and get a doctor to bring drugs for pain and some oxygen?'

The man looked along the wharf. 'Someone's coming. He's got a bag and a small tank. Is that what you want?'

'I hope so.'

The man was there in an instant, barely puffing despite

his sprint. 'I'm a doctor.' He hunkered down on the opposite side of Antoine's legs.

'Me, too,' Kristina told him. 'I was headed for the *Poseidon* when this happened. Kristina Morton.' She held her hand out.

His hand gripped hers briefly, firm *and* electric.

Shock ripped through Kristina. Rubbing her arm, she stared at him. What just happened? He'd sent fire through her veins with a handshake? Unreal. She was supposed to be focused on a man in distress, not this one with the most intriguing face she'd ever encountered.

A startled look was reflected in the dark depths of his eyes, too. Had he felt that spark? 'Chase Barrington, SARCO.'

Shock of another kind rocked her. This was Chase? The man who caused his family heartache on a regular basis? No one had told her he was hot! 'I met your sister when I was a locum at Merrywood Medical Centre. I finished a fortnight ago.' His brother-in-law, Jarrod, was one of the partners there.

'Libby told me.' He gave her a sharp look. 'Bring me up to speed.' Chase was taking charge.

Typical. She'd worked with enough male doctors in masculine environments to know the signs. 'There's a rod intruding into Antoine's groin that's attached to the grill. I'm hoping you've got morphine in your pack.'

'Yes, and compression pads.' Chase nudged the kit with his foot, and focused on the man needing his attention.

Leaving Kristina to get her breath back and stop feeling flustered by Doc Barrington's touch. She could tell him to get the pads himself, but time was of the essence, not her pride. Finding the morphine, she read the date out loud, gave the vial to her counterpart to cross-reference before drawing up a dose. Once administered, she opened packs of compression pads, ready for the grill to be lifted away.

Chase was methodically checking for further injuries on Antoine's body without jarring the grill. No wasted movements, his lean body muscular without being heavy. Picture perfect. So not good for her pulse. Deep breath, concentrate—on Antoine, not the SARCO. But he was so distracting. She closed her eyes, opened them and watched.

Without stopping those long fingers moving over Antoine, he told her, 'Ribs staved in, fractured femur and arm, blood loss from where the humerus protrudes, and I don't like the look of his mouth. It's possible he's bitten his tongue.' He was good, and thorough. Impressive in more ways than that magnificent body.

She nodded. 'Let's do this. The sooner we can get to him the better.' It was hard not to glance at Chase for another take on those muscles shaping his loose T-shirt but she managed. Looking behind to the men waiting to help, she said, 'On the count of three lift the grill—very slowly.'

The moment their patient was free she was pressing a pad onto the wound in his groin. 'The femoral artery's torn. Is there a catheter in your kit I can put in to keep the blood flow in the artery?'

'Unfortunately not.' Chase was gently removing the man's helmet in preparation for putting a facemask on Antoine for the oxygen. 'I haven't got a neck brace either.'

Kristina continued working on the haemorrhaging, making do with what was on hand, but the sooner help arrived in the form of a well-equipped ambulance the better. 'Has anyone called the emergency services?'

'*Oui,*' replied a man hovering in the background.

Like magic, the sound of a siren filled the air.

Kristina didn't relax. Antoine wasn't out of trouble by a long way.

A quick glance showed Chase working as hard, diagnosing all the injuries while keeping an eye on the man's breathing. There was a determined look on his face that

said, I am not letting you die, Antoine. Something they had in common.

But anything else? She doubted it. The little she'd heard from Libby and Jarrod indicated she and Chase were like north and south. She was looking for a place to settle down and feel as though she belonged, a place where she wouldn't be thrown aside at anyone's behest, while this man apparently did not have the time or inclination for stopping still. He was driven. Not that she'd been told by what.

The ambulance squealed to a halt beside them. Instantly paramedics were moving in, asking questions in rapid French she didn't understand. Continuing monitoring their man, she left Chase to answer them.

'How's that bleeding?' he asked her moments later. 'Still bad?'

'Yes.' She nodded around the relief that getting Antoine to hospital fast was now happening, as long as the paramedics didn't take too long preparing him for the trip there.

'We've done all we can. The paramedics are taking charge,' Chase said, his hands clenched on his thighs, his jaw tight, and his eyes fixed on the two men as they put a cardboard splint on the broken leg and a brace around their patient's neck. He wanted to remain in control, was itching to continue working on Antoine.

Kristina knew that feeling but moved back, knowing she would not be thanked for doing anything else. The paramedics knew what they were doing, and were used to working without the luxury of all the equipment an emergency department came with, but couldn't they get a hurry along? Glancing at Chase again, the same thought was reflected in his steady green gaze.

When Antoine was finally loaded into the ambulance, relief loosened the tension gripping Kristina and she was free to walk away, if only her feet would move. Staring

across the now quiet wharf, her gaze fell on the ship she'd be working on for the next three months, sharing the space with a man who had her hormones in a lather already. She'd be toast by the end of her time on board.

It had been Jarrod who'd suggested she do a spell with *Medicine For All*, instead of taking on the locum job in the far north of Scotland she'd been half-heartedly considering.

Watching men and women walking up the gangway laden with heavy packs for the start of the next three-week stint, tiredness enveloped her. She was weary of constantly moving from place to place, locum position to locum position, and not having somewhere of her own to return to after each contract finished. MFA was merely another diversion. It was harder this time because she'd finally found what she'd been looking for.

The quaint town of Merrywood and its friendly folk had sucked her in, made her welcome and comfortable in a way she hadn't known since she was ten and her family had imploded, leaving her bewildered and alone. She'd wanted to stay on, continue working at the medical centre and buy a cottage on the riverbank, only there was no job once the doctor she'd been covering for returned. However, Jarrod had told her to stay in touch and drop in when her time with MFA was up as he might know of a position for her. She planned on doing exactly that, fingers crossed and expectations high.

'Time to go aboard and meet everyone.' Chase stood beside her, legs tense, his eyes constantly on the move.

'I'm looking forward to this.' The organisation did amazing work with refugees and other people in need of medical attention in horrific parts of the world, and to be a part of it was awesome. And in case Jarrod didn't come up with the goods, she'd have time to research small towns and medical centres in the south of England in the hope of

finding that same enticing family-orientated atmosphere she'd found in Merrywood.

Why did she look to the man beside her? He wasn't the answer to her need to settle down. From what she'd heard, Chase Barrington could no more stop in one place than he could knit a blanket for a baby.

'What made you decide to give *Medicine For All* a go?' Chase asked as they walked out of the secure area.

'I'm getting tired of locum work. I start to feel settled and then have to pack up and leave again. Jarrod suggested MFA and how I might fit in. Once I started delving into the organisation I knew I had to give it a go and contacted Liam.' The director had been effusive when she'd volunteered. Though again she'd be moving on afterwards.

Fit in. Chase studied the slender woman before him. Get under his skin, more like. His brother-in-law had been chuckling when he'd told Chase how Kristina Morton was perfect for the summer operation in the Mediterranean. Yes, he'd known who'd put her up to signing up and until now had had no problem with it. All doctors were welcome any time. But now Chase had to question what fates had put *this* doctor on *this* mission. 'You want to get away from GP work?'

Her laughter was soft and sweet, and stirred him. Not that he wanted to be stirred by a beautiful woman. Or any woman. He'd put her where he put any female who managed to tweak his interest—out of his mind.

'Not at all.' Her shrug was tight. 'It's just that I would like something permanent, somewhere to get to know people beyond their headaches and high blood pressures.'

Good. The complete opposite from him. 'You like ships? Being at sea, getting tossed around in storms?'

Another shrug. 'Wouldn't have a clue, but I'm about to find out.'

There was more to this. For someone who wanted permanence she seemed to move around as much as he did. Not that he was about to ask her about it. That spoke of being interested and getting involved. Not his thing. 'Liam's a great advocate for our organisation. Without him we wouldn't get half the volunteers that sign up.' If not for Liam, who knew where *he'd* be working right now? For all he knew, it could've been in Africa, Asia, New Guinea, anywhere there were lives that needed to be saved. That was his mission in life. Not that he'd ever make up for the loss of his best friend, Nick, but he would keep trying. One day the guilt might run out. Might.

'I didn't stand a chance once he started in on me,' the woman matching his strides admitted. Then her eyes went a bit sad.

He wasn't asking about that either. They'd reached the security gate. 'Yours?' He nodded at a pack and roll mat the guard held out.

'Thanks.' She stretched for them.

'I'll take those.' Chase reached out at the same time. His fingers skimmed across hers before wrapping around a shoulder strap on the pack. A jolt of heat caught at him. Spinning sideways, he swung the pack over one shoulder and hooked the mat under his arm then headed for the ship, ignoring Kristina and the inferno in his blood. That was the second time he'd felt the heat around her.

Unfortunately she kept up with him. 'I don't expect you to carry my gear.'

Chase stopped as quickly as he'd taken off. 'I'm not trying to show you up as incapable. I'm exercising the manners I was taught as a lad.' If not in the polite way his father expected.

'It's just…' She hesitated, seemed to be thinking how to say whatever was bothering her. 'I'm ex-army. No one ever carries your pack there.'

He'd read in her CV about Kristina being ex-military. And the evidence was in front of him in her upright, controlled deportment—and apparently in her determination to carry her own pack. Because she'd heated his blood and stirred him with her soft laugh, he was going to rock her boat. 'You're not in the army now. I'll carry these to the ship.'

'Fine.' Her mouth drifted up into a lazy smile, stirring him tighter. He should've walked right past the blasted gear and its owner. It was as though she was poking him with sharp pins to wake him up from a long, deep sleep. But he wasn't asleep and as far as he could tell Kristina hadn't come armed with anything sharp, except maybe her tongue.

Chase pulled on his co-ordinator's hat; only way to go. 'I saw in your CV that you've worked in quite a few different medical jobs.'

The smile slipped away slowly, painfully. The light that had begun shining in her eyes faded. 'I have.'

Again, there was more to this than the simplicity the words suggested. If she wasn't saying anything else it had to be that something had happened to affect her badly. He'd respect that, because he understood too well about keeping fears close, and pain closer. Suddenly he wanted her smile to return. 'On board we tend to treat one another kindly, no ordering anyone to do anything.'

Her nod was abrupt. 'Good.'

Try again. 'The refugees are going to love that calm manner you showed with Antoine.'

'That's me. Calm throughout a crisis, a bit rocky afterwards.'

'No one would know that from helping Antoine.' There. A subtle lifting of those lips he'd have missed if he hadn't been watching for it. His heart lightened. Then her perfume wafted across his nose and he pictured pine cones

on the fire at home. Pine and roses. Yes, the strange mix that was home was this woman's scent. A scent he was not going to get out of his senses in a hurry. They'd just met, and she'd found a way to get under his skin already.

It didn't bode well for his sanity when they'd be crammed together for weeks with all the other medical staff in the small spaces that were the ship's medical facilities. They'd probably end up hating the sight of each other. It happened. There was little privacy, no space to think without being interrupted. Having no alone time did a number on everyone, especially on those used to their own company; like himself. Something about how Kristina held herself, self-contained, suggested she'd fit into that group.

Chase began striding towards the ship again. 'I think most people have arrived.' He automatically scanned the people at the gangway. And tripped. Ethan Reid stood at the bottom of the gangway, looking directly at him.

Chase's heart began a low thump, thump. So much of who he'd become was tied up in that man. And Nick.

The past charged at him in waves, winding him, curdling his stomach, raising the fear of not being able to save those he loved, bringing ice and snow pushing away the warm summer air, suffocating him. Death. Not his. Nick's. The crippling guilt.

I can't do this.

Yes, he could. He had no choice. He'd been the one to put out the feelers, asking Ethan to step up to the promise he'd made way back then. *If ever you need me, call.*

Right now Chase rued that phone call, even though it had been about helping others. But it was done. He needed to start moving forward, towards Ethan, the man he had saved instead of Nick, and the hideous past they needed to dispel, or at least subdue so they could work together. Would they be able to talk about what had happened that

fateful day in the Alps? About why certain people had survived when others hadn't? Why Nick had died, and Ethan had survived? Why he'd had to make that choice about who to save even when there really was no choice? Turning his back on Nick as the last breaths left his body had haunted him ever since, and made him go over it again and again looking for a way to change the outcome.

'Chase? Are you all right?' Kristina's question seemed to come from miles away. Her hand gripped his arm, shaking him, soft and endearing in her touch.

'Yes,' he lied, stunned at how easily she saw past his barriers, how she was there with him. No one did that. No one. He shrugged free of her hand, his eyes firmly locked on Reid. *Don't think* you're *getting the chance either.* His past rose higher, flared, threatening to overwhelm him. Bile soured his tongue. 'I've got to talk to that man.' It was that or charge past him to shut himself away in his cabin and not come out for six weeks. *Six weeks.* Why had he made that blasted phone call?

Ethan was walking towards him like they did this every day, but as he got closer Chase saw the tight lines around his mouth, the rigidness in his shoulders. Chase's heart was still drumming that slow, heavy rhythm as he nudged his feet forward. 'I'd have known you anywhere.' Even after sixteen years.

'Same.' Ethan did the unexpected. He embraced Chase, tight, strong, hard.

Tears sprang to Chase's eyes. He refused to let them out. Refused. And won, by a scratch. Stepping back, he stared at the other man who'd haunted him for so long. Thump, thump, in his chest. This was relief over finally meeting up. It was time. Not that he had any expectations of this being an easy ride. No, the coming weeks were going to test patience and forgiveness on both their parts.

'I'll take my gear,' came the voice of female reason from behind him.

He barely noticed Kristina lifting the weight from his shoulder, although as she began walking away and he was watching Ethan, she slipped into his mind, sitting on the edge, like she was not going to be easy to ignore. Right now that was about the only thing he was certain of.

Hell, Nick, what have I done?

CHAPTER ONE

Six weeks later

'KRIS, GOT A MINUTE? I'd like you to look at my patient.'

Kristina Morton ignored the man, even when his voice was like fingers picking at keys on a piano. Only that morning everyone had returned on board from a three-day break, and she'd missed him way too much for someone she wasn't involved with.

'Kris, over here,' Chase called again, a little less friendly and a lot louder.

She continued walking through the overcrowded cabin towards the steps leading out on deck. About once a week he used the abridged version of her name, winding her up something awful. He hadn't a clue to the depth of anger and hurt being called Kris caused her—neither was he about to.

'Kristina, your attention now.'

Kristina's back straightened, her chin jutted forward and her arm began lifting in a salute. *Stop. You're not in the army now.* Being the person in charge of personnel on this ship didn't give Chase the right to shout at her. Or shorten her name. But, she sighed, he had finally used the name she answered to. Slowly turning, she asked calmly, 'Which patient do you want me to see?'

Determination radiated out of eyes that reminded her

of an English forest on a damp day. Chase wasn't used to being ignored. Everyone complied with his requests no questions asked, but then they weren't usually delivered as abruptly. So it was *her* that got his boxers in a twist. Good. Because he certainly kept her panties in a knot. Those sparks she'd experienced on day one of this adventure hadn't died down one bit. Instead, they'd got brighter, sharper, hotter during the weeks of working together. Neither of them had made a move to explore where that raw attraction might lead. She did her best not to be alone with Chase, and suspected he did the same, but the relentless ache was getting to her, and she spoke more abruptly than she'd intended. 'Is it the pregnant lady needing help?'

'Sorry I yelled,' he growled around a wary smile. 'You didn't seem to be hearing me.'

'Really?' She tipped her head sideways, locked her gaze with his and tried to deny the surge of longing those eyes brought on. Another six weeks of working alongside him. Keep this up and she'd either dislike him intensely or have gone raving mad with desire by the time she left the ship for good. Somehow she doubted dislike would make it onto the ladder.

Chase blinked and his face relaxed some more. 'Yes, that lady. She won't let me near. No doubt because I'm male.'

'You know that's not uncommon.' The pregnant women who arrived on the ship via the rescue efforts weren't used to men pressing their bellies and listening to their unborn babies through stethoscopes.

'I keep hoping for a different outcome.' Chase smiled ruefully. She knew he ached for these people like she did. 'This woman doesn't speak English.'

'I'll find Zala and ask her to explain what we're doing and if it's all right to continue.'

Chase's chin lifted a notch. 'Zala?'

Kristina smiled to herself. Chase wasn't the only one who got onside with the refugees effortlessly. He just thought he was. 'She arrived yesterday. I overheard her asking for water in English.' Not that it had been easy to understand her mangled pronunciation, but when she'd handed the girl a bottle of water she'd received the most beautiful smile imaginable and a garbled thank you. 'I don't know how much she understands but any is better than none.'

'Agreed. Bring her in and see if we get any further with our patient.'

Kristina gasped. Why hadn't her senses warned her Chase had moved closer? Suddenly her body was getting up to speed with the fact that this man was too near, sharing the same air as her. Damn the attraction for those arms and legs, for the flat stomach and strong jawline nailing her feet to the floor. She'd spent six long weeks trying to kill off the annoying magnetism Chase's body had for her. Her mind had it worked out—he was not a man to get close to. He was self-contained in every aspect, appeared to work every hour day and night, was on a life mission to save people no matter where that took him—or so the gossip went. Gossip that fitted with what Libby had told her. She couldn't risk falling for someone who couldn't settle down in a place for more than one Christmas in a row. Because, while she wasn't any better, she was at least working on it.

Time to try some other tactic for moving past the unusual longing to get to know this man who dominated her mind so much. He was all wrong for her, as she was for him. He didn't have time for anyone who wasn't a patient in need of his extraordinary medical skills, so she had to stop thinking about him in any role other than the director from whom she took orders. *Instructions, not orders.* Whichever.

Dreaming about his body and what she'd like to do

with it didn't change the fact she had no room for people who didn't have time for her. There'd been enough already, starting with her parents. Adding someone else to the list was a recipe for disaster, especially when she had an uneasy feeling that she could get a weeny bit too intrigued by Chase.

Out on deck Kristina made her way through the hordes of people waiting patiently in the shade provided by tarpaulins strung from bulkheads to railings to be seen by the medical staff. Her heart ached for them and made her grateful she could help with their untreated deep-tissue injuries, burns from fuel, malnourishment, infections. Thank goodness Claire had left the ship. Her pregnancy made her vulnerable to illnesses she wasn't prepared for. Now, there was someone whose life had changed since coming on board the ship. Claire had found love and a wonderful future to look forward to with Ethan.

Kristina shoved aside her envy and focused on reality. 'Zala,' she called.

'Hello?' The girl glanced at her from under lowered eyebrows

'How are you?' She spoke slowly in order to be understood.

'All right.'

'Good. You had food?'

'Yes.'

Kristina again looked around at the people sprawled on the hard deck, hunger, fear, worry in every pair of eyes watching her. If only she could fix everything for all of them. Back to Zala. 'Can you help me talk to a woman who needs a doctor to examine…? To look at her baby.'

'I…' Zala tapped her chest. 'I say what you say my way?'

'Yes.' Kristina nodded. 'I'll keep it simple.'

'I don't know what you mean.'

'That's all right.' She reached for the girl's hand, hesitated. Touching didn't always mean the same thing to people from the Sudan as it did to Westerners. Retracting her hand, she said, 'Come with me.'

Back in the treatment room, persistent Chase had returned to his pregnant patient, holding out a water bottle and talking softly, even though not a word was being understood. Around here it was all about the tone of voice and not the words. 'I think we're in labour,' he told Kristina.

'How do you know?'

'The way her body stiffens every three minutes.'

Yea, she got her first smile of the morning. He should do that more often, it lightened the green of his eyes to that of a summer's day in the fields. And set her heart dancing. Damn.

'She's not going to want you here.' Kristina focused on the woman, avoiding getting tangled up in Chase's searching looks and that blood-warming smile. 'Do we know of any problems that could make delivery difficult?'

The woman caught her breath and pushed around the tightening in her extended belly.

'Minor fever. Exhaustion that's probably due to the pregnancy.'

'Fingers crossed the baby hasn't been infected with anything.' Kristina indicated to Zala to move closer. 'This woman's having a baby.'

Zala nodded as if to say, So what? Seeing a birth was probably part of everyday life for her. There'd be no racing off to a hospital or calling out the midwife where she came from.

'I'm clearing all male staff to the other side of the room,' Chase said. 'Call me if you need anything.'

'I don't think I've got much of a role here either,' she said, before turning to the woman Zala said was called Marjali. Light stretch marks on the skin covering the ex-

tended abdomen confirmed this was not her first pregnancy. 'She'll know what to do as much as I do.' *More than I do.*

Sweat shone on the woman's forehead as she pushed and groaned. Zala sat at her other side and chattered in short, sharp sentences before telling Kristina, 'Four babies. Two alive. On boat with her and father.'

'Are they all right?' What had happened to the other children? Kristina's heart squeezed. She'd never get used to the despair these people faced daily. There were times she felt so inadequate she wondered if it would be better to leave them to what they were used to and not offer promises through medicine. But she hadn't become a doctor only to turn her back on anyone needing her skills.

When her twelve weeks with *Medicine For All* were up she'd head back to England. She wouldn't do another stint on the ship. It was too distressing. Many of the medical people who worked in the organisation coped well with—or managed to hide—their emotions. She struggled to do either.

A sharp cry brought Kristina back to the marvel that lay before her. The baby's head was crowning while Zala chattered, excitement filling her dark eyes.

Kristina smiled as she watched the baby inching its way into the world. What was it like to give birth? To have a baby of your own? To hold him or her in your arms for the first time? She never gave much thought to it, afraid she wasn't capable of being a good mother. Her own mother had taken her to Los Angeles when she'd left her father, but had been quick to hand her back when the new man in her life said he'd marry her as long as *Kris* wasn't part of the package.

The man's wealth spoke strongly to her mother's lifelong fear of ever being poor again, and Kristina had been returned to England and her other parent, who'd immedi-

ately deposited her in boarding school because he'd been too busy to be there for her.

A sharp cry from Marjali and a tiny new life with the cutest face and a smattering of tight curls was delivered with one final push.

'Oh, he's beautiful.' Kristina's eyes moistened as she cut the cord and took the baby to check his temperature and general appearance before placing him on the scales attached to the nearby wall. Back home, with a weight of two kilograms, he'd have been admitted to the neonatal unit. Here all they could do was get nutrients into him so he might put on a gram or two before leaving. It could've been worse given the circumstances. Laying baby across his mother's tummy, she said, 'You made it look easy.'

Zala looked perplexed. 'Women have babies. It's normal.'

'You're right.' Again she wondered about the odds of having her own baby. Strange how she was thinking about this. She hadn't found a man to love her no matter what, let alone have a baby with, a man who wouldn't leave her to fend for herself while he went off to follow his own dreams. That should be enough to knock her attraction to Chase out of the paddock. Since joining this ship she'd seen him playing with some of the youngsters who came on board, laughing with them, chasing a football and making sure each kid had a turn at scoring a goal. He understood them, enjoyed them, so why not want a family?

Crossing to a cupboard for cloths to clean Marjali, she passed Chase. 'All done. One new little man has arrived in the world.'

'That was fast. Does the baby appear healthy? In as much as you can tell without doing tests?'

'A bit underweight.'

'We'll keep an eye on him while he's with us.' That was Chase-speak for making sure there were extra rations for

Marjali over the coming days. What happened after she left the ship was out of their hands. Their job was to deal with these people for the time they were in their care, and then move on to the next intake.

'Life's so complex, yet Marjali makes this seem simple,' she sighed, watching the woman cradling her son. Zala sat cross-legged, still talking non-stop, reaching out to touch the tiny bundle pushing into his mother's breast, not knowing what to do when he found a nipple. But his mother did. Soon he was suckling. Whether he was getting anything nutritious was unlikely given Marjali's malnourished condition.

'Very unlucky for some,' Chase said. Then looked directly at her, stealing her breath. 'Sorry if that sounds simplistic.'

'A lot of how our lives turn out comes down to where we are born, doesn't it?' There were the wild cards that life dealt when a person wasn't looking but luck did contribute to how and where he or she sorted out those problems.

'You think?' His eyes sparkled and his mouth lifted into a weary smile.

'I do.' She smiled back, enjoying the connection without her hormones doing their dance. Then her back gave a stab of pain, and she tightened up, held still.

'Hey, you okay?' His instant concern could undo her resolve not to give in to the attraction between them. 'You seem to be hurting more than usual.'

He noticed that pain struck her sometimes? 'I'm good. An injury I received in the army is playing up, that's all.' She gasped. She never, ever mentioned that, not even lightheartedly.

His concern deepened. 'Are you serious? Is that why you got out?'

She shook her head, wanting to deny the truth. But she couldn't lie. 'I took an honourable discharge. My back ac-

quired a dislike to humping around overweight packs and war gear.' She'd tried for light and friendly, thought she'd succeeded until she saw something in Chase's steady gaze that said he wasn't fooled. Something that drew her to tell him, 'I took a severe wound to my thigh and twisted my back. It's taking time but I'm coming right.' She turned towards her patient, needing to shut down this conversation.

Chase said softly, 'Glad to hear that, Kris.'

Her eyes closed and her head dipped. 'Kristina.'

He chuckled. 'Kristina.'

'You…' she spluttered as she turned back to him. 'You're deliberately winding me up.' She laughed, for real this time.

'Worth it to see your eyes widen as though I'd swiped one of your chocolate biscuits when you weren't looking.'

Which he had a penchant for.

As Kristina absorbed Chase's presence, her feet once again glued to the floor, the sparks that had flickered on and off between them since they'd met over Antoine suddenly became a raging fire in her veins. Worse, Chase was recognising her reaction.

Definitely time to put any dumb ideas about letting this attraction rule her head into the recycle bin. The only way to do that was to front up and explain she wasn't interested. In other words, lie her heart out. Tonight she'd do something about it, despite Chase never acknowledging the magnetism hovering between them. There were moments when he looked at her as though he wanted her. That was when her body really hummed; and her mind argued with it. Tonight she would not go to her bunk the moment she'd eaten dinner to get some sleep before the next draining shift began. No, she'd face up to Chase and deal with this annoying interference that crossed her day too often, sending her into an uncontrollable tailspin.

* * *

'Hey, Reid, how's things?' Chase settled his butt against the bulkhead of his private corner and stared out to sea, the phone hard against his ear.

'I'm good. You?'

Chase let out a long, satisfying breath. 'Another day almost done; more people helped, saved, fixed.' The relief was immense. He could rest easy—until the next day got under way. Ethan would understand where he was coming from. 'Not sure you're aware you left your tablet on board. I can send it out on the helicopter and have them courier it to you.'

'Keep it there till I come back. I don't need it for the next couple of weeks. Claire doesn't leave me time for reading.' Ethan chuckled.

'Glad to hear she's keeping you on your toes.' Chase grinned, and couldn't deny the envy sweeping through him. 'You decided where you're going to look for work after you finish with us?'

'I've been talking to the local refugee centre. If there's a vacancy coming up in Marseille then I want my name on it.' Ethan filled him in on what he'd been doing since he and Claire had left *SOS Poseidon*.

Chase listened avidly, enjoying the camaraderie— something he hadn't known since he'd withdrawn from getting close to people after the loss of Nick. He was still hesitant about letting loose and talking about anything and everything, but every day over the past six weeks when Ethan had worked on board they'd inched closer and the tension had eased somewhat. He still wasn't ready to let go the guilt about not saving Nick. And until he did that Reid would never get close.

For a span of time, standing here in his own small zone, letting Reid in, he could almost accept he'd made up for the past, could almost believe he deserved a chance at a

future. Almost. Until he hit the pillow and the memories came knocking, and Nick appeared in his head. Then he'd have to get out of bed to start over.

'Anyone special in your life?' Ethan asked. When Chase growled, he added sadly, 'Just learning about you. You know?'

Yeah, he knew. There was so much between them, and yet even more they hadn't a clue about. 'The answer to that should be obvious. There's no one for a very good reason.' Chase ignored the flare of pain. And the image of Kristina Morton that flashed into his mind. *She* might be as sexy as anything, but there was something about her that said don't touch unless you're serious. He was serious about having sex with her, but nothing more.

'So you're not interested in Kristina?'

Silence. He couldn't lie. Neither would he give Reid ammunition to give him a hard time.

Ethan sighed. 'She makes you laugh when no one else does. As for the sparks between the two of you, they had me looking for the fire extinguisher.'

Again Chase ignored him. Those comments were too close for comfort. If this was what having a friend was like, he didn't need one. Except over the previous six weeks he had begun to look forward to moments talking with Ethan. 'Nothing's going to come of those sparks. I'm all work and no play.' He already had parents and a sister who loved him and who he couldn't risk letting down—like he believed he had Nick even knowing he couldn't have changed a thing. The guilt did that to him. This getting a little friendlier with Reid didn't mean he was capable of allowing a woman close.

The breeze moved around him, fanning his face. 'Got to go. Talk to you again.'

Kristina slipped up beside him. Apparently she had no qualms about intruding into his private spot out here.

From the first trip of the summer it had got around that this particular corner was his, and no one encroached. No one until tonight. Sure, he'd rung Ethan, and been relaxed about talking to him here, because it had been his choice. But... 'Kristina?'

The breeze also held that scent of pine and flowers. That sweet and spicy aroma went with her all over the ship. Sometimes it followed him into sleep at night. Those were the times he woke restless and in need of a cold shower.

Why did she invade his privacy like she had a right to? Funny how he couldn't find it in him to care. Instead, he felt unusually happy she'd joined him, a feeling he couldn't explain, neither was he about to try. It didn't mean he was letting her close. He hadn't lost all his faculties. They might've locked eyes over breakfast, sending the temperature in the room off the scale, but he'd had to deny the need boiling in his gut. Had to. How they'd walked away from each other was a mystery. *So send her away before it happened again.*

'Please, don't call me Kris.'

'Kristina. Got it.' That morning he'd kept crossing paths with her as they'd gone about their patients, and the tension in his body had wound tighter and tighter. Calling her Kris had been a deliberate wind-up. He'd thought she'd be angry, but instead she'd made him laugh.

'Good.'

'Other people must shorten your name.' There had to be a reason *Kris* upset her. She wasn't the type to be precious about her name. She carried herself with confidence and the upright stance common to military personnel. That poise kept everyone on their toes, including him, until one day on the last trip he'd seen a wealth of pain glittering in her eyes as they'd watched a child being buried at sea. Her tiny heart had given up within hours of coming on

board—lack of food, too much sun, and who knew what else had taken the ultimate toll. It had been personally painful for him. Failing to save that girl despite doing everything possible and then some to bring her back to life had pained him.

He hadn't asked Kristina what was behind her agony. Things like that were too private to share. Hell, he was still getting used to the idea of him and Reid talking about the avalanche that had altered their lives for ever, and how Ethan had said they both had to learn to let go and move on. As if it was that easy. *It could be.* Oh, sure.

Leaning her elbows on the rail, Kristina stared out over the moonlit Mediterranean and breathed deeply, saying nothing.

A female who didn't talk the lid off a pot? Nothing like Libby, then. His sister never knew when to stop gabbing at him about why he should stop wandering the world and return home to be near the family. Chase sighed. He came out here for solitude while he went through his day and gave himself a pat on the back if he'd saved anyone. But right now he craved to hear Kristina's voice, couldn't bear this silence between them. He went with something innocuous. 'So you and Libby got on okay?'

'She makes the best blueberry muffins ever.' Kristina's head bobbed, and hair fell across her cheek. It was rare for her to let it free from the severe ponytail that was her signature style. Army style?

Many times over the past weeks he'd itched to flick the thick rope that fell down her back, pull away the band holding it in place to run his fingers through the golden waves. Shoving his fists deep into his pockets, he trawled his mind for something safe to say. 'What did you think of Merrywood?'

Kristina turned so the small of her back rested against

the rail and a soft chuckle winded him with its warmth. 'I loved it. Everyone was so friendly and welcoming, I wanted to stay on.' Her fingers intertwined across her belly, tightening his gut further.

So much for playing safe. 'It can become claustrophobic, though. Especially when you're a teenager and don't want your parents finding out you've been smoking down by the river with your pals.'

There was a wistfulness in her eyes as she said, 'Surely that's part of belonging somewhere?'

Yep, and it tied a person to everyone so that when things went wrong they all were affected. Chase watched her hands making slow circular movements over her abdomen. Was she aware she did that whenever she went all thoughtful?

This time the urge to make her talk, to break down her barriers didn't bat him around the ears. Instead he relaxed, leaned against the rail, and went with being beside her, trying to accept this was as intimate as they should get. He had nothing to offer her other than a quick romp in the sack and they weren't doing that. He didn't trust this *thing* gripping him to let him go afterwards.

But Kristina was unlike any other woman who'd pressed his buttons. *She* pressed them hard. Could that be the reason for his restlessness? He wasn't in the market for a partner. Not when he had to be finding more people to save, trying to redeem himself for Nick. How many more lives would it take to be free of the guilt?

Chase pushed the past aside, took a deep breath. The air was soft and warm, not cooling as the sun dropped below the horizon. Summer warmed his skin and his soul. There'd been a year when he'd followed summer around the world, working in countries where snow and ice were

alien, because he'd known how snow could destroy a person and he would never put himself in that position again.

But it hadn't been enough so he'd enrolled in med school to learn in earnest how to save people. London winters were cold but his heart had coped, had borne the pain that came with memories of a colder, icier, crueller place he'd never returned to. Not once. Never would. He couldn't. It wasn't in him to go there and bury the ghosts. They would never let him get away a second time. Except these past weeks, spending time with Reid, tentatively touching on what had happened, he'd begun looking at things in a different light. Would it be possible to put it all behind him one day?

Kristina's soft voice snagged him. 'I was called Kris in the army. When I wasn't sir or captain.' A tightness had crept into her tone.

'You let them?'

'Regardless of what the recruitment officers say, the military is still a masculine world. To fit in I was Kris. But I've objected to being called it since I was ten.'

'Am I allowed to ask why?'

'No big deal,' she answered in a harsh tone, suggesting it was. 'When my parents split up, my mother took me to LA with her where she met a man she was very keen on. When he proposed he told her in no uncertain terms that *Kris* was not part of the deal. The way he called me Kris was derogatory. I loathed it.'

Chase leaned closer, breathed deeply of her scent. He'd never call her Kris again. Not even as a tease. 'Did your mother tell him where to go?'

'No. I returned to England soon after.'

'To live with your father?'

'Dad was working twenty-four, seven trying to recoup the fortune he'd lost. I was sent to boarding school.'

'Geez.' She hadn't known the loving family environment he'd grown up with, had taken for granted, and now struggled not to put in danger by being near them. Lightly dropping his arm over her shoulders, Chase tucked her close. 'That's lousy.' A damned sight worse. His parents had stood by him through the days and years following the avalanche and still did. There'd been times they'd been so near he'd not been able to breathe, but he wouldn't have swapped that for what Kristina had missed out on. Yes, he was incredibly lucky to have such a loving, caring family.

'Yeah, it was.'

He daren't delve deeper, afraid she might sprint away, regret telling him in the first place. He didn't want her leaving his side, not until the tension in her stance softened and a smile returned to her eyes.

The silence returned, comfortable in an intimate way. Another first for him. The more he learned about this strong woman the more he wanted to know. Things like why she'd joined the army in the first place. Had she needed to belong to something, somewhere, to replace the lack of having a loving family around her? 'Were you ever deployed overseas?' He hadn't been going to ask any more questions so his words surprised him.

'I served in Brunei, where there are jungle warfare courses going on all the time.'

'I can't imagine being a soldier, charging around learning to kill people.' He shuddered. 'Not when my whole focus is on saving them.' Hell, she had *him* talking, wanting to tell her what made him tick. This was his time out, yet Kristina had sauntered into his space and *he* started gabbing on like he'd been on a desert island for months.

'It's not quite like that. I was a medic first and foremost. But sometimes I found myself questioning why I was there.'

'I'd be hopeless. Can't take orders from anyone.' Not since the day his skiing coach had dropped the ball when he'd been needed most. Coach Wheeler had phoned parents, tried to keep him from returning into the wrecked chalet, but he hadn't rushed in to help pull Nick free.

She turned under his arm and smiled up at him. 'Now, there's a surprise.'

He laughed, a belly-deep reaction that spread throughout his psyche. 'I know. Pig-headed is another term for the way I get things done.' Studying the sea, he asked, 'Do you miss the military life?'

'Not at all.' Her smile switched off. 'It wasn't what I wanted after all.' A little shiver and, 'See you in the morning.' Then she was gone, striding across the deck in that sharp, exact way of hers, heading for the hub of what went on day after day. Her leg left pulled a fraction higher on the upward movement. He'd noticed weeks ago how some days were worse than others, and how she sometimes winced or rubbed her lower back when she thought no one was looking. She wasn't one to complain or talk about her aches and pains.

She was back, a light smile on her face that heartened him. 'By the way, you'd make a lousy commanding officer.' Straightening, she mimicked him. 'Kristina, your attention—now.' This time she did leave him, flipping her hand over her shoulder on the way.

She left him chuckling yet bereft of company when he'd never before wanted anyone sharing this precious hour away from the cries and arguments and chatter that filled the ship twenty-four seven. Sometimes his head would be splitting apart with everyone's pain, his own grief and guilt working its way into the centre of it all, reminding him why he was there, and stressing that he'd never be able to

escape to a normal life back in England close to his family. He had to continue moving, keep finding more people to save. Working for MFA did that by bringing him and those people together. Day after day, week after week. There was no end to it. And not likely to be for the rest of his life. Which suited him perfectly.

Except Kristina didn't recognise his barriers, or ignored them, relentlessly chipping away, making him feel a little happier with life. Hell, he'd put his arm around her to give her warmth and support. Something more than her beauty, her confidence, her quietness, her heat-provoking body got to him—come on, it was a combination of all those.

Yeah, but there was an indefinable something else he couldn't put his finger on. When she'd told him about her name he'd known instantly she didn't talk about that to anyone, yet she'd told him. Not to shut him up, or at least not to let him think it was on a whim, but because she'd wanted him to understand there were heartfelt reasons behind her need to be called Kristina. She'd even told him those. Information he didn't want because it made him care. From now on he was done talking to her about anything deep. He had to be or he was doomed.

Chase tried to connect the dots between the doctor and her role as a soldier. Though the circumstances were poles apart, the requirements for patience and tolerance would be the same, yet he couldn't quite imagine Kristina issuing orders. Around here other medics did her bidding without question, her manner friendly and relaxed while underscored with determination, but a military officer would have to be sharp and firm. Bet she filled out the uniform perfectly.

Hell, he was in need of some diversion. Last time he'd

got like this a nurse had spent a night with him on their three-day leave from the ship. Eight months ago, at the end of last summer. That was the last time he'd had sex? So it wasn't sleep he needed, was it?

CHAPTER TWO

SO MUCH FOR confronting Chase about the frustrating attraction going on between them. Kristina stared at the bunk above her. Damn, but she was tired, kept awake by the shock that she'd wanted to take a risk and throw herself at him as they'd stood in the quiet of his corner. That she'd so nearly thrown aside her protective barriers and plastered herself against that sexy body, known every last inch of him, felt him take her deep. So, so close.

How could that happen when she'd gone to tell him they had to get past whatever it was between them? She hadn't gone to make it worse, stronger, *real*.

Because Chase had got her talking about herself. That was almost sexy, being something she didn't do. Like laying herself out naked in front of him, telling him personal stuff was as intimate. At least she hadn't mentioned her guilt, how a man had died on her watch. That would've been a passion killer—exactly what she'd gone to him to do. Damn, but her head space was a mess.

She'd nearly thrown herself at him. But it was all right. She hadn't. Somehow she'd managed to step away, with a smile even. But she had turned back, fighting the need to leave and the greater need to stay. To risk everything. It was that risk that had caught up with her at the last

moment and made her come out with the nonsense about him not making a good officer.

If only she hadn't. Glad she had. How had she done it? When her feet had been aimed in his direction, her blood thickening with desire, her fingers tense with the need to touch his skin? Guess looking out for herself was so ingrained it worked regardless of where her body wanted to go.

Kristina swallowed her confusion and rolled off the bottom bunk to stand hunched over, biting her bottom lip as pain jarred her back.

'You all right?' Jane, her cabin mate, asked from above.

'These bunks must've been designed by a sadist.' Knuckling her lower back, she began the ritual of straightening up, slowly easing tension from the muscles, not giving in to their stabbing protests. Then her left thigh got in on the act, shooting pain up into her butt.

'I wouldn't know. When my head hits the pillow I'm gone.'

Kristina's laugh was tight. 'I heard.' There'd been a lot of snoring going on during the night.

A pair of legs swung over the side of the bunk and Jane sat up, rubbing her eyes. 'What's with your back anyway? I often see you pummelling it.'

She gave her usual answer, not the one she'd told Chase. *Gave too much away there.* 'I haven't been doing the yoga exercises that keep me nimble.' No time or unpopulated space for those.

'Borrow Chase's bolthole when he's not around.'

Right, and be on guard in case he turned up? That would negate the purpose of yoga. He went there at some point every night. The plan was to turn Chase back into a man she could talk to about everyday things, not the deep or ugly, then walk away without a backward glance. Not

a man to get hot and edgy around. 'There's little room for stretching.'

'That's a shame.'

No, it was a relief. 'Isn't it?' Getting into Downward Facing Dog with Chase watching would have her heart going ballistic. And who knew what the sight of her backside poking skywards would do for him? He might be disgusted, but she doubted it. The physical friction between them that she'd done nothing to stop screamed attraction, intense and exciting and getting stronger; the mental not so much. He liked to be in control of everything around him, probably had to be since he was SARCO.

Would he be like that in bed? His guard had dropped while they'd talked last night. That hour had been comfortable in a way she'd not known with any man. As though the friction had been on hold, allowing room for getting to know each other on a different level. He'd been understanding about why she didn't want to be called Kris, and she'd swear he'd nearly laughed when she'd taken the mickey out of him over calling her to attention.

There was more to the man than she'd discovered so far. Lots more, and what she wouldn't do to learn it all. Perhaps she should've gone the other way last night and dragged him along to his cabin and put these feelings to rest in the only way possible.

Oh, no, you don't. House and job in the burbs, remember?

Jane's feet hit the floor with a thud. 'I need a long, hot shower, then I'm going to try for some more sleep.' All she'd get was short, wet and cool in the shower box.

'Me, too, for the shower.' Kristina tugged clean underwear and a white T-shirt with the MFA logo and shorts from her pack. The simple dress code was a bonus. Dressing for the locum role wasn't so bad, but as for the army uniform, she never wanted to see another, let alone wear

one. That'd taken her desire to fit in and belong to a whole new level. She hadn't belonged, she'd been submerged.

The knee-length shorts she shook out hid the scar running down her thigh to avoid the questions that'd invariably come when someone got an eyeful. Explaining that being thrown through the air by a bomb blast to land on a steel girder that had rendered her incapacitated wasn't happening. Not when it had meant she'd been unable to save Corporal Higgs from bleeding out, though it was unlikely he'd have survived anyway. She'd cried with frustration and despair until medics back at HQ had administered drugs that had taken her under. Unfortunately the drugs hadn't conquered her guilt.

A training exercise had gone hideously wrong that day, changing her for ever, altering the direction she'd been taking in an attempt to find the equivalent of family. The military wasn't it. People within the units were close, caring, and always had each other's backs, but something had been missing, something she'd spent most of her life looking for. Boarding school hadn't been able to make up for the loving family environment she'd known for the first decade of her life, neither had med school. Now she knew better, had grown up some, and understood she had to be comfortable in her own skin before anyone could share her life. She'd touched on that at Merrywood, enough to start believing it was possible.

Jane appeared in her misty line of vision. 'The showers are empty at the moment. Just saying, you know?'

'Thanks.'

When she arrived at breakfast, Chase was the only person there. 'Hey, where is everyone?' she asked.

'It's not six yet.'

Then they'd have a few minutes to themselves. That filled her with warmth when she should be taking her breakfast out onto the deck—alone. With a plate of scrambled

eggs and toast cook had just put up, Kristina strolled across to sit at a table with him instead, unable to resist spending a few minutes alone with him. 'Have you done a round of our patients yet?'

'I've seen the earache boy this morning. Dad slept the night on the floor beside him and was very amenable towards me, all thanks to you, I reckon.'

The father of a young boy had been having trouble letting anyone near his son, mainly because he'd been exhausted and struggling to cope with where he was. 'Guess I got lucky.' She wouldn't mind getting lucky with this man. *Thought I was supposed to get over him.* 'Or the father was tiring and needed someone to indicate what to do next.'

'You don't accept compliments easily, do you?'

She shrugged. 'Wasn't aware of it.'

'I'll have to give you some more.' He laughed. He was doing that a lot lately around her.

More warmth flowed over her skin. How was she supposed to walk away from this? Forking food into her mouth, she tried to make sense of what was happening to her. The eggs were dry and the toast soft. But her mind was on high alert. So she was admitting she felt something for Chase? Chew, swallow. Try some more, wash it down with tea. She couldn't feel anything for Chase. Mustn't. Wanted to.

Chase asked, 'What did you do in Barcelona, by the way? I hardly ever saw you at our hotel.'

Like he'd been hanging around, joining in with everyone. And she'd been looking. 'It was Barcelona.' She gave a strangled laugh. 'Shopping, tapas, shopping, wine. I was with Collette and Rani, and they made my shopping attempts look pathetic.' At the end of the three days the two nurses had come back to the ship laden with bags. 'I also took a day trip to the Pyrenees, driving through stunning countryside along the way. It was all a bit rushed so I'd like

to go there again for longer.' It had taken her away from the city and stopped her incessant scanning for this man.

'Spain's spectacular. I spent time there before I started my training. Surfing, jet-skiing, diving. All good fun.'

So he hadn't always been focused on nothing but patients and helping people. 'Time off before the real world took over.'

His hand tightened around his fork, and his face took on a strained look. 'Something like that.'

Wanting his smile back, she leaned over and stole a piece of his bacon. 'You emptied the dish, you've got to share.'

'Hey, first in and all that.' The strain disappeared.

Feeling so much happier, she stabbed another piece on his plate, held it at her mouth as she said, 'Pierre can't have cooked much if you got the last of it.'

'Keep this up and I'll hardly taste bacon.'

'Now you come to mention it.' She held her fork over his plate again.

Chase whipped his breakfast out of reach. 'I don't think so.'

'You want tea?' She rose from the table. 'Or coffee?'

'Coffee. Milk and one.' Then he glinted at her through eyes that seemed to see right inside her. 'Sugar, not salt.'

'Spoilsport.' She put the salt shaker back on the counter, and spooned sugar into a mug. 'Wonder how high the temperature's going to reach today. Yesterday was a scorcher.' A dollop of ice would help right now, tipped down the front of her T-shirt. Her body was steaming, all because of Chase, sitting there looking hot and yummy.

'The forecast's saying low thirties.' Chase looked happy. Not an ice man, then? 'I like the heat,' he added before she could ask.

Placing his coffee on the table, she sipped her tea and studied him, in particular those muscles shaping the front

of his loose T-shirt. Those dark curls falling all over his head needed shaping, too—with her fingers. She gripped her mug with both hands. Lowered her gaze to the light stubble darkening his chin. Tightened her grip further. Rubbing her palm over his face would really quieten the thrumming of her blood. 'Just as well considering the countries MFA takes you to.'

'I guess.' He was watching her. What did he see? Not the guilt, the pain, the need to be settled, please. Try happy, fun, lovable.

'Seems you two were up early.' Calvin strolled into the room. 'Pierre, can we have some more eggs and bacon out here?' he called through the hatch into the galley. 'These two haven't left anything.'

Kristina felt her smile shifting, away from Chase and into a general one. Their brief moment alone together was over for the day.

'I've scheduled you with me this morning,' Chase told her. 'There're a number of patients with fuel burns that require debridement. There's one young man whose injuries are particularly disturbing.' He placed his mug back on the table and turned it round and round between his fingers, his gaze now fixed on the depths of milky coffee, his meal forgotten.

She nudged him, ignored the force of heat where her elbow contacted his arm. 'Eat up. You've got a full day to get through.'

'You're right.' Picking up his fork, he took a mouthful of egg and swallowed it without chewing.

'Food is a tool to keep going, no matter what's thrown at us.' The eggs weren't wonderful. Not even a heavy dousing of salt helped, and probably only aggravated their BPs. 'What time's the first patient scheduled?'

'As soon as we're done here.' There he went again, tilting his mouth into that fascinating smile. As though he'd

shoved away whatever was bothering him and wanted to continue enjoying this break between patients and more patients without worrying about how to help them.

'Why me and not Abdul?'

'You're saying you don't want to help me?' A tightness entered his voice and turned his face into a scowl.

'Chase.' She tapped the back of his hand. No heat this time. 'That's not what I asked. But think about it. I'm a GP. Abdul might be insulted if I do his work.'

The tightness backed off, the scowl smoothed into a small smile. 'He's catching up on sleep after a long night doing minor ops. The last boatload we picked up came with a list of minor surgeries as long as my leg.'

Her gaze immediately dropped to his long, muscular legs with their tanned skin. She drank in the sight. *Get over yourself. They're legs. Everyone has them.* Yeah, but— She gulped her tea.

This was ridiculous. Chase's focus was firmly on helping those less fortunate, not on her. He was a man about whom no one on board had any grizzles. A regular guy doing extraordinary things to make life more comfortable for others. This attraction must've come from spending so much time in confined quarters surrounded by too many people. Like in the army when soldiers were jam-packed into bunkers for endless hours, watching for the enemy. Those times had always tested her patience. This growing need to get intimate with the most breathtakingly good-looking man she'd ever known would evaporate as soon as her contract was over—in a little over five weeks. An eternity.

What would it be like to leave the ship with him and go home? She wasn't going to know. She didn't have a place to call home, and when she did Chase would still be trotting around the globe.

How could her mind wander when Chase was still talk-

ing? But she'd been thinking about him, not the medical arena he was discussing. Time to focus on the practical, not the impossible. 'Right, I'll get ready for surgery.'

Surely the attraction vibes would shut up in the medical room where concentration on the operation and the patient was paramount?

Her hormones didn't get that message, sending heat zipping around her veins as she stood in the medical corner where they were working, listening to Chase explain which wounds they were to debride and which to leave.

'I'm concerned about infection, and working on every little wound will make him very vulnerable to bacteria.' Those strong hands described in fluid movements what they'd soon be doing to their patients. What would they feel like on her breasts? 'The larger wounds are going to be trouble enough.'

'Will you send him off with plenty of antibiotics and painkillers?' Chase dressed in blue, baggy cotton scrubs did nothing to quieten the excitement going on over her skin, in her moist places.

'Enough to get him through this crisis.'

In the meantime they'd do their best to counteract infection while the man was with them. She reached for the gloves and winced as her back protested. Definitely time to find somewhere to do a few stretches. Not on the open deck at the front when Chase could appear at any moment she was in her zen zone.

Chase peered at her. 'Back bothering you?'

About to die of embarrassment if he'd read her mind, she snapped, 'Just a twinge.' It was better when he hadn't noticed. Until Chase had asked yesterday she'd never mentioned her injuries to anyone on board, not even when filling in her application to work for MFA. So she'd fudged the truth, but it wasn't as though it caused problems for

others, such as covering her shifts. Besides, the injuries were improving, though slower than she would have liked.

'Right, we'll get started.' The shoulder he turned in her direction wasn't cold, neither was it warm and friendly.

She'd let him down by not sharing. 'I'm okay, truly.'

He glanced across. 'I have some massage experience if that'd help.' Then he straightened, shock registering in his face. 'I mean…'

Chase lost for words? It would've been funny if she wasn't feeling equally flustered. 'It's fine.' She shoved her hand into a glove with such force it split. 'I'll do some yoga later.'

'Here.' Chase held out the box of gloves. 'The offer stands if you change your mind.' He'd obviously got a grip on himself faster than she had.

'Thanks,' she muttered, turning to the table where their man lay, mouth open, snoring softly. Thank goodness for patients. Kristina picked up a scalpel and began cutting away the infected skin around a large wound on the right leg.

'Yoga, eh?' There he went again. Grinning like she amused him.

'Don't laugh until you've tried it,' she retorted through a smile.

Nearly an hour later Kristina stood back from the table. 'He is going hurt when he wakes up.'

'Morphine will help for a while, followed by strong pain-killers. Hopefully those wounds will be healing before he leaves us.' Chase dropped the scalpel he'd used into a metal dish. The clatter was sharp in the stuffy room.

The next patient was wheeled across and they were away again.

'The air-conditioning gone on the blink?' Kristina wondered aloud as they finished debriding their fourth

patient. Over the last thirty minutes the room had become
hot enough to keep a mug of tea warm.

'Seems like it.' Chase snapped off his gloves and tossed
them in the direction of the hazardous waste bin. 'Anyone
for a quick coffee on the outer deck before lunch?'

'Definitely,' the anaesthetist said.

'Not me. I'll check how the vaccinations are going.' It'd
take all day and half the night to get all one hundred and
something people inoculated. Chase would have it covered,
but she had to get away from him, breathe clear air into her
lungs and not the kind that was tainted with Chase scent.
Male, sharp, sometimes abrasive, sometimes seductive.
Definitely mind-blowing. And disruptive.

'See you at lunch,' Chase grumped.

'Maybe,' she gave back.

In the end, Kristina decided to avoid Chase and took
some sandwiches back to her cabin where she squashed
her yoga mat in the narrow gap between the bunk and the
wall. Sitting with her legs crossed at the ankles and her
hands on her knees, she tried not to bang her elbows and
closed her eyes to begin clearing her mind of everything.
Taking slow breaths deep into her belly, holding, relaxing,
gradually the tension in her aching muscles let go, and she
was able move freely. She began a workout of simple po-
sitions, allowing her mind to drift and her body to mend.

Placing her hands on the floor and pushing her butt up-
ward, keeping her legs straight, Kristina hung her head
between her arms. So relaxing, so freeing. When no one
was staring at her butt, that was, and in here she could be
sure of that.

Chase Barrington strolled through her head like he had
every right to be there.

Forget relaxed. Her body became a temple to ten-
sion. Every last muscle tightened. Dropping to her knees,
she stared at the mat under her hands. Damn him. Why

couldn't he leave her alone for once? All the good work had come undone in a flash. There wasn't time for any more. She should've been in the clinic ten minutes ago. Hauling herself upright, she dumped the mat on her bunk and headed out the door. At least her back and thigh felt better.

The same couldn't be said for her head space. Chase had settled in, and wasn't taking a blind bit of notice of her need for a clear mind.

He also had ideas about her next job. 'Kristina, could you examine Marjali? Zala says there's blood between her legs.'

Back up to speed, she answered, 'Hopefully it's normal post-partum bleeding. Zala mightn't know about that.' Slipping on gloves, she looked around. 'I'll talk to them, see if I am allowed to do an examination.'

'You will be.' Chase sounded so certain she turned to stare at him.

'There's no guarantee. We're the strangers in this situation.'

The shade of Chase's eyes lightened to summer and the corners of his mouth lifted. 'I wouldn't place a bet on this. I'd hate to take advantage of you.'

His belief in her ability to get along with a woman who lived such a different life startled her. It also lightened her heart, made her feel good. 'I promise not to deliberately skew the outcome of my discussion with Marjali just to prove you wrong.'

Wow. When Chase put a bit of effort into it his smile could light up the world. It certainly brightened hers, and she forgave him for crowding her head space. But she left him before she got carried away with this feeling of wonder and said or did something they'd both regret.

'Zala, help me pull these curtains around Marjali, will you?'

Zala grabbed a handful of curtain to tug along the metal rail. 'Is this right?'

'Yes. Now I have questions for you to ask Marjali.' Kristina drew a breath as she thought about how to word them in a way Zala would understand clearly to translate, and how Marjali would understand her intentions. 'Tell her I need to look at where the blood is coming from.'

'It's where the baby was,' Zala looked at her as though she was stupid.

'You are right, but sometimes after a baby there can be too much. Do you understand?' She had to or this wasn't going any further.

Zala gave an abrupt nod before talking to the other woman in a low, urgent voice, pointing at Kristina and then at the top of Marjali's legs.

Marjali regarded Kristina with a surprising intensity, her almost black eyes drilling right into her. Finally she nodded.

'You can look,' Zala informed her with satisfaction. 'I told her you are nice.'

Blink, blink. Really? Lifting her arms, she made to hug Zala, hesitated. Again she wasn't sure if it was acceptable. 'Thank you.'

Zala leaned in and put her hand on Kristina's wrist. 'It is good, yes?'

'Yes, it's good. Please tell Marjali everything I say.' Explaining in simple terms what she was doing, Kristina quickly found the source of bleeding. A tear had occurred since the birth. 'I am going to give her an injection.' Then she'd stitch the tear.

'Injection?'

'A needle to stop it hurting.'

Collecting the suture kit and drawing up a small dose of local painkiller, Kristina returned to the bed. Zala's explanation had gone down well. Within a short time everything was done and Marjali was sitting up.

'Slowly,' Kristina warned. 'What have you been doing since baby was born?'

'She's been carrying buckets of water to the men.'

'She's not to do that. That's why she was bleeding. There are other people to lift the buckets.' If any of the medics had seen Marjali hauling water around they'd have intervened, not that they'd necessarily be taken notice of. 'Tell her it's important to rest.' There might've been previous babies, but the woman wasn't in top health.

'I tell her.'

'What was Marjali's problem?' Chase asked as Kristina dumped her gloves, the used syringe and cotton pads in the waste.

'She's been hauling water containers around the deck when I thought she was resting with her baby.'

'Not any more she's not,' Chase growled. 'I'll talk to the man overseeing this group.'

'Maybe don't use Zala to translate that one. It might be seen as a female stepping into the men's shoes.'

'Good point.' Chase touched her lightly on the shoulder. A gesture that made her heart squeeze.

How could she close down these feelings for him? They were growing into more than attraction, more than the need to just have sex with him. But making love would be a great start.

Kristina put her plate in the dishwasher. 'That's it. I'll go and see Marjali and the baby then head to my bunk,' she said to the room in general. It was after nine. Dinner had been quiet, everyone lost in their own exhaustion.

'You're not going topside, then?' Jane asked quietly.

'No need. I did a few yoga moves in our cabin earlier.'

'I wasn't thinking about yoga.' The woman had the cheek to wink.

Jane knew she'd been up there with Chase last night?

Why was she surprised? The gossip mill spun well in the confined places crowded with people having nothing better to occupy their minds. Everyone required a diversion from their work at one time or another. If only it wasn't her. 'I'll be in our cabin.'

Marjali was asleep, her baby swathed in a cotton sheet in a crib beside her. Reluctant to disturb either of them, Kristina stood watching over them for a few minutes. Such an unimaginable place to be, and yet the woman had had a baby and was getting on with being a mother. Not that she had any choice, Kristina sighed. At least *she* did. Starting with finding her next job—preferably in another Merrywood, if not the real deal. The more she thought about the quaint town the more she wanted to be a part of it. Merrywood had firmly lodged in her heart.

Stepping outside into fresh air and the light breeze that had come up, she wandered around the crowded space. The noise was continuous and blocked her thinking. The idea of retreating to the stuffy cabin no longer appealed. Which left only one place that might be quiet, cool and empty. Except for one person, and he knew how to be silent without creating a strain on her.

'I wondered if you'd come,' Chase said as she slipped in beside him and propped her elbows on the railing, making sure there was a gap between them.

Touching him was not an option. It wouldn't shut down the lure of his body. 'I needed some quiet time.'

'Then I won't ask what you're thinking about,' he said around one of those devastating smiles she'd started looking out for, and seemed to find more and more often.

'Work, as in where to next,' she told him, because he was far too easy to talk to.

'You want to return home.'

'Yes.' They weren't meant to be talking. Even if it was

what she needed after all. He'd send her away. He'd started it, though.

'Pity.' He moved sideways a little, away from her, leaving her feeling she'd made a blunder. 'You're just what we need around here.'

As SARCO Chase gave more than most. Not everyone could be expected to do the same. 'If one percent of the medical profession gave six or twelve weeks out of their careers to work for *Medicine For All* there'd be an oversupply of staff.'

'Unfortunately it doesn't work like that,' Chase answered. 'What are you looking for this time?'

'I'd prefer a permanent position in a small town medical centre. But it's not as easy as I'd hoped,' she sighed. 'Merrywood spoiled me for choice. All the staff were welcoming and friendly. It was the same with the townsfolk.' Going to the pub for a drink on a Saturday had been relaxing and enjoyable, with people coming up to talk to her like she was a local. Now all she had to do was find something similar to make permanent and she was home and settled.

What about the love interest she'd started longing for? A man to come home to at the end of the day to share a drink and meal with while talking about what they'd done was a dream that slotted into the picture of family she'd waited for since her real family had fallen apart. The hazy memories of being hugged after school, taken out for a walk with the dog, being helped with her homework never quite disappeared, and always tugged at her, filled her with longing for another chance at that life.

Kristina's eyes moved sideways, towards Chase. Damn but he was gorgeous. Dragging her gaze forward again, she stared at the waters below. Dark and dangerous. Her gaze returned to the man beside her. His head was tipped slightly back and his eyes were closed. His hands lightly held the railing and his legs were splayed to counteract the

rolling of the ship on the low swell. Dark and dangerous? Maybe. Intriguing and exciting, for sure. Was this what she wanted in a man?

CHAPTER THREE

'REID, I'M CHECKING you're joining us aboard the *Poseidon* for the three weeks.' The man was busy with planning a wedding and finding a house to buy, Chase allowed.

'I gave you my word.' The underlying note in Ethan's tone told him that when he promised something he didn't go back on it.

'Sorry,' Chase admitted. He'd said that a lot lately. Ethan and Kristina had a knack of making him say things without thinking them through first. 'It's not you I'm worried about. People are pulling out of contracts and others getting ill so the roster I worked out before summer has gone to pieces.'

'Afraid I can't do more time or Claire will hang me out to rot. Though I'm really over choosing between lace or satin. And that's for the place settings at the wedding party we're having later on.'

Chase relaxed and laughed. 'I like it that Claire can wind you up.' His laughter died. He'd never have that. There was no one to blame but himself. He'd chosen the solitary road.

Yet lately there'd been occasions, especially since he and Ethan had begun burying the hatchet, when he'd give anything to forget the past and move on to something exciting and loving that could span his whole future. A re-

lationship, a marriage with rock-solid foundations, so that there were kids and a home to be proud of and go back to at the end of every day.

Kristina came to mind. He shoved her away. First he had to stop holding onto his guilt over having to let Nick die alone. It had taken a crane to lift the beam from Nick's chest the day after the avalanche had struck. While in Chase's head he knew what that meant, in his heart he couldn't quite reconcile himself with the truth. What would happen if he did relax on the guilt? Would the sky fall in? *Nick? Would you think I'd deserted you again?*

Ethan was muttering something.

Chase refocused. 'What did you say?'

'Being with Claire's taking some getting used to.' Ethan laughed. 'But I wouldn't change a thing.'

'Thank goodness she's stronger than you. She turned your head when you thought you had everything under control.'

'Don't get too wise, friend. The same could happen to you when you're least expecting it. How is Kristina, by the way?'

Chase winced. That was getting a little too close to the mark. 'She's good, as are Freja, Pierre, Mike, and Angel.'

'You might be fooling yourself, Chase, but you're not fooling me. The pair of you need your heads banged together. Six weeks and all that tiptoeing around as though you weren't remotely interested in each other, the air pulsing with electricity. Damned dangerous for anyone getting near. Kristina gets under your skin and you're not liking it.'

'Time I got back to sorting out the roster. I'll mark you as definite for the next three-week stint.' He already had. This call really had nothing to do with that and all to do with talking with this man who was rapidly becoming a friend—if he stopped giving him crap about Kristina. All part of letting go of the past, surely?

'You know the routine. I'll email the exact date for em-
barking. Catch you.' There were volunteers doing three-,
six-, nine- and twelve-week hauls. It would be a lot easier
if everyone signed up for the same length of time, but that
wasn't how the system worked.

'Chase, don't hang up,' Ethan shouted. 'Forget your
bloody roster. What's this call really about?'

About to hit 'off', Chase hesitated. It had taken too
many years for them to start burying the things they'd said
on that mountain for him to be stirring up more trouble.
Losing ground wasn't an option. He had stopped blaming
Reid for something he'd had no choice about—a huge step
forward. Ethan now accepted Chase didn't hate him for
surviving when Nick hadn't. Chase also understood the
guilt he'd put on Ethan by letting him believe he'd made a
choice between the two guys. Nick had never been coming
out of there alive. *Nick, help me here.* Nothing but silence.
The laden quiet he'd learned to live with, that crippled him.

Fill the hush. Try answering Reid honestly. Take a deep
lungful and just say it. 'I wanted to touch base.' Reid would
understand how big that was. They'd both admitted they'd
avoided close friendships since that horrendous night, and
that they weren't used to having someone to call just for
the hell of it.

'You don't have to make up excuses to get in touch,' the
man on the other end of the phone growled.

Chase grimaced. 'I'm still getting used to this.'

'You and me both.'

'Bet Claire doesn't let you go quiet on her.'

'Not a chance.'

How did that feel? Good? Frightening? Exciting? Kris-
tina came to mind. Again. She did that way too often. What
would it be like to give up this life and make a new one?
With her? *Go away.* 'How are you finding this no more
disappearing over the horizon at any moment thing?' He

needed to know. For future reference, in case he ever decided to take a chance on a relationship. *Go away, Kristina.*

'There are moments when the fear grabs me and I start to tap into sites for jobs in the heat.' Ethan went quiet.

And this was summer, no snow and ice. But Ethan was in France. Where he'd sworn never to return. Chase waited. The last thing he wanted was to say something glib. They were better than that now.

Finally Ethan continued in a subdued voice. 'Then I look at Claire and know I don't want to go. That staying here, with her, is all I want, need, look forward to every morning in that split second between waking and opening my eyes to find her beside me. She's worth everything. Including being at the bottom of a mountain.'

Chase swallowed hard. Then had to do it again. 'I'm glad.' One of them had finally got their life back on track. Was it possible to make that two out of two? Fear rose; sharp and solid. What if he had to choose between the woman he loved and someone else in another emergency? He couldn't do it. He couldn't. So he wouldn't put himself in that position. *Sorry, Kristina.*

There was a lot of throat clearing going on at the other end. 'I want you to be my best man at our marriage ceremony.'

Chase felt his legs soften. Dropping his butt onto the desk top, he took the weight off his boneless limbs. Best man? With their past? This spoke volumes about how far they'd come in a short time. It spoke of total forgiveness. He couldn't find it within him to be flippant, his usual way of dealing with difficult, emotional moments. This was do or deny. Working with Ethan, he'd learned he didn't want denial any more. Not with this man. They'd been through hell together, the outcome taken out of their hands by a larger force. Now they were taking tentative steps towards

a real, honest friendship and he wouldn't be the one to screw that. 'I'd be honoured.'

He might now be able to work at dropping the denial on living a settled life in one place with one woman. Huh? Too soon. Way too soon. He still had to steady himself over his friendship with Reid.

'Cut the fancy words,' Ethan croaked. '"Yes" would've been fine.'

'Send me the details. When's this happening?' The last wedding he'd been to had been when Libby had married Jarrod, her childhood sweetheart, and they now had a posse of kids that would drive an army commander to drink. Army. Kristina. The two words clashed and melded in his head. Would he ever get her out of there again? Had he transferred his denial from Ethan to her? Now, *that* was getting complex. Forget it.

'A month after the *Poseidon* ties up at the end of summer. Hope that won't mess with your plans for heading out to Africa.'

The contract lay in his in-box. He hadn't been able to bring himself to sign it. Every time this past week when he'd thought he'd print it off to scrawl his signature across the bottom, Kristina's beautiful face had slipped into his mind, and he'd put it off. But the day was coming when he'd have no choice. Liam had already emailed to ask where the contract was. All that had done was remind Chase how unlike him it was to dither. He'd do it today. It wasn't as though he was changing his career path because of Kristina.

'You still there?' Ethan asked.

'I'll be available for the wedding. No matter what turns up.'

'Thanks, Chase. It's not a wedding. We're getting married in the Marseille Town Hall, just the four of us there.

Then we'll have big bash back at the family's village later on.'

'Four?' His stomach was tightening.

'Better warn you, Claire's asking Kristina to be her bridesmaid.' He laughed as though that was the biggest joke of the week.

'You're winding me up.'

'Not much.' Ethan was still laughing. 'Catch you.' He was gone.

Chase stared at the phone, ready to hurl it across the room. He and Kristina were going to be beside Ethan and Claire as they publicly declared their love for each other. They were being pushed together, want it or not. Considering how well the two women got on, he should've realised this would happen. Apparently Claire didn't have lots of friends, or at least none she wanted to stand beside her more than Kristina. And she was searching for permanency in her life, making him the wrong man for her. Unless he followed in Reid's footsteps.

Impossible or terrifying? Both.

'Chase, the next load of refugees is alongside.' Kristina stood in the doorway, hands on delectable hips, looking amused.

Had she heard his end of the conversation with Ethan? Or had she already been talking to Claire and knew they'd both be going to the wedding—as partners, no less? 'You heard from Claire today?'

Her brow creased. 'No. Should I have?'

He'd put his large foot in it again. 'Ethan mentioned she might be phoning you, that's all.' Standing up, he slipped the phone into his pocket, though there wasn't anyone else he wanted to hear from today. 'Let's go deal with our new patients.'

Then he'd be able to focus on what was necessary and ignore the rest.

* * *

Kristina wiped her face with tissues. They came away sodden. 'This heat is unbearable.'

'Be glad you're not on land.' Chase put his empty water bottle aside. 'There's a heatwave going on in Greece, Italy and southern France, with temperatures hitting the low forties in some areas.'

'How do people cope? I prefer the cold.'

Chase shivered. 'I don't.'

'Then again, when I've had to walk through snow and ice on my way to work I wished for the heat.' She grinned.

'No pleasing you, then.' His breathing was rapid, his smile forced.

'I used to enjoy snowboarding, whenever I had a chance to get up to the mountains, but it's been years since I gave it go. I'd probably make a right idiot of myself if I tried now.'

'Not my idea of fun.' There was something wrong about his tone, like she'd pushed the wrong buttons, upsetting him.

Yet she persisted. 'You've given it a go, then?'

'Not snowboarding.' He wasn't giving much away. All part of the 'don't talk a lot' in their quiet space on deck?

To her it was *their* place now. Over the past eight days she'd joined Chase every night for time out and not once had he told her to go away. It was special and she looked forward to being with him, to the lack of expectations put on her to fill in the minutes unless she wanted to. 'That's a yes to skiing?'

'It was a long time ago,' he muttered. The tension that had been tightening his arms and shoulders increased.

Desperate to undo the damage, she said the first thing that came into her mind. 'I don't like clothes that are remotely green or tan.'

His nod was short. 'I get that.'

'Heavy boots are no longer in my wardrobe either.'

One corner of his mouth lifted. 'Replaced with ten-inch high heels?'

'Ah, no. I fall off those too easily.'

'I'm disappointed.' He turned and leaned back against the rail, his gaze fixed on her now. 'I still can't get my head around you, so feminine and kind and fun, in the army. Why did you enlist?'

She should've stuck to the unspoken no-talking rule: instead, that sense of reaching for Chase, of feeling close to him, had got the better of her and now she was in the firing line. Looking out to sea, she wanted to tell him to leave her alone, wanted to put him back in the box where all people getting close went before they could hurt her by dumping her first. But something held her back. The need to find that future she wanted.

While Chase didn't stack up when it came to settling down, there was no denying he was helping her find her way. Telling him why she'd chosen the military couldn't hurt, might even help her get past the pain she carried into every relationship. 'I was looking for somewhere to belong.'

He studied her for a long time, before asking quietly, 'Did you find it?'

'Not really. This will sound weird to someone who comes from a loving family…' She paused, collecting the right words. 'Libby was always talking about her and Jarrod and the kids, and about your parents and you. She made it sound wonderful, having people behind you all the time no matter what you did.' Reminded her of her childhood.

'That's our Libby.' He sighed. 'She's not always right about everything.'

Kristina nodded. 'Who is?' Of course he didn't answer. There really wasn't one. Her gaze returned to the sea. There was anonymity in the heaving water and the hidden depths. 'I had this idea that being a part of the army would

be on a par to belonging to a family.' She daren't look at Chase for fear there'd be mockery in his eyes. 'I wanted someone to have my back, to feel I belonged with them. I got all of that.' It still wasn't what she'd been hoping for.

'Where did it let you down?'

Chase got it. Again she watched him as she talked, basking in his ability to be non-judgemental, at least until he had all the facts.

'I *was* part of a dedicated group of people, working, training, playing together, and it appeared to be exactly what I'd been hoping for. Then I came to realise everything was on the army's terms, as it has to be. Going into battle as individuals would be disastrous. Every soldier has to be, and is, integral to each other.'

Then she had been discharged and the gate had closed firmly behind her. Bye-bye, Captain Morton. The two women she kept in touch with felt the same sense of being left out in the cold once they were no longer a part of the establishment, though they all agreed that could be their own fault because they'd expected too much.

'You obviously don't regret your decision despite not finding the right job yet.'

Again it sounded as though he understood where she was coming from. Just like that. With no follow-up questions about why, where and when. That earned him a lot of points. Other people like her father, who wasn't close by any stretch of the imagination, hadn't believed the truth, even knowing why she'd left the forces. Her mother had never understood her need to be loved for the person she was and not who her mum wanted her to be. Sitting on the Riviera or in the Bahamas, sipping cocktails, month after month with men who only wanted her beauty and body was not *her*. Yeah, her mum's American hadn't lasted more than a year.

Kristina could love Chase for his sensitivity alone. But

she wouldn't. Loving him for anything would only bring pain. At the end of the day he was still a man who didn't settle anywhere for long, didn't gather people around him, didn't want the same things she did. Though there was a real possibility he did want them, but wasn't prepared to risk finding them. He wasn't as straightforward as the man who presented himself as SARCO. That man was in charge, was friendly without getting involved. The man standing beside her hurt her deep inside where no one was allowed to go.

Again, she'd not be finding out why because to do so meant becoming involved, and as much as she'd like to be there for him, to make a difference, it would come with a price she couldn't afford. A broken heart was not on her horizon. Yes, getting close to Chase would mean love. Because she already felt twinges of emotion that only had one name whenever she was with him. Twinges only, not full-on, heart-totally-involved love. She remembered the lust that had dominated for weeks. 'I'm turning in. See you in the morning unless I'm required for an emergency.'

The haunting sound of a flute wafted over the air. She hesitated, listening as the sweet sound rose and fell. It was coming from the other end of the ship, striking her so that she didn't move in case it stopped.

'Kristina.' Chase's hand covered hers, his fingers slipping between hers. 'Stay with me for a moment.'

'It's beautiful,' she whispered, and slowly leaned back against him. Breathing deeply and slowly, she let the tension ease from her body while absorbing his warmth. A warmth unlike the heat from the sun that had finally dipped beyond the horizon. This was a warmth that filled her with longing and love and hope.

'It is.'

The notes rose and fell as though following the air. Who was playing the instrument? One of the medical people?

Or a refugee? They never brought much with them but a flute would take up no space in a small bag.

Chase wound his arms around her, tucked her closer to his body, his chest a wall for her back. His chin rested on the top of her head, his breaths lifting strands of her hair from behind her ear.

The music soared, and her heart rate followed the tempo.

Chase's hands spread over her waist, held her tightly yet gently.

She didn't want anything to move, could stay like this for hours.

Silence. Disappointment dripped off her. 'Oh,' she whispered. 'That was lovely.'

Then another note hung in the air, followed by more, a faster tempo, one that had her toes tapping.

Chase's hands were turning her, bringing her to face him. 'Let's dance.' He reached for her hands, drew her close as he stepped in time to the tune.

She went with him, unable to refuse, following his lead, hearing the music, hearing the beat in her veins, in her head.

When the music slowed, Chase slowed, held her close, and moved on the spot.

When the notes fell away, Kristina held her breath, waiting for the next tune.

Silence. This time it remained.

But Chase's hands were still holding her, his face coming closer to hers, and then his lips were touching her mouth, a light brush that woke her fully yet left her languid as his mouth covered hers and pressed harder, capturing her, teasing, sending waves of desire to her toes. To her fingers, her belly, her centre.

Winding her arms around his shoulders, she hung on

and kissed him back with all the pent-up frustration of the last weeks. She kissed him deeply, hungrily. Kissed him as though to imprint herself on his mind for ever.

'Kristina,' he groaned against her mouth.

She didn't answer. Couldn't for the longing in her throat.

Then she was being gently put aside. 'We have to stop.'

She didn't recognise his throaty voice filled with tension and need. Chase wanted her as badly as she wanted him. So why not do something about it? But as she opened her mouth to say so, she hesitated. He was right. They had to stop. Taking this any further would only exacerbate the differences between them. It would be a short-term thing, and knowing that would hover over her, make her feel uneasy instead of happy. She was too far gone over Chase to be able to have a fling and walk away in one piece. The pendulum was moving, from one side, lust, to the other, love, and she had to stop it going any further.

But couldn't she have one time with him?

He shook his head slowly, apparently good at mind-reading.

Stepping back, Kristina let her hands drop slowly to her sides. 'See you in the morning.'

His hand caught one of hers. 'Goodnight, Kristina.' His thumb caressed her skin, winding up the need tighter than ever. Then he let her go.

Loud banging on their cabin door had Kristina and Jane out of bed and pulling on clothes before hurrying on deck, where people from Libya were being brought on board after a small boat had capsized nearer the coast.

The scene was organised chaos. Small, bedraggled children sat crying and shaking in sodden clothes while distraught adults held them tight, their own tears tracking down ashen faces.

Across the deck Chase was doing CPR on a youngster, the strain in his face saying there was no way he would fail to revive the lad.

She rushed to join him. 'Want a hand?'

'Get the defibrillator,' he demanded, sweat streaming down his cheeks and forehead.

Snatching the machine off the bulkhead, Kristina dropped down beside Chase, placing patches on the boy's chest to attach the wires. 'Stand back.'

The limp body jerked off the deck, slumped back down. 'Again,' demanded Chase. 'Again.'

When the flat line started to rise Kristina's hopes lifted. 'That's the boy. Where's the oxygen?' she asked.

'Coming,' Chase informed her through gritted teeth. 'Someone else needed it first.'

There was more than one tank and fittings, but when she looked around the deck she could see them all in use. 'What happened?'

'The boat was so overcrowded that when a wave from a passing ship hit, it rolled and sank. Luckily the other ship stopped and tried to save everyone, but it seems some haven't been found.' Chase's face was grim. 'But I've got this one.' He reached for the boy's wrist and felt for his pulse. 'Too weak.'

The boy's eyes flickered open. Water spewed from his lungs.

Chase quickly rolled him onto his side to prevent choking. 'I thought we'd got all that. Seems he's taken in more water than the Mediterranean holds. How did he survive that?'

'Here we go.' Kristina took the gear a nurse was handing her and placed a mask over the boy's face, turning on the valve.

'Hello. My name is Kristina. This is Dr Chase. You are

safe now.' Hopefully her tone would do what her words couldn't and give the lad a sense of calm.

'Chase, over here,' called someone. 'We've got a major trauma.'

'You all right here?' he asked, but didn't wait for an answer, loping off across the deck like a wild dog was after him.

'I need a doctor when someone's free.'

Hearing Jane's voice, Kristina looked around. 'What's up?'

'Probably a fractured arm and torn ligaments.'

'Swap. This lad had heart failure, probable cause drowning. His lungs have been cleared, and he's breathing with aid from the tank. Can you watch him?'

'Be right there.'

Kristina counted the beats in her patient's wrist. Light, but regular. Was he really going to be that lucky? Her fingers crossed for him, she wiped his face and mouth.

Jane knelt down on the opposite side. 'Hi, there. I'm Jane. What have you been doing to yourself?'

Kristina headed for the girl with the fracture. 'Hello. I'm a doctor. Kristina is my name.' Her fingers felt the upper right arm that lay at an odd angle. 'I need to get you with one of the surgeons to put you back together.'

'I'll help you carry her down.' A nurse placed a stretcher on the deck beside them.

'Thank goodness for lifts.' Kristina nodded at him. Too much heavy lifting and carrying didn't do her back a lot of good.

'Kristina, over here,' Chase called. 'Now.'

'I'll get someone else to help me with this,' Bernie told her.

'What's up?' She squatted beside Chase, who looked fierce with determination.

'Blunt force trauma to the skull. He's not responding

to stimulus, BP's way too low. I'm going into Theatre immediately and need you on hand while we take him down. We can't wait for a chopper to airlift him to the mainland. He won't survive that long. Watch his vitals while I scrub up,' Chase added in no uncertain terms.

'Onto it.' This was like the day the bomb had blown up on the training exercise. With everyone in shock and frantic to do the right thing by the wounded, it had been chaotic. And she hadn't been able to move, to help. A chill settled over her. As long as the outcome was a hundred percent better. So far the chaos did appear to be under control, with everyone getting on with their jobs, all efficiency. She needed to relax. No one was dying from an uncontrollable bleed out. But she couldn't shake the sense of déjà vu, of not doing enough for the wounded. Which made no sense. Tonight she was not incapacitated with injuries and unable to help those who needed her.

As soon as Chase, his patient and a full tally of staff were at the operating table Kristina went looking for someone else to help.

'Over here.' Calvin waved at her.

'What's this one?'

'I suspect a miscarriage. There's heavy bleeding between her thighs and intermittent tightening of the gut at regular intervals. She's hypothermic, hence the survival blanket. We've stripped her of her wet clothes.' Calvin rubbed his chin with the back of a glove-covered hand. 'She's not responding to anything I say. Not a blink or a tightening of her hands. I wonder if it's because I'm a male.'

Kristina reached inside the blanket for a cold hand, and held it gently. 'Hello, can you hear me?' Where was Zala when she needed her? She'd disembarked along with everyone who'd come on board with her weeks ago, and Kristina still thought about her. If only they'd been able to keep

her with them, but that was selfish as the girl was getting on with finding her new life. 'My name is Kristina and I'm a doctor.' The words were starting to taste bland after so many times repeating them and not being understood.

The woman was shivering non-stop and her skin was frozen while there was a heatwave going on.

'Let's get her inside,' Calvin suggested. 'Away from the crowds she might be more receptive to help.'

'If that's possible. She's slipping in and out of consciousness.' Standing, she looked around for another stretcher.

In the full glare of the lights it was apparent Calvin's assessment was correct. The miscarriage was nearly complete, with the afterbirth coming away as Kristina began a thorough examination.

Calvin had put on a face mask. 'That way she might not see my masculine side and go all crazy. Though she's more settled since you joined us.'

'Seems pregnant women are my forté at the moment, despite having a midwife on board.'

'It's that soft, coaxing manner of speaking you have that gets them every time.' He grinned. 'I need to practise more.'

'I can see that working.' Kristina laughed. 'To be on the safe side, I'm doing a D and C.'

Calvin nodded. 'Onto it.'

'No problem.' They'd close the area off and scrub up after cleaning the woman down. 'You're helping me?'

'That's what I meant by *we*.' Again he grinned. 'Unless you want to do it alone.'

'Not at all.' They worked well together, and the woman was soon in a bed, tucked under a blanket with a nurse to watch over her until she woke.

'Back topside, I guess.' Kristina aimed for the stairs.

Chase was ahead, striding out hard and fast.

'Chase,' she called.

He didn't turn or slow.

'Chase, wait for me.'

His legs ate up the distance, his hands fisted at his sides. Why was he ignoring her? Or was he in a hurry to get to another urgent case? He should still be with the brain trauma patient. Uh-oh. She hesitated. Hadn't the patient made it? His injuries had been extreme, and they'd wondered if he'd been hit by the boat while in the water. Chase would be gutted if he hadn't saved the man. They all felt the loss of a patient but Chase seemed to feel it hardest. It was as though he was on a mission to save everyone who came under his care.

All doctors wanted that outcome, but with Chase she'd seen him go into despair when he'd lost a young girl even when the odds had not been on his side. Despair to the point of being over the top. Why? Was that just his nature? Or had he lost a patient he shouldn't have? Most doctors had failures on their conscience, but to the extent Chase seemed to go? No, there was more to this than he would ever let on.

Something terrible lay in both their pasts, something they'd both suffered, and still did, if Chase's reaction tonight was an indicator. He wouldn't tell her about it, she knew that. Didn't mean she couldn't offer her support. As soon as they were finished up he'd head for his—their— space, and she'd be right there for him.

Out on the deck there were few minor injuries left to deal with, and the nurses were handing out hot tea and bread with butter.

'We're done,' said Jane when Kristina came to a halt beside her. 'We're arranging bedding and dry clothes for those who need it and then we can stand down.'

'Sounds good to me. It's been quite a night.' From kissing Chase to fixing the wounded. Her gaze travelled the length of the deck and found Chase. He stood talking to

one of the new nurses, his stance tight and unforgiving, his voice low and controlled, yet anger was coming off him in waves. Anger at the nurse? Or because of whatever had gone on during the operation?

Jane turned her head to stare in the same direction. 'The head injury guy died on the table.'

'I wondered.' Kristina's heart went out to the young man's family. And to Chase. He'd be chastising himself for days to come.

'Want a mug of tea?' Jane asked, now watching her.

'Best offer I've had all night.' What would Chase say if she took him one? Only one way to find out.

But it wasn't going to happen. He went past without acknowledging her, yet she'd swear he'd seen her as he'd stormed away to head down to the cabins, not up to his space. He'd have a lot to see to before knocking off for what remained of the night. Then he did an abrupt about-turn and charged up on deck.

She could give him some time to collect himself. Or she could join him. 'Make that a tea and a coffee,' she told Jane as she watched Chase charge over to the stairs heading to the deck.

Did she go to him or let him be alone and unhappy? That had been raw pain darkening those eyes to thunder clouds. She didn't let friends down when they needed someone to talk to. Not that she had friends who came calling in hours of need, neither was Chase likely to talk to her. But, 'One tea and one coffee,' she repeated.

'Sorry it's not laced with brandy.' Kristina handed Chase a mug when she finally made it to their space a few minutes later.

'Right.'

At least he accepted the proffered coffee. Settling against the railing, she sipped her tea and stared out into the darkness. 'Rough night.'

She was met with silence. Not that she'd been expecting Chase to burst into conversation. But nothing? Yes, that was the man she'd come here to lend a shoulder to. She sipped more tea. 'It never gets any easier, does it?'

Nothing.

'We can't save them all all of the time, Chase.'

Coffee splashed over the deck as the mug jerked in his fingers. 'Yes, I can,' he roared. 'I have to.'

Kristina held still, watched the play of emotions warring in his face and eyes—pain, anger, frustration, need—and knew she'd gone too far. But she wasn't about to back off. He needed help. Not that she was any expert about this kind of pain, only knew from her own experiences how it could destroy a person. 'You're wrong. I've been there. I know.'

'Go, Kristina. Just go.'

So much for that kiss.

CHAPTER FOUR

HE MIGHT'VE KNOWN.

Kristina didn't budge, looked as if she'd stay all night if he didn't respond, if he didn't beg her to leave him alone with his pain. Did she think that because he'd kissed her she had the right to encroach? Chase wanted to slam his fist into a bulkhead, throw a tantrum, yell at her for caring enough to be there. People weren't allowed to care about him—he'd made a career out of pushing away anyone who tried. Not that he'd succeeded with his family. They ignored his outbursts, his cold shoulder, the physical distances he'd put between them ever since that night. They loved him, no question.

Was Kristina made of the same stern stuff? Did he want her to be? It would only lead to heartache—for them both. He was beginning to feel involved with her. To feel the possibility of a future. That kiss had only increased his desire for her, complicating matters further. He had to be strong and push her away.

Chase remained upright with his back against the bulkhead, his hands jammed into the pockets of his shorts and his chin jutting out like an arrow aimed at the distant, unseen horizon. Trying to pretend Kristina wasn't within reach was a joke. Lift an arm and his hand would be touching that creamy skin that managed to survive the

worst the sun sent her way without any blemishes. What he wouldn't do to touch, to taste, to kiss that sensational body. To take and to give, another kiss. To lose himself in her. Anything except surrender his heart.

'Chase? Talk to me.'

Why couldn't she leave him in peace? This was *his* place, not *theirs*. Though he had begun thinking of it as theirs. But right now he had to be alone to grapple with the bitterness of another failure. No one died on his watch. No one. Not any more.

But tonight a young man had. The odds of saving him had been long, too long as it turned out. But he should've succeeded. Even when he wasn't a neurosurgeon, and didn't have one on hand. Someone would be bereft, a mother, father, perhaps a wife. Because he'd failed. As he had with Nick.

'There's nothing to talk about,' he howled around the pain of his best friend lying trapped under an immovable beam, dying, pain that mixed with the loss of tonight's patient. 'Go away,' he shouted. Was it his memories he was hollering at? Or Kristina? Either, or: it didn't matter. It was imperative he turn her away before she saw through him to the guilt and fear that ruled him. It wasn't a lie to say there was nothing to talk about. It was called self-protection. Those wounds were not for opening.

They weren't open now?

'We work to save everyone, but it doesn't always pan out like that.' Kristina spoke softly, not daunted by his yelling.

'It has to,' he snapped. What didn't this woman understand? It was straightforward enough. Injured people came to doctors, to *him*, to be fixed, put back together, given another chance at living. 'It's what I trained for.'

'You're right, but sometimes it just isn't enough.' Did she take no umbrage with anything he said? 'Why can't you accept that?'

Get out. Stay. Suddenly he didn't want to push too far. Having Kristina on his side was like a balm he couldn't stop rubbing. Underneath that calm, friendly exterior was a will of steel. One he'd like to get to know. Damn it. Yes, he would. Around Kristina he didn't understand himself any more. It was as though by talking to Ethan so much lately he was allowing himself to dream. Hope rose when she came near. Was it possible to have a future with her? One where he planted his feet in the soil of his own property and felt like he belonged, like he had the right to stay and be happy with Kristina at his side? Deep breaths quietened his racing heart a little. Until he told her, 'Failure doesn't exist in my vocabulary.'

'Everyone knows that. It's the why I'm asking about.'

'Because the consequences are always unbearable for someone. A family, friends.' For me.

She waited. Not a movement, not a smile or a widening of those beautiful eyes. Nothing to get his back up. Nothing to make him believe she felt sorry for him. She was good.

Chase fell into the offer she was making.

'My best friend died. I couldn't save him. I blame myself regardless of the circumstances.'

Still Kristina remained quiet. No ranting about how that was silly, like so many had said to him in the past. Not Reid. He'd also lived with the consequences. Chase shuddered. Something he was accountable for.

'The national junior ski team was competing in the French Alps when an avalanche hit our chalet.'

Now Kristina did move, slipping beside him, her arm touching the length of his. Her warm hand wrapped around his cold one. Then she waited.

'I couldn't help him. Couldn't lift the beam that broke his chest and held him in snow and ice until he was frozen.' The memory of that ice and cold rippled through Chase, lifting his skin, turning his muscles taut.

Kristina's grip tightened. 'You were in the British national team? You must've been extremely skilful.'

'I was.' For all the good it did him or any of the team that night. 'But not the best. Nick Hariday held that ranking, and we were always after him to take over his position. Especially me and Ethan.'

'So that's where Ethan comes into it.' Kristina's nodded. 'Of course.'

'Of course what?' She intrigued him with her easy acceptance of his story. Had she read him correctly? He hoped so, or it was going to sting when he learned differently.

'The initial disquiet between the two of you during those first weeks he was on board. There was such tension between you. At first you both trod on eggshells whenever you were in the same room, but then something changed. You talked, didn't you? About what happened?' She shook her head.

Like he'd said, she was good. Where did that take him? Did he tie her to his side and never let her go so he'd always have someone who understood him to talk to? Or did he shove her away because he'd only drag her down as he hauled her all over the world, searching for more people to save? The one thing he was certain of about Kristina was that she wanted to settle, to stop wandering.

He answered her question in the vague hope it would turn her away. 'There were more beams on top of the one that pinned Nick down. He never stood a chance, but that didn't stop me trying, pleading with him to live. When the futility of my actions finally sank in I turned away to help Ethan. I had to save someone. But I resented him for that.' The words spewed out like poison and he let them come before the lump building in the back of his throat cut off all speech.

This was the second time in weeks that he'd talked

about that tragedy. Ethan had brought it up one night on shore during their first three-day break. They'd been downing bourbon, pecking around the past until Ethan had gone for the problem, boots and all, shocking Chase even though he'd known it had to happen. Ethan had put it out there about his guilt at being the one Chase had chosen to save thereby leaving Nick alone in those last precious moments.

For the first time ever Chase had admitted he'd been wrong to let him continue thinking that, how at the time he hadn't known how to cope with his loss and pain. Still didn't. After that they'd talked about the guys who hadn't made it, and the coach who hadn't had the courage to help anyone and who was now working for a charity gardening centre, possibly trying to assuage his conscience. It seemed every survivor from the tragedy had come away laden with guilt.

The resulting hangover had been a killer. Not something Chase was about to repeat, even if there was booze to be had on board, which as far as he knew there wasn't. It was MFA's policy, and anyone caught flouting it was politely asked to leave. Yet tonight, if there had been a bottle on hand, he might have been sorely tempted, needing the release that came with losing himself in the hit of alcohol. Not that he made a habit of doing that but occasionally it was okay.

Unable to resist her any longer, he drew Kristina close and wound his arms around that warm body, his chin resting on her head as he breathed in the salt air and her scent. As he waited for the lump to dissolve and his heart rate to return to normal, he absorbed her warmth, marvelled at the wonder of having a woman relax in his embrace, of not demanding anything for herself, letting him talk as he wanted to, or not if he preferred.

The lump of pain and despair slowly dissolved while

the throb of his heart began picking up its beat. His nerve endings came alive one at a time. His hands splayed on her waist. His mouth hungered for one more kiss. The rest of his body wanted everything, the whole naked, close, orgasmic thing. Tipping back in her arms, he gazed down into her eyes and asked, "Kristina?'

She must've felt the tightening in his body and known his need because she rose onto her toes and leaned forward. 'Yes.' Her husky voice brushed his skin, heightened his yearning. 'Yes.'

As her mouth opened under his he sank further into her embrace. She tasted sweet and strong and dangerous. He wanted to rob her of all awareness except for him. To take her where he was headed. To oblivion. Away from all that screwed him inside out.

There was no noise; no people talking or arguing, no birds squawking overhead, no boats heading towards the ship. Chase was deaf. And hot. And cold. And warm. He was lost in this woman who seemed to understand him when she shouldn't. She stole his ability to think, gave of herself and endorsed his feeling of being in the right place at the right time with the right woman.

His lips cruised over hers, devoured her mouth as he tasted. Her hands pushed under his shirt to caress and sensitise his skin, and he fell further into her. Rapid breathing made her breasts rise and fall against his chest, inflaming him more. He had to taste them. Her hips pressed against his rising, hardening need. Her scent swirled around them, enticing, erotic. His hands sought and found hot, bare skin, felt the frantic throb of a pulse, knew the warmth and care being given to him.

'Chase.' An urgent whisper against his mouth cut through the haze.

'What?' He wasn't stopping for anyone. He couldn't. Didn't have the brakes to haul on.

'Chase.' This time his name sounded urgent, and there was a cooling against his chest as the heat source pulled back. 'We've got company.'

His eyes ripped open. His hands dropped to his sides as he stepped back abruptly, the air suddenly chilly 'Who?' Damn it. Why couldn't he have one night to himself? With Kristina and no one to interrupt? *Because you're in charge of what happens on board this vessel where patients and medical staff are concerned.*

'Sorry, Chase, but we've got a problem below deck. One of the men is trying to steal food from the kitchen and the cook's going ballistic.' Calvin's words brought Chase back to reality faster than anything else could.

What had he been doing? About to do? Putting Kristina aside, he ran his hands over his face and straightened his back. 'On my way.'

'And that's that. He could've said something before rushing away. One word would've done.' Kristina stared after Chase as he bounded along the deck. 'Good to know where I stand.' Like a sticking plaster for his wounds that could be torn off at any moment.

Except the wound was a long way off healing. She wasn't so naïve as to believe she'd helped him on the first step towards forgiving himself. Only he could do that, and *if* there was anyone able to help him it was Ethan, not her.

Her fingers traced the outline of her swollen lips. Hell, could the man kiss. He'd exploded through her, taking away all sense of time, sound, location. All she'd known was Chase—and wanting more, wanting it all. His mouth, those large, strong hands doing a number on her skin, his erection hard against her soft stomach weren't enough. They'd been in a bubble. Until Calvin had turned up, spoiling the moment, bringing her back to reality in a flash. How she'd heard him calling Chase was beyond her.

If only he hadn't. Then who knew where she and Chase might've ended up? Or what they might've done? She should be thankful they'd been interrupted then, and not five minutes later. But she wasn't. She wanted him. Big time. Not sex. *Lovemaking.* She shivered. Yeah, she'd gone and lost sight of what she should be hanging onto and was starting to fall under his spell.

As for what Chase thought? Who knew? He'd rushed away without a backward glance, putting her in her place quick smart.

Chase had been through a lot. She understood his need to be in control, and wanting to save everyone who came his way. But he had to learn not to beat himself up when he lost a patient. As she'd begun accepting she couldn't have saved Corporal Higgs the day the owner of Merrywood's electrical business had been electrocuted while putting in wires at the garage she'd happened to be going past and she had made amends for failing Higgs by saving George.

Unfortunately, it wouldn't be her showing Chase how to move on. They might have shared kisses beyond her wildest imagination, their bodies might be hollering for each other, but they weren't *going* anywhere together. They had too many hang-ups to be able to have even a half-normal relationship. But she'd happily go for more here in their space. Though now she was coming down to earth she knew they wouldn't be making love here. Too risky that they'd be caught. Some people would say that was half the fun. Not her.

It was time to get some shut-eye. The horizon was lightening, and soon the ship would be alive with more people requiring attention. Another boat had been sighted and was due to be intercepted to remove the refugees later in the morning and she needed to be on her A game.

As if she'd get any sleep with those kisses so vivid in her mind. With how her body had reacted to Chase's touches.

She knuckled her back as she slouched along to her cabin. *Please let me sleep,* was her last thought for the night.

'Kristina, wake up. You're needed in the medical room.' Jane was shaking her arm.

Kristina rolled onto her back and stared at the apparition above her. 'What time is it?'

'You've missed breakfast.' Jane grinned. 'I'm not going to ask who kept you up so late.'

'Get a life,' she muttered. 'I was busy.'

'Sure you were. If it's any consolation, Chase looks terrible, too.'

'You're saying I look bad? How?' There was a low pounding going on in her skull, but how could she *look* a mess? They'd only kissed. *Only* kissed? Those kisses had been right up there with X-rated warnings. Her skin was probably scorched.

'Yuk, now you're looking dreamy. Definitely time you were downing strong coffee and dealing with malarial fevers.' Jane headed for the cabin door. 'If I don't see you in ten, I'll be back to prod you awake again.'

Kristina swung her legs out of the bunk and sat up to drop her head into her hands. Her eyes drooped shut. She forced them open. 'I'll be there. Give me five for a shower, and pour the strongest coffee that machine's capable of.'

'Will do.' Jane disappeared, closing the door behind her with a snap.

Hauling herself upright, Kristina's head floated and her body ached. If this was the result of Chase's kisses she was better off without them. Or had it been the reruns in her dreams that had wiped her out? Whichever, she didn't need any more.

Try telling that to someone who believes you. Imagine what making love with Chase would be like. Her imagi-

nation had already done that, now she was ready for the real thing.

The cold shower went some way to clearing the fog from her brain, and the coffee dispelled the rest, leaving her mind clear to focus on what was important around here—patients. 'That was perfect, Jane.'

'You're welcome.' Her cabin mate winked. 'Come and meet your next patient. He came on board yesterday, didn't complain of any ailments, yet during the night his temperature rose to thirty-eight point five and he developed sweats, chills and abdo pain. I'm thinking malaria so I've taken an EDTA blood and made a film. I'll stain it when it's dry.'

The thin, sweating man curled up on the mattress had a faint yellow tinge to his skin, suggesting his liver was reacting to whatever was causing the other symptoms. Kristina nodded. 'You're right. It looks like a case of malaria.' She'd seen a few since joining the ship. 'We need to determine which type but I'll give him a dose of chloroquine phosphate in the meantime.' It was the drug of choice for all but the rarest form of malaria and no harm would be done by administering it.

'I'll keep wiping him down and trying to get fluids into him. Shall we go for intravenous fluids as well?'

'Definitely. Dehydration needs to be kept at bay.' Kristina went to the drug cabinet and put in the code to activate the lock. Retrieving the chloroquine phosphate, she signalled Jane to check the vial and date, then returned to kneel beside the man. 'I'm giving you an injection,' she said, even though she wasn't sure he could hear her, and wouldn't understand her.

'Thank you.' His eyes flicked open, closed again.

He understood English. Yay. 'Have you had malaria before?'

'Yes.'

'Do you know what type?'

'Ovale?' Again he opened his eyes. 'Not sure.'

'Plasmodium ovale. I'll look at your blood film as soon as it's ready.' Sometimes a blood slide showed many parasites in the red cells, but more often they were difficult to find with less than one per field of a hundred or more red cells. This was work for a lab technician, and there wasn't one available. Chase had studied blood films and haematology so that he could diagnose some of the diseases their patients came with. She knew enough to recognise a parasite in the red cells when she saw one down the microscope and could run them by him for confirmation.

'I'm Kristina, a doctor. What's your name?' She pressed the plunger on the syringe she'd inserted into his arm.

'Abdal Matin.' A sheen of sweat covered his face. 'I worked in England five years ago as a reporter.'

How had he ended up here? It wasn't something she felt she could ask. 'Have you been taking prophylaxis?'

His mouth flattened and anger appeared in his unsteady gaze. 'I took chloroquine until it became impossible to get.'

Even when she had no idea where he'd come from or been, it was on record how difficult getting medical care had become in the places these people came from. 'Jane's going to set you up for intravenous fluids, and I want you to try and drink as much water as possible. You have a high temperature and those sweats aren't helping your fluid levels.'

'Thank you.'

Kristina got herself a top-up of coffee to take through to the tiny cabin where the microscope and glass containers of stain waited. A purple-coloured blood film lay on a blotter, ready to be looked at.

Perching on a stool, she applied a drop of oil to the slide and slid it in place on the microscope. Leaning forward, she focused the lens and began scanning the film, noting higher numbers of white cells than normal, mainly neutrophils and

band forms, confirming the infection her patient had. The platelet numbers appeared normal. The red cells showed no obvious abnormalities but, then, she was no haematology expert. What was important was finding malarial parasites and they weren't exactly waving flags.

Thirty minutes later Kristina stood up to stretch her leg muscles and rub her lower back where the familiar throbbing had started up.

'Nothing?' Chase asked from the doorway.

She let her hand fall away. 'There's still a lot of film to go over.' Glancing over at him, her breath stuck in her throat. At the moment that mouth mightn't be soft but she had the memories, and they were turning her stomach into a swirling mess of need.

'You had breakfast?'

'I'm not hungry.'

His head tilted to one side. 'I could remind you what you said to me the other day on that subject.'

'I need to keep looking for malaria.' Her stomach would reject any food she fed it.

'You can eat and study the slide at the same time.' That wonderful mouth slipped into a smile, aimed directly at her.

And finished off any last hope of eating. 'I'll grab something when I've finished here. The man speaks English, by the way, so we currently have another interpreter, or will when the fever's abated.'

'What nationality is he?'

'I have no idea.'

'Let's hope it's the right one to be of use over the coming days.' The smile widened, lifting the corners of those delicious lips further.

What she wouldn't do for another kiss. 'At the moment he's too ill to be worrying about helping us out.'

Chase stepped into the small cabin, tall and lean and

sexy as hell, making her want to throw herself at him. 'Kristina.' He spoke softly. 'About last night…'

'Kristina, your malaria man is asking for you.' Jane stood where Chase had been moments before.

'Right, thanks.' Her eyes were still focused on Chase.

'We'll talk later.' His smile hadn't faded so he couldn't have been going to say something she didn't want to hear, like 'Sorry for kissing you' or 'That was wrong' or 'Forget the things I told you'. Could he?

That would hurt, she realised in a moment of clarity. The few men she'd dated she'd usually left without a backward glance on her part. This was a jaw-dropping shock. Not that there'd been many males in her life, as in affairs or the like, and none had got close enough to touch her in a way that raised hope and awareness for those wishes of a home and family. Was this what it was like to fall in love? It had better not be. Chase was all wrong for her. Given her history of mucking up her big goals, like joining the army to find a 'family', there was every possibility she'd get this thing with Chase wrong, too. Her parents had not shown her how to get it right.

'Sure.' Stepping around him, making sure not to brush against that delicious body in case he thought she was making a play for him, she headed for the door. 'I'll see Abdal Matin and then grab a sandwich.'

'I've got a few minutes going spare. I'll take a look at the slide.'

'Go for it.' If he found a parasite she'd try not to be disappointed she hadn't discovered it.

'Get out of here. You're needed in the medical area.' There might be a smile beaming out at her but she still felt let down.

She'd been hoping Chase wanted her—in a totally different way from how a patient might. At least he was still smiling. That was unusual in itself.

She'd take what she could get. *Pitiful, Kristina. Really, really pathetic. You're almost begging for his attention.*

'Plasmodium ovale,' Chase informed her when she returned to where he was.

'You found it? Damn, I wanted to do that.'

He shrugged a shoulder. 'That's the knocks you get in this work. Come and have a look.' He pushed the stool back enough for her stand in front of the microscope and study the cells at the other end of the lens. 'The ring form could be any type, but that parasite in the centre of the field? Definitely ovale.'

The purple, blue and red shades of the circle and dots were strong. 'It's incredible how something unable to be seen by the naked eye can cause so much harm to a human.' She glanced over her shoulder and stopped breathing.

Chase's gaze was fixed on her backside, nothing but longing gleaming out of his eyes.

'Chase?' she squeaked.

His head jerked up. 'Um, what were you saying?'

'Nothing.' Important, she added silently.

'I'll get back to the operating table.' The stool rocked as he leapt to his feet and stepped around her.

'Chase, stop it. You don't have to rush away.'

'Yes, Kristina, I do. For your sake, if not mine.'

Watching him stride out of the room as though he was being chased by a malaria-laden mosquito, she sank onto the stool he'd just vacated. Chase had just told her where they stood. Bluntly and purposefully. His beguiling smile didn't mean they had something going between them, had not meant what she'd begun dreaming about.

You didn't want anything happening with Chase. Other than more kisses. And making love.

All off the menu, by the look on his face as he'd fled the cabin.

Might pay to stay away from Chase's corner on deck

tonight. Every night? He could think she was staying away because he was a lost cause. That she couldn't cope with his past. Or he might be relieved because one of them had to see sense and call a halt to this attraction steaming between them.

Tossing her sandwich in the bin, she went to find a patient who needed her undivided attention. Chase could wait. She wasn't done with him, though. Not by a long shot.

CHAPTER FIVE

'I KNOW I should've phoned days ago, but it's bedlam here right now. Anyone would think our quiet little marriage ceremony was competing with the latest British royal wedding. Don't tell people you're getting married until the deed's done,' Claire said breathlessly. 'Honestly, you'd think the whole village had been waiting for ever for me to announce this marriage.'

Kristina laughed away the pain at the idea of her ever having to plan her own wedding. 'Says she who sounds very happy.'

'I am so happy it's scary. And we will have a party at home sometime later, but I won't be wearing a lace train that's twenty metres long or carrying a bouquet that would require a crane to lift. A glass of champagne will be enough, though with junior on board the bubbles will be water, not wine.' Claire paused, then went on in a quieter voice, 'I didn't know people could be so caring. Ethan's having fits about it.'

'I bet he is.' Kristina could imagine him glancing over his shoulder for an escape route. 'But he'll stay. He loves you.'

'I know. I truly believe that.'

Again Kristina had to swallow hard. She was happy for

this woman who'd befriended her on the ship. 'I'm glad for you both.'

'I rang to say you're going to be my bridesmaid. I won't take no for an answer.'

'But you haven't known me very long. You must have other friends for this.'

'No, it's you I want, and shall have. We clicked from the beginning, and that's what matters. Not even the fact that Chase is standing by Ethan on the day will let you out of this.'

He hadn't mentioned it. Was he unhappy about having to stand by her, all dressed up? Come on, they'd kissed and were still on speaking terms. There'd even been a second round of kisses. A frisson of excitement ran through her. Even small weddings had a photographer, didn't they? She'd keep one of those photos of her and Chase in her drawer to take out on the rainy days. 'Thank you. I can't wait.'

'Thanks, Kristina. It means a lot to me.'

'You asking means a lot.' Gulp. *Don't do the sentimental stuff. It gets messy.* 'What am I to do about a dress? Have you got ideas on style and colour?'

'Soft blue and off the shoulder. Anything else is your choice. Don't forget shoes with heels to die for. Make the men salivate.'

'I don't need men drooling over me.' Kristina laughed. Her feet were still more used to heavy-duty boots than killer heels. It really was time to get a girlie life. This could be fun.

'Might make Chase take notice in ways he mightn't have yet.' When Kristina gasped, Claire continued, 'Has he already? Come on. How *is* it going between the two of you?'

'You'd better have a stand-in ready in case I decide not to turn up for your wedding.'

Claire just laughed. 'Touched a nerve, did I?'

It was fun talking like this, even if her friend ignored the boundaries. It could be time to let go of more of her hang-ups. 'We're getting on better than expected.' *Oh, please.* 'We meet every night at Chase's no-go zone on deck.'

'Chase letting you be there says heaps.'

'There have been one or two interesting conversations.' Not to mention those kisses.

Claire went to the heart of the matter. 'What aren't you telling me?'

'That I like Chase a lot, really like him. But I doubt we'll take it very far as he's not into long-term relationships and, to be fair, he's made sure I understand that.'

'Ethan wasn't into them either until I came along and changed his mind.'

'I am not getting—' *Stop. Claire will be upset if you finish that sentence.* It wasn't as though she'd deliberately got pregnant, but she might misconstrue what Kristina had been about to say. 'Chase has told me a little of what happened when their ski team was hit by the avalanche. He has some huge issues to work through. The way I see it, he's not trying to move forward, instead seems focused on the past and how to rectify the impossible.'

Chase had told her that in confidence, but she needed to air her concerns, and to whom better than Claire, who already knew what drove their men? Their men? Chase wasn't hers. Yet there was something between them that went further than she'd ever experienced. Resisting him would be nigh on impossible—if they were ever to get hot and bothered together again.

'I shudder every time I think about that avalanche,' Claire agreed. 'I know the guys are still dealing with what happened and how they sort of hated each other, and are now becoming firm friends, but don't let Chase hold that

up as a reason not to get involved if you're beginning to feel something for him.'

The many times Chase dominated her mind, not to mention her body, had not distracted her enough to put plans on hold for finding somewhere to settle and get a job. There was only one person looking out for her on that score, and that was her. 'You'd make a great agony aunt,' she joked, while the weight of what she might be losing out on dragged at her heart.

'Any time you have questions, you have my number. But, seriously, be open-minded about this. I'm speaking from experience here.'

'Thanks, Claire.' Swallow. Friendship. Wow. 'I've got to go. There's a boatload of refugees coming on board. We'll talk more about the wedding soon.' Without waiting for an answer, Kristina ended the call and slipped the phone into her pocket. Claire was too easy to talk to. Like Chase.

Looking around the deck, her gaze instantly found him. Standing with a nurse and a young man holding his meagre possessions in a ragged pack, Chase looked alone as he issued details of medical requirements. Tall, imposing and in control of all that was around him, there was no doubting his ability to oversee the comings and goings of the ship and its occupants. He was achieving what he desperately wanted, yet there was something sad about his stance. It spoke of disconnection, of deliberate composure to keep everyone at bay, of not letting anyone see the real Chase Barrington.

She was beginning to see behind that mask to the longing and fear, even the love he was capable of if only he'd risk himself. Strange how he allowed her into his corner. Only once had he told her to go away, and she'd chosen to ignore him, and look where that had led. Revelations followed by electric kisses, almost followed by making love. Most times he seemed pleased when she turned up.

Sometimes she thought he was almost relieved, as if needing reassurance she wouldn't let him down. Since he wasn't into relationships it didn't add up. Could be she read too much into what for him was simply a friendship. A friendship with hot kisses and nearly sex? No, they'd moved beyond being pals. What came next was anyone's guess.

Chase turned, his eyes meeting hers. Then his mouth lifted into a soft smile that warmed her to her toes. That smile was genuine, and to be treasured. Bit by bit the man behind the caution was coming to light. Their kisses had softened her determination to remain strong against people who could hurt her, and had her wondering if Chase might be the one to eventually tear all her barricades down. Talk about a huge leap of trust that she wasn't ready to chance this side of the next ten Christmases. But she could give him a smile filled with happiness in return.

His eyes widened and his smile deepened. She'd get on with the day in a cheery frame of mind, and stop wondering if Chase was right for her. If he was, then things would unfold at the right time. If he wasn't, they'd move on from each other, maybe cross paths occasionally at events like the wedding. The naming ceremony for Claire and Ethan's baby perhaps. As if it would be that simple.

Claire had found her soul mate. What was that like? Finding a man who'd accept her for who she was and give her the love she craved? She'd have to love him back as strongly, or what would be the point? A rigid relationship like the one Kristina had with her parents wasn't happening. Chase might be aloof but he didn't do cold, much as he tried to pretend differently.

Did she truly believe that? The dreams that romped through her head at night where they were always together— working, playing, living—said so. In those he was always fun, kind and laughing. Which wasn't likely to become real.

Dreams were nothing more than uncontrolled hope flitting through her mind when she wasn't in a position to stop them.

Moving away, she vowed to get on to looking into GP vacancies as soon as she had time to herself. It wasn't fair to expect Jarrod to come up with what she required.

'Why aren't there any jobs available where I'd like to live?' Kristina muttered as she shuffled her backside on the hard deck and leaned against the bulkhead, trying to stay out of the sun, still strong as it slid beyond the horizon.

'You being too picky?'

Chase. Where had he come from? How long had he been standing there? Why hadn't her radar warned her? 'Probably.'

'What are you looking for?' He sat down beside her, stretching those long legs for ever, and folding his arms across that expansive chest that stretched his T-shirt over interesting muscles that she itched to touch, to kiss, to lick.

In other words, diverting her attention to places it had no right to go. 'Something permanent.'

'So you've said. Are you sure you want to settle down? No more travelling the world, using your medical skills to help others?'

Did he have to make it sound so dull? So ordinary? It was what she longed for. 'Yes. My skills are just as useful at home, working in a medical centre, as here.'

'Home as in Manchester?'

'I have no wish to return to Manchester.' Now she looked up from the website listing medical positions all over Britain that she'd been scrolling through and focused entirely on her inquisitor. 'I prefer the south of England.'

'A small town like Merrywood.' When she gasped he added, 'It's written all over your face.'

She looked away. 'It can't be.' She'd become an expert at hiding her feelings.

'Was your boarding school in Manchester?'

'Yes, but Dad wasn't most of the time so no weekend catch-ups. Anyway, that's history, doesn't pertain to anything here. My problem is that I'll be unemployed in a little over four weeks, and that makes me nervous. I like to know where I'll be at any point in time. I plan my year to know what I'll be doing and where I'll be doing it, except I only got close to six months sorted this time.' She stared at him, hoping he'd understand her need to find her little spot in the world, a place that didn't require major worries about how to survive while making sure others could, too.

'You just argued with yourself. Your past is driving your future.' Breaking eye contact, his head tapped the bulkhead as he tipped it back and stared out in front of them.

The sea and sky had merged on the horizon so it was impossible to tell where one started and the other finished. 'Sometimes that's how I feel,' Kristina conceded. 'What you said is true for everybody.'

'Why this need to settle down?'

'It's what women in their thirties do.' She glanced at him. 'And, no, the biological clock's not ticking. I've been looking for somewhere to call my own since the day I overheard the girls at boarding school saying I didn't belong in their dorm, that I was dumb.' Following on from her mother not wanting her and her dad dumping her into someone else's care, the girls had only confirmed what she'd learned. She wasn't lovable, or likable.

Chase took her hand in his, clasped them together on his thigh. 'So why the army? Why *Medicine For All*? Why didn't you buy a house in any town and join the local medical practice when you qualified?'

'Shouldn't you be checking on patients? Or organising rosters?' She couldn't find the strength to withdraw her hand. It felt as though it was in the right place. Neither

should she continue talking about her past. But there was nothing of interest to divert her attention on the medical jobsite. She closed that down with her free hand.

'The rosters are up to date, all vacancies filled again. The refugees are in capable hands or sleeping.'

Rare indeed for Chase to be letting go that easily. The blue in the sea was darkening to black, whereas in the sky it was as though the colour was slowly draining away to leave behind a star-studded canvas. Relaxing, she gave in to the need to talk.

'A recruitment officer for the armed forces was at a school where I was working on an immunisation programme and we had lunch together at the back of a classroom away from raging teenagers and bored teachers. He talked about the services and how he'd belonged to the army since he'd left school and it felt more like family than his parents and brothers ever had.' That had struck a chord with her. 'He mentioned how everyone in the unit always had his back in a way he'd never known before. I signed up within two months.'

'Was he right?'

'Yes.' She sighed. 'And no. I always knew the men and women around me had my back, wherever we were stationed. I belonged to them, to the greater picture. We ate, drank, worked together twenty-four seven, to the point it got claustrophobic and I'd wish I was out in the real world again. Until I was discharged. Obtusely then I wanted back in.' Much like the day her father had deposited her at that boarding school and told her she had to stand on her own feet and not be so needy. Apparently wanting to be loved by her parents was wrong.

'There were no jobs you could've done if you'd stayed in?'

'Nothing I wanted. The medical side was basic on home base. My back injuries stymied me from ever again being

able to carry a twenty-five-kilo pack for hours on end. There were desk jobs, except pen-pushing didn't appeal.'

'It's always the paperwork that rubs me up the wrong way, but there's no avoiding it, I'm afraid. Not that I've found anyway.'

'When you do, copyright the idea. You'll make a fortune.'

'Now, there's a thought. But what would I do with said fortune? I'd want to be philanthropic but it takes time to look into charities and make decisions about who to donate money to. Time that would keep me away from surgeries and medical cases.'

'Which is what keeps you moving.'

Chase's hand jerked around her fingers. 'Yes.'

Kristina left it at that and studied the stars appearing in their thousands.

'There's a shooting star.' Chase pointed to the west.

The glittering light shot across the sky. 'I'm making a wish,' she chuckled. *To finally find what I've been searching for.* Her hand tightened around Chase's.

'Don't tell me what you wish for or it won't come true.'

Not a chance. Some things were best kept secret regardless of the consequences. Now she wanted another star on the move, because suddenly she really, really wanted to wish for Chase to kiss her. She could make the first move but what if he pushed her away? What if he told her the other night couldn't be repeated? Instigating a kiss then being rejected would humiliate and hurt. To hell with it. She'd take the risk.

But as she turned toward Chase he stood up and leaned down to tug her gently. 'Join me up here, will you?'

Then she was in his arms and his mouth was covering hers. No need for another shooting star. Certain dreams came true because they were meant to. Kristina gave up thinking and succumbed to Chase and his mouth, his chest

pressing against her breasts and those hands splayed across her back. The hard rod pressing into her stomach. Heat spread slowly throughout her body, warming her in places that had been cold for far too long. This she could get to like permanently.

Her lungs squeezed tight. What?

Chase's mouth left hers. 'Kristina? You all right?'

Permanently? With Chase? It wasn't happening. *Am I all right?* 'Absolutely,' she whispered, before returning her mouth to his, afraid he'd walk away before she'd finished with him. More than all right. As long as she didn't think about that permanent word.

Chase deepened the kiss and she forgot everything except the man delivering this wonder. Forgot common sense, disregarded the warning bells clanging in the back of her head, and went with him to some place she'd never been before. And that was only with a kiss.

'Have you decided what you're doing for your days off?' Jane asked Kristina as the two of them worked on a young girl with a fever related to an infection in a wound in her thigh.

At the next bed Chase palpated a man's belly and held his breath as he listened for Kristina's answer. It was a question he'd been pondering, with an idea he wasn't certain was right brewing in the back of his mind.

Kristina drew up a dose of antibiotics. 'I'm thinking I'll do some sightseeing around Marseille, might even go to Nice for a day or into Italy. The trains run all the time. And I'll soak for hours in the spa at the hotel where MFA has booked our rooms.'

He had his answer. Two days before everyone headed off in different directions and he was already thinking how much he'd miss Kristina. Those times they had to themselves on the deck held him enthralled. 'The idea of the

break is to get well away from the ship and the problems it's connected to.' The words spilled out of his mouth. True though they were, he suspected Kristina might be avoiding going back to England for her time off because there was no one she especially wanted to catch up with.

'I won't be on board, I'll be at the hotel. What's everyone else doing?' She was good at redirecting a conversation when it got too close for comfort.

Jane answered, 'I'm heading to Majorca, where my boyfriend's got an apartment. He's flying out from London to be with me. Three days of sun, swimming and lots of sangria. What more could a girl want?'

'It sounds sublime.' Kristina laughed, but there was a hint of sadness in the depths of her eyes.

Chase hated seeing that. He wanted to cheer her up, make her laugh. Stepping away from his patient, he told them, 'I'm going to my mother's sixtieth birthday shindig.'

After hearing about Kristina's sad family life, he'd rethought how lucky he was and had given in to the demands from Libby and his father to turn up for his mother's special occasion. Feeling like the heel he was for avoiding most family gatherings, he'd been mortified at his mother's joy. He really had become a terrible son, and while he believed he was protecting himself from further pain there no denying he'd hurt his family in the process. 'I'll be staying at my parents' farm.'

'Nice.' Kristina wiped the girl's arm and slid the needle in. The girl didn't wince.

'Want to join me?' he asked into a sudden silent moment. It was awkward because whatever her answer everyone would hear it, and know he'd got friendly with her when it was general knowledge he didn't do friendships. Except now he did. Reid had refused to be pushed away, had insisted they had a lot to work on and an underlying

respect for each other despite Nick's death hanging be-
tween them. Despite, or because of?

During the weeks Ethan had been on board he'd begun
to question everything he'd held onto since the tragedy and
had realised how much he admired Ethan and always had,
that what he'd believed to be strong dislike when they had
been teens had actually been envy because the guy had
been a better skier than him. None of that made him feel
any better about himself.

Kristina's eyes widened and the empty syringe shook
in her hand. 'What did you say?'

Here was the chance to backtrack, to reword the invi-
tation. He didn't do inviting women to his parents' home
on those rare occasions he visited. His mother and Libby
would be asking questions there were no answers to. 'Want
to go to Somerset for our down time? You already know
half the clan.'

*Get that, anyone listening in? Kristina's no stranger
to my family. This is a friendly invitation, not what you
might be thinking.*

Kristina stared at him as though he'd lost his mind.

He had. He was going to regret it if she answered yes.
Though right now disappointment was gathering like
storm clouds the longer she remained quiet.

The silence around them grew, as if everyone was wait-
ing for Kristina's answer. When Chase glanced around he
saw one or two people watching them but most were en-
grossed in patients—or pretending to be. Returning his
gaze to Kristina, he held his breath.

'Thank you for offering but I'll stay in France.'

His gut dropped. So did his heart. Why? 'Okay, if that's
what you want, but in case you change your mind the offer
remains until nine tomorrow morning when I leave for the
airport.' Relief should be flooding in at her turning him
down. Instead he felt piqued. Did he really want Kristina

visiting his parents? Libby wasn't known for keeping her mouth shut when it came to her brother; all part of her agenda to make him get over the past and return home to settle. As for his mother, she'd see Kristina as a challenge, a woman to get onside. Still, the disappointment at his offer being declined was growing.

'Thank you.' The syringe rolled between her fingers.

'Careful. You could do yourself some damage with that.' Returning to his patient, he was soon left looking for something else to do. Seeing the doctor rostered to assist him with some minor surgical procedures shortly, he tracked through the waiting refugees. 'Calvin, see you in ten?'

There was a list as long as the table of these procedures to be done but since the cleaners had taken over scrubbing out the area after the last shift knocked off, they weren't able to start earlier.

'Not long now,' Chase told patients as he strode past, hands forced open, a tight smile stretching his face. What was wrong with joining him for a few days' R and R? 'Afterwards there'll be meals waiting for you,' he added when he noticed one of the men repeating everything to the others. Worried smiles broke out. They had yet to learn that when he gave his word it would be kept, and by the time they did they'd gone from the ship and on to whatever awaited them next.

A little after two, Chase and Calvin downed tools and went to grab a bite to eat. 'That was some line-up,' he muttered around his sandwich. He ached from head to toe from standing over the operating table for so long, but at least this intake would be ready to leave the ship when they docked at Marseille. 'You'd think I'd be used to it.'

'Throw in the late nights we work as well and the hours stack up really quickly.'

Kristina and Freja wandered into the room, picked up

plates of salad and bread rolls and came towards them. Both of the girls looked as exhausted as he felt. It was definitely time for that break.

'We had twin girls this morning,' Freja told them with a smile. 'So pretty.'

Kristina sat at the furthest end and tore into her roll hungrily.

'You helped with the birth?' Chase asked, because he wanted to hear her sweet voice.

Her ponytail swung as she shook her head. 'I've been assisting Jorge with vaccinations. Hope that's all right?'

'Of course it is.' He couldn't remember what she was rostered on, but he had no problems with what she'd done.

'I'll get to the children and their check-ups as soon as I've finished lunch.' Kristina lifted a water bottle to those wonderful lips and guzzled half the contents, her eyes closed.

Desire swiped him; hard and sharp. The air hummed. His lungs didn't know whether to breathe in or out. It would take one look from her and he'd be leaping up to sweep her into his arms and race along to his cabin where he'd make love to her, long and deliciously slow—if he had the stamina to hold on for long and slow.

Kristina yawned. 'Sorry.'

Chase collected his scattered brain cells and pulled himself together. This was absolutely silly. Losing control in front of staff in a place where he couldn't do a thing about what was ripping him apart, with a woman who kissed like a she-devil and had then said she wouldn't go home with him was doing his head in—not to mention other parts of his taut body.

Why wouldn't she go to Somerset? Though if this was how he reacted in a dining room where half a dozen medics were eating lunch then he should be grateful. He wouldn't

be able to keep his hands to himself as they walked in the fields or sat at the local, having a beer.

Right now he needed to be busy. Very busy. Carefully adjusting his trousers before standing, he took his plate to the dishwasher, trying not to watch Kristina as she sat, chewing slowly, her eyes still half-shut, exhaustion leaking out of her like sauce on an upside-down pudding.

Grabbing a coffee, Chase headed for his office and the pile of paperwork that had come in on the helicopter that morning. Along with the papers there'd been a load of medical supplies they'd run out of due to the unprecedented number of minor surgeries performed over the last three days. At the time he'd have preferred that the satchel had been dropped on the other side of the railing so it could have sunk to the bottom of the sea, but now he was glad of something to occupy his restless mind.

Not that work calmed his rampant hormones. Hopefully getting deeply engrossed in refugee numbers and the amount of flour Pierre needed would eventually settle everything back into place. Until next time Kristina was in his breathing space.

'Chase, got a minute?' Kristina stood in the doorway.

No, his mind roared. 'What's up?' he said aloud. Now, there was a loaded question. He shifted from one foot to the other.

Her tongue wetted her bottom lip. 'Please, don't think I'm being ungrateful, turning down your offer.'

'I don't. But the dogs are going to be disappointed.'

'What?' Her head flicked back so she was staring at him, and then a soft smile lightened the moment, made him fight to stop himself wrapping his arms around her. 'You've got dogs?'

'Not me, my mother. She's bananas about her two German shepherds, and they go crazy around visitors, especially those who take them walking in the fields.'

'Low blow, mister. I love dogs. Once I settle I'm getting one, maybe two.' Her eyes were alight with excitement.

'So you might change your mind about going to the farm—because of dogs, and not me?' He grinned to show no hard feelings, and made a mental note to buy the biggest, juiciest bones in the village if she said yes to going with him.

'You push a hard bargain. But...' Her shoulders rose slowly. 'But I have a dress to buy, and I still need to look into finding a job.'

'You can do that in Somerset as easily as in Marseille.' At least his knees weren't on the floor as he all but begged. 'I know how much you want to resolve the employment problem, but there's nothing wrong with having some fun while you're doing it.'

'You're persistent, aren't you?'

'I've been known to be.' Usually when it was to get something for a patient, not when it came to a beautiful woman he couldn't get out of his head. But he'd never been faced with this dilemma before and was like a blind man trying to follow a track through the forest.

'Jarrod told me to drop by once I'd finished with MFA.'

'Kristina, can you take a look at Abdal Matin when you've got a moment?' A nurse appeared between them. 'His temperature's spiking again.'

'Coming right now.' She locked thoughtful eyes on him. 'Talk later.'

His heart sank. That meant she was still saying no to his invitation. He had to accept it, or risk looking like a prize prat.

So Jarrod kept in touch with her. He'd sung Kristina's praises when she'd worked for him. Who wouldn't? She'd do anything for her patients, and Chase believed she'd do the same for a partner and any children they might have. Lucky guy, whoever that man might be. Because she would

meet someone to love and care about her. How could she
not when she was so beautiful, inside and out?

You could be that man.

Using his heel to slam the door shut, he stomped across
the narrow space to the desk. He did not want to be that man.

You're sure about that?

Very. His heart might get a few palpitations when they
kissed, his body definitely lusted after hers, his dreams
were filled of images of Kristina, his hands always want-
ing to reach for her—but he would not get emotionally in-
volved. He wasn't ready to stop roaming the world, saving
injured people. He never would be as long as the night-
mares about that night on the mountainside persisted.

Nick had never got to win gold at the skiing champi-
onships, hadn't fallen in love, or studied to become the
architect he'd wanted to be, or had had children—all be-
cause his best friend hadn't been able to save him, try as
hard as he did.

Sorry, Nick. So damned sorry.

Time to sign the contract that'd take him to another
continent at the end of summer.

Chase dug his phone out and punched a number. 'Ethan,
got a minute?'

'Sure. What's up?'

Not answering that. He shifted in his chair. 'Nothing.
Just thought I'd give you a call.' No excuses needed this
time. 'I could do with some sensible talk.'

'So Kristina's giving you grief. I like it.'

He should've left the phone in his pocket and sat on it.
'I don't.'

'We going to talk about this?'

Deep breath. 'I invited her to the farm. She turned me
down.'

'Don't give up at the first knock, man. Be as stubborn
about this as you are about work.'

'Like you?' Finally Chase began to relax. This was why he'd phoned his friend. 'I recall you opting to be there but not as a couple when Claire announced she was pregnant and keeping the baby whether you wanted it or not.'

'Watch and learn. If you want Kristina, go after her, be persistent until you win or lose.'

There was the million-dollar question. Did he want her? 'Yes.' The word sighed out of his throat. Yes.

CHAPTER SIX

'I'M GOING SHOPPING in Marseille tomorrow for my brides-maid dress,' Kristina told Claire over the phone. 'I'll take photos if I find something special and email them to you for your approval.'

'Whatever you're happy with I'll like,' Claire replied. 'Have you docked already?'

'The city lights are getting closer by the minute.' She leaned on the rail in the space on deck and wished there was something more exciting to look forward to than buying a dress. Which was grossly unfair to her new friend. She dug deep for enthusiasm. 'Is sky blue still your colour of preference?'

'Unless you think you'll look hideous in it then yes. It's fashionable this season so it shouldn't be hard to find something.'

'If I don't have success here, I can try Nice or Genoa.'

'Remember to get something sexy, blow Chase's socks off. And his boxers.'

Kristina laughed hollowly. 'Yeah, right.' Her palm rubbed the scar line on her thigh.

'Kristina? Are you all right? Is something wrong?'

The concern in Claire's voice nearly undid her. 'I'm fine. Truly. With three days' leave about to start, why wouldn't I be?'

'Because you'll miss Chase.'

'Says who?'

'You weren't listening.' Claire paused. When Kristina neglected to fill in the silence, she continued, 'Still fancy him?'

'Yep.'

'The two of you need to get on with it, work whatever this is that you're denying out of your systems. Or make it something that's impossible to walk away from.'

This time Kristina was quick to speak, afraid of what else her friend might have an opinion on. 'Forget writing for an agony aunt column, you should try writing a romance. You've got the talent for making up stories.' Impossible to walk away from? She was already starting to think leaving Chase at the end of her twelve weeks was going to be hard.

This time Claire didn't laugh along with her. 'What's the problem? You're not sounding one hundred percent happy, so spill.'

Kristina glanced around, mindful Chase would come out here once he'd finished his paperwork. She was alone. But then her extra-sensory perception had already told her that. Chase only had to step onto the deck and her body would thrum with excitement. 'He invited me to go home with him. It's his mother's birthday and there's a party planned.'

'That's wonderful. You'll have a great time. Don't you already know his sister and her family?'

'You weren't listening,' she remonstrated. 'I'm staying at the hotel MFA has booked in Marseille to go sightseeing and shopping.'

'Come on, Kristina. Take this opportunity to have some fun. As in real, let-your-hair down fun.' Her laughter was naughty and left nothing to Kristina's imagination about what that fun should be.

She wanted to agree, to accept Chase's invitation and enjoy herself without worrying about getting a job or finding the right dress for the wedding or whether she'd ever find a town to call home. But the consequences? Suddenly she said, 'I was hasty in turning him down.' Then hadn't known how to retract without showing Chase how her increasingly mixed emotions were screwing with her head.

'You're afraid of where it might lead, of being hurt. But you'll get nowhere if you don't take a chance. Look at me. I was afraid Ethan would walk away and now I'm planning a wedding and dealing with morning sickness every afternoon.'

'Whoa, slow down, will you? It's only a weekend with people I mostly don't know, not a love fest with a man who has me in the palm of his hand.' Scratch that last bit. He only had to look at her and she'd melt into a pool at his feet, into his arms, against that lean, muscular body.

'Stop holding back. Get out there and live a little.'

Could she do that without coming a cropper? She'd give up parts of herself for him, but not her need to be in control of her life. Going to Somerset with Chase would be like putting a match to petrol, and she'd grab it with both hands. It was the afterwards that frightened her. There were no guarantees. They might fall head over heels in love with each other and ride off into the sunset, or they could say that was good, thanks very much, and get on with the last three weeks on *SOS Poseidon*, but most likely she'd settle further into the depths of love beginning to spread through her head and her heart, and then she'd be lost. Unable to get back on track and finally make her life happen. 'It's not that simple, Claire.'

'Yes, it is. What have you got to lose that you haven't already?'

My heart. 'My sanity.'

'Sure you haven't already?' Claire asked in all serious-

ness. 'A little nudge in a different direction doesn't necessarily mean getting hurt, and it might find you something fabulous you've never expected.'

Kristina cut in. 'Don't you dare say look what happened to you two again.'

'I don't need to. You're already thinking about it. Now, a certain someone is indicating it's time to go for a stroll around the village before hitting the sack. Text me when you make up your mind about what you're doing.'

'I already told you.' But Kristina was talking to herself. The distinct sound of a phone being cut off was the only reply she got. *Thanks, friend.*

She stretched her legs one at a time, the left one protesting at the effort, then she stood with feet wide and bent over into the V pose of Downward Facing Dog. With her hands flat on the deck and her butt sticking up, she tried to clear her mind of everything but banishing the aches in her leg and back. She needed quiet space in her head to get back on track.

'I brought you tea.'

She whipped upright, wobbling on her feet as her head caught up with the sudden change from hanging down to being upright. Chase stood a metre away, holding two mugs, looking like he was caught in headlights. How long had he been there? Her cheeks burned. He should be in his office, not gaping at her rear end. 'I hoped you were giving this a miss tonight.'

He shook his head abruptly, and tea spilled onto the deck. His eyes were still too wide, and there was a distinct look of want turning them to forest green. 'I've finished the paperwork.' His voice had darkened. Sexy.

'Oh.' She hadn't got that message.

'That stretch helping?'

It had until he'd turned up. Though now she could forget the aches in her back and thigh because the tension in

her stomach was taking over, sending pulses of heat to her core. She nodded, speech beyond her.

'Here.' He pressed a mug into her hand and turned to lean on the rail, his mug clasped in both hands as he stared across the narrowing gap between them and Marseille.

It was a miracle she didn't tip the tea all over the place. Her knuckles whitened and the mug steadied. Now what? Keep quiet and see what he said. That wasn't hard considering the block on her brain and the pounding in her chest.

'That's a beautiful sight.'

He was talking about the panorama before them, wasn't he? 'Cities look so exciting from a distance. All those lights have me guessing at what's going on in the streets.'

'Want to go see when we dock? We could have a drink in a wine bar or go to a jazz club.'

Definitely talking about the city. Not her butt. 'You're into jazz?'

'What's not to like about it?' He continued watching the approaching shoreline, like he didn't know where else to look.

'I wouldn't know.' Music wasn't her thing.

'Then it's time to find out.' He glanced at his watch. 'Meet me at the gangway in thirty.'

She hadn't seen that coming. 'You're on.' Just like that she had a date—with Chase Barrington. The only man she wanted to go out with. What to wear? Her pack hadn't come filled with dresses and fancy shoes, just T-shirts, shorts and sneakers. 'See you soon.'

She tore down the stairs. 'Jane,' she yelled as she shoved their cabin door wide. 'I need clothes to wear to a night club.'

'I've got a skirt that might fit you—don't dance too vigorously unless you want to show what you've got. Who are you going with?'

Kristina caught her breath and eyeballed her cabin mate, trying for stern. 'Chase.'

'Brilliant.' Jane held her hand up, palm out.

Caught up in the moment, Kristina raised her own hand, slapped Jane's in return. 'Let me see this skirt. And thanks. I'll have it back before you leave for your flight in the morning.'

'Don't worry. I can replace it in Monaco. It's not the prettiest skirt you'll have ever worn but it beats those denim shorts you're so fond of. Now, a top. We'll go and see Freja. She's got enough clothes to go round all the females on board.'

'Really? Why?'

Jane's laugh would've been heard all over the ship. 'She likes to be prepared. Why not when the men are falling all over her?' She knocked on a cabin door. 'Freja, you in there? We need help.'

Chase watched the vision coming towards him and felt the tension holding him stiff let go and a low whistle rush across his lips. 'You look stunning.'

Kristina grinned. 'Not a bad effort considering what was in my half of the shoebox-sized wardrobe.'

He held out his hand. 'Let's have some fun. I can't believe you haven't listened to jazz.' He couldn't believe they were going on a date.

Her fingers tightened around his. 'I'm open to new experiences.'

There was a plus. Though how many new ones they'd face tonight was anyone's guess. One step at a time. Chase blinked. How many steps did he plan on taking? He wasn't thinking only about tonight. But she'd already turned down his invitation for the weekend.

He waved down a taxi and helped Kristina inside, trying not to stare at her delightful derrière. But how could

he not when it was right there; rounded, filling out the red skirt perfectly?

The jazz club was heaving when they arrived, standing room only and a queue for the bar. 'Welcome to downtown Marseille,' he said against her ear so he was heard. That he got a whiff of pine and roses was a bonus. 'What would you like to drink?'

'A mojito would be great.'

'Wait here, and I'll try to be quick.'

'I'm coming with you or we might never see each other again.' Her hand slid effortlessly back into his and she stayed close as they pushed through to the bar.

'There's a bar upstairs and one through that door,' the barman told Chase as he mixed Kristina's drink. 'Different bands at each and you might find some seating upstairs.'

'*Merci,*' Chase said. 'We'll take a look.'

The only available chairs were at a table with three other couples, who happily let them join the group. Chase settled Kristina before sitting beside her and propping his elbows on his knees, his chin in his hand. 'This is a jazz club.'

'No complaints so far.' She tossed him a saucy smile.

Was she flirting with him? Two could play that game. 'I don't intend to give you anything to criticise,' he gave back, and felt strangely happy when she laughed.

'Sure of yourself, aren't you?'

'Oh, yeah.' What sort of man would admit to the butterflies that had come to life in the last minute? A woman didn't want an insecure guy trying to woo her. Wait, he was wooing her now? He sure was. Only for tonight. He'd see where they got to on mojitos and bourbon and loud music and hot moves on the dance floor. If they returned to the ship and separate cabins with the narrow uncomfortable bunks then that was how it would end. Standing, he held out a hand. 'Let's dance.'

'This could get tricky. These shoes aren't mine and

they're a little tight.' But she was already heading for the dance floor, her hand pulling at his.

Chase couldn't take his eyes off her as she raised her arms and rolled with the music. She mightn't be familiar with jazz but her body certainly knew how to move. He felt clumsy beside her, his own movements heavy and awkward, and he'd thought he knew what he was doing on a dance floor. But it didn't matter. No one would be watching him, all eyes would be on his partner. But, boy, did she know how to swing those hips and push out her breasts and move her hands in time to the music that seemed to get louder and louder. He was lost. In her. In the picture before him. In the music that she was responding to as though she'd been dancing to jazz all her life.

When Kristina whirled around and wrapped her arms around his neck his hands found her slender waist and he leaned in to kiss her. Who needed bourbon when he had this woman in his grasp? She was an aphrodisiac in a tight skirt and low-cut top, balancing effortlessly on ladder-high heels. Chase tipped his head back and laughed. He had not been this happy in a long, long time.

Kristina heard that laugh, felt it all the way to her toes, and smiled around the bubble of excitement bouncing up her throat. This was Chase as she'd never seen him, letting go and relaxing, having fun, truly enjoying himself. With her. Right now life couldn't get any better. Right now was what it was about. Not yesterday. Not tomorrow. Tonight. Her hands gripped together at the back of his neck and she stretched up to kiss that teasing mouth, to put a stop to the rampant sensations his smile caused in her belly. Much more and they'd have to find a bed, fast.

As her mouth caressed Chase's, those sensations went into overdrive, spinning through her body, touching everywhere, bringing her alive beyond what she'd ever imagined. Yet her limbs still moved in time to the jazz filling

the air. Her feet hadn't stopped from the moment she'd walked onto the dance floor, while her eyes had been fixed on this sexy man holding her with those wicked hands, like he had no intention of letting her go. It felt like they were meant to be together, here, in this club, this city, on this night.

Then the lights flicked off then on again. A loud announcement broke through and brought her upright, still holding onto Chase, afraid to let him go in case that was the end of their time together.

'They're calling final drinks,' Chase interpreted. 'Let's get out of here and grab a taxi before the rush starts.'

She'd have hesitated, reluctant to go, but Chase took her hand in his and rubbed a thumb across the back, and her skin sat up to attention. 'All right.' Did he mean this wasn't the end of their night? 'We could walk. Our wharf's not too far away.'

'Are you sure your feet can stand it? Is your back playing up? You're walking a little lopsided.'

The concern in his voice touched her. She wasn't used to someone noticing and caring. Her back ached like mad and her thigh wasn't happy but she'd get over it. She was not spoiling a wonderful night by moaning about what couldn't be fixed. 'I don't want the night to end, that's all.'

'You're sure about that?' he asked.

'Absolutely.'

'I'm with you.' Chase pulled her up against him and kissed her forehead, then each cheek and finally, finally her mouth.

Oh, yes. She melted against him, kissed him back with all the passion pouring along her veins. So much for not getting involved. Right now there was nothing capable of stopping her. 'You're right. We need a taxi. Now,' she whispered from the side of her mouth, and went back to kissing him.

When she felt one arm lift from her shoulder she continued kissing him, pausing only to clamber into the cab and resume the instant Chase pulled her against him.

Then they were tipping out of the taxi at the security gate on the wharf. Kristina looked around. In the east the sky was beginning to lighten on the dark horizon. 'I can't remember the last time I was out all night.'

Chase placed an arm around her waist. 'I'd say you haven't been living, but it's the same for me. All work and no play makes for sad puppies.'

The guard waved them through. *'Bonsoir, Docteurs.'*
'Bonsoir, Louis.'

They reached the gangway. Chase murmured against her lips before his mouth covered hers, 'Come on. I can't wait any longer.'

'Chase, where the hell have you been?' a robust male voice interrupted them.

Chase ripped his mouth away from hers, though he kept his hands on her shoulders as she wobbled on those shoes, and asked the ship's captain, who was standing at the top of the gangway, 'What's the problem?'

'I've been phoning you for hours. Liam wants to talk to you urgently. He's in Manila and he isn't happy about something,' Josip told him.

The man was never happy about anything. Chase's hand automatically went to his pocket, pulled his phone free. 'Five missed calls.'

'You wouldn't hear it ringing inside the club. We couldn't hear ourselves think.' Not that she'd been doing much of that, unless it had involved the hot male body dancing before her. Hot and full of the promise of more heat. Kristina straightened, stepped back from those steadying hands, a sinking sensation going on in her stomach. Chase was back at work, whether he realised it or not, wanted to be or not. Being available twenty-four seven

was what he did. Tonight had been uncharacteristic, not normal. She followed him up the gangway, trying not to drown in the disappointment flooding her.

He was telling Josip, 'I'm on leave. Have been since midnight.'

'Tell that to Liam. He's in a real mood, I'm warning you.'

Kristina reached the deck and stood watching Chase. The heat between them was gone, evaporated in a dose of reality. Though why should Chase let someone demand he phone them when he was on leave? But she already knew he would never walk away from his responsibilities. This was a timely reminder of how it would be if she took this any further. Her feet weren't yet back on the ground; she still wanted to follow through on their promises to go downstairs together. For her the night was not over. It might be out here where the sky was lightening to a grey shade of blue, but not within herself. No, her body was still afire with need. She laid a hand on his arm. 'Chase?'

Her heartbeat quickened as she watched the play of emotions on his face. Determination was winning. He was going to ignore Liam's calls and finish the night with her.

Then regret took over. 'Kristina, I'm sorry.'

'No, Chase. You don't have to be.' *You can come with me.* 'Phone Liam. I'll wait.'

He leaned in and kissed her. When he drew back his mouth lifted in a wry smile. 'I'll be as quick as I can. If I don't call back, Liam won't stop harassing Josip.'

Relief had her heartbeat slowly quietening. 'Remind Liam you have a life.'

'Unfortunately I don't really. Not outside MFA.' He leaned down to place the softest kiss ever on her lips. 'But for the first time I can remember, I want to. Thanks to you.'

'I'll be topside.' Could they make love in their space?

Most personnel were long gone. No, most likely they'd head to Chase's cabin.

'See you shortly.'

She watched him stalk across to the stairway leading to his office, her hope of finishing the evening in his arms making love still there but cautious, uncertain. So much for having a great night out and then getting over him. All she wanted was more. 'Chase?'

He paused, turned back. 'Kristina?'

'Is your invitation to join you in Somerset still open?' Her heart stopped, her lungs waited.

Caution crept into his eyes. 'Yes, of course.'

Thump, thump. Breathe. 'Then I'll be at the gate at nine. What airline do I book a seat on?'

'Leave that to me. I'll do it while I'm talking to Liam.' The next thing she was being lifted up and swung around in a circle before being placed back on her feet and receiving another kiss, this time on the tip of her nose. 'Somerset, here we come.'

'Multi-tasking? But you're a man.'

'Glad you noticed.'

How couldn't she? 'I'll fix you up for the flights.' They weren't in the sort of relationship where she'd accept him paying for her trip. Probably never would be. No reason not to have a load of fun over the weekend, though.

Up in 'their' space, Kristina toed off the shoes, which were killing her. It'd take more than one night to get used to glam footwear. Leaning on the railing, she soaked up the lights and tooting horns and shouts that was downtown Marseille at this hour, and let her excitement grow. How long would Chase be on the phone? Tempted to go down to his office and sit on his lap while he talked business, she wavered. That might be pushing the boundaries too far, too soon. One fantastic night would not change Chase into a relaxed, let's have fun with no consequences kind of guy.

She hadn't changed that much either, and being tense and nervous would spoil the moment. She'd wait here, let the anticipation in her veins grow and keep her warm.

'Liam, what's so important you have to phone in the middle of the damned night?' Chase growled. The phone was on speaker to allow him to pace around the poky office, trying to pacify the tension in his body that was all about Kristina and her seductive body, and nothing to do with work.

'Interrupt something, did I?'

Damned right you did. The best thing that's happened in a long while. Like for ever.

Chase held back on shouting. Liam would wind him up relentlessly. When he didn't feel like killing the Swiss national, they were friends. 'I'm on leave and was out having a drink with friends.'

Make that a friend who's within minutes of being my lover.

'My apologies. I didn't think beyond needing to talk to you before you left for England.' Liam paused.

Chase didn't rush in to forgive him, just waited and paced.

'We've got a lot to do in the Philippines. The people here are in need of urgent medical help.'

Chase clicked onto the internet and the airline taking him home in a few hours. Might as well get Kristina's ticket sorted while listening to Liam's rant. Once he started there'd be no stopping him. Except this morning his call wasn't going to be a long diatribe. *He* had somewhere to go, a woman to be with, and frustration was making him edgy. He could feel Kristina under his hands, taste that sensational mouth on his lips, wanted, needed her body joined to his. 'Liam,' he snapped.

'I need you in two places at once. We're short of doctors. These people, Chase, they'd break your heart. Today

I saw a three-year-old digging in the gutter for food. The boy needs urgent surgery for a displaced hip.'

The words came through the haze in Chase's head. There was a child who needed *him*. His skills. He pressed 'buy' on the flight details before him. 'You want me in Manila or Ghana next?' He'd be too late for the boy Liam was talking about. There were still weeks to go on the *Poseidon*, helping equally distressed people, but he'd go wherever he was most needed after that. It was why he was here, and would be there, or anywhere come tomorrow and all the days after.

Liam's sigh said it all. 'I guess Ghana. Who knows where you'll go after that? It's months away.'

'Whatever.' Chase saved Kristina's ticket, forwarded it to her phone. Kristina. She was waiting for him. Out in their space. 'I've got to go.' He wanted to make love with her. And then? Walk away? He stared at the screen where his copy of her ticket waited. There'd be no walking away for the next three days. And afterwards? After making love, and the party, and sharing his family, then what? Nothing would change. He still needed to save people.

Those demons still need to be placated, Nick. I can't stop moving from one crisis to the next. Can I?

Liam came through loud and clear. 'I don't like it when you go quiet. What's going on?'

'Sorry, doing two things at once.' It wasn't a lie, but it was the first time his mind was more focused on himself than on what Liam wanted. His gut churned with longing and the sense of missing out on something sensational. His trousers were uncomfortable, evidence of where his mind had been. Kristina.

'You need a break from all this? More than the three-day leave you've started?'

'Not at all.' But did he, though? The last nine weeks had knocked him around. First with Ethan landing in his

life and insisting they sort out the past. That alone was enough to turn a man on his heel and have him running for the Sahara. Then along had come Kristina. Beautiful, mysterious, kind, fun and sexy. Don't forget the sexy. Like that was happening. She had his blood constantly running hot, and his ideas about his life sitting up and scratching at his head, as if to say, 'What am I doing? Do I want to spend the rest of my life going from one tragic place to another, to be always looking after those who can't look after themselves in faraway countries?'

Yeah, he did, because he had to.

'That's a relief.'

No pressure. He couldn't take any more. 'Talk to you later.' Stabbing the 'off' button brought that conversation to an end. But no relief.

Tonight had started out as an evening of drinks and dancing and music, and had ended with kisses, and sex about to happen. Except they'd been interrupted. He should've ignored Josip and Liam. Then he wouldn't have been responsible for the disappointment that had filled Kristina's eyes and face and tugged at her shoulders when she'd realised he would put work before her. He'd said he'd join her on deck, but he'd also let her down. Hell, he'd let them both down.

Chase took the stairs two at a time. Kristina was waiting for him.

But she wasn't. The space was empty, only a hint of her scent to confirm she'd been here.

His heart plummeted. Did she believe he hadn't intended to join her? Why had she left? Looking around, he could see the outlines of bollards and chains. The sun was coming up. His watch showed it'd been nearly an hour since they'd parted at the top of the gangway. Really? Liam had talked for that long?

Kristina must have thought he wasn't coming to her.

He wanted to rail against her for not trusting him, but couldn't. He should've cut the conversation short and joined her, but he hadn't.

He couldn't let the night finish like this. Couldn't. Sex was probably out, but an explanation—no, an apology was needed.

Kristina didn't answer his knock on her cabin door. The handle was locked.

Back in his office he texted her.

Liam took for ever.

No. He deleted the words, started again.

I am truly sorry. Can we try again? In Somerset? Airline tickets in your inbox.

Now he had a weekend to rectify things. If Kristina gave him a chance, which he so wanted. Of all the dumb things to have done, tonight's blunder had to be right up there. How close would he allow Kristina to get if she forgave him? Did they have a great time and walk away from each other come Sunday? Or did he give in to this crawling need coursing through his veins? For the first time in over a year he was going home, taking a woman with him who had his boxers in a twist and his heart holding its breath.

For the first time ever he was beginning to feel there was more to life than sick people in need of him. And it was scary.

CHAPTER SEVEN

'I'VE PREPARED YOU the bedroom next to Chase's,' Verity Barrington told Kristina much later. 'I wasn't sure if you two were friends or something more, so I've covered the bases.'

Kristina squirmed under the older woman's scrutiny. Was a man's mother supposed to say things like that?

There was a twinkle in Verity's eye that did nothing to quieten the hope knocking softly in Kristina's heart. It had started when Chase had apologised deeply as they'd waited for the taxi to take them to Marseille Province airport and it became real when his father, Alec, pulled up in front of the large double-storeyed farmhouse in Somerset and she'd climbed out of the four-wheel drive to stare around, with Chase standing beside her. The green fields where sheep grazed and the large implement sheds where tractors and machinery were stored made her feel she'd done the right thing in coming here. She was spending a weekend in Chase's territory.

'Watch out,' Chase had warned when German shepherds had charged out to greet first him and then her, making her welcome. His parents had accepted her without a barrage of questions, even hugged her on introduction. But that hope lurking in Verity's eyes when she'd mentioned the

sleeping arrangements had Kristina questioning if she'd done the right thing in coming here.

'Thank you so much. I really appreciate you having me to stay.' She wasn't saying a word about bedrooms. For one, she didn't know the answer herself, and, secondly, Chase would put her on the next flight out if she talked about him to his mother.

'This couldn't get further from my cabin. It's enormous and I'm not sharing with Jane, who snores like a hungry pig. Nor are there people all over the place needing attention and fearful of asking for it.'

'It must get quite intense, dealing with those poor people.' Verity's eyes turned in the direction of her son, who was sitting in the conservatory with his father now that dinner was over. 'I know it takes a toll on Chase. Not that he's ever admitted it, but we see it in his demeanour. He's always tired, and doesn't laugh as much as he once did.'

'He takes his work very seriously.'

'Too seriously. While I'm not saying it's wrong, it breaks my heart that he doesn't lighten up a little. It's as though he doesn't want to enjoy life to its fullest.'

Kristina knew exactly where she was coming from. However, it wasn't her place to get involved in a deep and meaningful discussion about Chase. 'It's hard to put aside the things we see on a daily basis, which is why we have these breaks. They're essential to coping.'

'How long have you been on board the *Poseidon*?'

'I've done nine weeks, with three to go before I return to England and find a permanent job.'

'I wish Chase would do something similar.'

How long had it been since this woman had talked about her son to someone other than family? Why choose her? Hadn't she got the message that there wasn't a relationship going on, even if they were spending the weekend together? 'I'm sure he knows what he's doing,' she

said softly, trying not to sound critical. The last thing she wanted was for Verity to turn her back on her. She liked the woman, and not just because she was Chase's mother. She was a charming, warm soul who adored her family and made strangers feel comfortable.

'I'll make a pot of tea. Would you like a cup?' Disappointment clouded the older woman's face.

Regret at having cut Verity off, but having had to before the conversation got out of hand, Kristina smiled. 'I'd love one. Shall I ask the men if they want one?'

'Alec will, but I don't know about Chase.' It was obvious she didn't know a lot of things about her son any more.

So he'd cut himself off from his family in order to stay true to his goal of saving people. Didn't he understand he could do that by living and working full time in Somerset? In the same country even? Saving people didn't mean only those who were in jeopardy of their lives because of politics. Helping a young girl overcome pain from a broken leg was as rewarding as removing a melanoma from a man's back before it metastasised.

'Where have you gone?' Chase stood in front of her.

She shook her head. 'I was coming to ask if you wanted a cup of tea.' Then, before he could ask more and she'd have to lie, she added, 'I'm looking forward to seeing more of the farm.'

'You ever been on one?'

'A couple of times when I was at boarding school I went home for long weekends with a girl who's a distant cousin. I didn't like the horses, too big and scary. But the cows and farm dogs were all right. More importantly, I loved the wide open spaces and how I could yell and laugh and no one heard me.'

'I'll take you to the farthest field tomorrow.'

'Or you could wait until the grandkids get here and

they can compete with Kristina.' Alec laughed. 'Those kids don't know the meaning of quiet.'

'I can't wait to see them again.' She meant it. It would be interesting to watch Chase interacting with them, too. Aloof, or down on his knees, hugging and playing, like he did on the ship? Could he remain uninvolved with them? Or would they knock his memories and fears aside for a short while? 'I met the boys at the medical centre. They certainly know how to create havoc.'

'Sounds like my nephews.' Chase grinned.

Suddenly Kristina's body slumped with exhaustion and it was hard to concentrate. A lack of sleep and being on edge about coming here was taking its toll. Now she'd relaxed everything was catching up. 'I know it's early but I think I'll go to bed, if no one minds.'

'Of course not. Take your tea with you,' Verity said. 'Make yourself at home and don't hesitate to use anything you want.' It was what any good hostess would say but it came with a huge dollop of kindness.

Kristina's eyes watered, and it took strength not to throw her arms around the woman. But she didn't. It might make her seem needy. Which she probably was. Why hadn't her mother been half as loving? Or her father? They did love her. They just had never shown it in the way she needed. It had been there in the trust funds and the expensive education her father had paid for, and the holidays to the luxury apartments her mother lived in with her latest billionaire. They didn't understand she'd have swapped it all for hugs and being cuddled when the cat died and having them watch when she acted in the school play. 'Goodnight, everyone.'

She scarpered to her room before emotion got the better of her, making her act like a blithering idiot. Coming here was beginning to look like a mistake.

'Kristina, wait,' Chase called as she began to close

the bedroom door. 'Are you all right?' He leaned an arm against the doorframe, studying her closely.

'Why wouldn't I be? Your parents are lovely.'

'So it's not their fault you're about to burst into tears?' His smile was gentle and undid the final cord holding in her emotion.

'No way,' she managed as those now familiar arms closed around her and drew her against the broad chest she'd touched last night. Why did she have to get so emotional? 'They're so open and friendly. It's not what I expected since they don't know me.'

'They're always like that, especially Mum. So, now what? Do I walk to my room and forget you're upset? Or shall I stay here and kiss you better?'

Kristina stepped backwards, her arms now firmly holding Chase, not wanting to let him go anywhere but up against her in her room. 'Option two.' She was only referring to a kiss, wasn't she? Yes, she had to be. For the sake of her head and heart. Not that she'd given those a thought last night when they'd been speeding back to the ship.

Bending towards her, Chase brushed his lips across hers and drew back a little. 'What made you sad?'

'Don't talk. Please,' she added, breathless around the electricity zipping throughout her body. Placing her mouth on his to shut him up and abate that current now debilitating her, she closed her eyes and went with the kiss. Went with being lost in Chase's arms, letting go of everything else, aware only of them.

A groan erupted between them, and opening her eyes she saw the happiness on Chase's face, in his eyes, and was happy to have given him that…and because his hands were circling her waist and his broad chest pressing against her breasts and awakening her further.

Kristina ripped her mouth away from his and stared at him. Making love was moments away—if she gave in to

what she was feeling. It would be as easy as taking two steps and sinking onto the bed. She wanted it, needed Chase naked against her, pushing into her, taking her to great heights. And yet… 'Can we talk? I mean, I don't think I'm ready.'

His thumb rubbed across her lips. 'Damn.' He smiled. 'But it's okay. I think I understand.'

'I don't,' Kristina admitted, reluctant to remove her hands from him, wanting his strength and warmth. She backed away. 'I'm sorry.'

There was confusion and something she couldn't identify in his gaze. His voice was rough when he replied, 'Don't be. You're being honest, as you always are.'

If she was honest she'd admit to being afraid of where this could lead, scared of having her heart broken, of being left alone again. Better not to have loved than to love and lose him. Yet all she wanted was to fall onto the bed with Chase in her arms and forget the nagging memories from the past, to believe in a future filled with hope. She'd had time to think about this on the flight. She looked at him long and hard. If only she had the guts to follow through on the longing filling her from head to toe. If only. Early that morning nothing would've stopped her. What a difference a day could make. 'Goodnight, Chase,' she whispered.

'See you in the morning.' But he didn't move, remained standing there, watching her, a question in his eyes.

'What?' she asked finally.

He shook his head. 'It doesn't matter.'

The door clicked shut behind him and she was left feeling that she'd missed something big. 'I'm sorry,' she whispered.

She'd been looking out for herself. Sinking onto the bed, she hugged herself tight. And cursed silently. The more she came to know Chase the more she believed he was right for her—if he wasn't so determined to be alone.

Not that Verity had intended to but she'd reminded Kristina of the reasons she shouldn't fall in love with him. If it wasn't already too late. Double whammy, that. If this emotion that kept flooring her, stalling her was love, she'd found it with the wrong man. It had sneaked up and snared her when she wasn't looking.

Crawling into bed, she tugged the covers up to her chin and concentrated on forgetting Chase and his potent kisses, tried to think about the email she'd received from Jarrod that morning, asking if she'd drop into the medical centre tomorrow and catch up with everyone. There was something he wanted to discuss with her. Could there be a position going in Merrywood? A permanent one? If there was, how did she feel about it? Ha, that was one thing she did know the answer to.

It was exactly what she wanted, would be the perfect opportunity to get on with her life. She knew the staff, liked the locals, and could buy a cottage to suit her needs. She'd live alone. She'd meet people, and maybe a man would come along she would fall in love with.

Chase.

No, not Chase. She should never have come here. Now she had something else to put behind her.

Could be that she was getting ahead of herself. Jarrod might only want to catch up and offer her more locum work. And these feelings for Chase might be a figment of her overactive imagination.

Chase got up with the sun to take the dogs for a walk along the lane leading around the copse behind the house. So much for catching up on sleep. Impossible when Kristina reigned supreme in his head.

They'd come close to falling into bed together. So close he could still taste it on his tongue, feel it in his veins. But she'd backed off. That had nearly crushed him. He'd

wanted her very badly, and he'd have sworn she felt the same. If not for Liam's phone calls the night before, they would've made love in his cabin. He'd have touched her everywhere, tasted her skin, felt her need, and held her to him as he pressed into her. He'd have known her intimately.

But he hadn't, though he wanted to more than ever. But he'd never force her to do something she wasn't one hundred certain about. Kristina had to come to him willingly. And had to want to make love as much as he wanted her. That was the scary thing. Because he did want Kristina, all of her, so damn much it hurt. He longed for the lovemaking, the laughter, the sadness, the history—and then a future.

'A future?' he roared at the blue sky looking down on him.

The dogs leapt, stared at him, their legs tense and shaking.

'Sorry, boys, but you don't know what it's like to be so damned afraid of grasping the chance at a future that might be on offer.' If only he could find the guts to front up to Kristina and lay these mixed-up feelings before her.

What do you reckon, Nick? Am I being stupid to think there might be a future with Kristina?

His head moved rapidly from side to side. It couldn't happen. That'd be a disaster. The desire crawling through his veins would become love, and he couldn't honour that in the way Kristina deserved. She needed a man at her side all the time, not when it pleased him to come home. She was not interested in travelling to different countries to put her medical skills to good use and he could not imagine himself staying in one place for ever. See? They were poles apart in their needs, and those poles could not be moved closer. He knew this in his bones. Nick was in the way.

The cool morning air made Chase shiver. Or could it be the sense of loss washing over him? Strange, when

what he might be losing he hadn't actually gained in the first place. Deep conversations and off-the-scale kisses, a night on the town in a jazz club—that did not add up to a full-on relationship where both of them gave everything of themselves. Kristina had demons, too, but she was trying to work through them, unlike him.

Chase picked up his speed. He'd prepare breakfast, save his mum time when she already had plenty to do for the party.

'*Woof, woof.*' The dogs began trotting faster.

'Smell a rabbit, do you?' He turned and the air stuck in his throat.

Kristina stood in the ankle-high grass, hands clasped at breast height as she swung left and right from the waist, that stunning light hair, free for once and swishing back and forth across her back.

His mouth dried. 'OMG…' What little air was in his lungs hissed over his lips. Parts of his anatomy went rock hard. He couldn't move but he had to or she'd see him staring and think he was perving. He was. Couldn't help himself. 'Kristina,' he gasped. When she didn't acknowledge him he tried to swallow. It was impossible when his mouth was like a desert. Putting one leg in front of the other, he closed the gap, tried again. 'Morning, Kristina.'

Her eyes flew open and her arms fell to her sides. 'No wonder I couldn't rouse you. You were already out here.'

'You're up early.'

'Old habits. I never sleep late.'

Not lack of sleep because of thinking about how they could've spent the night together? Her eyes were puffy and dull. He sighed. They weren't doing each other any favours. 'Neither do I. I'm heading back to do something about breakfast.'

'Verity's got it in hand. She said it would be ready in

forty-five minutes and not to be late. I thought I'd limber up with a few yoga exercises before taking a short walk.'

'Want company?' He held his breath.

'I'd love it.'

Chase breathed again. 'We'll head to the top of the copse, then follow the track that comes out behind the farmhouse.'

'This place is wonderful. You were lucky to grow up here.'

'I know.' He tried not to stare at her butt filling those tight denim shorts as she strolled along, but his eyes had a mind of their own—until he tripped over a sod of grass-covered soil and nearly fell flat on his face. What had they been talking about? Oh, yeah. 'As kids Libby and I used to raise any calves rejected by their mothers for one reason or another. We had to do all the work and when they were sold at market we received half the money. The rest went to Dad to cover costs, though he was soft and didn't hit us with a large share of the expenses.'

'He was teaching you that nothing comes to you without working for it. I like that. My parents, especially Mum, thought the more they gave me the more I'd love them and not argue about who to stay with during the school holidays.' Kristina stopped to look around. 'Luxuriant green for miles and miles.'

Following the direction of Kristina's gaze, he admitted, 'I don't always see it like that. It's a big part of me, and still I don't get lost in being here.'

Drawing her eyes away from the view, she started walking again. 'You obviously weren't meant to be a farmer. Did that bother your father?'

'Dad's never been anything but encouraging in what ever I chose to do. This farm hasn't been in the family for generations like some around here. It was Dad's dream, and he went after it with everything he had. Then let his

children follow their own dreams. I think he's hoping one of Libby's boys might be interested, but they're a few years off making those kinds of decisions.'

'The freedom of it all.' The wistful note in Kristina's voice caught at him.

'What did your parents want from you?' She can't have let them down by becoming a GP.

'Nothing I was prepared to give my soul for.' She strode out, leaving him behind.

Chase lengthened his steps and caught up. 'I hope you like a full English breakfast, because Mum's not going to let you away with anything less.' He wasn't going to follow up on that terse comment. There'd been pain in every word, pain she wasn't ready to share. Hopefully one day she'd find it in her to tell him. If he was still in the same country as her. Which wasn't going to happen so he wouldn't be hearing about her parents and how they'd raised her.

'My mother thinks marrying a millionaire is the only way to go.' Her laugh was tight. 'Lying by a pool for a couple of days a year is fine, doing it year round isn't my idea of fun.'

'I can't see you filling in time for the sake of it.' Surprised she'd given him a snippet, he waited to see if there was more.

'Dad wanted me to work with him, his company's specialty being hedge funds.'

Chase chuckled. 'Sitting in a high-rise, glass-encased office making millions online to please wealthy men who own fancy yachts isn't you either.'

'Dad isn't any good at knowing what makes me tick.' Again sadness tainted her voice.

And made him want to cheer her up. 'Do you want a lift into Merrywood this morning? I hear Jarrod wants to catch up with you. We could have lunch at the pub afterwards.' He was getting the hang of this dating caper.

Her mouth curved upward. 'Family, eh? Knows every-thing about everyone?' Then she blanched. 'I didn't mean I was part of your family.'

'Relax, Kristina,' he said, hating the worry clouding her eyes, wanting to see any other emotion there, even anger, toward him. 'No one's expecting more of you than to enjoy the time we're here and to join in all the fun.'

She suddenly grinned, a bright light in the cloud that had fallen over her. 'I'd like a ride into town, and espe-cially lunch with you.'

With you. Two simple words and his chest was filling with pride and excitement. 'You'll be doing me a favour. Mum has a list a mile-long of groceries, meat, flowers and a million other things that need to be picked up.'

Her knuckles rapped his upper arm lightly. 'My shout at the pub.'

'It's a deal.' His blood warmed, his heart squeezed. Was this a second date with Kristina? So what if it was? He'd promised to have a good time, and not think about the future. 'We'll leave straight after breakfast.'

'I need to hit the shops. I haven't got anything to wear to the party.'

'Now she tells me,' he groaned. 'Is this going to take all day? Or are you a speed shopper?' Then it struck him as odd that she had no clothes for anything other than work. 'You must own more clothes than the shorts and shirts you carry in that backpack.'

'There's a wardrobeful at my father's Manchester apart-ment where I have a bedroom I use about once a year. Mostly it's for storing my gear. Another reason for find-ing a town to settle in, a home to live in. I'll be able to buy furniture I like, clothes I'll wear more than once before putting them in storage, collect recipe books and serving dishes.' She gathered a breath. 'Cooking isn't my strong point, mainly because I've never done any. Put that on

my sheet of things to do—when I start one—take lessons on how to make duck *à l'orange* or tortellini in smoked mussel sauce.'

'You don't want to start with porridge or ginger-nut biscuits?' His mother had insisted he learn to make basic meals because cooking was her passion. Kristina obviously hadn't been given the chance. Because there'd been servants? Or no one could be bothered or patient enough to take the time to walk her through a recipe?

'Why start at the bottom?' She grinned in that way of hers that hit him in the gut and rattled his bones.

'Fair enough.' He opened the gate before them and breathed her in as she went through, her arm brushing his. 'Follow this path and we'll be through the trees and at the back door in minutes. Hopefully we haven't kept the bacon waiting.' What would that hair feel like on his skin?

Kristina felt a nudge in her belly as her arm brushed Chase's. Her feet tangled and she stumbled. Why hadn't she made love with him last night? She'd spent every hour until the sun rose regretting her decision.

'Careful.' Chase's hands caught and steadied her. His thumbs drew leisurely circles against her skin. His mouth was close, so close.

She had to kiss him, to feel his heat. 'Chase,' she whispered against his stubble-covered chin before her lips touched his. 'Chase.'

'Hell, Kristina, I've been wanting to do this since I saw you in the field.'

Her mouth peeled away far enough for her to reply, 'Good,' before she returned to kissing, this time trailing a line from the corner of his mouth to his chin and down his neck to the edge of his shirt. She yanked the shirt up and continued the kisses over his chest, down to his stomach where her tongue circled his belly button. They should've

done this last night, she thought. Well, she wouldn't be stopping for anything this time.

'Those shorts should be banned. They cradle your butt like my hands need to. They outline your slim legs to the point that if I don't touch them, I'm going to die.'

'Help yourself,' she murmured against his stomach, while her hand sought the button holding his shorts closed and preventing access to the hard rod of need she had to touch, to wrap her hand around.

Chase groaned against her as she worked the button free.

Then his hands were on her pants, trying to push them down. 'Here.' She shoved his hand aside and tore the zip open, before returning to Chase's throbbing reaction to her. Reaching inside, her hands found him and slipped slowly down the satin skin stretched tight. She gasped at the wonder of his hardness, the heat, the throbbing need for her.

He dropped to his knees, his mouth finding her. Kristina gripped his shoulders, her head tipping back as Chase licked and nipped first one thigh and then the other. As his mouth reached the puddle of desire making her shake, her fingers grabbed his head, clung to him as he touched her, a lick, then another, and another, and she melted and tightened and let go all at once as hot, hungry need rocked her.

Chase rose before her, and gently laid her in the thick grass. His eyes were dark and intense, his erection throbbing when she enclosed it in her hands. She had to have him inside her. 'Now,' she cried.

Chase held himself above her. Winding her legs around him, she drew him down until his tip touched her. When she gasped he pushed, slowly, firmly, inside. Withdrew, pushed in. Her arms, wrapped around his shoulders, convulsed in time with her need exploding around him. Chase pushed hard, shuddering as he came.

Slowly her heartbeat returned to normal. Tipping her head back, she drew a long, unsteady breath. 'Wow.'

'Yeah, wow.' Chase rolled onto his back, sprawling her across him.

She clung to him, absorbing his heat. 'Guess we're officially late for breakfast now.'

'I don't think Mum will be too worried. She doesn't start cooking eggs until everyone's seated at the table. But we'd better get a wiggle on or there'll be a load of unwanted questions to deal with. If the dogs haven't already told them what's going on.'

Kristina laughed as she scrambled to her feet. 'What dogs?'

'Exactly.' Chase took her hands in his. 'What happened to "I don't think I'm ready"?'

'I spent the night regretting it.'

His smile devoured her. 'I nearly knocked on your door at three this morning.'

'It took till three?'

'Nah. I was playing hard to get, but it backfired.'

Winding her arm around his waist, she smiled for the short distance to the house, and then in her room where she quickly tidied up, and throughout breakfast, subtly ignoring Verity's amused glances coming their way. She was not sorry she'd made love with Chase. No, all she wanted was to do it again. Unfortunately the day ahead was about preparing for a party and catching up with everyone at the medical centre. Not that that was a bad way to spend a day, it was just that now she knew there was an even better one.

CHAPTER EIGHT

'Kristina, you're here.' The medical centre's reception-ist flew around the counter and engulfed her in an enor-mous hug.

Kristina's heart melted at the welcome. She felt like crying. 'Hey, Wendy, good to see you.'

'You're in time for morning tea. Libby sent blueberry muffins in with Jarrod.'

More tears threatened. Kristina straightened her back and dropped her hands to her sides. 'I am being spoilt.'

'Watch out, they want something from you,' Chase teased. 'Believe me, I know how this lot operate.'

'Dr Kristina, hello. Do you want to see my baby? She weighed in at four kilos and hasn't stopped gaining weight since.' A young woman held up a baby dressed in pink and held her out. 'We called her Lily.'

'Sherry, it's lovely to see you both.' Kristina took the soft bundle in her arms. 'Hello, little one. Aren't you the cutest thing? Look at all those blonde curls.' In the weeks Kristina had worked there she'd seen Sherry regularly.

'Lily came in a real hurry and I didn't make it to hospi-tal.' Sherry was smiling, her eyes full of love as she gazed at her daughter.

Kristina's stomach turned to goo. *I want that.* Hand-ing Lily back, she managed, 'I'm so glad to see you both.

I really am.' There was a sense of completing a circle, something that didn't usually happen for a locum.

'Me, too,' Sherry acknowledged. 'You were so kind to me when I panicked and cried for hours about my swollen ankles.'

'It was only minutes and every pregnant woman is allowed those moments.'

'Hello, Kristina. It's great to see you. Libby'll be along shortly. She's bursting to catch up on everything you've done since leaving here.'

Kristina turned to find herself slap bang in the middle of another hug, this time from Jarrod. When she was released she asked, 'Is she at the market?'

Jarrod nodded. 'Otherwise she'd be on to the list I presume is burning a hole in Chase's pocket. Come through to the tearoom where everyone's waiting.'

'But it's Saturday.' Merrywood Medical Centre had obviously been rostered to cover weekend emergencies for the area, but that didn't explain all the staff.

'They weren't letting you get away without seeing them.'

'Oh.'

Chase was biting on a smile. 'I prefer chocolate muffins so I'll leave you to it. Mum's list will take some effort to get through.'

'I said I'd help with it.' Kristina didn't want to let him down.

'I'm not tramping around behind you while you trawl the dress shops. Pick you up here at twelve-thirty, okay? We'll have lunch, then I'll put you to good use working on what's left of the list.'

'Sounds good.' Hopefully there'd be an outfit for the party in the first shop she went into. If there was spare time, she'd look for a sky-blue, full-length dress as well.

'Thanks for coming in when I know it's bedlam at the

farm.' Jarrod led the way into the tearoom, where two nurses hugged her.

Were the hugs adding up this morning, or what? 'Verity's got everything under control, no sign of panic. How's everything here? I've missed this place.'

'Give this lot five minutes and then we'll go through to my office. Thankfully it's not too busy for a Saturday morning so we'll have some time to ourselves.'

Interesting. A fizz of excitement tickled her, and made the next five minutes the longest she could remember even when feeling so welcome.

'Bring your coffee.' Jarrod was on his feet and heading out the door.

As Kristina took a seat in his office the mug shook in her hand. Tension tightened her stomach. Was she about to get the offer of a lifetime or be sorely disappointed?

'Hey, there you are,' Libby bounded into the room and banged the door shut behind her before embracing Kristina. 'I'm glad you came with Chase for the weekend. It's great to see you again.'

This was getting out of hand. Kristina hugged her back fervently. 'Me, too. I thought you were selling cheese this morning.'

'I have been, but a friend's taken over. Jarrod wants me here while he talks to you. Probably thinks I can twist your arm for him.'

She straightened her back. This meeting was serious, then. *Please, be what I'm hoping for.* She waited, her breath stalled in her throat.

'I'll cut straight to the point. Campbell's leaving us, heading to New York where his wife's got a power job at some financial conglomerate.'

Kristina relaxed a notch. 'No surprise there. She's supposedly a whiz at that stuff. But can Campbell practise in the States?'

'He'll have to sit some papers, but he's decided to be a stay-at-home dad until the kids have settled into their new way of life, which will be very different from little old Merrywood.' Jarrod steepled his fingers. 'So, are you still looking for a permanent position as a GP? Because there's one going here and we'd like you to join us. Everyone would. You were so popular with the staff and patients during your two months, and I'm tired of patients asking when you're coming back.'

Lay on the feel-good stuff, why don't you? A smile split her face. 'I do want to work in a medical centre where I get to know patients for more than one visit.' Come on, say what you really think. 'Okay, truly? Merrywood feels right for me, and I would like to move here.'

Jarrod was watching her closely. 'Campbell intends to hold onto his partnership for now, in case things don't work out in New York. But even if he returns, this position is permanent. Our patient numbers are high, and could grow more if we opened the books again.'

'I don't need a partnership.' Maybe later on when she was settled in her own home with those dogs she'd begun thinking about. What about Chase? He was the snag in this otherwise perfect solution to her needs.

'Say yes, Kristina,' Libby said.

'So you're interested in working with us? Permanently?' Jarrod asked, before dangling a carrot in front of her. 'Campbell has suggested that whoever takes his place here might be interested in renting their home.'

That would take the pressure off finding her own place, give her time to look around and decide where best to put down roots. Kristina stared at her entwined fingers, looking for the answer to the main question, because now the offer had come, there were other things to consider.

These people were Chase's family. Libby and Jarrod lived nearby, his parents a few kilometres down the road.

He'd come home for visits, even if only occasionally, and she'd have to deal with seeing him, unless she took annual leave whenever he appeared. Despite the high she was on from that morning's lovemaking, come the end of her time with MFA their fling would finish. And it was definitely a fling. Chase was not ready for anything else.

Lifting her head, she looked at Libby, then Jarrod. 'Thank you so much for this opportunity. It's exactly what I want.' Deep breath. 'But there are things I need to consider. Can I have a few days before I give you my answer?'

Jarrod nodded. 'I didn't expect anything less. Just know that you're wanted around here by everyone, and that we'll all do whatever we can to help you settle in.'

'You're off to a head start, knowing my family,' Libby pointed out.

The snag in this whole deal. 'True, but I also have a need to see myself sorted, to find my feet. This would be a permanent move, and I want to get it right.'

'No problem.' Jarrod glanced at his computer and stood up. 'Sorry to rush you but I've a patient waiting.' He handed her an envelope. 'We haven't talked hours or salary, but it's all in there. Any questions or uncertainties, give me a call, or talk to me over the weekend.'

'I will.' She stood, surprised to find her legs a little shaky. Was this what finally finding what she wanted in life felt like? But it wasn't everything she hoped for. Until Chase, falling in love, possibly having a family, had been a distant dream to be followed when all else was in place and going well. Now she couldn't imagine life without Chase and yet that was exactly how it would be.

Libby slipped an arm through hers. 'Come and have another coffee, then we'll go to my favourite clothing shop because I hear you need an outfit.'

Two friends now? Special women she could talk to about anything. Except she couldn't with Libby because

she had a brother who'd made love with her only hours ago, who no doubt would again before the weekend was up, and who, in the end, would walk away from her. No, she wouldn't be talking with Libby about what mattered. Unfortunately. But they could have fun shopping.

Sunday dawned wet and misty, and Kristina couldn't have cared less. Chase had taken her to his bed after the party had wound down and she was still there. He had one leg thrown over hers like he never wanted her to leave. That was an illusion, like the one that said summer was only about sun and warm temperatures.

'What are you looking so happy about?' Chase nuzzled against her neck.

'That was some party.' She grinned.

'The Barringtons are famous for putting on a good bash.' He was watching her now.

'I'll 'fess up. The after-party bash was even better.' Leaning over, she kissed his chin, felt the rough texture of beard growth.

'Glad you mentioned it. My ego was getting a little worried.'

'I'm glad I came. To the party,' she added as a grin began widening his beautiful mouth. 'It's been quite a weekend so far.'

'A great party, amazing sex, and then there's Jarrod's offer. What more could a woman want?'

'There is that.' The air dribbled out of her lungs, taking some of her happiness with it. To accept the job was the right thing to do. Yet she still hoped for something more with Chase. And if that wasn't possible then living in this district might encroach on his hopes for the future. Not that she could say why, but she did think that if she moved here he might stop visiting entirely and she wouldn't be responsible for that.

'Hey, if you don't want it, say so. You're not obligated to Jarrod.' Chase sat up and tucked an arm over her shoulders, drawing her close.

Why couldn't he see what they had? This easy rapport, a simple gesture of holding her, a kiss on his chin as they woke to a new day. 'We'd better get up. Your mother will need all hands on cleaning-up duties.' Kristina swung her legs out of the bed.

Chase took his time removing his arm from around her. 'You're avoiding my question. Haven't we moved past that?' He shook his head. 'Spill. What's bothering you?'

This so wasn't the time. But when would it be? Twisting to face him, she placed a hand on his arm, felt his strength and warmth. 'The job is perfect, the location is ideal, the future looks good.'

'But?'

No. She couldn't say she was falling for him. He'd shut down completely, and she wanted what was left of their time together. Today at least. Call her selfish, but this sense of belonging had never come along before. Why not make the most of what little time she had left? *Am I being greedy?* Yep.

'I get a little scared when I think about how lucky I am to have this opportunity. It's what I've been looking for and I'm scared it'll be snatched away. Part of me thinks if I don't say yes to Jarrod yet, the bubble won't burst too soon.' Now he'd think she was mad, but she always told him the truth—about most things. Those she didn't she avoided.

Chase's arms wrapped around her and drew her close. His lips caressed her brow, then trailed down to her mouth where he kissed her softly. 'Believe in yourself, Kristina. If this is what you want then grab it with both hands and never let go. You're strong because of what you've faced in the past. Draw on that strength. Keep on smiling and

winning people over because that's also helped get you to where you can make a decision about your future.'

Tears streamed down her face. See? No wonder she loved him. Yes, full-blown love. That falling for him thing had arrived at its destination. She loved Chase Barrington. So tell him. Always truthful, remember? Avoidance, remember? She didn't need him saying, 'Thank you very much but nothing's going to change'. Her pride had taken enough knocks over the years to know when to look out for herself. Now was one of those times.

'Thank you.' She sniffed. 'I needed that.' If only she could give the same back. But they weren't talking about him and his plans after the *Poseidon*. Hopefully she'd get an opportunity over the next three weeks to do something about that. Who knew? She might even find the courage to tell him how she felt about him.

'Any time.' He grinned. 'Now, go shower. There's a party to clear up.'

Chase watched Kristina head out of his bedroom, his heart heavy despite that grin he'd given her. Go, Jarrod, for offering her the position at the medical centre. It was exactly what she wanted, and needed. She'd be mad not to accept. So why the hesitation? He didn't believe her explanation. Or rather he did, but it was only half the reason. What was the other half? He'd wanted to push for an answer but was wary of spoiling the wonderful time they were having together.

They'd be flying back to Marseille in the afternoon. No wonder he felt dispirited. He wasn't ready to go back to work, and that was such a rarity. He put his hand on his brow. Temperature normal. He and Kristina had hit it off so well the idea of giving it up so soon rankled. Hell, he'd come to enjoy her in his space, not only on the ship but also here amongst his family. She was special. Could

they have a relationship after all? One that went beyond this weekend, further than the next three weeks on board the ship, out into the real future?

Chase leapt out of bed and snatched up his shirt. Pulling it over his head, he grabbed his shorts and jerked them up his legs. Time to give his mum a hand downstairs. He'd shower after all the hard work of packing up chairs and tables and taking down the marquee was done.

'Where do you want me to start, Mum?' Chase sauntered into the kitchen minutes later, a tight smile fixed in place.

'With eating breakfast,' he was told. 'Then you can do a rain dance in reverse, get the sun to beat away those pesky clouds and dry everything out.'

'Sure thing.' He hugged the woman who'd been there for him all his life, had never backed away when he'd lost his mind over Nick's death, who still believed in him no matter what he did and how often he hurt her. His throat started closing as he said, 'Happy birthday, Mum. You're the best mother a guy could have.'

She blinked, patted his face and said, 'I'm the only one you've got, that's why.' Then she smiled that special mum smile that always hit him hard, especially since the tragedy that had changed his life for ever. 'You're my best son, too.'

'I'm the only one,' he croaked the expected reply, and pulled her into another hug.

'Come on, you two. Haven't got all day to be mucking about, real birthday or not.' His dad strolled into the kitchen and dropped onto his usual chair, pulled the pan of bacon towards him and began dishing some onto a plate.

Chase sank onto a chair and tugged the dish out of his father's hand. 'You reckon?' Then the air crackled around his ears, the skin on his forearms tightened.

Kristina had arrived. 'That smells so good, Verity.'

'Help yourself, and don't be mean about it. You're going to be so busy you'll need all the energy you can muster.'

'Me, busy? I told the dogs I'd take them for a stroll down the lane, maybe sit in the field for an hour. Might even take them to the pub later.' She began buttering some toast, a soft smile lighting her beautiful face.

Damn, she fitted right in here. Almost as easily as he did, maybe more so considering those moments he got edgy about trying not to hurt his parents even knowing he would when he left to return to work. His mother always smiled and pretended she was all right with him heading off to places out of the norm to feed his need to fix people, while his dad would shake his hand, say 'Have a good trip' and go out to the shed.

Watching Kristina fork breakfast onto her plate as she chattered with them, Chase knew happiness. *She did fit in here.* And in doing so she was making him feel there was a chance he might, too. 'The dogs really enjoy a good burger and chips washed down with a beer.'

'I thought they might.' She fixed him with a dazzling smile, no trace of her worries of earlier darkening her gaze. 'Verity, what job have you got lined up for me? As long as it's got nothing to do with food, I can do pretty much anything.'

'I was hoping you'd bring the flowers in from the gazebo and arrange them in the lounge.'

She winced. 'I might be better employed dealing with the tables and chairs.'

Chase laughed. 'No flower arranging in the army, then?'

Kristina biffed him on the arm. 'I'll help your dad and you can take care of the flowers.'

His mother laughed, too. 'Whatever. As long as it's all done today. I see Jarrod's pulled up. They'll all want feeding.'

Chase leaned back in his chair and sipped his tea, soak-

ing up the atmosphere. Even when the calm was shattered by three young boys racing into the kitchen shouting 'Happy birthday, Nana' so loudly his eardrums seemed about to burst, he felt the most relaxed he had in…well, in for ever. Funny how his eyes turned to Kristina. Come on. They were always looking her way, seeking her out, watching the play of emotions on her exquisite face, storing images for the months ahead when she was here and he was somewhere else.

Pushing up off his chair, he took his plate, cutlery and mug to the dishwasher. 'Right, let's get this show under way.' He had to get out of here, away from Kristina and her sweet voice as she chatted with *his* family. She was doing his head in, tinkering with his resolve to go solo for ever.

Placing fresh sandwiches and leftover bacon and egg pies on the table hours later, Chase pulled out a chair and sank onto it, trying to ignore the way his body ached in places it had no right to. It showed how out of practice he was when it came to making love. 'Anyone seen Kristina?'

'She took the dogs for a walk,' Libby answered. 'Said she'd be back shortly.'

'One of the dogs has probably taken off after a rabbit. She won't come home without them both in tow.' Tempted to forgo lunch and follow her, he remained seated. Like him, she sometimes needed time alone. He wondered if she was thinking about their lovemaking. It had been out of this world, and a running film kept going across the front of his mind. But with all that came decisions to make. He knew it, and so would Kristina. Nothing had changed in that they still weren't getting together permanently. He had obligations to fulfil—if he ever got around to signing that damned contract. Not once had he taken so long over something as simple as scrawling his name across a piece of paper. Hopefully Kristina wouldn't take so long with

Jarrod's offer. She wouldn't be doing herself any favours by procrastinating when it was exactly what she wanted.

His mother was pouring the coffee he'd forgotten. 'Jasper, naughty boy.'

Libby growled, 'No, Jasper, you cannot put all that in your mouth at once. Eat properly.'

Chase's nephew was working at shoving a whole bacon muffin in his mouth. 'Cute.' It was. All part of the family thing, everyone sitting around the table picking at food in a desultory fashion—except for Jasper—mulling over the party and generally relaxing together. He could get used to this all too easily. Where had that dumb idea come from? Usually he was bursting to get out of here before his family dragged him under with their love. But he'd never brought home a woman about whom he cared a lot, hadn't made love in his childhood bedroom since he'd been a horny teenager, and that had been more about sex than love. Face it, he hadn't felt so at ease with the whole scene in a long time.

'It's not cute at all,' Libby growled at him. 'Jasper, behave. You're disgusting.'

The kid couldn't reply with so much food in his mouth.

Chase wanted to laugh because he remembered doing something similar as a boy, but Libby would probably box his ears for encouraging him. Where was Kristina anyway? It was time she came back from her walk and joined in the fun. He'd seen in her demeanour how much she enjoyed interacting with this lot. 'Do you think Kristina will take the position you've offered her, Jarrod?'

'You'd know as much about that as I do,' his brother-in-law answered. 'I know she wants to, but something's holding her back.'

'That'd be Chase, I'm betting.' Libby added her two pence worth.

The hackles rose on the back of his neck. 'Anything

Kristina decides has nothing to do with me,' he said a little more forcefully than he'd intended. 'She's quite capable of making up her own mind.'

'Didn't say she wasn't.' Libby grinned. In other words, *Got you, big brother.*

'The job's everything she wants,' he said. 'She likes the town of Merrywood, too. She'll be wanting to buy a house as soon as possible.'

'We're all here for her,' Verity added. 'She can visit any time.'

His family liked getting involved with other people's business, whether asked to or not, but this went further. It was as though they'd accepted Kristina as one of them. He'd witnessed how comfortable she'd been at the medical centre yesterday. The staff had been fighting each other to talk to her. 'Kristina will make up her own mind without anyone putting pressure on her.' She didn't need this lot surrounding her with advice and—

Love?

Yes, from what he knew about them, they probably did love her in their all-embracing way. 'Her independence is important to her. You'd do well to remember that before you try to smother her.'

'Sure you're not talking about yourself, bro?' Libby really had sharpened her tongue overnight.

'That's ridiculous, and you know it,' he snapped. Sometimes Libby went too far. He didn't need to be reminded how he let his family down on a regular basis. 'I'm happy doing the work for *Medicine For All.*'

'Yeah, and when you're done with them you'll find another cause to hide behind. Don't you think it's time to come home and be a part of us again?' Libby gave back as good as she got, more so perhaps.

She had him between a rock and a hard place. Say no and he was telling his family he didn't care about them.

Say yes and they'd have interviews at the hospital lined up within days. He went for neutral. 'I'm not ready to stop what I'm doing yet. There are people who need me.' Then the hairs lifted on his skin. Twisting around, he swore under his breath.

Kristina stood in the doorway, sadness darkening her lovely face. Her gaze touched him briefly before she looked away, swallowing hard at the same time. As though she might've been thinking things between them had changed since they'd made love, and had now learned everything was exactly the same.

Guilt had him standing up and pulling out a chair for her. 'Come and have some lunch. Tea?' How much had she heard?

She stepped up beside him and smiled, a slow, soft movement that didn't reach her eyes. Then she turned to his family and said, 'What Chase does for *Medicine For All* is truly amazing and very important. They'd be lost without him.' She sat down and reached for a sandwich.

Libby stared at her, a slow smile finally breaking out and taking the sting out of her next words. 'So, big brother's got to you, too. Don't let that stop you coming to work for us. We need you.'

Kristina chewed and swallowed. 'There's only one person deciding on what I do next and that's me.'

Chase's hands were unsteady as he poured Kristina's tea. She'd had his back in front of his family. He should be squirming. He didn't need anyone taking his side, but while his head railed against that, his heart was lifting, softening. It felt good to have someone who wasn't family caring enough to support him. If he'd thought it was going to be harder than usual to leave the farm today, it was going to be a whole lot harder to say goodbye to Kristina in three weeks' time. Might be best if he backed off before then, stopped seeing her as anything other than a

colleague, possibly a friend, but definitely not a woman to make love to in his cabin after he'd finished with the people needing his services.

But first they had the rest of the day to enjoy. Placing the cup in front of Kristina, he said to the room in general, 'How about we go to the pub for a beer before someone drops us at the airport? Let's have some more birthday celebrations. Family only. And Kristina.'

A wicked glint filled his sister's eyes and he wanted to growl at her but refrained. They'd always pressed each other's buttons, and this time he wasn't letting her win. Today was about him and Kristina, before he packed her away and got on with his real life. No, he wasn't exactly proud of himself, but there was no denying the need coursing through his veins.

CHAPTER NINE

'Big day.' The air was heavy as Kristina leaned on the railing in their corner of the deck. The horizon was lost in grey cloud. Her head was thick due to lack of sleep and a never-ending line of refugees requiring her attention since nine that morning. Many of today's boatload were suffering from fuel burns, and there'd been an outbreak of gastric flu on their cramped boat before they'd been picked up in the Gulf of Sirte.

The sleepless night had been exciting. For most of it. Chase had taken her to his cabin and made love to her with passion and hunger, and a need so great she'd wanted to hold him for ever, reassure him he was safe with her, but she'd held back, uncertain of his reaction. When he'd made love to her a second time he had been so excruciatingly gentle she'd cried. She'd been right to stay quiet. He was saying goodbye to their brief fling. Goodbye to the woman he'd taken to his bed, not to the doctor he'd still be working with.

Around four she'd kissed him softly on his cheeks and forehead, and lastly on his lips as he'd slept, then she'd crawled out of his bunk to head back to her cabin. He hadn't moved at all.

Now Chase was staring out to sea. 'They happen.' He hadn't budged an inch when she'd joined him. 'It's going

to be as hectic throughout the night when the Sudanese refugees arrive.'

The message was so loud, so clear she wanted to shrink in on herself and pretend she was with a complete stranger passing the time of day before going below deck and catching up on much-needed sleep. Throughout the day they'd been so busy the only conversations had been about patients, and those had been abrupt. It was as though once she'd left his cabin that morning she'd left the man she loved, the man who'd let her in close.

Coming up here when it was obvious she wasn't wanted had been a mistake. Was she naïve, thinking he might miss her if she didn't? Damn, but she was pathetic. And hurting, and wishing she could change him, and knowing some things were plain impossible. She'd thought they'd have another three weeks together. Wrong. There weren't going to be any more stolen kisses up here. This area was reverting to *his* space. No making love in his cabin. Nothing.

Well, he wasn't getting away with not talking to her. Kristina watched Chase. 'I got my invitation to Jasper's birthday party today.' She'd checked her emails while downing a hurried meal between patients.

'Me, too.' Still no movement in that lean body she'd touched all over.

'I emailed straight back saying I'd be there.' She'd be living in Merrywood by then. 'His first day of school on the following Monday. How cool's that?'

'They grow up fast.' A sudden yearning flitted through his eyes, then was gone so fast she might've imagined it if she hadn't known what to look for.

Kristina swallowed the hurt she felt for him. She had her own to deal with. He loved his family, and if he thought they didn't know he was fooling himself. He needed shaking—hard. But was it her place to instigate

it? No, but when had she ever let something like that stop her? Pressing on, she said, 'You'll be going to the party?'

'I'll be in Africa.' Again that yearning flared, died.

'So you've finally signed the contract?'

He winced and finally looked at her. 'No, but it's lying amongst the paperwork. I'll get to it later tonight.' The bleakness in those eyes was frightening. Did he not understand how much he was hurting himself, let alone everyone else, by being so stubborn about staying on his mission?

'Tell me again why you want to go so far away from those you love?'

'I've told you of my need to help people in difficult or dangerous situations. Nothing's changed, Kristina. There are people all over the world needing urgent medical help that's not easily available. Someone has to be there for them, to save them.' There was a warning in his voice. *Don't step any further over the mark.*

That wound her up fast. 'You think I won't save people in Merrywood? That being a GP in an English town won't rank up there with helping the sick and needy in your foreign locations? That diagnosing a heart condition before it becomes life-threatening isn't saving a life? You think you have to be at the coal face of danger all the time to be a great doctor?' Her disappointment in him, and knowing he wasn't about to change because of anything she said, further cranked up her temper, made it easy to say what she'd held in for days. 'Would you be more accommodating of a relationship between us if I followed you around, doing what you do?'

'No, Kristina, I don't think that. You're brilliant at what you do. I can't imagine you doing anything else. And before you even think it, I am not being condescending. The world needs more of you than of me.' His chest rose slowly. 'Further, I would never expect you to sign

up for the work I do—if I even wanted us to be together in a permanent relationship.'

'*Even* if you wanted us to be together?' she choked.

'I don't want to hurt you, but you've never hidden the fact you long to settle in your own home with a career you can become completely involved in. That's what you need, hanker for, have to have, and should make happen. What's more, if you take up Jarrod's offer you're halfway there. Those are the things I don't look for.'

'Avoid, more like.' He hadn't told her anything she didn't already know. But heck. 'Don't turn the conversation onto me,' she snapped around the ache building in her throat. 'You can't handle the heat whenever anyone starts talking about *your* future, can you? Fine, I'll shut up, but don't...' She poked her forefinger into his chest. 'Don't start on what I should be doing.' She'd find a way to accept that she was about to achieve half of what she wanted, which wasn't bad going. Not everyone was so lucky. Unfortunately she'd had a taste of what the other half could be like, and wouldn't be forgetting it in a hurry.

'Fair cop. Talking about my past is the hardest thing I ever have to do, so mostly I don't.' He was in his staring out to sea stance, arms folded across that chest she'd spent so much time kissing, his chin jutting forward with its tempting cover of light stubble, those long, sexy legs tense.

Even in the middle of this she was turned on. Damn him. 'You told me some of what happened in the French mountains.'

His nod was short and sharp. 'I don't regret it. Neither do I regret everything else we've shared,' he added almost as an afterthought, surprise shining out of his eyes for a moment.

Good to know. If it didn't hurt so much. But there was no point carrying on this awkward, snappy conversation. It only undermined the friendship and closeness they had,

and if she could keep those alive she would. 'I also emailed Jarrod, accepting his offer.' Somewhere between leaving Chase's cabin and giving her last patient intravenous antibiotics she'd realised the decision was still hers alone to make, and if becoming more involved with Chase's family was the result then she'd grab the opportunity with both hands. He wouldn't stay away because she was there—he already did that.

'It's the right thing to do.' No heart-wrenching Chase smile for her this time. 'If I'm allowed to say so.'

Her heart rolled over. If only it could be different. They understood each other so well they really would work out as a couple—if they weren't looking for completely opposite lives. 'You take care of yourself. I'm sure Libby will keep me up to date with wherever you go and what you do.' To her own ears it sounded like she was saying goodbye. Which she was, despite the weeks ahead on the ship before she left for the final time.

There'd be no resolution for them, no seeing a path they could follow hand in hand. This was not a romance story with the predicable happy ending. Just her luck to fall in love with a man who could not meet her requirements. He was more intent on bashing his head against a brick wall, trying to save every endangered soul on the planet all by himself.

She took a step towards the stairs. It was time to accept what she'd known all along.

'Kristina,' Chase called, and when she turned he was watching her with an intensity that curled her toes and told her heart to move on. 'I am sorry.'

Did he love her at all? A tiny, weeny bit? They'd met equally on more levels than the physical. There'd been gentleness, kindness and, yes, something like love, if not total love, in everything they'd done together, including the times up here. This was the last time she'd come. Why

prolong the agony? Stretching up on her toes, she leaned in and kissed him lightly on his mouth. 'I know.'

Then she was gone, out of there, away from the temptation to grovel. She'd only come off worse than she already felt. 'Goodbye, Chase,' she whispered.

Goodbye while they still had to work together. Should be a picnic.

Chase read all the documents that had come in with the medical supplies by boat that morning, signed the ones that were going back in the next outward mail bag, and dropped the rest into the cardboard box that served as his filing cabinet. The clock on the wall read seven-fifteen. Time for dinner, except he wasn't hungry. It had been a week since Kristina had slipped out of his cabin after a night of lovemaking. A week since he'd let her know that whatever they'd had was over. A week of wondering if he'd made the biggest mistake possible, of wishing she'd sneak back into his bed and ignore what he'd said about running alone. A week of growing tired and edgy, of avoiding her, and trying not to let Ethan's presence on board get in the way of his goals and his foul mood.

Pulling a large, over-full envelope towards him, he emptied the contents onto his desk. 'More damned forms to fill in. Why did I train as a surgeon?'

Yeah, why did he? Because of the driving ambition to save people's lives, to put them back together when life had made a mess of their bodies, to make their loved ones happy again. And had it made him happy?

Ramming his fingers through his hair, he dropped his head forward and stared at the tobacco-coloured carpet between his feet. He didn't have the right to be happy when Nick had lost out on so much.

The door opened and the sound of voices and laughter reached him before the door clicked shut again. 'Thought

I'd find you in here, sulking,' Ethan said conversationally, before banging a tray down on the desk.

Chase raised his head and stared at the man who'd finally become his friend, not his enemy. 'I'm not hungry.' The smell of sausages and chips made his nose screw up in distaste.

'Sure you're not, but you've got to eat.'

There were two laden plates, two glasses of iced water and cutlery for both of them. Ethan had returned for a final stint, as he'd said he would. He'd been working every hour he could, and still found time to harass Chase whenever he thought he needed reminding there was more to life than this.

'You been talking to Kristina? She told me the same a while ago.'

'Funny, that. I just gave her the same speech as I'm giving you. Eat.' Ethan sat down on the other side of the desk and used his fingers to pick up some chips. 'You two had a spat?'

'Not at all.' It was true. They hadn't.

'Then why are you burying yourself in work twenty-four seven? We're busy, sure, but there's more than enough staff to cover everything.'

'I need to catch up on all this.' He waved a hand at the files and documents Ethan had had no compunction about setting the tray on top of. 'I should've been an accountant or statistician, not a surgeon.'

'Getting withdrawal?'

From Kristina? Definitely. 'I sometimes wonder what it might be like working full time as a surgeon in one place, occasionally seeing repeat patients.' His head jerked back and a bleak smile lifted the corner of his mouth. 'Don't know why I'm telling you. You'll find a way to use it against me.' Something Ethan and Kristina had in common—taking

what he told them and putting the onus back on him to do something about it.

'Because I know where you're at by rite of the same passage. I'm still getting used to the idea of putting my feet down in one place for as far ahead as I can see. I'll tell you this for nothing. I'm glad I'm doing it. More than glad. Happy beyond anything I could've imagined.'

'I'm happy for you.' Ethan deserved Claire and their unborn child, deserved that happiness.

'So am I.' Ethan chewed on a sausage and watched him. 'It's been quite a roller-coaster ride but I'm glad of every moment so far. I even look forward to the next phase: marriage and parenthood. Who'd have believed I'd be saying that?'

'Not you.'

'Isn't that the truth?' His eyes were still locked on him. Looking for what?

Chase began to feel uneasy, as though Ethan found him lacking. Picking up a handful of fries, he began to eat them one by one, swallowing with difficulty. He'd wait this one out.

Finally, 'You sent that contract back yet?'

It had been lying on the desk for five days, signed and ready to go to head office, gathering dust and more crinkles whenever he fossicked for particular documents to deal with. He shook his head. 'Not yet. But…' he shoved chips into his mouth and picked up the paperwork that would see him fixed up for work over the coming months '… I'll do it right now.'

Ethan's eyes were dark, unreadable as he watched him, more worrying than if he'd been angry.

Chase couldn't help himself. He had to ask. 'What?'

'Why did you ask me to do a spell with MFA?'

Kathump. The sound of his gut hitting the floor was deafening. 'There was that promise you'd come whenever

I needed your help. All I had to do was ask.' No cross-examination required. Or wanted.

'What took sixteen years for you to ask? And why ask me for help with something any doctor could do?'

His head joined his gut. 'Could be I wasn't ready to see your face or hear your cheek before.'

'Could be you're starting to think there might be more to life than how you're living? That in order to move on you had to deal with me, with your past—our past—first.'

'Never crossed my mind.' It hadn't. Not once. Never. Why would it?

'I'd been waiting for a damned long time to get that call. Thought it would never come.' A wealth of sadness dulled Ethan's words.

And sapped the resistance out of Chase. 'I wanted to call you, picked up the phone often enough, but then I'd think, Why spoil your day? Then one day I didn't put the phone down, just let the number ring. And here we are. No regrets. Don't ask why that day was any different from the others. It just was.'

'Sure.' Ethan stretched his legs out. 'Make sure you put in the dates you have to be in France for my wedding before you send in that contract.'

He was off the hook, yet relief wasn't rushing at him. 'Plus three days for my nephew's birthday and first day of school.' He owed Libby for upsetting her the morning after their mum's party. Nothing new in that, but he'd decided to go home for Jasper's birthday. If only he'd seen Libby's face when she'd read the email. Probably took an hour to close her mouth.

He had Kristina to thank for this. She'd managed to get him doing things with his family no one else had come close to. Could that be because she'd slotted in so effortlessly? Strange when she wasn't used to a close family who accepted a person for who they were. But if she hadn't had

that, it made sense she might grab the opportunity when it came along.

'That's good news.' Ethan shrugged and put his empty plate back on the tray and stole some chips off Chase's. 'What are we expected to reach the next boat of refugees?'

Relief lightened Chase's mood and he stabbed a sausage with a fork. They'd moved past the sticky conversation. 'About six, just in time for breakfast.'

'Then I'll get things set up tonight.'

'You do that and I'll stocktake the pharmaceutical cabinet.' Something else to keep his mind occupied and off Kristina Morton. 'Then Josip wants to go over docking days and when the ship will be laid up for maintenance.'

'I'm sure you can come up with enough to keep you busy until six if you try hard enough.' Ethan sauntered out of the office like he hadn't a care in the world, so unlike the Ethan he'd thought he knew. This new Claire-enhanced version was slowly relaxing into the world around him. Did the man still think back to the avalanche? Of course he did, but he'd learned to go a little easier with what had happened and was beginning to live in the present without having to justify himself and his actions.

All assumption, really, based on how *he* reacted and lived, Chase admitted. He and Ethan had had too little to do with each other over the intervening years for him to be certain about the other man's thoughts and reactions.

Snatching up the drugs list and keys to the cupboard, he headed out of his office.

Less than twenty-four hours to go. Kristina sighed. The weeks since she'd left Chase's bunk had seemed endless and yet now, suddenly, it was all but over, and she'd leave for good in the morning.

The boat was quiet, and time lay heavily on her hands, with no patients needing attention. She'd done a round of

those who were left, waiting for tomorrow and disembarkation. She'd accepted thanks and smiles in ever-increasing discomfort. These people deserved to be treated well. No one knew what lay in store for them next.

'Slow night.' Ethan looked up from a book he was reading. 'Claire's looking forward to you visiting for a couple of nights.'

This had felt like the longest period she'd done on the ship, all because Chase took up so much of her mind, and nothing else. The sooner she didn't have to see him countless times, work with him on patients, or hear his voice everywhere she went, the better. 'It'll be great spending time together. Talking baby things and dress shopping for my bridesmaid outfit.' Merrywood Fashion hadn't produced a sky-blue anything, let alone an off-the-shoulder dress fit for the occasion.

Ethan's eye-rolls were quite eloquent when he put in the effort. 'Think I'm washing my hair that day.'

'Thank goodness for small mercies,' she gave back. 'We really don't need your advice.'

'I *am* deciding what I'm wearing to my wedding. Though Claire has given me instructions.' He grinned.

It was amazing how much Ethan had relaxed since meeting Claire. He wouldn't have forgotten anything about the past he shared with Chase but he was so excited about the future it was lovely to see. If only Chase would take the risk, preferably with her. But it wasn't happening, and she had to remember that—all the time.

'Have you got Chase fixed for a suit?' Why ask? Because he was constantly in her mind. It wasn't because she needed to know the groom and his best man had their clothes sorted for the wedding. Claire was more than capable of doing that and, determined woman that she was, she had probably arranged weeks ago everything right down to the socks the men would be wearing.

Ethan's eyebrows rose and he tipped his head ceiling-wards. 'What do you think?'

'Yeah, I figured the moment I asked.' Wiping a tissue across her face, she laughed. 'This heat is diabolical. I still haven't got used to it.'

'I know what you mean, and yet we'll be complaining about the cold soon enough.'

'Probably.' That'd be when she was back in England, working as a GP and settling into a routine, maybe even moving into her own little house with lawns and gardens. Like she knew anything about plants and how to look after them. But wasn't that part of putting down roots? Not only her own but those of plants? Learning the day-to-day care and maintenance, pushing the barriers, extending her horizons. Exciting, if she didn't overthink it all. 'I'm heading up on deck for some air.'

Tomorrow she'd step off the ship for the last time. There'd be no coming back. Not that she hadn't enjoyed her time on board. It'd been a great experience, and she'd met lots of wonderful people, including Claire.

Chase. Yes, well. What could she say? She'd found the love of her life, and would be walking away from him. Not that they were together but, still, when the realisation of what little they'd shared was over and got too much to handle she could seek him out, breathe him in, file away more pictures of him working with patients or talking to crew, and pretend she was coping, pretend that her heart would recover, though bruised and wary for a long time to come.

'Your back playing up?' Chase asked from behind as she reached the railing.

Looking around, she gasped softly. She must've been in a different world to have walked into their space without realising he was here. It was the first time since the night she'd said goodbye to Chase and their relationship.

'You're doing the lopsided walk.'

Her hand automatically went to the spot where a steady throbbing had set up in the muscles an hour ago. 'I moved too quickly getting out of the way of some boys chasing a football. I'll have physio when I'm back on land.'

'Not a bad idea.' His smile was friendly, and warmed her down to her toes until he said, 'There was more to the story than being blown up, wasn't there?'

'Why ask now?' Was he tidying up loose ends?

His shoulder lifted. 'I feel I'm missing something.'

'It happened up north in Scotland. No enemy in sight. Something went horrendously wrong and a bomb exploded when there should've been no way it could. Corporal Higgs took a hit in his neck and I was impaled by a steel bar so I had no chance of helping him. I could only focus enough to tell others what to do.' She swallowed. 'Later, I learned nothing would've saved him, but I blamed myself for a long time, even though I understand how it was.'

The bright light from the sun reflecting back at them from the ground, the dust in the air, the silence moments after everything had literally blown up in their faces, the pain, the inability to move—it all raced back to her.

Chase remained where he was, but his arm was now somehow touching hers. 'Leave it if it's too hard.'

She shook her head. 'One day in Merrywood George Baines was electrocuted as I was walking past and I saved him. That made me realise I couldn't win them all and to be grateful for the ones I could. I started getting over the guilt that day.' Something Chase should try and understand.

'We have the guilt in common.'

But not how they dealt with it. 'We do. But neither of us deserves it.'

Chase went back to being silent. What was he thinking? That she'd done what she could and got on with her

life in a way he hadn't? Or was he simply wondering why she hadn't settled down in a town as a GP from the moment she'd left the military? Or, even more simply, why was she standing here, talking to him?

'When do you head to Africa?' Might as well jump in and learn all she could to stop those pesky questions zipping around her brain.

'After I've seen Jasper go to school for his first day,' Chase said defensively.

Surprise made her gabble. 'You're going to be there? That's wonderful. Libby will be stoked. So will Verity.'

'Cool it, Kristina. It's no big deal.'

Okay, so he wasn't happy with her. Too late to retract a thing. 'It is to your family.'

'Once you get going, there's no stopping you, is there?' A hint of amusement took the sting out of his words. 'I should be used to it by now.'

'Chase...' How did she put this without sending him running for the stairs?

'Don't, Kristina.'

That automatically stirred her along. 'I was only going to say I'd like it if you'd call in to see me whenever you're visiting your parents. I don't think we need to break contact entirely.' Now she was being pitiful, clutching at any opportunity to see him and thrashing her heart all over again.

'You can count on it.' He gave her a small smile.

'Really?' Down, hope, down.

'Really.'

She'd have to be happy with that.

CHAPTER TEN

THE SHIP ROCKED, causing the gangway to roll as Chase made his way down it for the last time this year. Next stop Ghana.

He paused, waited for the rush of excitement. His heart rate remained the same, his stomach quietly went about its business. Sighing, he continued onto the wharf and stopped, placing his bag at his feet and his hands on his hips as he stared up at the *SOS Poseidon*.

'Will I see you here next summer?' Josip called from the bridge.

'Probably.' Again the exhilaration let him down, not a buzz in his veins at all. 'You take care.'

'I intend to. My wife says she's nailing me to the bed for at least a week.'

Chase laughed. 'Lucky man.' The laughter faded. It wasn't that he was jealous. But not having a woman waiting for him at home, to make love to and talk and laugh with—that made him feel even lonelier than he'd been every damned minute since Kristina had disembarked four weeks ago. No one could ever have made him believe how much he'd miss her. As though she'd taken his heart with her, leaving him struggling to breathe.

The days had crawled by, the nights hadn't moved at all. The hours spent in their space had been cold, despite

the soaring temperatures blitzing the region as summer gave one last shove before handing over to autumn. He'd missed Kristina so damned much he ached in every part of his body.

'You going to stand there all day?' Ethan stood near the security gate, hands in his pockets, shaking his head. 'There's a cold one on tap waiting along the road.'

Hoisting his bag, Chase strode across to his friend. 'You're talking sense for once.'

'Who? Me?' Ethan laughed.

Suddenly a lightness settled over Chase. For the next twenty-four hours he could relax, enjoy being with his friend whose best man he'd be as he pledged his love to Claire in a week. 'My shout.'

'Already had that planned.'

They walked along the street until Ethan indicated an English bar. 'I'm missing beer from home.'

With frosty glasses in hand, they settled into a dark corner. 'Thanks for staying with us,' Ethan said. 'It means a lot.'

Chase took a deep mouthful of beer and swallowed slowly. It felt good, hearing that. 'We've come a long way in a short time.'

'No regrets?'

None whatsoever. 'We should've made the effort years ago.'

'Everything has its time and place.'

'Getting a bit sage, aren't you?' Chase wondered why they'd been at each other's throats so much as teenagers. The need to compete against each other had been huge, but at the expense of friendship? Who understood teenagers?

Ethan stared across the room, the fingers of one hand tapping on the table top, in the other his glass turned round and round. 'How're things with you and Kristina?'

What? 'I'll catch up with her in Merrywood.'

Slowly Ethan brought that inscrutable gaze round to fix on him. 'I don't think I'd have made it with Claire if you and I hadn't begun to repair the past, if we hadn't started to become friends. Without that happening I was too far off the rails, too afraid to trust my instincts when it came to love.'

Where was he going with this? Guys didn't talk amongst themselves about love. There was an awful feeling in the bottom of Chase's gut suggesting he wasn't going to like whatever came out of the man's mouth next, and he rushed in to halt him. 'You're moving on. That's enough.'

'You're in love with her.'

Chase sucked in stale air, stared at the apparition he'd thought he was getting to know. 'You think?'

'What are you going to do about it?'

'Nothing.' Was that admitting he did love Kristina? As in with all his heart loved her? 'I'm heading to Ghana straight after your marriage ceremony. Do you seriously think I should persuade Kristina to join me when she's finally found the life she wants?'

'What's wrong with you stopping in one place long term with her?'

'You know why I can't do that. More than anyone, you understand.'

'Before Claire I'd have agreed with you. Even after Claire I might've for a while. Not now.'

'Okay, you've found what you were looking for but—'

'I wasn't looking to settle down, certainly didn't intend to get married and become a dad for the same reasons you're denying yourself love. I was always looking for places to be, towns to slip through on the way to the next hellhole where people needed my undivided attention to make them better.' He banged his empty glass on the table. 'I was you. You are who I used to be.'

Chase sat back, gobsmacked. There was nothing to say.

He didn't understand, didn't *want* to understand the message Ethan was banging him over the head with. He could admit to himself he loved Kristina. To tell her would only hurt, because he'd have to follow up with the statement that he didn't intend to do anything about it. She already knew that. 'Want another?' He nodded at the empty glasses between them. If only that was all that lay between them, but it seemed Ethan was hell bent on prodding old wounds.

'Sure.'

Moving through the throng of men standing at high tables eating lunch with their beers, Chase fought the urge to run for the exit. What right did Ethan have to talk about his love for Kristina? He'd never admitted his feelings out loud, afraid that by voicing them he wouldn't be able to keep them under wraps. That was where they had to stay. For Kristina's sake. If that wasn't love, what was?

Back at the table they sat in silence as the beer slowly disappeared down their throats. Chase began to relax. That conversation was done. Now he could enjoy a night with his friend and Claire. It was such an alien idea that it excited him. 'How long does it take to drive to Claire's apartment?'

Ethan downed another mouthful of his beer, drew a breath, and locked his eyes on the table between them. 'Stop trying to save everyone, Chase. It's not possible. I know. We're sorry examples of men when it comes to what we want from life, but Claire has shown me otherwise. You...' his finger tapped the table top '...can have what you're hankering after—Kristina and love and a family, all in your own corner of the world. You want that as much as you want to save those people, so go about it differently. Get a job back home. I'm learning that saving a child by removing a ruptured appendix in a big hospital is as rewarding as debriding a refugee's burns. You can have it all. Go for it, man. You're entitled to happiness. We both are.'

There wasn't anything to say. It would take time to absorb the sincerity in Ethan's words, and even then Chase doubted if he could accept the possibility of following suit. 'You're staying on in France, not moving back to England?'

'Claire needs to be where she is, and that's enough for me. Have to admit I'm not keen on spending too much time with her family with the mountains that loom over their village, but as long as I don't go climbing or skiing I'll manage.' He drained his glass. 'And I need you here next week. I'm not waiting any longer to get married.'

There he went again. It all came back to the love of a good woman. Apparently Ethan would do anything to make his woman happy. Anything.

Wasn't that what he was doing by staying out of Kristina's way? Making her happy rather than dragging her around the world as he saw fit?

Ethan picked up their empty glasses. 'Let's hit the road. Gridlock starts when everyone heads out of the city at the end of work, and Marseille in gridlock is hell on wheels.'

Conversation was on hold until Ethan pinged the locks of his SUV. 'One last thing, then I'll shut up. We can't undo the past but we can change our futures. Start doing something about that now. Not tomorrow, not next month, now. Go home, stop wandering the globe.'

Chase's pack dropped into the back of the SUV with a loud thud. 'Never knew you could talk so damned much,' Chase snapped around the pain that was flaring in his belly and spreading throughout his body. Did Ethan believe he could change his life with the snap of his fingers? When he knew better than anyone what held him back?

But he does know. That's the whole point.

Was it possible to turn his life around?

Did he want to?

He was beginning to think he did.

And he knew where he had to start.

* * *

The hut sat on the brow of the hill behind the copse, the door closed but not bolted. The front was bathed in weak sunlight. The weatherboards had recently been painted. Dad doing his regular upkeep even when this particular tiny building had not been used since Nick had died.

Chase sat on the edge of the veranda and leaned back against the wall, deliberately letting the ache come and the memories start opening. Gazing out over the green pastures, he wished he'd brought a bottle of beer to raise to Nick. 'We were going to conquer the world, live in the fast lane, you as an architect and me a plastic surgeon. Women were going to fall at our feet, we were going to make millions, own our own houses and take holidays in exotic locations.'

Despite the tears tracking down his cheeks, he laughed. 'We were morons. Normal teenagers from secure backgrounds who knew the only way to get ahead was by working hard, and then harder still, and yet we dreamed.'

What a lot of fun they'd had up here, drinking illicit beers and talking nonsense. At least they hadn't been on the street, doing drugs or getting drunk, robbing the local grocer.

The biggest and likeliest dream had been that the team would win the European under-eighteens ski championships. 'You would've made it, mate. It was a given. You deserved to win.'

He sat looking down on the world that had been his childhood, his safe place, his home, and thought about Nick, then the night that everything had changed for ever, Ethan, and lastly Kristina. 'I love her, Nick. Everything about her. She's gutsy and strong and sweet and sexy, and why am I telling you this?'

Focusing on the farm, a sense of belonging stole through him. This *was* his place. He'd never live in the house again.

His children wouldn't grow up with these paddocks to run around in, and this hut would not be their hideaway, but his heart belonged here.

It also belonged to Kristina. If she'd accept him as he was—flawed, wounded, and willing to give life a go with no guarantees.

The sun was dropping beyond the distant hedges when Chase finally roused himself. Time to get started on the future. But first he had to close the past. He stood, hands in his pockets, feet splayed, and his eyes closed. 'Nick, I'm sorry, buddy, but the time has come for me to let you go. It's not fair you didn't get to do any of those things you wanted so much, and I've done everything I can to make up for that in other ways. Now I'm done.' He opened his eyes, looked around and felt okay about what he was doing. 'Goodbye, Nick.'

That night Chase slept the deepest sleep he could remember having. In the morning he joined his parents for breakfast then borrowed his father's four-wheel drive and headed into the city.

'Thank you so much, Dr Morton. Sorry to be a nuisance but I panicked when Lily went limp and quiet.' Sherry bounced a now happy baby in her arms.

'Stop apologising. I'd rather you came in and there was nothing wrong than you stay away because you're embarrassed and we find there's something to worry about. Most first-time mothers are the same.' Kristina tickled Lily on the chin. 'Your mother loves you, gorgeous.'

Sherry nodded. 'I still can't believe how that just happens, no warning, nothing. One day I was pregnant, and the next I was holding this precious little bundle I'd give my life for if I had to.'

Kristina's heart squeezed. Would she ever know the same love? 'Let's hope it never comes to that.' Placing

Lily's file on the receptionist's counter, she picked up her next patient's notes. 'I'll see you for Lily's six-month check-up. Unless you're worried about anything before then.'

Sherry nodded. 'I'm so glad you're back.'

Sherry's words registered in the back of her mind as she scanned the waiting room for Mrs Winter and instead found Chase sitting, watching her. Every thought went out of her mind as her blood heated and her body turned in his direction. He was sexier even than her memory of him, and that was off the scale. Those magical hands lying loosely on his thighs dried her mouth as more memories flooded her head. 'I've missed you so much.'

'I've missed you, too.' Chase crossed to her, those hands reaching for her, taking her close to that wicked chest.

She hadn't seen him move, didn't know she'd spoken aloud until his reply. He'd missed her? Really? In the way she hoped? 'I didn't know you were in town.' Libby hadn't mentioned it. Though Claire and Ethan were getting married shortly, so she should've figured he'd turn up.

'I got in yesterday.' His hands dropped away. His hug had been brief but warm. Friendly.

Ah, friendly. He hadn't come specifically to see her. But he'd said he'd missed her. What was going on? 'You're waiting to see Jarrod?' Not her. They weren't an item. She was getting on with her life, not stagnating while waiting for Chase to make random appearances.

'No.' His hand reached for hers again. His tongue licked his bottom lip. 'I—I'm hoping you'll spare me some time after you finish up. Go for a meal at the pub?'

'Oh.' She gulped. 'Oh.' Where was the strong, know-what-I-want Chase? This nervous version was new to her. 'I'd like that.'

There was relief going on in that gaze locked on her.

'I'm early, but I didn't want to risk you leaving before I saw you.'

'I've got two more patients.' Kristina dragged her eyes away to look around the room for her next patient, trying to get her brain functioning properly.

'I'll be here.'

She began to turn away.

'Kristina?' She turned back, still trying to fathom what was going on. "I'm glad you missed me,' he said quietly.

Thud. Was that her heart hitting the floor? 'Meaning?' She needed to find another doctor quickly because she was in no state to take care of patients. Not after that. Chase was either building her hopes up or about to kick her feet out from under her.

'Talk to you later.' His hand cupped her chin for a moment, dropped away. 'I'm not here to hurt you, okay?'

Okay? Her head dipped into a nod without thought. 'Fine.' Whatever that meant. First she had to get a grip. Just because Chase had strolled into her day didn't mean forgetting what, who her day was meant to be about. 'Mrs Winter?'

An elderly woman rose stiffly, and hobbled her way. 'Hello, dear. Are you Dr Morton, then?'

'I am. Pleased to meet you.' With all her willpower Kristina remained focused on the lovely lady before her and ignored the man who'd once again thrown her mind into a flap. 'Come through, and tell me what's bothering you today.'

Removing what appeared to be a basal cell carcinoma from Mrs Winter's lower arm took half an hour and made Kristina late for her last patient, who didn't seem fazed.

'I've been talking to Chase Barrington,' Tony Webster told her as he sat down by her desk. 'We went to school together. He always was a great guy. If only he'd come home.'

See what you're missing out on, Chase? People who know you and want to be a part of your life are as important as the ones you see briefly before they disappear over the horizon on their own journeys.

'He's doing a wonderful job with *Medicine For All*.' Why had he asked her out for a meal? 'What can I do for you today, Tony?'

'It's my hip, Doc. It's getting more painful and I need to increase the diclofenac.'

The joint had been fractured a year ago when a cow had charged him, and he'd had problems ever since. 'It might be time for that hip replacement.' The wait-and-see approach hadn't worked and Tony needed to face facts. 'Up on the bed and I'll have a look.' After getting him to lift his leg, push sideways as she assessed his resistance level, Kristina returned to her desk and brought up the radiology request form. 'Get dressed. I'm sending you for an X-ray and referring you to the orthopaedic department.' She typed in details, printed off a radiology form and a repeat prescription for his anti-inflammatory drug.

'Only old people have hip replacements.'

Men. Stubborn creatures. Why *was* Chase waiting for her to finish work? 'Let's see what the X-ray shows, shall we?'

'I can't afford to take time off from the farm.'

'You'd rather lie awake in pain every night and hobble around the fields at half your speed. I get it. Make that appointment with Radiology today.' Then she glanced at her watch. 'Tomorrow. I'll be following up on you.' She smiled to soften the blow.

'I'm docking sheep tomorrow.' He limped out, a scowl on his face.

'Nice try,' Kristina called after him, before closing down the computer. Picking up her bag and keys, she slung

her denim jacket over one shoulder and went to find Chase. And learn what this was about.

Pausing at the door, her gaze filled with the sight of him leaning against the reception counter, talking with Jarrod. Even knowing Chase was here hadn't prepared her for the simple need to throw herself at him and wrap her arms around that tall, lean body, to feel his muscles under her palms and breathe in his man scent, just... Oh, just whatever. She'd missed him beyond reason. Missed the intimacy, his sexiness, their talks, everything about the guy. *Settle down, girl.* One evening sharing a meal wouldn't change a thing. He'd still head away on another adventure come tomorrow.

When he took her elbow, sparks flew up her arm. 'You all right to walk?' he asked calmly. No sparks for him?

'Definitely. I need to get the kinks out of my back. There's a lot of sitting with this job.' Which was never good.

'You been going to physio?'

'Twice a week. There's a physiotherapist connected to the medical centre, which is handy.' And the woman knew what she was doing. Always a bonus.

Chase placed two beers on the table and sat opposite Kristina so he could watch her face. He'd missed how her expression lightened when she laughed, how her eyes went deep blue in serious moments, how she scratched whatever surface was available with her forefinger when discussing those things that had shaped her life.

The moment he'd seen her in the waiting room he'd wanted to scoop her up and run to the nearest hotel room to make love, to show her how special she was. 'Jarrod tells me you've settled into the medical centre without any hitches.'

'It's early days yet.' She blushed.

He hadn't seen that before, and tenderness stirred throughout him. 'You've made the right move.'

The light blue shade of her eyes turned dark as she gave a sharp nod. 'It's working out well. I'm going to look at two houses next week that have just come on the market. In for the job, in for everything.'

'You don't think you're rushing things?' She could come a cropper if she suddenly wanted to up stakes and head off somewhere else. Houses didn't always sell overnight.

'If I don't back myself, how can I expect anyone else to?'

She had an answer for everything. Way ahead of him. But he was racing to catch up. 'Point taken.'

'Hey, Kristina, see you at the make-up party on Saturday?' A woman in her thirties stood by their table.

'You sure will, Pam.'

See? She was fitting in in a way he struggled to envisage, yet was finally willing to give a shot. He'd listened to the young mother with her baby talking to the receptionist about how kind and caring Dr Morton had been, and how she was glad to have her as her doctor, and felt he was missing out on something big. When Tony came out of her room looking like he'd lost a battle, and grumping about Doc thinking she knew best, Chase had known exactly how he felt.

Weeks back when Kristina had had a crack at him about how he could do as much good for people here as anywhere he'd gone all defensive, believing she didn't understand what drove him. He wasn't going to be sucked into her way of thinking that home was best, didn't want to get involved with her or the town he'd run away from. Then Ethan had added his two euros' worth, saying the same thing even more directly. Who knew better than Ethan where he was coming from?

Throw in the four longest, dullest, most boring weeks

of his life out at sea, and he knew he had to stop holding
out for the lonely path he'd chosen when he'd been at his
lowest. He had to do something different or end up a bit-
ter, lonely old man with only himself to blame.

Kristina. He loved her. Without reservation.

Would the woman hurry up and leave? He had things
bugging the hell out of him to share with Kristina. Now.
Not later.

'Thanks for the invitation.' Kristina lifted her glass
and took a sip.

The woman got the hint and said goodbye.

'You're popular already.' He needed to provoke that
sweet blush, and was instantly rewarded.

'Join the medical centre, join the whole town.' Her smile
was strained.

'That's how it is here, people watching out for each
other.'

Her eyebrows rose, but she kept quiet.

'Everyone turned out to support me after the avalanche.
I was overwhelmed by their compassion.' And his grief,
but he'd put that to bed yesterday. 'I've spent the day visit-
ing hospitals and surgical practices in Taunton and Frome.
I'm looking for a job.'

Kristina leaned back in her chair, her eyes locked on
him, disbelief warring with hope in her expression. 'Say
that again.'

'I'm coming home, Kristina. It's time.'

'Why?'

'Because if I don't do it now, the chances are I never
will, and I need to as much as I needed to stay away be-
fore.' Everything was so clear—how he'd wasted his life
rushing after causes, how he'd let his family down when
all they'd ever done was love and support him. But more
than that, 'It's you. I love you. I want that future you're

following. I want to...' He ran out of words as he watched Kristina's reaction.

Never a big talker, she was now silent. Shocked might best describe her. Her eyes remained locked on him, her hands tight around her glass.

'Say something,' he croaked.

She picked up her drink in unsteady hands and gulped a mouthful, all the while watching him.

Raucous laughter broke out on the other side of the room.

Chase stood up and took the glass out of Kristina's hands, placed it on the table, then took her hand and tugged gently. 'Let's get out of here.' What had he been thinking to drop that on her when surrounded by people that had nothing to do with this conversation?

Outside he led her to the four-wheel drive he'd borrowed from his father that morning, and held the passenger door open as she climbed in. 'Where're you living?'

'Are you sure?'

'That I love you? Yes.'

'It's a bit sudden, isn't it?' Her tongue worried the corner of her mouth.

'I believe it started the day we worked together to save Antoine on the wharf. I didn't recognise love for what it was, or, if I did, I didn't want to.' She had to believe him. He wasn't making any of this up.

Kristina turned her startled gaze forward, so he couldn't read her any more. Not that he was having much luck interpreting what she was thinking anyway. 'Take me to the river. I need to walk.'

It would be dark soon, but the idea of being shut inside the house with Chase while she absorbed what he'd told her made Kristina feel hot and cold all at once. She needed space, not walls closing in on her.

Chase loves me. Who said dreams didn't come true? Her wildest dream had been that he'd fall for her and want to settle down here. So why wasn't she falling into his arms with excitement? Did she love Chase? Without a doubt.

Chase loves me.

So he'd been looking for work in the area. How long would he stay in one job before that crippling need to be actively helping those unfortunate people took over? Would he be able to stop in one town long term?

You have. It was early days, but she already knew she'd found her corner of the world. She was happy here—when she wasn't thinking about Chase. Sure, there'd be times when things went wrong, but this was home. But could Chase do the same?

He was pulling over. 'This do?'

'Yes.' The river walkway was devoid of locals, thank goodness. Now was not the time to be making idle chit-chat. She slid out of the vehicle and pulled on her jacket, zipped it up against the cool evening air. 'How did the job hunt go?' she asked as they began strolling along the river's edge.

'I have an interview tomorrow with the head of surgery at Collingwood Hospital. There are no positions right now, but there might be one coming up. In the meantime, I'll keep door knocking. Jarrod's contacting two surgeons in private practice he knows well.'

'You sound…excited.'

Chase looked down at her. 'You know what? I am. Now I've made up my mind I'm keen to get cracking on starting over.' Then his smile faded. 'You're not certain I'll stay around, are you? You're worried that I'll wake up one morning and wonder whatever possessed me to give up the life I've led for so long.'

'Yes, that's exactly what's going through my mind.' *I'm terrified my heart will be broken.* At the moment she

could walk away and it would only be badly bruised, but to believe they had a future and then have it torn away—no, she couldn't survive that. 'I'm sorry.'

'It's right that you're looking out for yourself. I understand that.' Wrapping an arm over her shoulders, he pulled her out of the way of a cyclist. 'I'm going to Ghana the day after Ethan and Claire tie the knot.'

Her heart slowed. See? He hadn't made the change yet, was still hanging onto the old life. 'You finally signed the contract.'

His body touched the length of hers, strong and warm, making her want to believe in him. 'Yes, in a fit of uncertainty I did. I was grappling with missing you so damned much it hurt. Do I regret it? No, because I owe Liam time to find my replacement. Anyway, the contract is only for four weeks.'

Not long enough to know he'd made the right decision. Or was it? Was she being fair? Just because it had taken her a couple of years to realise the army couldn't give her what she'd been looking for, it didn't mean Chase needed as long. Kristina began walking again, pleased when Chase's arm remained around her shoulders. She'd missed him so much there'd been days when she'd wondered if she should walk away from what she'd found and re-join him on the ship. 'Four weeks and then you're moving to Somerset.'

'For good, Kristina. For good. This is where my heart is.'

She stopped in the fading light and turned into him, looking up at that face that was seared into her mind. 'I'm glad. You belong here. I've wanted to bang you over the head so you'd see what you've been missing out on.'

'Trust me, you did that more than once.' His smile was wry. 'Verbally, and in the way you fitted in with people I care about. That woke me up more than anything. If you could let your past go and be happy in a town that was new

to you, slotting in as though you'd always lived here, why couldn't I return to where I'd grown up and have known people my whole life?'

'Because you're stubborn?' She raised an eyebrow and grinned, letting the wonder of his love take hold.

'There's that.' He grinned back. Then sobered. 'Kristina, I meant what I said. I love you with all my heart.'

She'd never told him how she felt. True, she had doubts about his ability to stay put, but while she'd only known his restless side she'd seen his strength in dealing with the day-to-day dramas and tragedies on the *Poseidon*. And he loved her.

'I want to marry you and settle into a home of our own and eventually fill the spare bedrooms with kids that have fair hair and summer-blue eyes,' he added.

Tears streaked down her face. 'Really?' she choked. Wasn't this what she'd been searching for?

'What do you think?' he asked as his arms wound around her.

Drawing herself up and taking a deep breath, she told him, 'You need to know I love you, too.' She'd always wanted the chance to love someone and to be loved back. And here it was. *Chase.* 'Yes, Chase, I love you,' she repeated.

'Oh, sweetheart.' His mouth touched hers, soft and warm and filled with love. The kiss when it came was long and slow and made her heart melt.

She didn't think it could get any better.

Chase lifted his mouth away from hers. 'Kristina, please say you'll marry me.'

Seemed she still got things wrong. This went beyond better. 'As soon as you return home for good.'

'Better start planning the wedding. From what Ethan tells me, it's quite a process.'

'Claire doesn't have Verity or Libby alongside her.'

'True.' Chase smiled. 'Family. They're going to be thrilled about this.'

'Want to go tell them now?'

He shook his head. 'No. We're going back to your place and I'm going to make love to you all night long.'

'Perfect answer, husband-to-be. Perfect answer.'

EPILOGUE

'I DECLARE YOU man and wife,' the marriage celebrant announced with a smile. 'You can now kiss your— Oh, right... Well, it seems I was a bit slow off the mark.'

Kristina would've laughed but she was too busy returning Chase's enthusiastic kiss. They'd done it. Gone and got themselves hitched, surrounded by family and friends.

'Okay, you two. There are children present.' Ethan clapped Chase on the back. 'Plenty of time for that later.'

Chase dragged his mouth away. 'Go and annoy *your* wife, will you?'

'Oh, no, you don't,' Claire shot back as Ethan reached for her.

Kristina grinned as she slipped her arm through Chase's. 'Get in line, you guys.'

'Did I tell you she's ex-military?' Chase turned back to Ethan.

'Didn't need to. I've known who's in charge in this relationship right from the start.'

'You haven't seen anything yet.' Taking her first step in her now complete life, Kristina tugged her husband and began the walk down between the chairs where everyone important to them stood and cheered.

Even her father, who reached out and placed a gentle dad kiss on her cheek. 'You're beautiful, my girl.'

On the other side of the aisle her mother dabbed at her eyes and nodded. For once her mum appeared to be in tune with her father.

Tears spilled down Kristina's carefully made-up face and she couldn't have cared less. The photos would show the real emotions of the day, smudged mascara and all. Her family mightn't know how to express aloud their love for her, but today they'd shown it by being here. It was all she asked.

Outside the tiny village church in the wintry sunshine they crossed the road to the wedding reception venue and were met by a waiter holding a tray of glasses filled with champagne and one with sparkling water for Claire. The four of them formed a tight circle and clinked the glasses. 'To the four of us,' Chase said.

'To us,' Ethan agreed.

After taking a sip, Chase dropped a kiss on Kristina's cheek then locked his gaze with Ethan's. 'We did it. Both of us.'

Ethan's hand splayed across against Chase's back. 'No regrets. This is real, and wonderful, and, yes, we made it.'

Chase looked at Ethan, then her. And raised his glass as he looked upward. 'To Nick.'

'To Nick.' Ethan nodded.

Kristina's tears grew heavier, but her heart was light. 'They're special, our men,' she whispered to Claire.

'I'm so glad they're happy, and have found a way forward.'

'I'll drink to that,' Kristina agreed.

'So will we,' Chase added as he smudged a streak of mascara off her cheek.

'Big ears.' His wife grinned. Tears maybe, but nothing today was going to wipe the smile off her face.

Then Libby was nudging into the group, breaking the moment, only to replace it with another. 'Welcome to the

family, Kristina.' Then she broke down. 'And thank you for making Chase see sense at last.'

'Another glass required over here.' Chase beckoned a waiter.

Then they were surrounded by people congratulating them.

'It doesn't get any better than this, does it?' Chase whispered in Kristina's ear.

'Well…' She tapped her mouth thoughtfully.

'Don't.' He laughed. 'I love you. That's all you're getting.'

'That's all I need.'

* * * * *

COMING SOON!

We really hope you enjoyed reading this book. If you're looking for more romance, be sure to head to the shops when new books are available on

Thursday 25th July

To see which titles are coming soon, please visit

millsandboon.co.uk/nextmonth

MILLS & BOON

MILLS & BOON

Coming next month

DR RIGHT FOR THE SINGLE MUM
Alison Roberts

'I learned then that you just had to get on with it,' Laura said, her voice soft enough to make Tom lift his gaze to catch hers. 'You get to choose some of the cards you play with in the game of life but others just get dealt out, don't they? There's nothing you can do about that except to play the absolute best game you can. And you have to fight for the people you love. For yourself, too.'

It was impossible to look away from those warm, brown eyes. She totally believed in what she was saying. Laura McKenzie was quite prepared to fight to the death for someone she loved. There was real passion there, mixed with that courage and determination. He was seeing a whole new side to the person he was so comfortable to work with and it was more than a little disconcerting because it was making him curious. Apart from being an amazing nurse and clearly a ferociously protective single mother, just who was Laura McKenzie? No... It was none of his business, was it?

The half-smile that tugged at one corner of her mouth made it seem as if she could read his thoughts and sympathised with his small dilemma.

But she was just finishing off her surprisingly passionate little speech. 'I guess that's the same thing, isn't it? If you're fighting for yourself that means you can't do anything other than to fight for the people you love.'

Okay… That did it. Tom had to back off fast before he got sucked into a space he had vowed never to enter again. He didn't want to think about what it was like to live in a space where you could love other people so much they became more important than anything else in life. That space that was too dangerous because, when you lost those people, you were left with what felt like no life at all…

He had to break that eye contact. And he had to move. Making a noise that was somewhere between a sound of agreement and clearing his throat, Tom slid off the corner of his desk.

'I'd better get back to the department.' He opened the door and there was an instant sense of relief. Escape was within touching distance. 'As I said, we'll work around whatever you need. Send me a copy of the chemotherapy calendar and I'll make sure Admin's on board for when you're rostered.'

Laura nodded as she got out of her chair. 'Thank you very much.'

Her formality was just what Tom needed to make things seem a little more normal. 'It's the least I can do,' he said. 'The least we can do. You're a valued member of this department, Laura. We'll all do everything we can to support you.'

Continue reading
DR RIGHT FOR THE SINGLE MUM
Alison Roberts

Available next month
www.millsandboon.co.uk

LET'S TALK
Romance

For exclusive extracts, competitions
and special offers, find us online:

- f facebook.com/millsandboon
- 🐦 @MillsandBoon
- 📷 @MillsandBoonUK

Get in touch on 01413 063232

For all the latest titles coming soon, visit
millsandboon.co.uk/nextmonth